Write Me a Murder

JAMES MURPHY

First published in 2024 by SpellBound Books Ltd
Copyright © James Murphy
The moral right of the author to be identified as the owner of this Work has been asserted by them in accordance with the Copyright, Designs and Patents Act, 1988.
All rights reserved. No part of this publication may be reproduced, stored in a retrieval system, or transmitted, in any form or by any means, electronic, mechanical, photocopying, recording or otherwise, without the prior permission of the publisher.
This is a work of fiction. All names, characters, places, locations and events in this publication, other than those clearly in the public domain, are fictitious, and any resemblance to actual persons, living or dead, or any actual places, business establishments, locations or events is purely coincidental.

For Heather & Bella.

PROLOGUE

"YOU CAN'T GO BACK AND CHANGE THE
BEGINNING, BUT YOU CAN START WHERE YOU
ARE AND CHANGE THE ENDING" (C.S. LEWIS)

CHAPTER
ONE

HANWELL, WEST LONDON - 2001

It wasn't the extent of his injuries that had paralysed Daniel Knox with fear on his brief return to consciousness. Nor was it the realisation that his life was about to end. The thought that had him pinned to the cold concrete floor with every bit as much pressure as that being exerted by the weight of the Harley Davidson he was trapped beneath was for one thing only. Victoria's safety.

Vaguely aware of the words being directed towards him but oblivious to what was actually being said, he tried hard not to drift away. Tried and failed. In the moments before the blackness finally took him he felt powerless, experiencing the scene of his demise as an anguished bystander to it. In a different setting the scene would have resembled a fatal road traffic accident. He could have dealt with that, perhaps even seen it as a fitting, albeit a premature way to go. Death by Harley Davidson, he could certainly hear that been eulogised. This was no road traffic accident though. The horrific head injury that would no doubt be cited as the primary cause of his death was not the result of driving beyond the limits of his or the machine's capabilities. It was the result of a violent blow to the head delivered via a tyre iron by the person, who like he, was now watching him die. He wouldn't have thought them capable. At least not physically. He'd been wrong. Anxiously willing his unconscious body to wake, to get up, his final thoughts were consumed by one question. Where was Victoria? He needed to protect her. To warn her at least. When he'd woken alone to the sound of the doorbell he'd presumed that she had gone to get breakfast takeout from the deli across the street. After all, that was her weekend thing and they were celebrating right? Clearly she had forgotten her keys, *again*. He hadn't given a moment's thought to trotting downstairs and opening the door wearing only his boxer shorts and a smile. A smile that quickly faded to extinction, his life soon to follow.

CHAPTER TWO

Mariticide wasn't a word that I was familiar with before my arrest. In the days and weeks that followed though, I would become only too aware of its definition and the enormity of the weight of the allegations being levelled at me. To be suspected of killing one's husband, boyfriend, or in my case fiancé, was a strange situation for a newly qualified police officer to find themselves in, to say the least. Yet here I was. What was worse, I could entirely understand the logic and methods being adopted by those sat across the table from me in their approach. I especially understood the accusatory tone and the suppositions being presented to me as fact.

In their place I would be doing exactly the same, had done exactly the same to some capacity throughout my training. It was textbook. Murder 101, it was more often than not the partner who was responsible. Start your investigation with them then work your way back.

Taking the evidence into account, circumstantial as it was, of course I would feature highly on the persons of interest list. It didn't take any police training to work that out. The partner is practically always the prime suspect and often with good reason.

The thing was though, the last time I saw Daniel Knox, he was very much alive. My arrest and detention for questioning on arrival for my shift at Ealing Police Station less than 24 hours later however, made it emphatically apparent that it hadn't been the case for much longer afterward.

The eyewitness account placing me at the scene around the supposed time of death had been enough to secure me firmly in the frame as a feasible perpetrator. Of course the eagle eyed crone from the apartment above the deli, with her front windows facing ours would have seen me in the vicinity. I lived right opposite the interfering old biddy! To be fair, my actions on the day hadn't helped my case. Still, despite my situation, I had faith that my innocence would be enough to free me from suspicion. Faith and a naive confidence in the justice system that had been instilled in me through my own police training. Misplaced I would later learn. That said, if cutting the cancer that was my relationship with Daniel Knox out of my life was a crime then I would have happily raised my hands in submission. Mia Culpa! Guilty as charged Your Honour. His murder on the other hand, that was an entirely different story, and not mine to tell. It would, however, be one I would be unwittingly complicit in whether I liked it or not, through my decision making on that fateful Saturday morning.

The events of that Saturday morning, the first part at least, now that was my story to tell...

...the hazy recollection of the previous night's proposal as I straddled the void between dreams and consciousness had been enough to stir me towards the ominous reality of a new day. It was the raging hangover that truly started my morning though.

Tentatively blinking my eyes awake brought the first dilemma of the weekend... and a pile driving headache. Was it to be a long drink from the hi-ball glass of water on the night-

stand to relieve the chemical dehydration, the arid conditions inside my mouth and the leatheriness of my lips? Or was the more favourable option the one that would have me exiting the bedroom post haste, hoping against hope that relieving my stomach of the burden of its contents would restore me to pre-hangover normality? As it turned out, it was the nausea that had tipped the balance in the end. The recollection of the copious amounts of cider, cheap white wine and the obligatory Donner kebab that had been consumed, coupled with the realisation that I was about to reacquaint myself with each in turn, though not necessarily in that order, resulted in my only just making it.

In conveyancing parlance my destination could have been best described as a water closet. In real terms, it was the unglamorous partition of the toilet of an already small bathroom to create two, separate, more practical but no less appealing amenities within the space allotted. At the moment though, the environs were irrelevant to me. Holding the falling strands of my dark hair away from my face through the retching, vomiting and seemingly endless dry heaves that followed, I heard his voice in my head. The predictable attempts at humour referencing my "calling God on the big white telephone" and his no doubt mocking my overindulgence in the form of "humour" for the remainder of the day. Thankfully, he slept like a rock and was still deep in an alcohol induced slumber as the low rumbling snores attested to. Probably just as well. I recalled the advice offered by the proverb about sleeping dogs and, at the moment, certainly planned to adhere to it. I needed to turn my attention to the second and more difficult dilemma of the day just as soon as I could focus my alcohol addled brain. A coffee would help. Some paracetamol too. I needed time to think. Time to plan. Time to frame how to best unsay that one word that I regretted allowing to escape from my lips more than any other utterance in my entire existence. The word, Yes.

He hadn't moved or stirred since I left, still deep in the post-coital slumber he had succumbed to moments after rolling off me with a parting grunt last night. The "celebration sex" hadn't been worthy of the occasion from what I remembered, but that hadn't necessarily been a surprise given our collective levels of inebriation from the free bar at my passing out parade celebrations. Not that it was ever euphoric if the truth were being told. My return to where the "magic happened" and sliding carefully back in beside him, coffee in hand, had brought a slight grunt. Nothing more, thankfully. Carefully, I slid open the drawer of my nightstand and reached for the paracetamol. As quietly as I could manage, I twice burst the blister pack and popped the tablets into my mouth, washing them down tentatively with a small mouthful of coffee, careful to resist the urge to gulp for fear of inducing any further gagging or the possibility of roasting myself. Both the tablets and the caffeine would bring some solace from last night's overindulgence. They would do little to solve the other problem I faced though.

Watching him sleep as I sipped at the coffee, I reflected on his drunken proposal. I'd been happy last night when he'd popped the question, aside from feeling a little irked at his selfishness in finding a way of making my day about him. Why not so happy now? Deep down I already knew the answer.

It had come as a bolt from the blue when he had dropped to one knee amongst my fellow former cadets and friends, and I guess I'd gotten caught up in the romance of it all. And of course I loved him, right? Now though, the reality of my predicament couldn't be ignored. Yes, I loved him, but was I in love? No, not if I was being honest with myself, and him. Hardly the basis for a marriage, especially when we were both still so young, not yet twenty in my case. Our relationship was comfortable, secure, but love's young dream we weren't. I'd met him early on in my time in London, having been introduced by a mutual friend, and although he wouldn't have been my type, if I had one, he was tall, handsome and had a hipster charm that I, as a fresh faced young police cadet from Northern Ireland, had soon been won over by.

It had been exciting at first, me completing my police training at the Met whilst he carved out the beginnings of a successful career path in engineering. The fact that my mother would never have approved made it all the more enticing of course.

Now though, in this moment, reflecting on the proposal, brought with it a decision that in reality I had been coming towards reaching for more than a year on some level or another. It wasn't only that I couldn't marry him. I simply couldn't be here anymore. I'd lost myself somewhere in the cosiness of the relationship and now it was time to reclaim my identity and my hard won freedom. The more I thought on it, it had been he who had been so enamoured by the idea of living above a shop that dealt in reclaimed wooden furniture. It had been him who had presumed that the studio space behind the shop that came with the rental would be used to house his motorbikes. Even the Aerosmith t-shirt that I was wearing now, picked from the banister to cover my modesty as I went to make the coffee, was a reflection of his interests. I couldn't last another day here, let alone the rest of my life.

The combined aromas of varnish and engine oil emanating from below were suddenly new to me again and were not welcome. The lack of natural light and the rough texture of the unvarnished wooden floorboards that I've received countless splinters from, now silently mocked me where I lay. I was incensed. Not so much with him as with myself. It had been almost 18 months since I arrived in London against the better wishes of my mother, stubbornly governed by a "what's the worst that could happen" attitude. If Northern Ireland society couldn't deal with a young catholic girl joining the newly formed Police Service of Northern Ireland, then I'd be damned if I stayed there. It was that attitude that was still getting me noticed within training for a role on the force, so why had I fallen so easily into a life of docile subservience in my relationship with him. It needed to end and it needed to end now.

For the second time this morning I found myself slipping swiftly out from beneath the duvet, keen not to wake him. This time I peeled off the t-shirt, grabbed some clothes from the chest of drawers nearest my side of the bed and quickly dressed before stuffing a few more hastily chosen outfits into the duffel bag I'd pulled from the top of the wardrobe. The depositing of one harshly scribbled note on the kitchen table and I was free, about to embark on a new life. What was the worst that could happen? I would find that out soon enough.

PART ONE - "WE WRITE IN ORDER TO UNDERSTAND" (C.S. LEWIS)

CHAPTER
THREE

Antrim, Northern Ireland - October 2015

Head in hands as he sat on the edge of the bed, the growl of his profanities still reverberating through the pencil thin walls of the council house bedroom he attempted to gather his thoughts. The girl lay lifeless beside him, her head tilted at an awkward angle off the edge of the pillow from where he had tried to shake her back to consciousness. Her right arm flailed across the mattress from where he'd desperately grabbed at her in a vain attempt at pulling her back to him. Back to life. No amount of shaking her disrobed body or panicked swearing at her was going to rouse her, he now realised. Taking in her face, still bearing the pained anguish of her death he reached a painful conclusion. He wouldn't be able to charm his way out of trouble this time. That was more than apparent. At the moment though, that thought paled into insignificance in comparison to the guilt that was cascading over his body, seeping into and consuming every fibre of his being. The flash of adrenaline at the moment he felt her pass had brought with it a combined sexual climax of an intensity he had never experienced before, and an emotional high of rapturous proportions. In that millisecond he had felt like a Demi-God. Now though, he was racked with a myriad of feelings, none of which were welcome. Fear and panic fought to consume him. It was guilt that came to win that particular contest though. A crushing, soul destroying guilt that would be his price to pay for his actions. Except he hadn't been the one who had ultimately paid it. It had been her. In ending her life, albeit unintentionally, he had taken away the prospect of any future that either of them had. For now though he needed to suppress that thought, those feelings. Ignore them to the best of his ability, and quickly. Now he needed to focus, to think clearly, methodically. He needed to strategise a way forward. Ultimately everything now came down to one thing. Could he get away with murder? He thought so. After all, he had done so once before.

CHAPTER FOUR

Antrim, Northern Ireland - October 2022

'What's the worst that could happen?' Beth Shaw's parting words, the wry humour dripping thickly from them echoed in my mind as I guided the battered Transit van up the dark narrow lane that led into Antrim Castle Gardens. She knew full well that phrase was the one to use to push my buttons and she knew why too…sort of. Yet here I was, parking up in the pitch black, almost empty car park, my most prized worldly possessions separated from me only by a thin wooden partition dividing the cab of the battered hire van from its load space.

Facing me stood Clotsworthy House, every bit as beautiful as Beth had described. Set against the inky black of the October night sky and under a thin pall of mist illuminated in a fiery orange by the streetlights surrounding it, the long red bricked exterior was punctuated by a sequential pattern of windows, interior light emanating from only a mere few of them, adding to the already hauntingly beautiful attraction it exuded. It was a fitting fortress like extension connecting old and new, the original building itself a Gothic masterpiece protecting the newly refurbished gardens. I'd been here many times in my youth, our annual family Easter break bringing us camping in the nearby Loughshore Park before we discovered the beautiful Langford Villa B&B and upgraded our annual Summer holiday to include accommodation there. Despite it's being situated a mere 20 mile drive from our Belfast home, an annual stay in Antrim was a must for my parents and I. Dad's ancestral routes were deeply embedded across several generations in nearby Randalstown before some had spread their tendrils toward Antrim, his birthplace, making our annual excursion a homecoming of sorts for him. It was here where he had felt grounded and through his love for the place I too had become besotted. Perhaps that was why I had returned, I wondered fleetingly. An attempt to retreat to the bosom of a family that I no longer had, to a place that had always made me feel safe and secure at a time when those were two of the very things I needed most. That was a different time though, and this, a different place.

Antrim Castle Gardens was now a modern and vibrant mix, a welcoming community hub for all, despite the darkness and fog it was currently enveloped in. Welcoming for all that was, except me. For me, the glowing light of the arched entrance held nothing but dread, the darkness, fog and distance between here and there only serving to compound my rising anxiety. That wasn't the building's fault, nor was it the fault of the people within it. It wasn't my fault either if I was being honest, though I very much felt like it was. That's what she'd managed to reduce me to. Even now in death she still lurked in every shadow, waiting, watching... ready.

'Get a grip Carolyn. She can't hurt you now. You made sure of that.'

Reaching inside my leather messenger bag on the passenger seat bench beside me, fingers busily searching out my phone within its contents, I felt my hand brush past the still chilled glass of the miniature wine bottle, one of two that I'd liberated from the mini bar in my hotel room. The other not long ago consumed before I'd left the hotel. Perhaps some more courage of the dutch variety would take the edge off. Give me the fire I needed to cross the forbidding expanse of the car park.

'Please don't let it come to this, please', I chastised myself, feeling the tears come. I'd seen first-hand how alcohol dependency can ruin a person, kill them, in the guise of an emotional support crutch.

'You're better than this', I told myself. 'You're not your mother.'

Finally gripping the phone instead, I drew it out to check on the time. The screen illuminated, simultaneously confirming my suspicion that I was ridiculously early and alerting my attention to a missed call and a voicemail from Beth.

'Good Luck Tonight. You'll ace it! The class are lovely. They've already reclaimed you as one of their own. They can't believe that THE Dr Carolyn Harkin is going to be taking over while I'm away. Enjoy it and remember that this town IS big enough for both of us. Looking forward to a catch up when we get back. Much Love. Beth.'

Beth's words of encouragement were exactly what I needed to bring me to my senses. Now one of my closest friends, we had met only a few years ago when she, a fellow crime fiction author, had been included on the same discussion panel as I had at the Theakston's Old Peculiar Crime Fiction Festival in Harrogate. We'd been close ever since, and the fellow Belfast girl, also now being Antrim based, had figured in my decision to come live here. Now the small Northern Ireland town found that it could boast not one, but two bestselling crime fiction authors amongst its residents. Instinctively I set myself to return the call before thinking better of it. Best to wait until later. No doubt that even whilst in Boston, Beth would be awaiting a debriefing after the class. Besides, I should take advantage of the adrenaline boost that her message had brought before it wore off. Better that than the wine. After all, I had a class to teach.

CHAPTER
FIVE

BELLA MASKULL WAS DOING HER BEST TO APPEAR FRIENDLY AS SHE watched the sullen Receptionist scan the screen in search of her name, seemingly most put out at having her small territory encroached upon, and worse still, having her attention taken from the well-thumbed paperback she was currently consumed by. The Dark Room by Sam Blake. Bella too was familiar with the book, having been a fan of Sam's since the Cat Connolly trilogy. For a brief moment Bella entertained herself with the thought that it would be unfortunate if she let slip the ending. The face of Clotsworthy House already resembled that of a bulldog chewing a wasp as was. The body beneath it reminding Bella of the political incorrectness of the phrase pleasantly plump and calling to mind the mirth filled voice of her much missed Uncle Dan to her ears. "You wouldn't want to go home to her twenty quid short in your wages." His views and humour of course were of their day but that hadn't made life without him any easier. It wasn't that Bella was normally unfriendly, quite the opposite in fact, but since realising that she couldn't find the confirmation email on her phone, all sense of affability toward the Receptionist had been replaced by a nervous angst.

'Isabella Maskull' the Receptionist droned in a nasal monotone without looking up, 'Yes, I have you here. I'll just tick you off my list. Isabella Maskull, 6 sessions attendance for, A Life of Crime (Writing) with Dr Carolyn Harkin. You're in the Foster suite.'

Feeling the knot in her stomach loosen a little, she waited, presuming instruction on how to get to The Foster Suite would follow, though it soon appeared that unless the directions had been secreted inside the foil wrapper of a KitKat bar that Miss Clotsworthy House 2023 had turned her attention to, she had presumed wrongly.

'How do I get to the Foster suite?' She heard herself ask politely, though the tone and language choices currently being employed by her inside voice were conveying her feelings much more accurately and colloquially. Preoccupied by the incredulity of the Receptionist, she hadn't noticed the other woman enter.

'That's exactly what I was about to ask.' The woman smiled by way of greeting.

'Oh, are you attending the course too?' The Receptionist's question sent debris from a mini explosion of chocolate particles and wafer radiating toward the surface of the Reception desk.

'I'm teaching it' the woman said enthusiastically, 'I'm Carolyn Harkin'.

Finally, an utterance worthy of commanding the full attention of the Receptionist. Regarding the latest arrival into her tiny domain with scrutiny, she seemed surprised. Bella wasn't. She already knew exactly who the woman was as soon as she had set eyes on her. She'd been looking forward to and dreading meeting her in equal measure all day. What was more, their meeting had a lot riding on it.

CHAPTER SIX

I'M NOT EXACTLY SURE WHAT I EXPECTED FROM THE FOSTER SUITE, BUT what I got wasn't it. When your usual workspaces are comprised of a heady mixture of lecture theatres, crime scenes, mortuaries or occasionally, a draughty home office, a cosy classroom space is a refreshing change.

'Wow, this is a nice place' remarked the first of my students to arrive, Isabella, or as I discovered on the way upstairs, Bella to her friends, of which it seemed I now counted. She took the words from my mouth.

'It's quite homely, isn't it', I answered, taking in the dandelion coloured walls, oatmeal carpet and small, pinewood fitted kitchen to the rear of the room. It looked like someone had already set the teaching space up for me. Four large banqueting tables had been laid out portrait style from the top of the room, to form a large rectangle topped and tailed with two more, the one nearest facing a wall mounted whiteboard, presumably my "stage".

'We kick off in twenty minutes, you need a hand with anything?' Bella asked, her voice a mixture of urgency and excitement.

'Yeah, that'd be great. Could you boil water for the tea and coffee pots while I connect my laptop to the projector?'

'Sure, no problem.'

As I fumbled with the wires and connections that would hopefully make my laptop speak to the projector provided by the venue, I became aware that she was working serenely and with an almost noiseless efficiency at the back of the room. Her back to me almost the entire time, ponytailed blonde hair shimmering from the eyeball lighting under which she was working, it was almost like she was deliberately trying to radiate calm vibes to neutralise the anxious ones that were screaming from me.

'Do you get nervous doing this sort of stuff?' she asked softly as she turned away from the hot water urn that was now hissing into life. Her tall, slim frame, yet shapely figure and the piercing pale blueness of her eyes reminded me of a younger Beth Shaw and I fleetingly wondered if they were related before dismissing it. After all, one of the two would have mentioned it, and besides, like me, Beth originally hailed from Belfast. Bella had already told me that she was Antrim born and bred.

'Not usually. I'm all over the place tonight for some reason though.' Some reason? I heard my inner voice mock me. I knew exactly the reason, and it had nothing to do with teaching a class.

Tea and coffee urns filled, milk jug removed from the small fridge and biscuits placed on a plate beside the sugar bowl, Bella was now effortlessly displaying the small selection of signed author copies of my books on a nearby table.

'You'll be fine' she replied with a warm smile.

I nodded.

'With you here, I think I might be.'

Moments later, the remainder of the small class arrived, each regarding me then the first slide from my presentation illuminating the whiteboard behind me in turn, firstly with curiosity, then a welcoming smile. I felt my muscles relax slightly, what had been the beginnings of a tension headache begin to recede and my breathing return to normal. I was going to like this group I think. Most importantly, it was show time.

'Ok! Welcome Everyone. My name is Carolyn. Let's plot some murders together!'

CHAPTER
SEVEN

FEELING HER CHEST TIGHTEN A LITTLE AND HER MOUTH DRY, BELLA Maskull hesitated slightly before beginning to share her response to Carolyn's first writing task of the evening. "Write Me A Murder" had been the instruction and for Bella the words had flowed with a redemptive ease. Reading them aloud though. That was a different matter altogether.

My name was Sarah, when I had a name. Sarah Clark. Not any more though. I lost my identity along with my life. Very few speak it now. It only brings with it grief or guilt...or both. Now, I'm only referred to as she, or the victim, or that poor girl. That was his doing. He was responsible for that, and more. He made me a victim. I fought back in the only way I could, though as the time neared, I'm ashamed to say that I was willing myself to pass. Willing it to end. An unhappy release. I wish I'd been stronger. Wish I could have fought harder. Wish I hadn't been a victim. That wasn't the type of person that I was. Feisty, passionate and intelligent were the kind of words I'd heard myself being described with in life. Descriptions that those who knew me, loved me, still use now after my death. In the past tense.

I thought he loved me. He told me often that he did. He didn't. He's a monster. A cold, unfeeling, self-serving, heartless monster. I know that now. I had my whole life ahead of me. We had our whole lives ahead of us. We'd made plans. I loved my life. I loved my job. I loved him. Now I'm here. Cold, alone, used and abandoned. Undiscovered. I need your help. I need you to find me. I need you to find him.

CHAPTER
EIGHT

'Write Me A Murder.' That's usually one of the first writing tasks that I ask my students to complete. Fifteen minutes of creative time where they get to fulfil their darkest desires...well, in a manner of speaking. It's typically a great ice breaker and friend maker in one fell swoop. After all, the participants in this type of class would normally already have an interest in the consumption of crime fiction from films, tv, or books like mine. They never seem to realise though that writing crime tends to involve, believe it or not, writing a crime, usually a murder, until it suddenly becomes the elephant in the room. For me, the outcome of this task usually gives me some idea of the types of writers that I'm dealing with and their level of knowledge of the genre. Usually the responses are archetypal. Tonight though, two of them had me floored.

Firstly, there was Bella's giving voice to the murdered, Sarah Clark. Such an interesting approach. It brought a chill to me. I was really looking forward to working with my new friend on developing that voice. The other, brought a chill for a very different reason, transporting me back to the London of yesteryear. A previous life, and a previous me. Back to a time and a place that I had tried to keep buried, and with good reason. Tried and failed; and was still being consumed by the consequences on a daily basis. Not like this though. This brought my anxiety and paranoia to a whole new level. Each word had placed me more and more firmly into a state of shock as they were read to the group. It was like he had been there. Present not just in place and time, but in my thoughts too. His words remained seared into my memory long after they'd been read, distracting me as I tried to listen to some of the other responses to the task from within the group. Still, there they were. Front and centre, replaying over and over again.

It was the closure of a crisp white envelope and its placement on a reclaimed wooden dining table that had ended the life of Victoria Harkin. Her fate had been sealed, literally. It had been no more than she deserved. For Carolyn Harkin, the middle name she had always preferred over Victoria, placing the Dear John letter right where he wouldn't miss it was where her life was set to truly begin, and that was no more than she deserved.

Despite the limitations that the hangover had placed upon her she was ecstatic. Was she really doing this? She certainly was. After all, what was the worst that could happen, right? She paused briefly to admire her handiwork. The deliberately heavy lipstick mark double sealing the envelope, a hot red beacon that would instantly draw his attention from where it sat beside the keys of his real true love, the Harley. Smiling, she snapped a mental polaroid she would revisit fondly in the future. At least that had been the intention.

Swinging the hastily packed duffel bag up onto her shoulder from where it lay on the hardwood floor, she purposely avoided her reflection in the vintage mirror as she made her way across the open planned kitchen diner-come-living space of the duplex apartment they shared. She didn't want to see herself. She wouldn't see herself. She would only see the Victoria that he'd moulded her into, and as of a few moments ago she no longer existed. Turning on her platform sandalled heel she walked out onto the first floor landing of the apartment, doing her best to wear a smile as she did so. The words of the popular proverb, "Feel The Fear and Do It Anyway" reverberated through her thoughts. Still, it didn't stop her casting only the merest glance toward the stairway leading to their second floor bedroom where he lay. A glance that brought with it a wave of angst. This was the right decision wasn't it? She couldn't allow herself to buckle now. Recalling her late father's mantra, "What Would Elvis Do?", she could almost feel her Dad's presence there with her, willing her on. The answer to that particular question in this case lay within the lyrics of one of The King's most popular hits. "It's Now or Never" she decided before striding purposefully along the bare wood first floor landing and descending the staircase that led to the exit.

 The leaving of what was now, her former home, brought her through the small garage area at the rear of the furniture shop used to house his motorcycle collection and the abundance of unfinished projects collected along the way as his engineering career and hipster lifestyle began to flourish. Finally outdoors, she scurried through the small unkept garden into the already scorching sunshine of a typical Saturday morning in July, her Northern Irish lungs struggling a little more than normal to acclimatise to the heady mixture of humidity and pollution filled air typical of the capital as she did so. Squeezing past the huge, white, 1970s Mercedes E Class that took up half the kerb in front of the shop, another of his unfinished projects, she had felt her heart sink a little at the sight of it. The decaying grandeur of the vehicle a perfect metaphor for their relationship. Onwards and upwards she told herself. She'd be fine she *told herself. They both would. Her leaving would be the making of them both. If she'd stayed it would have been the breaking of them. One of them at least. Next stop, Boston Manor Tube Station. The walk there would give her time to decide which side of the Piccadilly Line platform she would stand on. Was she Heathrow bound for a return to Northern Ireland? Her mother would like that. Her arrival with her tail between her legs would bring hugs and blessings...and I told you so's. No thanks.*

Whatever her decision, it would be better than 'Winter Wedding' that he had apparently planned for them. He had planned. She was only 19 for God's sake, and she'd only just gotten her foot in the door at The Met. Her career in policing had barely started. No matter what her future held she wasn't going to sacrifice that. It had been too hard won. Pushing away a stray strand of dark brown hair from where it had caught in the perspiration on her face, before adjusting the weight of the bag on her shoulder as she struggled to balance the weight over her slender frame as she walked, she started to become aware that all feelings of apprehension were beginning to abate. Today was the day she would take her life back.

Of course it could have been coincidence, stranger things have been known to happen. At least that's what I'd been telling myself as I had listened to him read aloud, fighting to keep my composure all the while. It wasn't though, I knew that from somewhere deep down inside me. Besides, the detail, everything was almost exactly as it had happened. He had confirmed my suspicions with a cold, hard, stare as he lifted his head from the notebook, the beginnings of a smirk unmissable at the corners of his mouth and his eyes narrowing in question. He was looking for a reaction, it was written all over his face. He wasn't about to get one though. At least not the type he'd been expecting. It was taking every bit of emotional strength I could muster, but he wasn't going to see me shocked. My game face was staying firmly on. That was of course if I could bring the flight part of my fight or flight instinct under control, which at the moment, I wasn't sure I could. Still, at least he didn't get to Daniel's death, my arrest...or Jess. I'm not sure if I could have held it together if he had.

'A perfect setting of the scene and I'll forgive your use of my name for your character...for now' I had heard myself say. He would be constructively critiqued just like everyone else had, 'what about the murder though?' He craned his neck back slightly, furrowing his brow as he did so. It was almost like my words had had a physical impact on him. Then the corners of his mouth curled back into a smirk.

'Apologies for borrowing your name. I had toyed with calling the character Jessica Farnham, maybe Jess for short, but your name seemed a better fit. The murder will come later. I know exactly what I have in mind for it, but that's a story for another time.'

CHAPTER NINE

'There we go. I think you've more than earned this' Bella said as she set the large glass of Marlborough down on the table in front of me before sliding into her seat and placing her tipple of choice, a pint of Magners cider, onto the beermat in front of her.

I smiled before lifting the glass and taking a long sip from the wine.

'Jeez, tonight was intense.'

The adrenaline was still awash through my bloodstream and I was a little wired, which was normal for me after delivering a workshop, but tonight's took the spike to a new high. Some food and some alcohol usually helped prepare me from the inevitable dip that was to follow and I was glad that Bella had agreed to join me for a late bite back at my hotel. Though I'm not normally the type to be so sociable with someone I've only just met, there was something about her that made me feel a connection. Perhaps it was her comment on there being safety in numbers as we found ourselves last to leave and contemplating the potential danger held in the dark and rainy isolation of the car park between us and the relative safety of our respective vehicles. She seemed like such a strong young woman, a reflection of what I had been up until a few years ago, yet she held the same fear that I had. The same vulnerability. In truth it mostly came from my being scared witless from the moment of hearing Jess' name being uttered by the seemingly clairvoyant class delegate, and the gnawing thought ever since that said member of the class could have been waiting for me outside. After all, it wouldn't be the first time a man has used the cloak of darkness and isolation to assert power over a lone woman, and he'd already inferred, although subtly, that intimidation and menace over me was what he was aiming for.

'You were great. What about that new guy though? What was all that about?'

Of course, everyone was new to us, but Bella and the mystery man in question were the only ones who were new to what had been Beth's group, so I knew exactly what she meant. I was glad too that she had noticed that something wasn't quite right about him. I was about to share my thoughts on just how weird and intense the whole situation had been, but hesitated, thinking better of it. Aside from not wishing to delve into my past with a virtual stranger, I needed to remember that I was the person delivering the course, and thus must maintain a level of professional discretion. Still, I did need to acknowledge it.

'I know, right? I'm glad you noticed that. I think he'll be one to watch' I frowned.

'Oh, I think I could manage that ok' she laughed.

I rolled my eyes before laughing too. Admittedly, I'd noticed that our mystery man was a bit of a looker. At around 6 feet in height, his slender, muscular body made him a perfect clothes horse, and his chosen attire, smart casual as it was, looked good on him. The ash blond hair and piercing grey eyes, an almost perfect complement to Bella's own, helped. Still, not that I was in the market, after tonight, it was safe to say that he wasn't my cup of tea.

'His story was really strange though, I mean, you were pretty clear. Write me a murder you said.'

'I know. I do occasionally get someone who writes outside the lines though, so it's not that unusual. Sometimes it's a refreshing change from the endless permutations of the gnarly but brilliant police officer with a complicated family life, alcohol dependency and a slew of equally stereotypical murder cases to solve, usually involving partially clothed young women.'

Bella laughed..

'Not that you're in any way cynical' she joked. It was easy to be in her company.

'No, not at all...well, maybe just a little' I chuckled, 'maybe I'm a bit gnarly myself. Joking apart though, I do love my work, especially the workshop part. Murder's been my business in one way or another for most of my professional life and I love all aspects of the work I do. I just sometimes wish that not everyone in the world would consider themselves as forensic experts or master sleuths just because of what they see on their screens or read in their books. Anyhow, I'm ranting, time for a change of subject. So, who was the girl? A friend, family member?'

Bella shifted uncomfortably before placing the rim of the condensation frosted pint glass to her lips, an apparent effort to appear relaxed.

'What girl? What do you mean?'

'Sarah. The girl in your story. She was real, wasn't she?' I answered, watching her expression intently.

'Yeah but, how..?'

'Call it years of police experience, or crime writer's intuition, but mostly a doctorate in psychology, and like I say, murder is my business.'

'Ok, you got me' she replied meekly, 'It's kind've why I joined your course. Though I am a huge fan of your books, and of course, who doesn't love Netflix's hottest new detective series.'

Her face blanched as she sheepishly fumbled her words and struggled to maintain eye contact with me.

'Relax. You had me at Yeah, now let's order some food and you can tell me all about it.'

The relief in her expression was immediately obvious and she instantly appeared to be more at ease. I'd sensed that there was some element of reality in her story as she'd read it and had been intrigued then. I was more so now.

'Thanks. I really am a fan of your work though, and the show.'

'Me too. I'm pretty sure my agent and bank manager are fans as well' I joked, 'Now, tell me what's good on the menu.'

CHAPTER TEN

Glenn McGinley's sense of smug self-satisfaction peaked after ending the reporting phone call. 'Now we're sucking diesel' came the voice on the other end of the line, a satirical reference to a popular TV crime drama filmed in Belfast. McGinley took the phrase as an indication of approval for his part in what would be his very own story. The one that he had started to plot a considerable time ago and was already orchestrating future instalments of from the first instant of setting foot into Carolyn Harkin's class. He didn't need approval of course, especially from her, but to have it was a bonus.

'You haven't seen anything yet. If the good doctor thinks she's fucked up in the head now, she won't know what's hit her by the time I've finished with her. She will know who though?'

CHAPTER
ELEVEN

THE BAR-RESTAURANT AREA OF THE HOTEL DIDN'T LOOK NEARLY AS homely and appealing in the harsh light of morning as it had last night. Doubling now as a breakfast room, the morning sun streaming in from the wall of glass on its left side caught virtually every one of the numerous particles of dust as they floated in a semi-suspended animation above the dance floor. The large blocks of sunshine cast across the floor and furnishings too were unforgiving, putting the threadbare furniture under a spotlight and showing the dated decor at its garish worst.

Seated at the same table I had shared the evening before with Bella, I waited whilst my order, the traditional cooked breakfast that was the famed, "Ulster Fry" was processed. The tea in the small silver pot that sat on the table in front of me would be brewed nicely by the time the food arrived, which should be shortly, given that I was the only person in the room, and the assurances from the waitress who took the order, that Rusty, the chef would be right on it. The name, no doubt a nickname conjured images of a flame haired cook akin to the Swedish Chef character in The Muppet Show in my mind. As I waited, I couldn't help but think that as I was attired, I probably fitted in with the decor perfectly. Dressed in skinny dark blue jeans that had seen better days, my favourite oversized Jack Wills hoodie and vintage Converse trainers, my dark brown hair scraped back into a loose ponytail, and wearing not a pick of make-up, I could probably be most flatteringly described as shabby chic this morning. Still, I was moving into my new house today so was dressed for purpose. Unlike the decor of the room though, on the whole, I was probably wearing well, though admittedly since reaching the age of forty one earlier this year I'd noticed that there was now a little more work involved in maintaining a "natural" look. Still, I could turn heads if and when I chose to, I smiled to myself. Today, as with the majority of others, I chose not to.

The arrival of my breakfast brought with it a sense of nostalgia as the sight, smell and taste of the fried potato bread and soda bread transported me to the kitchen table of my youth in South Belfast. A firm favourite of my dad's, I could almost hear my mum nagging him as she picked over a bowl of muesli whilst lecturing him on the clogging and hardening of his arteries, and the risk of a coronary that he was placing himself at the mercy of. Equally, I could hear his stock reply that he would walk it off easily and bemoaning the fact that the young nurse he had fallen for as a hospital porter now never completely allowed herself to be off duty. Of course, she had been right, a fact that she appeared to revel in telling the mourners as we waked him at home before the funeral that would be held the day before my seventeenth birthday. That was just her though. I don't think she could help it if she tried. Equally, I don't think she ever did try. Always right, even when she was wrong. I felt a flush of anger at the thought of the irony of her own passing. The gradual poisoning of her body in a slow suicide in years of committed alcoholism. Of course alcoholism was an illness, I got that. It didn't stop me thinking though that if she'd been as committed as a wife and mother as she was to pickling her liver and adding further bile and acid to an already sharp tongue, fate might have dealt her a better hand. I tried to get her out of my thoughts, annoyed with myself that I had allowed her to invade my consciousness again. She didn't deserve to be there.

As I ate, I tried to stop my thoughts returning to the other place they were desperate to go. The same place that had robbed me of the majority of my sleep last night. The Writing Group. Him...and Jess. I did need to process what had happened alright, but now was not the time. My fractured psyche couldn't cope with it any more now than it could then. Instead, I occupied my thoughts with Bella and her story. I totally got why she wanted to give Sarah Clark, her friend, a voice. From what she had told me so far, I agreed that there was more to the young woman's disappearance than the missing persons case label warranted. I also agreed that what she had theorised as a possible murder, with a definite suspect in mind, had merit. I had been resolved to do what I could from the get-go and that had been before Bella had told me of the impact that the disappearance of her friend had had upon her own life; ending her career in nursing before it had barely began and condemning her to a string of failed relationships stemming from a deep anger towards, and a mistrust of men that came from, what she thought, the fate of her friend had likely been. The one exception of her skewed view of men, it had transpired from our conversation last night, being her employer, the man who had saved her sanity and offered her an unlikely career in building renovation and interior design. The man, who as it happened, was currently under contract to me in readying my new home. Now I was determined to persuade the powers that be within the PSNI, that this would be the first case I would consult on, alongside writing my next novel. That would be a job for tomorrow though. Today was about settling into my new life and I could hardly wait a minute longer. Especially since I was about to be reunited with the house of my dreams. Langford Villa...and of course there was Uther.

CHAPTER
TWELVE

THE CLOUD OF CONDENSATION FROM THE STEAM RISING FROM THE COFFEE changing state as it hit the cold glass that was the inside windscreen of the Mini had gone unnoticed by Bella Maskull. Nibbling at the Sausage McMuffin held in her left hand, her head tilted downward toward the phone held in her right, she was engrossed. A passer-by in the McDonalds car park could have been forgiven for the presumption that it was her social media that had captivated her so. After all, the majority of us could be increasingly and accurately accused of zombified scrolling of our feeds whenever time allowed or boredom came, running the gauntlet of early onset arthritis in our thumbs as the result. It wasn't the banal pictures of others depicting their lives as being more glamorous than their reality that she was perusing though. Nor was it the endless stream of gifs, videos and fake news that permeate so much of our social media, taking their places among the other sources of micro-aggression that is often parodied in advertising. Instead, the image that had transfixed her was that of a young girl. A local girl. A dead girl, who according to the article beneath it, written just a month before, had died supposedly by suicide, having been found drowned in the nearby Sixmilewater

River at Antrim Castle Gardens. If the article was to be believed, the young woman had a history of familial abuse, a problem with alcohol and bouts of poor mental health, all of which may or may not have been true. Whether they were or not had been of little consequence to Bella. What she had been questioning was the cause of death. Suicide as stated, perhaps, but the fact that the woman had borne such a striking resemblance to Sarah and was of similar age to her at the time of her disappearance made her doubt it strongly. She too had been murdered. She was convinced of it and had become obsessed by it. A deadly mistake had been made. Her mistake, and perhaps an innocent party had paid much too high a price for it. She had thought about mentioning the news story to Carolyn last night but had decided against it for fear of sounding manic. It was difficult enough to get up the courage to tell her about Sarah without adding any further complications into the mix. She would tell her though when the time was right. For now, she needed to quickly finish up on her breakfast and make her way to work. The Langford Villa job was almost complete, which was such a shame. She had really fallen in love with the place, though her blossoming friendship with Carolyn may allow further visits. She hoped so.

CHAPTER
THIRTEEN

THE ENTRANCE WAS EXACTLY HOW I HAD REMEMBERED IT. The high stone walls and tall overhanging trees that made up the perimeter of the property remained divided at the front entrance by two grey stone pillars standing sentry on either side of the metal framed, heavy oak gate, forbidding entry to the single track gravel driveway that led to the house. The butterflies in my stomach danced even more enthusiastically than they already had been as I pressed the button on my key-fob that would activate the newly installed motor of the now electronically controlled gate. As it slowly opened to allow access to my battered rental, I fought an urge to retch as the fluttering in my stomach churned a fried breakfast that I now realised was a bad idea. I did my best to ignore it, choosing to focus more on the sight that was about to be revealed to me by the open gate as opposed to the internal machinations of a battle between my digestive and nervous systems.

I didn't wait for the gate to open fully, opting to impatiently cross the threshold as soon as a gap wide enough to squeeze the van through became available. It was just as I had remembered and I was as awestruck at the sight of it now as I had been in my youth, where I would take in the view of the house ahead and grounds and gardens either side of the drive annually through the windscreen of a range of equally battered and tired vehicles that had made up my father's car history.

At the end of the drive, the single track opened into a larger circular expanse at which the house was central. Built from the same stone and echoing the Edwardian Gothic style of Clotsworthy House, the centrepiece of Antrim Castle Gardens, and home to its aristocracy, the majestic two storey Langford Villa had once been part of the Clotsworthy Estate and had been named in honour of Lady Marian Langford, bride of Sir Hugh Clotsworthy, of whom it had been said, had a particular liking for this part of the estate. The reason why lay behind the house where in lieu of a back garden was a small sandy cove and a short wooden jetty that extended out onto the magnificent body of water that was Lough Neagh. Aside from its name, the building that I still struggled with the idea of calling home bore other hallmarks of Lady Langford, the most notable of which being a statue mounted high on a plinth overlooking the gardens at the front of the house. The statue, the unmistakeable likeness of an Irish Wolfhound was a scaled version of its considerably larger counterpart that currently rested at the centre of the Castle Gardens. The sight of it called to memory the former owner of the house, Eileen Magee, herself the owner of an Irish Wolfhound that I had befriended as a youth and maintained a closeness to into my mid-teens until the animal passed or had crossed Rainbow Bridge as Eileen had put it. Eileen too had been smitten by the house and owned it as a B&B with her husband for many years. It had been her who had told me of the folklore around the statue. The stone representation was in tribute to an Irish Wolfhound who had become legendary after twice appearing from out of the blue to save the life of Lady Langford. The first saw the hound in a fight to the death with a wolf that had cornered the woman and was set to pounce. The hound though victorious almost died in the battle. In appreciation Lady Langford had nursed it back to health and had given it a home with her. The animal later once more saved her life and that of her husband by alerting them to an imminent attack upon Antrim Castle. The dog from that point onward had been heralded as mascot and protector of the estate and upon its death, was celebrated in stone, the statue itself entering into folklore. It had been said that whilst the statue stood in one piece, the estate and its people would be safe. Areas of the estate, such as the Villa, that were held in particular esteem were each awarded a scaled version of the statue for further protection. I was as in love with the story as I was with the statue. The fact that it nicely tied in with my memories of Eileen and her own mighty hound made it all the better. So much so that as soon as the property had become legally mine, I immediately decided that I would have a living companion in the form of an Irish Wolfhound pup. Uther had subsequently been sourced and would be ready to leave his mother for his new home with me in just a few days' time. Of course I would be lying if I'd said that folklore and sentimentality were my only reasons for bringing him into my life. After all that I'd been through lately I would rest easier with the protection that he would provide.

CHAPTER
FOURTEEN

It was only after he had clicked the save and print icons on his MacBook that Glenn McGinley became aware of the stiffness across his shoulder blades and at the back of his neck. Using the middle three fingers of his right hand he kneaded the muscle at the back of his neck before repeatedly rolling his shoulders. It brought only light relief. Still, the stiffness and pain would be worth it. The tension he was feeling within his muscles was nothing in comparison to the tension that the document currently running through the printer was laced with. Dr Harkin wanted a murder to be written. That would be exactly what she would be presented with in the next workshop. The tension for her wouldn't lie in the story though. After all, what happened there should be familiar to her. The fact that he had written about it though, that he even knew about it, that's where the tension would lie for her. He smiled to himself, picturing her reaction to the piece of work he'd prepared ahead of the class. He visualised the potential range of emotions being displayed on her face as he would watch her read it, visualised also the range of possibilities of what might happen next. He was looking forward to seeing the lovely Carolyn again. For now though, he would content himself with rereading through the manuscript. Picking the document from the floor in front of the printer from where the machine had unceremoniously spat out the art that was his words committed to paper, he moved to the sofa. The famed words of the BBC's, Listen With Mother programme, for some reason entered his mind.

'Are you sitting comfortably? Then I'll begin.'

As her partner responded to the tinny distorted voice originating from the control centre pulsating through the small speaker in their car radio, the young sergeant gunned the engine of their Batonberg liveried Vauxhall Vectra, adrenaline already beginning to coarse through her veins. The call, a report of a domestic disturbance brought with it a sense of urgency, especially when she heard the address. She'd been there before. Just days before. Saw the visible evidence of battery across a tear streaked face, already inflamed and swollen. Saw the young woman tremble with fear as she had held the door ajar, insistent that it had just been an argument. Insistent that she was fine as she gripped the door tightly, peering around it for fear they would ask to come in. Saw the relief in the young woman's face as she moved to leave, both knowing full well that everything was not ok. Would not be ok.

They were right.

Now as her colleague cuffed and mirandised the man, she regarded him for the first time. Small but heavyset and muscular, the skin on his head pale in comparison to the skin on his face indicating that it had recently been razor shaven, she found herself wondering if it was the small man syndrome or the male pattern baldness that had caused the insecurity. There had to be some reason behind the steroid inflated bulk and the need for exertion of power over a defenceless woman. Maybe he was making up for another inadequacy. Perhaps he was the owner of a large car too. She continued to watch as he tried to struggle against her partner as he tried to lead the man from the scene; the thug voraciously protesting his innocence all the way. Her colleague was more than up to the challenge. For her part she was zoned out from the actual words, no doubt the usual diatribe about her having provoked him or that it had been accidental, or just some other equally pathetic excuse. Whatever the case, the remains of what had been a young woman with her entire life ahead of her, were now splayed across the kitchen floor. Her job now was clear. She was to secure the scene and make the necessary calls that would allow an investigation to begin in earnest. Yet here she stood, rooted to the spot, unable to face the young woman even in death. Especially in death. There was no more she could do for her now. Yes, she could work to bring the perpetrator to justice, but that wouldn't bring her back. She'd failed her. What's more, she knew she was failing her as she had walked away that night. She half remembered the famous quote about evil triumphing when good men, or women in her case, do nothing, and wondered what the now dead, young woman would have done if their roles had been reversed.

'You wanted a murder my dear Carolyn. Let's see how this one grabs you.'

CHAPTER
FIFTEEN

OBVIOUSLY I'D EXPECTED A CERTAIN AMOUNT OF NOSTALGIA UPON returning to Langford Villa. What I hadn't been expecting was to be confronted by the first major crush of my teenage life. Following the noise coming from behind the house I moved to the rear courtyard in search of the cause. What I found on the face of it was a man on a ladder, seemingly installing an intruder alarm as per my instruction. It wasn't just any man though, it was him. The object of my teen affections and the source of seemingly endless blushes when I was in his presence. One Sam Moran. Despite having his back to me and being at a height, his figure was unmistakeable. What's more, it was every bit as toned now as it had been when I'd last set eyes on him more than two decades ago. I hadn't made the connection when Beth Shaw had recommended him to project manage the restoration to the house, nor had I made the connection when we had exchanged almost daily emails regarding the project specifications and minutiae, right down to the colour palates and kitchen design. I supposed I could be forgiven for that. After all, I had no reason to associate the name, Sam Moran with anything. Back in the day, to me he was just plain old Sam.

'Oh, Hi Carolyn' came Bella's voice, drawing my attention away from him whilst alerting him to my presence, 'I hadn't expected you for a while yet.'

'Oh, Bella, you startled me.' I instinctively tapped the flat of my hand across my chest several times as if trying to calm palpitations.

'Yes, you were deep in thought' she smiled before tipping her head in the direction of the man now descending the ladder.

'Victoria' I heard him murmur, his head craned forward, eyes narrowed and tone questioning. I blushed.

'Vickey...it is you isn't it?' I blushed further if that was possible, as he closed the distance between us in what seemed like just a few strides.

'Yes' I heard myself reply, raising my right hand to brush an imaginary loose strand of hair over my ear, one of my nervous tells, 'I, I mean...well, I haven't been called that name in a while. I use my middle name now. Carolyn.'

I offered my hand in greeting as I said my name. An effort to diffuse my embarrassment and regain control the situation. It didn't work.

'You! You're Dr. Carolyn Harkin?' He looked taken aback to say the least. He wasn't the first person to address me in this way when matching my name to my face and definitely not the first man. Still, in his case there was a more genuine reason for his surprise.

He smiled and reached to lightly grip the tops of my arms, regarding me more closely.

'I can't believe it's you. I mean, I didn't think to...'

'No, me either. I'd no reason to...' I let the sentence trail off, not quite sure how to finish it.

Sam had worked here around the house in its B&B days and had been one of the main reasons, *the* reason why I always looked forward to our holidays here as a girl. Then, he had borne a more than passing resemblance to Morten Harket, the Scandinavian pop heart-throb who not only was the lead singer of my favourite band, A-ha, but if the fates would allow, had also been set to be my future husband. Obviously even the pre-teen me knew that was never really going to be the case. Sam on the other hand, he was at least a bit more obtainable. Just a bit.

For his part, he was fully aware of the looks that he had been blessed with and equally aware of the wide eyed girl who mooned around the place after him, besotted, who became a wilted wallflower with even the merest hint of his smile in her direction. He was confident, nonchalant even, but never unfriendly or unkind. I'd always been sure I wasn't the only girl who he'd had that effect on. I wasn't that naive. Nor was I foolish enough to think that he didn't have a string of girlfriends. Still, he'd always been...nice. In actual fact, he still bore more than a passing resemblance to Morten Harket, both men having aged exceptionally well.

'Why don't we give you a tour of the house?' I heard Bella say, no doubt attempting to escape the awkward reunion she'd stumbled across.

'Great idea' I replied, a little more gushingly than I would have wished.

'Then maybe I'll show you how to use that fancy new coffee machine of yours inside, and you can catch me up on all that's been happening the last...20 years?' He hadn't lost his ability to disarm tension or dissipate awkwardness with his smile and the warm, softness of his voice. That voice.

I returned his smile. 'Sounds like a plan. Then we can look at compiling a project review' I answered without missing a beat, making him aware that despite an initial stumble in meeting him again, I was now fully aware that I was no longer a teenage girl.

CHAPTER
SIXTEEN

Despite Sam's earlier offer, it had been Bella who ended up manning the coffee machine in the end. She had accompanied them on the grand tour of Carolyn's newly remodelled home, watching as Carolyn Oohed, Aaahed and Wowed in all the right places. She did seem genuinely blown away with the quality of the finished house, and why wouldn't she? It would have been a clear contender for Northern Ireland Home of the Year if she chose to enter it after all, and of course, would have been hankered after by many as a dream home. Still, as they progressed through the house Bella had become more and more aware that increasingly, Carolyn's interests lay elsewhere and Sam was talking less about colour palates and finishes, or anything else, leaving the talking of shop to her as his assistant, as he became more preoccupied with the new lady of the house. Bella couldn't blame him. Her almost perfectly symmetrical porcelain doll features were flawless, her narrow frame one to be admired and envied; Bella suspected that Carolyn was completely unaware of her natural beauty. Either that or there was a reason why she seemed to try to conceal it. Sam was completely fixated by her. What's more, the conversation was now flowing easily between them, and dare Bella think it, there seemed to be evidence of the beginnings of a spark there. So much so that they had barely acknowledged her as she served coffee to the dining table, Carolyn chatting easily and Sam completely captivated.

'I'll leave you two to catch up then so' she said as she set the milk jug, sugar bowl and a small plate of assorted biscuits down beside the steaming cups of freshly brewed Lavazza. Waving off Carolyn's polite protestations, she grabbed herself a coffee and made her way outside, grabbing her notebook and pen from the windowsill in the hallway as she went. She wouldn't be able to enjoy the views afforded by the house for much longer so she may as well make the most of them while she could. Besides, it would give her time to ponder on how her writing would develop and how she could further tell the story of Sarah Clark. She already had an idea. Carolyn had mentioned that in the next workshop they would be exploring the creation of a hero or villain character. She'd had more experience of the latter than the former and one in particular was textbook. Putting pen to paper she began to give Sarah a further voice.

I was never aware if Cillian Moran's mother had known the meaning of the Christian name she had been insistent upon bestowing upon her newborn son. I doubted it. If she had, she may not have followed through on her choice. Regardless, his name was an apt one. Of Celtic origin it was equally as associated with war and strife as it was with Churches and Monasteries. That was him right to the letter. The picture of innocence and light, though interact with him at your peril. Unfortunately for me, I'd been one of many poor souls who had become embroiled in the storm at which he was the centre, and I'd paid most dearly for it.

I hope there have not been others like me. Others who have suffered my fate at his hands. I wouldn't be surprised if there have been. He was a skilled lady's man after all. Women gath-

ered around him like moths to a flame. And of course, he didn't look like a murderer, did he? Whenever I'd heard someone say that on news reports or TV programmes I often wondered what they thought a murderer did look like. In my case he looked decidedly like Cillian Moran.

CHAPTER
SEVENTEEN

Unpacking the boxes marked "Study" in my new writing space had given me a little time to reflect on my return to Northern Ireland. Langford Villa had been everything I had hoped for and more. Sam and Bella had done an extraordinary job in the refurbishment. Not an easy task it had to be said, given my exacting specifications and written in stone decree that the final look was to be a perfect marriage of original and modern features. They hadn't just met the brief, they'd smashed it. What was more, the place was already feeling like home. My home, despite my continued carrying of the monkey on my back that was imposter syndrome. When I'd heard that the property had become available I was desperate to own it, yet my agent had practically had to beg me to put an offer in on it. I'd been the same at every stage of my career development. Not worthy of any of the offices I'd held, despite reaching the rank of DI in the police and all those which preceded it, by merit. I probably could have smashed through that particular glass ceiling too if I'd put my mind to it, even though the police service in those days might well have been described as an old boys network, well a boys network anyway. I'd been the same too when awarded my Doctorate in Investigative Psychology. The award had been a reward for all the hard work and study that I'd put into the qualification, yet when it came to it, the title of Doctor hadn't sat well with me at first. After all, I was just a working class girl from the streets of Belfast. Surely at some point I would receive a tap on the shoulder from someone much more worthy than I, who would tell me to, as we would say in Belfast, "catch yourself on". I'm surprised I ever had the confidence to send that first crime novel manuscript off to the publisher in the first place, yet without it, I wouldn't be here where I was today, a bestselling novelist with a huge publishing deal, an eye-watering Netflix deal and a new consulting role with the PSNI. I was grateful, I truly was, but I would gladly have traded it all to have some of the events that have happened to me in my adult life, particularly in recent years, not to have happened. Maybe that was the Catholic guilt heaped upon me by my mother. Between that, the imposter syndrome and her disappointment that I didn't reflect her archaic views on gender, I'm surprised I ever achieved anything, let alone feeling undeserving or guilty at having done so.

'Looks like you're settling in nicely' Bella said from the doorframe, 'the people from Irwins are here to pick up the hire van. Is there anything else you need to get out of it?'

'No, it should be good to go, I'll come down now and give them the keys.'

'Cool' she smiled, 'speaking of keys, they also have a delivery for you.'

The excitement on her face was unmistakeable and I knew exactly why. I'd been like a child in a toy shop when picking out what I suspected was now sitting on the front drive of the house and had been looking forward to this particular delivery for a while, albeit with a tinge of not being deserving. Just a tinge.

The Irwin family, owners of the local Ford dealership had overseen the details of the sponsorship vehicle that came with my

Netflix series, and my additional purchase, and now three generations of Irwin men were stood outside the house. The youngest, knowing his place had already made his way toward the hire van they had arranged for the transport of my worldly goods whilst his father and grandfather stood proudly alongside the vehicles they were about to present. That was a picture in itself, though the faces agog reactions of Sam and Bella almost rivalled it.

The vehicles instantly transported me to my American muscle car fuelled TV obsessions of childhood. Never would the 8 year old Tomboy me have ever dreamt that I would be the proud owner of not just a Ford Ranger Pick-Up Truck, but also, the pinnacle of American auto engineering, a Ford Mustang. They were breathtaking. The Ranger, finished in flat grey with two metallic grey Mustang style racing stripes running right down the centre of the bodywork, and huge black, matt finish alloy wheels was an excellent choice for country living for Uther and me when he arrives. The other vehicle, the Mustang, my self-indulgence and what I told myself would be my urban ride was nothing short of stunning. Finished in shadow black with iconic matt black racing stripes running down its centre, I'd requested the addition of a thin strip of red piping at the outward edge of both stripes as well as black, bowling ball style alloys in homage to the star of my favourite 80s TV show, Knight Rider's, KITT. I'd always been a Mustang fan but it's choice as the hero car in the 2008 Knight Rider reboot made it a must have for me if I was ever in the position to do so. The show itself, as a reboot had been a disappointment. Over sexualised and aimed at fans of the Fast and Furious franchise, it had completely missed the ethos of the original show and had unsurprisingly been cancelled midway through its first season. The car though, had been perhaps the only good choice. A natural successor for the Pontiac Trans-Am of the original that had held a fond place in my heart. If another reboot set in Antrim with a female lead was on the cards, then I could now well be the woman for the job.

'I think it's fair to say that we're going to need to upgrade security in the garage' Sam japed.

'I hadn't thought of that, but yes, you're right. There are a couple of other things that have occurred to me this afternoon too that it might be good to add to your jobs list' I replied.

'I have a jobs list now too.' He arched his eyebrows in feigned surprise.

'Yes, we'll combine it with the jobs that come up in the contract review. We'll discuss it over dinner maybe? The least I could do for you after you helping me move in would be to cook for you both'.

'Sounds like a plan' he nodded; lips pursed slightly.

'Don't mind him Carolyn, we'd love to. It's not like he has any pressing engagements for the evening is it?'

'Hey...'

'I'll need to do a grocery shop first though' I added, realising that there would be nothing in the house.

'Brilliant, I'll come with. We'll take...the Mustang. You drive there and I'll drive back' Bella replied, only half joking at the expectation of taking the wheel for at least part of the errand. A woman after my own heart.

CHAPTER
EIGHTEEN

My first outing as host of a dinner engagement in my new kitchen diner had involved more heating up than actual cooking, but that was fine with me, and as far as I could tell, my guests too. Courtesy of the M&S store adjacent to Belfast international Airport and just a short drive away from Langford Villa, our menu consisted of a Prawn tempura starter, Chicken and Bacon Carbonara main, a side of Garlic Bread and dessert of Key Lime Pie, all of which I had been assured in the store by Bella, would be more than agreeable with Sam. She was right about that. It seemed that they'd approved of my wine choices too. I'd teased her a little about her relationship with Sam, receiving a ribbing from her about my blushes when I saw him for my trouble. Still, they seemed close and I was determined to find out more about how Bella, a former nurse, had ended up working as a builder-come-interior designer with a former B&B handyman, which was where I was now steering the conversation as we sat around the dining table, glasses freshly charged and surrounded by the remnants of our meal.

'It all stemmed from my work around here in the B&B days' Sam said by way of introduction on his part, 'As the time went by there were more and more little handyman jobs that needed doing around here, then word got around and other people started asking me to do work for them too. Eventually the jobs started getting bigger and more complicated, and to cut a long story short, after a few years at the local Technical College, I was ready to set up on my own. Things have been going from strength to strength.'

'Evidently' I smiled, 'you're not on your own now.'

'I guess that was more by fate than design, eh Bella?' He nodded across the table at her, a look of paternal pride evident on his face. There was something else there too I guessed, trying to curb the psychologist in me. A hint of sadness would have been my initial conclusion, the glassiness of his gaze and half smile the giveaways.

Bella flushed.

'Sam's been really good to me' she said, 'especially since Sarah's disappearance and...Cillian.'

'Cillian?' I asked to her now slightly bowed head.

'My son' Sam answered on her behalf, a weakness in his tone now, 'Cillian. He died a few years back, an accident on a job I'd been working on. He came to the site and...anyway, we lost him.'

'Cillian had been Sarah's partner before she disappeared, and we were all friends' Bella interjected, 'after she disappeared I was really struggling. Cillian was too. We really helped each other out and we started seeing each other until, until he died too. Like I say, Sam's been great. He's really helped me through it all.'

'We've helped each other' Sam corrected, handing her a fresh napkin to dab away the tears that were beginning to form.

'I'm sorry, I shouldn't have, I mean, I was just curious about how you came to be working together. I'm so sorry for your loss too. Both of you' I said.

'No need to apologise' Sam replied. Bella nodded her agreement as she tried to regain her composure.

'When Sarah went, I couldn't continue in nursing without her. Sam provided me with support through distracting me with helping with house dressing etc. I eventually got bitten by the property refurbishment and development bug, and here we are.'

Bella's eyes though still red rimmed, brightened as she spoke. News of Cillian's existence and death had stunned me a little. Why hadn't she mentioned him before? I mean, she'd mentioned that she had suspected Sarah's boyfriend as her killer but as I recall, hadn't mentioned him by name, or that she too had a connection to him. Interestingly, I also noted that when she referred to his death using the word too, the implication that she thought Sarah was dead had been obvious. There had been no sign of any reaction to the statement from Sam. I wondered what his take on the situation was and had made a mental note to find out when the time was right.

'Here you are indeed, and aren't I glad of it' I quipped, raising my glass. It was true, I was glad. Not just for the newly formed and rekindled friendships, or the excellent job they'd done on the house. I was truly glad of the company. Despite the state of the art security and alarm systems, I hadn't been looking forward to being left alone. Some good company whilst I steeled myself with the dutch courage I needed to get through the night alone was exactly what this particular Doctor ordered.

CHAPTER
NINETEEN

'Dr Harkin, so nice to meet you. We've been looking forward to your arrival. Please, come in.'

Assistant Chief Constable Brian Hannon rose from the seated position behind his cluttered desk, beckoning me into the small office cubicle that served as his base. I'd once heard someone say that the measure of how busy someone was could be directly reflected in how messy their desk was. I often wondered if it was rather a reflection of their time management. In his case, I suspected the former to be the truth.

'Thank you, it's nice to finally meet you' I replied, hand outstretched to meet his, 'I'm looking forward to getting started.'

'Let's have a seat over here and we can have a chat. Coffee?'

He gestured toward the rear wall that partitioned his office off from the open planned workspace beyond it. Just in front of it sat a small, circular coffee table, a chair at either side, all of which smacked of inexpensive but functional Swedish design.

I nodded my acceptance and seated myself on the chair to the left as he temporarily exited. To arrange the coffee I suspected. As I waited I took in the space around me. Although at a premium, it had been thoughtfully utilised, though with the exception of the chairs and table at which I was now seated, the room and its contents looked to have seen better days. It occurred to me that his office was not befitting for his office. I smiled at the thought of how clever I had been in the lexicon of my thought, though was also aware that had I been seated in front of my laptop drafting my new novel, that the words invariably wouldn't come so easy.

Thinking further on it, Hannon himself seemed at odds with his position. At around five feet eleven with a paunch, thinning mousy hair and outfit comprised of navy chinos, a plain, sky blue shirt, navy wooden blazer and burgundy tie jarring with his modern choice of spectacles, he certainly didn't conform to the stereotype of the higher echelons figure of policing that my experience of several throughout the years had led me to form. Momentarily he returned carrying a small tray which he shakily set down on the table between us before lowering himself into the seat opposite me.

'There we are. The coffee and Danish from the canteen here are a must' he smiled, 'I almost said are to die for, but given our line of business, perhaps that would have been a poor choice of words. Anyhow, they almost make up for the shortcomings of the place. Almost.'

It had almost been like he'd read my mind, and although it wouldn't have been a massive leap for him to have guessed what had occupied my thoughts in his absence, it irked me a little, nonetheless. I'd had quite enough of coming into contact with the seemingly clairvoyant after my encounter with the mystery man at the writing class.

'I'm supposed to be based at the new Field Centre & HQ in East Belfast' he continued, 'I am most days, just to keep the Chief happy, but I like to work from here when I can. I've spent so many years of my career here that it feels like home. More importantly, it's closer to home.'

I hadn't yet visited the Field Centre HQ but I'd seen the

pictures from the website and it was certainly clear from those that the building was a reflection of the corporate face of policing, so would not necessarily appeal to those who have been seasoned by their experience on the front line.

'You've sold me' I said, nodding toward the pastries as I lifted the tiny milk jug and whitened my coffee. In truth, as he had been speaking I was already being seduced by the delicious aromas emanating from the fresh pastries and what was quite obviously a quality coffee filter. As he followed suit with the milk and in his case, sugar, I couldn't help but exercise the little area of my brain reserved for character profiling. I knew little about the man who bore the stereotypical informal title, "Boss", but given that he had just as good as admitted to feeling uncomfortable in the environs of the PSNI HQ and the fact that he was dressed more like a kindly English Teacher about to provide a roadmap to success to a misguided Sixth Former, I suspected that he hadn't been a career cop. Most likely he was just a nice guy who happened to be exceptionally good at his job and that his progression through the ranks had been a natural one, most likely being bestowed rather than sought. That said, I was also fully aware that to maintain such a career trajectory, one needed to have exceptional people skills, an extraordinary resilience, a highly functioning bullshit detector and an unwavering attitude of not suffering fools gladly. In that instant I knew we would get along. I also knew from the expression that he now wore, that the niceties were about to be dispensed with.

'Dr Harkin, I'm not sure what has already been explained to you in relation to your consultancy role, but I'm sure you're aware of the financial pressure that forces UK wide have been placed under in recent years. The PSNI are no exception.'

I nodded, mouth full of Danish, which was indeed, to die for. There was no hostility in his tone but I suspected that if my consultancy fees could be directed elsewhere in his budget, he would have done so.

'I suppose what I'm saying is, the role may not always be as hands on as you might have been led to believe. We're not the FBI. There's not a great deal of need for criminal profiling here. Though in fairness, that particular aspect of your skillset may be called upon from time to time.'

He stopped, as if checking my understanding. I swallowed.

'I'm not under any illusion Sir. I'm fully aware that the role will have its limitations in accordance with budget and other constraints. By its very nature consultancy is an as and when arrangement and I'm happy to work within those parameters.'

My response appeared to bring with it a flicker of relief on his part before he was down to business again.

'That said, one of our key objectives is to dramatically increase our hit rate for prosecutions so we will, as I've said, from time to time, need your experience in the field. For the most part though, I'd like your role to be two-fold.'

I raised my eyebrows and nodded slightly, intrigued at where he was taking the discussion.

'Go on.'

'First and foremost I would like your role to be as an educator. Our new recruits and seasoned employees alike would do well to develop their understanding of the psychology of offenders and their sociological characteristics.'

I liked his thinking, and truth being told, I'd already facilitated similar training throughout my career.

'And the rest?'

'Cold cases and case reviews. I'd like to you take a look over cold case files and undertake a review of cases that couldn't be taken forward to prosecution or weren't successfully prosecuted, to analyse the investigative and legal processes and the decisions made. In short, increasing our prosecution hit rate.'

'Sounds like a challenge, well a series of challenges. I like what you're proposing' I conceded, 'I'll work up a training programme and schedule for you to have a look at as soon as I can. Do you have any particular cases in mind?'

'Good, I'm looking forward to working with you. We'll get your remote access to the IT systems and server set up today and take it from there. As far as particular cases go, I'll leave it to your judgement for the moment.'

With that I seized my opportunity to put forward the Sarah Clark case for consideration, wasting no time in giving him an outline.

'Certainly have a look at the files' came his response, 'though don't reopen the case or interview anyone without my consent. From what you describe the young woman may simply have left of her own volition and there's nothing untoward at all. She wouldn't be the first, nor will she be the last.'

'With the greatest of respect Sir, I do think there may be more to it' I answered politely.

'There may well be and I trust your judgement. Just tread carefully though. Antrim's a small town and nobody will take kindly to you wading in too deeply with unfounded suspicions. Thinking on it, if my memory serves me correctly there was another incident in the locale recently, a similar one. A young girl reported missing within the last few weeks. She was found though. Suicide, though those closest to her refused to believe it, which of course they wouldn't, given the circumstances. You might want to look into that too, though again, at file review level at the moment.'

'Yes Sir, I understand' I replied before taking another sip of coffee. I'd barely drank any of it but got the distinct impression that I'd been politely but firmly dismissed, 'I'll leave you to it.'

'Thank you Dr Harkin. Like I said earlier, I'm looking forward to working with you.'

He stood and extended his right hand, emphasising in doing so that my allotted time was now up.

'Thank you Sir' I replied, shaking his hand firmly as I did so, the voice of my father in my head advising against weak handshakes and providing judgement on those who delivered them.

'And Carolyn, remember. Be careful. You don't want to stir a hornets nest.'

'Sir.'

CHAPTER
TWENTY

Although Sam Moran was no stranger to his thoughts, conscious or otherwise being dominated by events of the past, they didn't normally centre around the girl he knew from there as Victoria Harkin, and now as Carolyn. In the short time since she had come back into his life, his thoughts had been continually awash with memories of Summers gone, regrets at what could have been and excitement at the possibilities brought by their reconnecting. At the moment though, his logical reasoning was being governed by worry. As he checked the installation of the newly extended security system and made final adjustments to the CCTV cameras now nestled within the garage, he wondered what had happened to Carolyn that had changed her so. Something was different about her, something was...broken. He got why a woman living alone in an isolated big house like this would want a high level of security, but it hadn't escaped his attention that she seemed much more jittery than he remembered and she definitely was trying to delay his and Bella's leaving her last night. Not to mention that she increased the speed and amount of her alcohol consumption as time had worn on toward midnight. He didn't need a psychology degree to see that she was self-medicating and that she was afraid of something, or someone. It had begged the question for him as to why she had come back to Northern Ireland, Antrim in particular. Whatever the reason, he intended to get to the bottom of it. He also intended to support her through it, just like he had with Bella.

CHAPTER
TWENTY-ONE

I couldn't decide if Hannon's parting words were intended as advice or a warning. Either way I liked him despite now feeling like I'd just left the Headmaster's Office having received a dressing down for my sins. I wasn't about to dwell on it. I was champing at the bit to get started on the Sarah Clark case too much to let that happen. If indeed there was a case. It wasn't without worry though. My main reservation being that opening the file could well be the equivalent of tossing a hand grenade at my newly formed relationship with Bella and rekindled relationship with Sam, not to mention their relationship with each other, and would almost certainly go against Hannon's direct orders, though technically I'd already done that, albeit not in any formal way. Still, I wasn't about to tell him that.

What I really needed to do now was to chase away the post-pastry slump in blood sugar that would invariably come after the insulin spike at having consumed it, and I knew just what would resharpen my focus before I got down to work. Breaking the Mustang in a little more on my motorway cruise home would be the perfect antidote. That was of course as soon as I could free the vehicle from the two pairs of eyes currently ogling it. I sighed as I approached the two young males, clearly plain clothed officers, only too aware of how the next few moments would play out. The smart-arse remarks about the car belonging to a woman, and a woman in her forties at that, would be inevitable. Low level, overt sexism in the guise of banter. God, I hated that word. They probably wouldn't even realise what they were doing, as was my experience. Like generations before them they would have been conditioned to see their behaviour as being acceptable, just like generations of women before me have been conditioned to let it go unchallenged. Until now. True to form, the banter wasn't long in kicking in. It disappointed me but I'm long past being angry about such instances. I've been dealing with them since my pre-teens after all, and I certainly wasn't the exception to the rule. It still managed to piss me off without fail though, which left me wondering. Should I scowl at them whilst silently continuing about my business, or was I pissed off to a level where my interaction with them would result in their asking, can we have our balls back please?

I decided on a happy medium, but by the time I was tearing out of the car park to the satisfying growl of a V8 engine, they were left in no doubt as to who I was and had made what could be best described as a lasting impression on them, the condescending quip #metoo from one of them being met with a #fuckyou in the process.

CHAPTER
TWENTY-TWO

'You said what?' Bella cackled as I recounted the story of my morning to her and Sam over lunch.

'Fair play. Bastards', Sam nodded his approval, as if I had been seeking it, 'I like Carolyn Harkin's style. The Victoria Harkin that I knew would've blushed and scampered away.'

'Then I'm glad she scampered away permanently', Bella replied, 'You still haven't told us the story there you know.'

'Not much to tell really. In fact you have already heard it, just not from me.'

Her quizzical look prompted yet another recount from me, this time of exactly how much I'd been creeped out by our mystery man from the writers class and why. Their friendship merited as much, I decided, though I took care to leave what had happened to Daniel and my meeting of Jess out of the tale.

'How could he have known that, and in such detail?'

I had already been feeling really unnerved by it, but the concern in Sam's voice as he asked, and the signs of worry across his face made me think that despite those feelings, I maybe hadn't taken it quite seriously enough.

'I don't know, I mean it could be coincidence but...'

'I doubt it. Surely you would have told someone about it at some point?'

'No, not a soul. Never. I drew a veil on that life that day. I moved away, changed my mobile number. Obviously I told my family I had moved on but the rest was between me and my conscience.'

'Conscience? It doesn't sound like you should have had anything to regret'

'No' I answered, less surely than I'd meant to, stopping Bella in her tracks, briefly before she continued.

'In that case, I think we should get to know our mystery man a little bit more next time, and I know just how to do it.'

'And are you going to share that particular nugget of information with us?' I asked.

'No. All you need to know is that you will need to arrive fashionably late. Leave the rest to me.'

'Fair enough' I shrugged, 'I need to get working on solving another mystery anyhow.' I nodded subtly at Bella in silent affirmation of what that particular mystery was.

'Whatever you both get up to. Be careful' said Sam, the concern still evident in his voice.

'Yes Dad' Bella joked with an eye roll.

For me, it had been the second time I'd heard words to that effect within just a few hours.

'We will' I answered as much in reassurance of myself than of him, 'now back to work you two, and don't think I'm going to be providing lunch every day.'

'Yes, boss.'

'You're the boss, boss.'

Their response made me smile and certainly lightened the mood albeit temporarily in my case. Unfortunately for me, as I headed off to my study with the intention of getting my head back into the game, I was about to walk down a very dark path. It hadn't been the first time though, and I'd be very surprised if it was the last.

CHAPTER
TWENTY-THREE

By the time Bella had adjusted the hem of the curtains she'd made for the narrow window of the least spacious of the large bedrooms, they were perfect and ready to hang. What's more, her plan to get to know as much as possible about the mystery writing class delegate was fully formulated and all set for implementation. It would, of course need more than a sprinkle of charm, a dollop of humour, not to mention a good pinch of flirtation. That would be fine though. She was familiar with that particular recipe, or as she preferred to think of it, this wasn't her first rodeo. She was already looking forward to the next class even more than she had been.

For now though, it was time to look at further dressing and accessorising the room. It was a task that she would enjoy, but more importantly, it would continue to distract her from the knowledge that in a room not very far away from where she was in the house, Carolyn was beginning her reinvestigation into the disappearance of Sarah Clark, an investigation that she herself had instigated and that she hoped against hope the outcome of which would be the one she was desperate for, despite the possible dangers held within it. Cillian Moran's guilt needed to be confirmed in the public domain, regardless of the impact on Sam and what it would do for the memory of his son. Besides, in proving his guilt it would justify what she had done. Wouldn't it?

CHAPTER
TWENTY-FOUR

USING MY NEWLY ALLOTTED PSNI LOGIN CREDENTIALS, I NERVOUSLY navigated the central IT system, familiarising myself with its operation as I went. Locating the Sarah Clark file brought with it a spike in my anxiety levels. When Bella had initially asked me to help her find justice for Sarah, it had been a no brainer. Now with the possible implications for Sam, it felt much more like a poisoned chalice. If I were to find enough evidence to suspect foul play, it would be likely that Cillian would be considered a suspect. If I were to subsequently reach the conclusion that he was guilty, then not only would it destroy Sam, the fact that it had been Bella who asked me to look at the file would devastate him further. Then of course there was what it would do to her. From what I had gathered her relationship with Cillian had been a complicated one. Love hate at best and complicated by what she obviously suspected he had done. Yet she had remained with him until his death. If I were to find that he was guilty, the impact on her, let alone that on her relationship with Sam could be catastrophic.

Having finally gathered the courage to dive in, I opened the digital folder containing all documents pertaining to the case. I had expected there to be more to it but the contents were scant at best. Deciding it would be most logical to start at the beginning and work my way through, I firstly opened the missing persons reporting document. Aside from the description of Sarah, details of when she'd last been seen and what she had been wearing, the main thing of note had been who had reported her missing. That person, her mother, had reported that Sarah was last seen on Halloween night. Dressed in skinny blue jeans, a blue plaid shirt, red neckerchief, Stetson and boots; she could hardly have been described as being subtly dressed, though given the October 31st date of her disappearance, she would not necessarily have stood out too much. She had been on her way to meet her boyfriend, who I presumed to be Cillian. Apparently the plan had been that they were meeting for a drink at his house before attending the fancy dress party of a friend in the guise of a cowboy and cowgirl couple. According to her mum, she had been in great form and had no worries or issues in the lead up to her disappearance. She was at the start of a promising career as a nurse and was very much in love. In short, everything to live for and nothing to run away from.

By and large, the remainder of the file was made up with interviews of other people close to her, including Bella, all pretty much echoing the words of her mother and very much reflecting her image as portrayed by the picture she had provided of the beautiful and vivacious young woman. The facts were though, that according to Cillian, she never arrived at his house, nor did she turn up at the party. According to him, when she hadn't turned up at the house, he tried several times to call her on her mobile. When she hadn't answered, he presumed she had been delayed somehow and texted her to tell her to meet him at the party. He continued to call her throughout the night but the phone was directed to voicemail each time. He also tried calling her at home, where there had been no answer either. Finally, when he got back home himself, he noticed that the clothing, toiletries and cabin bag that she kept at his house for when she stayed over, were gone. Interestingly though, during the time the investigation was live, her bank cards hadn't been used and there had been no attempts made by her to contact anyone that were recorded. My instincts were telling me that she had died that night. They were also telling me that Cillian's statement and the fact that there didn't seem to be any log of him trying to push the investigation forward in any way smacked of guilt. The long and the short of it would indicate that the investigation team at the time should have opened a murder enquiry and investigated accordingly with Cillian as a person of interest. Instead, it appeared that they used the convenient excuse of the lack of a body and the missing personal effects, as a means to shelve the case.

I puffed out a sigh. I needed to drill down into Cillian's character and whereabouts on that night and the days and nights either side of it. How I was going to manage that without stepping on a metaphorical land mine, I had yet to work out. Regardless, the one view I had that had not changed, was that Sarah needed a voice. Needed justice, despite the fact that the person most likely responsible for her murder, was himself deceased.

Logging out of the system, I was about to have a break to decompress a little when I remembered Hannon's mentioning of the recent discovery of the body of a young girl in the Sixmilewater River. A google search and the clicking of the link to the Belfast Live coverage of the story sent me reeling. Before I even got to the accompanying story, I needed to get my head around the picture of the victim that preceded it. If I hadn't known any better, I would have sworn that the young woman staring back at me from the screen, was none other than Sarah Clark.

Surely Bella would have known about this. Why hadn't she said anything about it? Also, the more I thought of it the more I became irked by why Bella hadn't said that her employer was the dad of the person she had suspected of murder, and that her suspect also happened to be her boyfriend? I didn't like being played, especially by someone who had come into my life in the guise of a friend, which I guess was why the anger was rising in me at a rate of knots. Something wasn't adding up and I had every intention of getting some answers, starting now.

CHAPTER
TWENTY-FIVE

'What's up Doc?' Sam joked as I came thundering down the stairs.

'Like I haven't heard that one before' I retorted, 'What are you doing?'

Stood, with what looked to be a manual in his hand, he was beside the alarm control panel in the hall with the front door wide open, a chill draught flowing in from behind him.

'Just ironing out a few wrinkles in the security system. We're good now though.'

'Have you seen Bella?' I asked, 'She's not anywhere around upstairs.'

'Yeah, she's just popped out Cameron's to pick up the lamp and mat you had her eye on for the box room. She wanted to surprise you. She shouldn't be long. You ok? You look a bit stressed.'

'Yeah, I'll catch up with her later. It'll keep. I could be doing with a bit of decompression though. You fancy a walk?'

'Sure, but if it's decompression you want I can do better than that, come with me. Actually, I'd better leave Bella a note.'

Taking a pencil from one of the seemingly endless number of

pockets in his work trousers he closed the manual and on the blank page at the back of it scrawled, "Gone Fishing" in large letters on it before stuffing it half into the letter box.

'Really?' I asked.

'Don't worry, she's used to it' he winked, 'now let's go, it's not far.'

'What's not far?'

'You'll see' he grinned.

A short walk to the back of the house and a descent toward the jetty soon revealed what he meant. Not visible until the edge of the garden dipped downwards towards the sandy bank of the lough, there, moored to the jetty it bobbed gently. The most beautiful small cruiser boat I had ever seen.

'Really! Of course you have a boat' I japed, though to be fair, I was a little surprised.

'She's called, "Scoundrel Days" though she might just as well have been called, "Mid-life Crisis" if I'm honest.'

He blanched a little as he smiled, something I had never seen him do before. I liked it. Despite the embarrassment his excitement was clear in the speed of his stride as he walked to the end of the jetty before stepping down onto the boat and holding his hand out to me as I shakily followed.

'Welcome Aboard' he grinned before saluting me in jest.

'I love it' I heard myself gush, aware of the increased blood flow bringing a rosy hue to my own cheeks and neck. Thankfully he hadn't noticed, already busy with the undoing of the rope which kept us moored before turning his attention to starting the motor. Within a few minutes we were seated and I watched as he manoeuvred the juddering steering wheel to expertly guide us away from the jetty and out onto the still glass majesty of Lough Neagh. It was beautiful. The surroundings, the boat, the company, everything. Seeing Langford Villa from this angle was new to me, and this moment summed up everything which drew me back to Northern Ireland, but more specifically, here. Home.

'Penny for your thoughts' I heard Sam say.

'I'm just taking stock. Smelling the roses if you like.'

'And?'

'I'm lucky.'

I was too. Not only had all thoughts of frustration at Bella, the Sarah Clark case and the mystery writer, pun intended, vanished from my mind, the emotional scars of the last few years were finally beginning to feel like a soothing balm had been lathered upon them.

Cutting the engine, Sam looked at me warmly before rising.

'I know just the thing that'll make you feel even luckier' he said before disappearing down into the cabin and returning with a folded blanket tucked under his left arm, a half empty bottle of Black Bush whiskey in one hand and two glass tumblers pinched between the finger and thumb of the other.

'The temperature tends to dip about this time of the evening. We don't want you catching a chill.'

He gestured for me to take the blanket from him, which I did, before placing it half across my lap and holding the remainder back before gesturing for him to sit down beside me and putting the remainder across his as he did so.

'We best share. You're right, there is a bit of a chill in the air, and they say older people feel the cold more' I joked.

'You're too kind' came his playfully sarcastic response.

I took the glasses, freeing him up to pour a generous measure of the whiskey into each before propping the bottle in the space between us.

'Cheers' he offered as he clinked his glass against mine.

'Cheers' I returned.

'Feeling decompressed yet?'

I took a small mouthful of the drink, savouring it before swallowing and enjoying the satisfying warmth it brought to my throat as I did.

'Definitely' I finally replied.

'You want to talk about it?'

'Yeah, but not yet. Let's just take in the view and the liquid refreshment for a wee while longer first.'

He nodded slowly before taking a drink himself, and for a relatively long time, that's exactly what we did. Until I was ready.

My interrogation of Bella would keep. For now I wanted to delve a bit more into the character of Cillian Moran and I knew just how I wanted to broach it. First though, I wanted to take a photograph of the house from here on the Lough. It would make a fantastic print for one of the many walls I had to find something to hang upon.

'If someone had told the teenage me all those years ago that I'd be sitting here with you like this, here now, I would have said they were mad' I began.

'But here we are.' He smiled warmly.

'If someone had told me this time last week that I could be sitting here with you, I would have taken their arm off for the chance of it' he continued.

'Really?' I asked, feeling myself flush again, more so than the whiskey could have been blamed for.

'Really... You know, you weren't the only one who would maybe have had things turn out a little differently than they did back in the day.'

'You would never have thought it. You were always so cool and nonchalant. I'm surprised you ever noticed I was there.'

'I noticed ok, but you never stayed in one place long enough for me to tell you.'

'I always got so embarrassed. Why would you have ever been interested in chatting to me?'

'But I was, more than you'll ever realise, and then you were gone and yes there was always the promise that you'd be back, another year, another holiday. Until you weren't.'

'And then what?'

'Then I eventually met Helen, Cillian's mum and to cut a long story short, a quick courtship and an unplanned pregnancy later we were walking down the aisle and all dreams I had of being an architect disappeared in the exchange of vows that created a loveless marriage. 7 months later I was a new dad and handyman by day, and a construction student by night. Then within a few months beyond that I was adding widower and single parent to my list of titles when she drowned.'

'Sam, I'm so sorry.' I lightly gripped his forearm as I shifted closer into him like it was the natural thing to do. Perhaps it was. He remained silent, though put his arm around me, gently pulling me in closer still, at least as close as the bottle between us would allow.

'You really didn't love her?'

He drank before answering. Perhaps needing some more alcohol on board to deal with the question I wondered? I'd been there too.

'I was infatuated I guess and briefly, yes, I thought I was in love, but no, I don't really think I did love her. I just got swept up in it all I guess. She was the prettiest girl on the estate and she was determined that we would become Antrim's answer to a royal couple. I liked the idea and we had fun for a while. A holiday romance without the holiday. Then Cillian came along and the fractures that had always been there in the relationship became gaping fault lines and not long later she was gone and it was all about Cillian.'

'It must've been tough on you both?'

He shrugged.

'What can you do? We had to just get on with it. We did ok

though. He was a great kid, which was a help, though not everyone shared that opinion.'

I noted how his voice cracked at the use of the word was.

'It was such a tragedy that you lost him. So young too. His whole life ahead of him' I offered.

'I still can't bear to think that he's gone. Not a day passes that I don't curse his loss. He should never have been on the site that day. I still can't get my head around that. I mean, I know more than most how freak accidents can happen on building sites but...'

I nodded before sipping again at the fiery brown liquor, my silence allowing him to continue.

'You seemed a bit pissed at Bella' he rasped in a change of subject that I wasn't expecting.

'Something and nothing' I replied with a soft shoulder shrug, reacting to the change of subject and leaving me wondering just what had happened to Cillian.

'Take it easy on her if you can. She plays the independent young woman well but she's just a broken kid underneath it all.'

'You underestimate her' I replied, 'she's stronger than you think and I suspect she might have you to thank for it.'

'She's great. She's probably helped me more than I've helped her in truth, and besides, I kinda feel responsible for looking out for her, for Cillian's sake.'

'Has there never been anyone else? For you I mean.'

'There've been a few relationships but nothing that ever really amounted to anything. I guess no-one could ever really compare to the girl who stole my heart and took it as a holiday souvenir all those years ago.'

I laughed nervously at his goofy attempt at flirtatious humour, part of me wondering how much truth there was to it, if any.

'What about you? I've been wittering on about me all this time. I want to hear everything.'

I didn't doubt that he did. The questions were more, where would I start and indeed, if I wanted to.

'Well, you already know that I gave my life a reboot and took a new name in my late teens. The rest, that's a story for another night. You don't have enough whiskey for that one. Besides, we best get back.'

He raised his open hands in a disarming gesture.

'No worries, I didn't mean to pry.'

'It's fine, but just not tonight ok' I replied, more angst in my voice than I would have liked.

'Ok. Promise me something though. Please be careful with that guy in your class. Something there just doesn't quite stack up.'

'I know. I promise. I'm going to look into him a bit more before the next class in addition to whatever Bella has planned.'

'I suppose I'd better be getting you back' he sighed.

'Actually, maybe we could spare another ten minutes' I smiled, motioning my almost empty glass in front of him, 'and another little nip. For medicinal purposes of course.'

'I like your style Doctor Harkin...and your company.'

CHAPTER
TWENTY-SIX

CAROLYN HARKIN WAS A MASTER AT WHAT SHE DID, THERE WAS NO doubting that as far as Bella was concerned. She was even more sure of the fact now that she too had been subjected to a dose of good cop and bad cop rolled into one, in what only be described as an impromptu interrogation. She'd survived it though, that was the main thing. What's more, the air between them was now clear. It had been naive of her to think that Carolyn would've been anything other than annoyed with her given the things she'd held back from her in their initial conversation. Obviously her connection to Sam and the recent disappearance of another girl would have come to light early on in Carolyn's investigations, but if she'd been upfront with everything at the beginning, she would have come across much more manically, and surely that would have spooked Carolyn into not getting involved. The fact that it turned out that Carolyn and Sam knew each other had only served to complicate things further. Still, she'd been straight with her this time round. Well, as much as she could be given the circumstances.

Commanding her smart speaker to play an essentials collection from Billie Eilish she decided to turn her attention to something a little less emotionally taxing. She had a full weekend of baking ahead of her if she was to properly initiate Operation Mystery Man Uncovered and creating a batch of cupcakes whilst getting lost in the lyrics of Bad Guy was as good a place to start as any.

CHAPTER
TWENTY-SEVEN

SATURDAY MORNINGS FOR ME WERE USUALLY THE STUFF OF LONG LIE INS followed by lazy brunches and curling up on the sofa with a coffee whilst James Martin filled my screen with masterclasses on creating gastro delights with a Yorkshire twist and portion size, whilst effortlessly interviewing the celebrities of the day. The media aspect of my writing career is one I normally shy away from. Even more so in recent years. An invitation to Chez Martin though would be one engagement I would make an exception for, that's for sure, not that one would ever be forthcoming. This morning though, I was awake, showered and dressed by 07:30 and was now nibbling on a piece of toast and sipping at my orange juice in the dining area snug whilst the coffee maker did its thing in the corner. Breakfast was very much being consumed at breakfast time today and despite my not normally being an early breakfast person I was consciously making time for it. Admittedly it was only to kill some time before Uther's arrival but it was nice to have an early morning bite safe in the knowledge that my morning was unlikely to include a visit to a gruesome crime scene, a ripe custody suite, or worse, the morgue. Like a child waiting for Christmas, I was struggling to be patient, silently willing the hands of the clock be swifter in movement, hastening his arrival, despite the memory my Dad's voice in my ear chastising me for wishing my life away. In an effort to distract myself from clock watching, literally, I decided to amuse myself by looking at the photographs of his progress that had been sent to me by the breeder. The most recent picture was already a firm favourite and a contender for a pride of place spot on a hallway wall, housed in a frame befitting of the decor.

After some time spent scrolling images, then frames for those images, double checking I had everything prepared for his arrival, it was finally time to hit the road out to Lisburn to bring my boy home. I decided to take the back road over the mountains and the road locally referred to as the Seven Mile Straight, a road that relatively lives up to its name in being approximately seven miles long and directionally straight. What the local name doesn't describe in its title is the fact that it is perhaps one of the most uneven roads in Ireland, a series of peaks and troughs in quick succession that make a journey across it at pace, a thrill seeker's delight on a par with any rollercoaster. It was a favourite experience from my childhood that I'd kept with me and was excited to see how the Explorer would handle it on my outbound journey, knowing that having Uther with me on the return journey would mean a slower pace.

'Dr Harkin, we weren't expecting you until next week. He wouldn't be ready to leave yet.'

Sonya Wilson's feigned surprise at my arrival almost had me fooled. Almost!

'The look on your face was priceless' she giggled as she beckoned me in, 'Uther, look who's here' she called down the hallway. I followed her toward the sound of the excited movement of unsteady paws on a ceramic floor as she made her way to the large kitchen-diner. Locking eyes on him I wasn't sure which of the two of us was more excited to see the other until he attempted to bound toward me on those impossibly long legs across the smooth tiled floor. For a second I thought he was bound for a cartoon style fall. Thankfully he didn't but it didn't stop me closing the distance to him quickly for fear he would hurt himself.

'Hey Boy. Look at you. You're gorgeous' I told him as I instinctively rubbed the side of his face and ear, a muscle memory from my time as a teen with Langford Villa's previous wolfhound resident perhaps. That was it. That was all that it took. We'd bonded and I think he found himself falling for me as quickly as I had him.

'I can't believe how quickly he's grown in comparison to your last picture' I marvelled to Sonya.

'He's becoming a big boy alright, aren't you Uther?'

He raised his head proudly as if he knew what she was saying, seemingly ignorant of Sonya's family pet Springer Spaniel, Penny running around and through his legs playfully.

'Come, let me get you a coffee before we go over the papers and routines. Take a seat over there at the table, if they let you' she nodded toward the dining table as she lifted the kettle and began to fill it.

Padding after me and continuing to ignore the increasingly impatient Penny, Uther sat at my side, awaiting further pampering. He didn't have to wait long. His smoky grey fur was a soft, thick down that gave me as much pleasure to run my fingers through, as my actions clearly brought to him. His eyes, two beautiful, polished emeralds locked knowingly on mine. I'd fallen for him hook, line and sinker, and he knew it. His look seemed to silently communicate that my feelings were reciprocated.

'His name suits him perfectly' Sonya said as the kettle clicked to a boil behind her, 'where did you get it from?'

'Arthurian legend' I replied, 'I'm a bit of a geek that way. He's named after Uther Pendragon, King Arthur's father. I've been a huge fan of all things Camelot all my life' I blushed, though couldn't help but continue with my nerdish self-indulgence, 'in fact the legend has kind've followed me around in a matter of speaking. Some of my pop culture obsessions have a grounding there, and bizarrely my books are published by Excalibur Press.'

'The pen is mightier than the sword then I guess. Or the keyboard at least.'

'Not always' I smiled, 'not if the progress to date on my new book is anything to go by. Still, maybe this guy will give me some inspiration.'

As if he heard me, Uther moved closer to my side, though the fact that my phone rang as soon as he did so sent a shiver through me, making me wonder if there was indeed any truth to the notion that dogs have a heightened sense for impending danger. True or not, I knew instinctively that the call would not be good news. The voice of Assistant Chief Constable (ACC) Hannon on the other end of the line immediately confirmed it.

CHAPTER
TWENTY-EIGHT

Less time in the field was to be one of the few benefits of Brian Hannon's recently acquired senior policing role. Today though, a return to the front line couldn't be avoided. Not with a case of this magnitude and a victim of this level of popularity. Despite being long past the stage where he could be described as being jaded by the number of crime scenes he had attended in his time, he couldn't help but feel a little excited at the prospect of that which lay ahead. It certainly beat the alternative, an audit of regional policing budgets hands down. Adding his service vehicle, a tired Volvo V90 to what already looked like a makeshift PSNI vehicle depot outside the majestic St. Anne's Cathedral, he made his way towards the cordon erected across the adjacent Writer's Square.

'Jesus, so what did we do to deserve the honour of your presence?' The familiar gruffness of his career long frenemy and seasoned lead Soco, Matt Osman brightening his day, despite his being only too aware that the scene he was about enter into, through the newly erected evidence tent, would be enough to ruin it again: Ruin it even further than the news of the discovery of the victim who currently resided within already had.

'Somebody needs to keep an eye on you, a man of your

advancing years.' Hannon returned with a smile. His instinct was to embrace his old comrade but they were both too professional and too long in the tooth to risk compromising the scene or their authority with those their junior.

'What've we got?' he asked.

'Come, have a look' Osman answered, gesturing to the officer manning the cordon to raise it for them. Within a few steps Hannon found himself inside the tent and being confronted with the sight of the victim, and the sickly metallic sweetness of the blood loss that he had suffered, though apart from that apparent on his clothes, which were saturated, there was relatively little of it at the scene. Bizarrely he found himself gagging despite the depth and breadth of his experience.

'And they say you never forget that smell' Osman joked.

'It's true, you don't. What they don't tell you is that when you've been out of the game for a while your gag reflex normalises its response to it' Hannon heard himself explaining matter of factly. In truth he was embarrassed at his reaction to the smell and his need to defend it. He paused, allowing himself a few deep breaths before bending down on his haunches as if taking a seat on an invisible stool to properly take in the scene.

Before him lay a familiar face, one he had last seen just weeks ago when his wife and daughter, both huge fans of the growing Irish Country Music scene had persuaded him to attend coun tryfest.ie at the SSE arena in Belfast. The victim, Ryan Casey had been the hotly anticipated headline act at the Irish Country Music event. Now the ascendency of this particular young star had been halted and the light of it snuffed out in one fell swoop in the seemingly violent altercation that had resulted in his death.

Sliding into the easy routine between the two men despite Hannon's new title, Osman began to talk him through preliminary findings as he observed.

'Looks like he's taken a hell of a beating both pre and post-mortem. Multiple stab wounds too as you can see.'

Hannon now leaning closer over the side of the body, nodded.

'Looks like some traces of cocaine around the nostrils. I wouldn't have had him down for that.'

'Ah, sure there's no telling what people get up to in this day and age. Not much surprises us in this game Brian, you know that' Osman replied.

'I don't know. Just when you think you've seen it all, there's always a new shock in store. Especially with the young ones. It wasn't like in our day old friend.'

'Ah Brian, would you ever fuck off' Osman laughed, 'you're making us sound like a right couple of old codgers. You might be edging closer to the pipe and slippers but you know my motto. It's ok to grow up just as long as you don't grow old.'

Hannon craned his neck to look at Osman.

'You're only as old as the person you're feeling eh.'

'That's exactly right' he smiled broadly.

'Well, that might go some way toward explaining your penchant for wedding cake. What are we on now, is it marriage number three?'

'Separation number three as it goes' he shrugged, his smile fading.

'When will you be finished up here do you think? I've arranged for our new Investigative Psychologist to give the scene the once over before you move the body' said Hannon.

'What! Oh for fuck sake Brian, we could be doing without some jumped up Crime Writer coming here and telling us how to do our jobs. Sure why doesn't she teach her granny to suck eggs while she's there?'

Standing, Hannon asserted every extra inch in height he had over Osman as he moved a little closer into his personal space.

Just the right amount. Not too close to be intimidating, but close enough to remind him who was in charge.

'That's for fuck sake Sir' he replied through a very thin smile, 'and let's make no mistake, we need every advantage we can get on this one. As soon as it breaks there'll be a media frenzy and I've already had Chief Constable Collins pressing the urgency of getting this one resolved quickly. Besides, it might be time you woke up to how things are done now. Modern Policing we call it. You'd better watch out my friend, especially if you want to avoid that old codger label, or worse, the dinosaur of policing one. After all, you know what happened to the dinosaurs don't you?'

With that Hannon left the tent, though not before hearing Osman calling after him.

'Enough said...Sir.'

Exactly the response he was looking for, though he suspected that considerably more was being said under Osman's breath.

CHAPTER
TWENTY-NINE

THERE WAS FASHIONABLY LATE AND THEN THERE WAS DOWNRIGHT ignorant. At the moment I was bordering on the latter. Pausing to catch my breath just short of the Foster Suite I saw a sign on a door beside that I hadn't noticed before marked, Toilet. Just the place I needed to compose myself a little and freshen up before stepping into the relative limelight that was session two of my Crime Fiction Writing class.

The cooling water splashing against my face as I bent over the sink was exactly what I needed. My first Saturday with Uther had been so far removed from what I'd planned for us it had been unreal. Instead of the long walk in the countryside designed to tire him out while I was at the class this evening, he had spent the entire day being looked after by the two morons who I'd called out on their overt sexism the last time I'd clapped eyes on them, whilst I undertook a lengthy analysis of a crime scene in Belfast's famed Writer's Square, trying to avoid the strange combination of dismissive comments on the role of an Investigative Psychologist from the CSO as he simultaneously and clumsily tried to hit on me. Then of course there was the obligatory drafting and typing up of the profiling report on the likely traits of the perpetrator in the nearby North Street Station whilst Uther was fawned over by those on duty. Now with the day gone, I was running late, almost literally, for a class that I hadn't had the time to properly prepare for, whilst Uther was either pining for his former home, or for all I knew, demolishing his new one. Thankfully from the laughter and bustle coming from the room next door, it sounded like Bella had the other delegates in the palm of her hand. I smiled to myself as I dried off with a handful of blue paper towels that had all the softness and absorbency of sandpaper. The glamorous life of a writer, I mused. Still, at least I looked halfway presentable now, ready to meet my public, and even more ready to see exactly what Bella's intelligence plan had entailed.

'Surprise' Bella chimed as I entered, a greeting which resulted in a chorus of repetition of varying degrees of enthusiasm from the other members of the class.

'Oh my Goodness!' I heard myself gush in response as I took in the scene before me. Instead of the tea, coffee and bog standard selection of biscuits provided last week, Bella had taken it upon herself to create quite a buffet. Taking in the platters of sandwiches, sausage rolls and chicken bites at the centre of the adjoined tables, the array of cupcakes, scones, crisps, nibbles and the range of soft drinks beside them I couldn't fail to have been impressed...and intrigued.

Each of the other course delegates, nine in total, the names of the majority of whom I was frantically trying to recall, had already availed of the buffet somewhat, each with a paper plate of food in front of them and a plastic cup containing their soft drink of choice, or so it appeared.

'I decided that we could extend a warmer welcome to our new tutor than you got last week, particular a tutor of such standing' Bella smiled, 'besides I thought it might be nice to welcome you back home to Northern Ireland too. The guys here, the girls most definitely there, and Glenn agreed.'

And Bingo, she'd already gotten his name, and I suspected, much more from our mystery man.

Moving toward the paper plates, napkins and cups at the back of the room near the tea and coffee pots Bella lifted a plate and napkin before addressing me again.

'Now! Tea, coffee, soft drink…or wine?' She broke into a grin as she opened the cupboard beside her to reveal several bottles of wine, some of which had already been opened.

'We decided to stash them in here in case we get ourselves thrown out.'

'Or me sacked' I laughed, 'After the day I've had a paper cup of red wine is exactly what I need.'

'Oh? Do tell Dear' one of the older women near the top of the table said, her interest clearly evident, though her tone mildly empathetic too.

'I'd love to…'

'…Gladys.'

'Gladys', I replied, 'unfortunately its police business, so my lips have to remain firmly sealed.' I gestured as if closing an imaginary zip across my lips before smiling.

'Too bad' she sighed, brow furrowed before breaking into a smile, 'I'm joking' she added, though I suspected that was only half true, 'Come, take a seat Dear and have some food before we get started. It'd be a shame for Bella's efforts to go to waste.'

'They won't' I replied as I edged into the seat beside her, 'I'm famished.'

'I'm sure poor Glenn here is delighted to see you' Bella said, gesturing to my mystery man, 'Gladys and the other ladies at the front here have been interrogating him to within an inch of his life, the poor man.'

With that he blushed and smiled, and for me the penny dropped as to what Bella's plan had been to find out more about him. What better interrogation team than three female friends of a certain age who had been provided with a wet buffet and the company of a younger man that they knew little about. I was beginning to think she was a better psychologist than I was.

'I don't think we'll need to bother about police interview techniques if that was part of the course' he laughed nervously.

'Well that's tonight's lesson ruined' I replied, returning his laughter, wondering how far I should allow my guard to drop.

'Oh no Dear, you keep it in. He used the same trick as you with the whole lips are sealed thing. We'll break him yet, and you.' Gladys laughed loudly at her own joke, prompting her friends to join and the rest of us to follow politely if not wholeheartedly.

'Tell Dr Harkin and the others your story you two' she prompted her friends. These three ladies and their obviously close friendship seemingly gave them a relative ease to be more outgoing than those other more established members of the group. Either that or the others had grown tired of their leading lady in Gladys.

'Oh, yes, oh you'll like this one' said the woman I now half remembered from last week as Edith...I think.

'Kate and I' she began, gesturing to the woman sitting closest to her, 'were sitting in the canteen at work the other day having a conversation about our writing since the class last week. Of course one of the young girls who works on the checkouts wasn't to know that when she came in for her lunch. I was wondering why she was looking more and more uncomfortable as she went about her business and we were both surprised when she made a hasty exit with her lunch as soon as it had been prepared. It was only afterward it dawned on us that what she would have heard from our conversation had been along the lines of Kate asking me "if I'd managed to do it yet", and my answering, "Oh Yes, I've murdered him ok, but I still haven't worked out what to do with the body."'

Edith barely managed to finish the story before collapsing into a fit of giggles, prompting us all to join her.

'Oh, the poor girl' I tried to sympathise, struggling to stifle a snigger as I did so. As well as apparently getting some information out of Glenn, which I hoped to be filled in on later, Bella had also succeeded in getting some of the class members new and old to further gel. I felt myself relax a little. The alcohol possibly helped. Either way, it wasn't to last.

CHAPTER
THIRTY

THE START OF THE EVENING HAD BEEN AN UNCOMFORTABLE ONE FOR Glenn McGinley though it had been worth it in the end. Worth every one of the relentless questions friendly but pointedly posed by Antrim's answer to The Golden Girls. What they had gotten from him was of little consequence. What they, and by his presence he got from the lovely Bella on the other hand was a mine of information. Not just on her life, but the recent goings on in the life of the good doctor too. It would all prove useful to him in the future. More than any of them would ever know. It never failed to amaze him how much of their lives people carelessly divulge via what they see as harmless chit-chat and more so via their social media. Still, he'd made a living from human behaviours and the folly they can lead one to, and a decent one at that. This time it wasn't about the money though. This time it was personal.

Biding his time until the others had become engrossed in the writing task she had set them he took his opportunity.

'Oh, Carolyn, I hope you don't mind, I promised you a murder, so I worked on it over the last few nights. Would you mind?' The feigning of sheepishness in his voice sounded convincing, even to his own ear. Stomach churning, but convincing, nonetheless.

'...of course, I can have a look. I'm already looking forward to it.' She feigned interest well, but the hesitancy in her response was audible to him. Her failure to disguise the nerves brought by his approach had also been duly noted.

With her carefully unfolding the typed script and quickly immersing herself into his words, McGinley returned to his seat. He couldn't afford to watch for her reaction this time. Hopefully it would be pretty clear afterwards. For now though he had no time to waste, not if he was going to hit her with a double whammy of his "imaginings" as planned. Now, like the others in the group, it was time for him to get plotting, literally, as they tried to create the timeline for their story that would aid its plot development. At least that's what the good doctor had suggested. He was going to enjoy the group feedback discussion when they were done. He was however, to be disappointed. He certainly hadn't expected Carolyn's snap decision that had been shared with them at the end of the evening. That had sent him reeling.

CHAPTER
THIRTY-ONE

THE TRICKLING STREAM OF HOT COFFEE BEING DELIVERED THROUGH THE open eyelet of the travel mug was as much an elixir to me now as the wine had been earlier. It would do little for my ability to sleep upon my return to the house, but it was making Uther's late night walk in the company of Bella around the grounds of Langford Villa a much more pleasurable experience. The heat combined with the much needed caffeine hit that came with it was reviving, though would not promote restful slumber. I was ok with that; I was used to sleep deprivation. Besides, the events of today and more especially tonight had already conspired to make sure that the only REM I would experience tonight would be the sounds of Georgia, USA's most famed sons through my smart speaker as I worked.

Uther, on the other hand, I suspected would soon be sound asleep, despite his valiant efforts to disguise his sapping energy levels. It had been a busy day for him I figured, and an exciting one at that. He'd clearly enjoyed exploring his new home and meeting lots of new people, including his most recent friend, the one who as we walked, he was quite happily allowing to partake in frequent, affectionate rubs of his head. He and Bella were already becoming close it seemed.

'He likes you' I smiled. It was a blatant effort to get her talking again. She had noticeably retreated into herself after reading some of what she'd been writing about at the class earlier. As well as the beginnings of a timeline, she'd created a villain, one that I was familiar with by name and was increasingly building a picture of. Now she was clearly withdrawn. Not a trait I'd seen in her before and one I was wondering how to manage.

'I have that effect on animals... some people too' she joked, 'if I'm honest, I'd rather deal with animals though. At least you know where you are with animals.'

I couldn't not agree.

'Cillian?' I asked, pointedly.

She nodded, and though I could barely see her expression in the relative darkness, her upset was clear.

'Was it true? I mean the stuff that you shared with us in your writing earlier. I know you were using your victim's voice but is that what he was really like? Is that what you thought of him?'

She sighed heavily before stopping, Uther silently following suit.

'He was a real piece of work but when I wasn't busy hating him I loved him' she answered, the anger, grief and despair suddenly laced into every word as she continued.

'What does that make me? I saw the damage he was capable of but I let it happen. I let him get close to her. I let him kill her. I let myself be lined up as her replacement. What does all of that make me?'

Her voice was raised slightly now, the anger and despair building towards a desperate peak, yet Uther stood sentry, silent, almost knowing.

Her description of Cillian was not the first time I'd heard of or come across such a character, nor was it the first time I'd heard someone who had been close to them speak in such a way. As victims of their own decisions as well as the behaviours of those they had become entangled with, the emotional scars she bore were more normal than she realised.

'I get it' I said quietly, though sensed that she needed to say more. I started to walk again slowly, silently towards the house, Bella and Uther falling into step a little behind me.

'I'd known him practically all my life. We grew up together. Went to the same schools. We'd even talked of buying a house together at one stage. The three of us were so close but it seemed like I was the only one who could really see him for what he was.'

'And what was that?' I heard myself say, realising that whilst I was trying to be a consoling friend I had inadvertently put my psychologist hat on.

'Trouble' she answered, matter of factly. 'The worst kind.'

'The unavoidable kind too it would seem. Have you ever shared any of this with Sam?' I asked over my shoulder as she and Uther walked a few steps behind.

'No. I couldn't... I mean I tried but... Anyhow, he wouldn't believe me if I had. Not his perfect boy.'

'Every parent wants to see the best in their child but they're not blind to the worst' I offered as I stopped to face her.

'True, but what happens when they want to be blind to it? What else could explain how Cillian went through school with a colossal chip on his shoulder, an unhealthy disdain for every female he came into contact with and strong held belief that the world owed him a living?'

'You mean...?'

'...Sam played the little boy lost, poor motherless victim act on his son's behalf at every opportunity. Right through from all the potential suspensions from school to the potential exclusions, the succession of visits from the police and the charges levelled. Yes, that's exactly what I mean. At least until he couldn't.'

There was a coldness to her last sentence that wasn't lost on me.

'There must still be some resentment there, with Sam I mean' I questioned.

'He was doing what he thought best I suppose. Anyhow, let's get back indoors and let this fella get cosied up by the fire. I presume you'll want to hear what I found out about our friend Glenn?'

'Of course I do. I just wanted to make sure you were ok first that's all.'

'I'm fine, now let's get ourselves thawed out a bit and I'll fill you in.' She offered a half-hearted attempt at a smile.

'Wait. There's something that I need to find out first.' I locked my hands around her upper arms and deliberately fixed my gaze firmly on hers, 'Why are you doing this? Really, I mean writing the story, persuading me to look into Sarah's disappearance, what are you hoping to achieve? Is it justice for her, redemption for you, revenge on Cillian, what's it all about?'

'All those things...and more' she rasped; her eyes still fixed on mine.

'And what about Sam? How does he figure in all this? Is it worth breaking him even further? After everything?'

'I love Sam, you know I do. He's been more of a dad to me than my own father, but when it comes down to it, he could have done more. I know it must've been tough on him raising a troubled child as a single parent, but he could have done more. He should have done more to stop it. He would never admit to it, but he knew deep down. Yet he continued to provide the fake alibis, continued to block any chance the girls Cillian had victimised had of getting any closer to retribution. Not that the odds weren't ever stacked irrevocably against them, but still... He created and harboured a monster whether he intended or not, and if what you find proves that, then he'll need to deal with the consequences like the rest of us. Like it or not.'

It was a fair and convincing response but I wasn't quite done with her yet. There was something else I needed to know.

'Why now? Why are you stirring it up now? What happened to Sarah, if anything has, was years ago. Why has your crusade for justice only started now?'

'I tried in the beginning, but I didn't get anywhere. Everyone was saying that she'd just left, that the horrible scenario I had in my head was the product of an overactive imagination. Then there was Cillian's death. By that time we were in a relationship and although I was heartbroken when he died and devastated by how he died, part of me thought it as a natural justice of sorts. Lately though, there was the other girl found at the river. She was so like Sarah and the circumstances were so similar I didn't know what to think. It brought everything back to the surface, all the feelings I've tried to keep bottled up. It also potentially put Cillian's guilt in doubt. Then I heard about your course. It seemed like it was fated.'

Her tone was level and she seemed sincere but there was something off. I couldn't quite put my finger on what just yet. She wasn't lying, but I suspected that she wasn't telling the entire truth either. That said, my gut was telling me to trust her, just not necessarily her motives. It also told me that I needed to find out more about how Cillian Moran died. Now though, was not the time.

CHAPTER
THIRTY-TWO

With his pleasure boat anchored at much the same spot that he'd brought Carolyn to, Sam Moran sat at his vantage point around a mile off the coast adjacent to the mooring area of Langford Villa watching the building with interest. Despite the hour, the cold and the choppiness of the tide, he couldn't help himself. Seated in exactly the same seat he had been beside Carolyn, he sipped on a whiskey decanted from the same bottle he had shared with her, under the blanket that still held the scent of her perfume. He was fixated on the house. Fixated on her, despite every effort not to be. From his prolonged observations Bella had returned with Carolyn as he had expected. He was glad of that. He was glad to have caught a glimpse of the dog earlier too. Uther, if he remembered correctly. A companion and protector for her rolled into one. He approved. Despite her feistiness and intelligence, whether she cared to share the reason or not, it seemed that protection was exactly what she needed at the moment. If not from the mysterious male member of her writing group or whatever had happened in her past, then from...him.

He still had feelings for her, that was the danger. That had always been the danger. Feelings that had never abated despite losing her in his younger years. Feelings that if he acted upon now, could place her life under a very real threat, just like the others before her. He needed to make sure that that didn't happen. Whether he would succeed or not would be in the lap of the Gods though. He took some consolation in that. He only knew he couldn't trust himself, nor her for that matter, but he equally knew that he couldn't stay away. The course had been set, leaving him only to hope that they could navigate safely through it for both their sakes. If not, then so be it. He would deal with it as he had done so before if needs must.

CHAPTER
THIRTY-THREE

'Ok, so here goes' Bella said as she removed some folded sheets of paper from the back pocket of her jeans before taking a seat in the armchair and unfolding them and placing them down before spreading the three A4 sheets across the coffee table. From my place on the sofa beside her in the kitchen snug I pulled the MacBook toward me in anticipation of needing to use it, whilst Uther snored softly from his place on the mat in front of the wood burning stove.

'What've we got?' I asked, noting that our earlier chat had changed her mood for the better and that she was now buoyed with the thrill of the hunt for information on Glenn McGinley.

'Ok, so as you know I arrived early. Well, given that I had so much stuff to carry with the buffet etc, it was quite easy to convince the Receptionist that I was assisting you in setting up the room and that you had asked me to pick up a copy of the delegate information list for the course. She was reluctant at first, you know, client confidentiality and GDPR regulations and all that, but the offer of a coffee and scone with jam and clotted cream courtesy of the buffet seemed to make company policy much more flexible in the end.'

I snorted a laugh.

'What she printed off for me was a list of the details given by each delegate as they booked the course.' She leaned forward and tapped the first piece of A4 where it rested on the table, its fold marks dividing it into eight roughly equal squares.

I nodded. 'So?'

'Well, that's the first interesting thing. Not only does his name not appear on the list, the names of the people on the list are all female.'

'That's not actually all that uncommon' I replied, 'sometimes people use the booking account of a partner if they don't have one, or sometimes it's the partner who makes the booking on their behalf. Still, it's good to have the list of names to see if we can make a connection to him from them.'

'When I noticed that he wasn't on there I had another bright idea' Bella continued, unfazed, 'When the others arrived I got a piece of paper and asked everyone to write down their contact details on it so that I could set up a WhatsApp Group and mailing list for us to stay in contact and share work. Bingo, we now have an email address and mobile number for everyone, which I presume you can trace.'

I pursed my lips and nodded, before breaking into a smile.

'The girl did good' I said.

'Wait, I'm not finished yet' she answered with a raised hand and a grin, 'Before I went out, up to the conference room, I asked the Receptionist if we could use the smaller room next door as a breakout room. Thankfully she agreed... grudgingly, and I was able to go in there, turn out the lights and watch from the window as each person arrived. The result, one vehicle description and registration number for his car.' She tapped the final piece of folded paper with enthusiasm.

'At this rate, you'll soon be taking over my job' I laughed, 'Ok, first thing's first' I said as I lifted the sheet nearest to me, the one with the delegate booking details. My smile was soon to be fade on a cursory glance down the list.

'Carolyn, what is it? You look like you've seen a ghost.'

In a manner of speaking I had.

CHAPTER
THIRTY-FOUR

Bella Maskull was no Investigative Psychologist but she knew fear when she saw it and there was no mistaking, whatever Carolyn had seen on the delegate list had shaken her to the core.

'Are you ok? What is it?'

'Tilly', she whispered, her stare fixed still on the paper, 'Talitha Khatri.'

'I saw the name. It doesn't match with anyone on the course. You know her?'

'Knew her. She's dead now. Because of me.'

'And her name is there as one of the delegates? I don't get it. How can that be? What exactly is going on Carolyn?'

Carolyn's already ashen face began to crumple as the tears came. Tears that perhaps had been kept back for too long Bella sensed. She moved to beside Carolyn and put an arm around her, comforting her until her sobs became low whimpers and finally subsided.

'I'll get you some water' she offered before rising without acknowledgement from Carolyn.

'You want to talk about it?' Bella asked as she returned,

placing a glass of water on the table before again taking her original seat in the armchair.

'No. It's ok, I don't want to lay any of this on you. I've already burdened you enough, more than enough. Besides, it's really late and I don't want to keep you up.'

'Carolyn it's fine, I'm a night owl', Bella smiled in reassurance, 'Anyhow, we both know that we're too wired to sleep now in any case and I know you'll try to deny it but we both also know that you really don't want to be alone at the moment. So, what's it to be? Are you going to tell me about this...Tilly, or are we just going to sit here in awkward silence?'

'Ok, you win' Carolyn replied huskily before taking a sip from the water and shakily handing the glass back to Bella.

'I'll tell you what, if you agree to turn this into a Shiraz and agree to road test one of the guest rooms tonight, then I'll fill you in.'

'Water into wine I can do, and with a bed here for the night I've just cancelled out my commute to work tomorrow morning so it's a win win. As they say in the movies, "I'll be right back".'

Carolyn forced a weak smile at the implied joke, a pop culture reference to horror films where the person who utters those infamous words invariably finds themselves the next victim of whichever crazed fiend is the chosen subject of the film. Fleetingly Carolyn hoped that Bella wasn't being ironic.

CHAPTER
THIRTY-FIVE

GLENN MCGINLEY ENDED HIS VOICEMAIL WITH A DEEP, SINISTER LAUGH that he knew would have been appreciated when it was retrieved by its recipient. Recalling the events of tonight's writing class to her had been pleasurable, though he would have much preferred that conversation to have been two-sided and would have been absolutely ecstatic if it had been face to face. Still, to adopt the American phrase that had too easily become Anglicised with gusto, "it is what it is". Besides, she would be here soon. He'd made the arrangements himself.

Dr. Carolyn's reaction to the creativity of his writing efforts had been intriguing. From his study of her, not entirely surprising, but intriguing, nonetheless. Her announcement that she would plot a new novel herself by way of taking part in the class and completing the very exercises that she would set the others alongside them had clearly been an unplanned reaction to what she'd read. Of course the old biddies and the wannabe bestsellers in the class had lapped it up as an admirable demonstration of leadership by example. He, on the other hand, knew the sound of a gauntlet being thrown down when he heard it. If the good doctor wanted a good old fashioned game of cat and mouse, then she would happily get one. Just as long as she realised which of them was the cat and which was the mouse in their particular relationship.

Then of course there was the aptly named Bella. The would be, glamorous assistant of Dr. Harkin had managed to throw him a curve ball tonight in her intelligence gathering. He had to hand it to her, she was subtle. The others hadn't a clue that she was harvesting information for her friend. A regular little teacher's pet, she'd forced him into expediting his plans a little more quickly than he'd intended. No matter, he could strategise around that, and besides, her intellect had endeared her to him. Actually, she was in possession of many of the qualities that he found attractive in the fairer sex. Brains, looks, humour, empathy, she had in spades, and through her writing, it would seem, evidence of a scarred past. She would prove a worthy challenge when the time came. For now, he would enjoy getting to know her, allowing her to think she was getting close to him before he made her another of Carolyn Harkin's victims. Another strong young woman left broken and devastated by the actions of the good doctor.

CHAPTER
THIRTY-SIX

'Tilly was a witness' I finally began. Bella who had patiently waited while I found the strength to compose myself within the wine glass, leaned forward in anticipation. The contents of the glass had been more than half consumed before my senses were dulled enough to revisit that particular memory.

'A witness and a victim actually', I corrected myself, 'she got caught up in a sex trafficking ring in the West Midlands. I was the DI overseeing the investigation. She's one of too many reasons that made me realise that I needed to leave the force.'

I paused for a little more liquid courage before continuing, swallowing the mouthful of wine down hard in the hope that it would stop the well of sadness and regret from rising. It didn't.

'She and some of her friends, girls from both the UK Asian and White communities had become the teen victims of a group of young UK Asian traffickers. The young men would woo them and shower them with gifts, building trust, the illusion of attraction and the implication of a long term relationship before becoming controlling of them and eventually forcing them to attend parties where they would be prostituted to the even less morally scrupulous. By the time I had become aware of their situation, they were trapped in a cycle of violence and abuse. A cycle which I promised to break if Tilly helped me to.'

'Which she did?' Bella interjected. I nodded a heavy agreement.

'Not without some persuasion', I answered, 'she was so brave from that point onward though. From providing us with intelligence through to testifying in court she did everything I asked of her without question and persuaded the others to do likewise.'

'Should she have questioned?' Bella asked, her tone a little harder.

'No, at least not my motives, but still, I let her down. We made the arrests, broke the ring and made it to court. We even got a conviction. Not for all of them though. Tilly's would-be suitor-come-monster got off due to a technicality relating to my questioning in his interrogation. He walked free that day and despite my promises that we would protect her, we couldn't...at least not from herself. She took the law into her own hands. She stabbed him to death in front of his young wife and family. She later took her own life in custody, using her shoelaces to hang herself. It had been a horrendous oversight from the arresting officer not to make sure she had no way of harming herself. A failure in standard procedure from an officer under my direction.'

'Oh Carolyn, I'm so sorry. For her and for you. It must've been terrible' said Bella.

'It was. I still think of her virtually every day. She's one of the reasons that I retrained in psychology.'

'So there would be no more like her?' Bella offered.

I nodded again.

'To stop myself and others repeating the mistakes of the past' I answered.

'He must have some connection to the case' Bella said, unknowingly vocalising my thoughts.

'Time we knew more about him I think' I answered pulling

my MacBook decisively a little closer before booting it up and logging in to the PSNI portal within the DVA computer system. Clicking the link to vehicle registration checks with determined enthusiasm I was soon typing the vehicle registration details in as Bella dictated them to me. It was time we knew where Mr McGinley lived so we could turn the tables on him. I needed to start being able to delve into his life, retell him what I'd learned of it, regain some sense of control of what had escalated from a worrying situation to that of a potentially very dangerous one. When I saw the name and address of the registered keeper of the vehicle though, my world imploded. His earlier mention of Jess wasn't just a cruel taunt. She was back. The reason for my return to Northern Ireland. The reason I nearly died. The reason I'm afraid of my own shadow had somehow forced her way back into my life. It couldn't be.

'Jessica Farnham' I finally managed to mouth the words softly, my brain delayed, struggling to process the information I'd literally just read.

'But she's dead?', I croaked as I turned to look at Bella, her face a mixture of enquiry and concern as she watched me.

'She's dead. I know she's dead. I waited and I watched her die. I saw it happen. I watched her die. She's dead, I watched her die.'

'It's ok Carolyn' I vaguely heard Bella say as she moved toward me again. As the tears came I realised that I must've sounded demented to her. There was a reason for that. I was.

CHAPTER
THIRTY-SEVEN

The panic attacks that have been a regular feature of my existence for a little over a year now have been unpleasant at best, but the one that woke me from my fitful sleep in the early hours of this morning was welcomed as an old friend. At least I was familiar with the panic attacks. I knew how they manifested themselves in me, knew how long they would last, how an episode would develop and how it would eventually pass. Most importantly I knew that it would do exactly that, pass. If at times fiendish, then at least they were predictable. There was something oddly comforting in that, especially now. Even as I had been jolted from my sleep, a literal rude awakening and was being pitted against the wall of terror, choking and gasping for breath in the relentless respiratory assault contracting my trachea whilst I struggled to fight it, drenched in a cold sweat that I had so often heard being referred to as death sweat, I was thankful that the attack had plucked me from the nightmare of reliving something much more frightening. The Past.

As Uther's growl changed from fear to concern, his presence helped sooth me and I was soon past the stage of greedily gulping down air and moving toward pants of respiratory recovery. I'd obviously shocked him with my jumping up from the sofa where I'd finally fallen to sleep having chased Bella to bed a few hours earlier in spite of her endeavours to find out who Jessica Farnham was, and why sight of her name had troubled me so.

'It's ok boy' I puffed, ruffling his head as I sat down again, 'everything is ok?'

It wasn't though. Jessica Farnham, Jess had somehow forced her way back into my life and I wasn't sure how I was going to deal with that, or if I even could. I did know where to start though. I needed to find out if she could have survived. Was she alive? It was a thought I struggled to comprehend, especially since I saw her die. At least I thought I did. I also needed to find out as much as I could about Glenn McGinley. Urgent as both those things were to me, there was something else I needed to do first. Uther's show of alert and concern had earned him an early morning walk and nothing could quite beat a dawn walk around the lough with the eerie, early mist rolling at its banks. It would be like a scene taken directly from Conan-Doyle and I had my very own Baskerville hound.

CHAPTER
THIRTY-EIGHT

THE NOISE OF HIS SMART SPEAKER HERALDING HIM INTO THE DAWN OF A new day indicated to Brian Hannon that it was not going to be a good one. He considered his body clock to be as precision tuned as a fine Swiss timepiece and always awoke naturally just before the 06:00am alarm was due to go off. On the rare occasion, like this morning, where he slept through until the alarm, his experience was that he would soon be under the influence of a migraine and that the fates would continually conspire against him throughout the time between his rising and his return to slumber tonight, at whatever unearthly hour that might be.

Trying not to disturb Mrs H as he got up, though knowing that he probably already had, he tried to muster the enthusiasm to greet another day. He'd increasingly struggled to do so lately and in recent mornings had been debating internally if it was his advancing years or bearing the weight of his new responsibility that was the root cause. He didn't dare think about the other reason. Her diagnosis. The cancer that had put an hourglass between them, forcing them to watch the last remains of her life to ebb away as each grain of sand fell was killing them both and like the job and his age, was taking its toll. Still, if not as spritely of body and happy of mind as he once was, the one thing that hadn't dulled was his professionalism, which was why his thoughts were soon occupied with the murder of Ryan Casey and his duty to get to the bottom of what had happened to the young singer. More precisely, his thinking was of Dr. Carolyn Harkin. Her insight into the psychology of the perpetrator in her report had been an education for him, and invaluable to boot. He needed her on the team for this case budget constraints or not.

CHAPTER
THIRTY-NINE

'I heard you leave' Bella said with a shrug of her shoulders by way of explanation for why she was awake, dressed and seemingly responsible for the delicious aromas of breakfast that were filling the kitchen.

'We approve don't we Uther' I replied with a smile as Uther scampered towards the breakfast table, or more accurately the steaming pile of American pancakes piled high on a plate adorning it.

'Can he?' Bella asked tentatively, both of us knowing the answer should be no but was always going to be yes.

'Just this once.'

I'd hardly managed to get the words out before she had lifted one of the fluffy disks of gorgeousness and to a yelp of delight, presented it to Uther who wasted no time in wolfing it down.

'How about you, you hungry?'

'Famished. Nothing like a brisk early morning walk to build an appetite.'

'Did you sleep?'

'Like a log' I lied.

'Good, now that you're well rested and have had a refreshing constitutional, we can have some breakfast and you can tell me why the name Jessica Farnham has put the fear of God into you.'

I hadn't been expecting that, but she was right, seeing Jess' name on top of the reminder of Tilly had rocked me to the core and she deserved to know why. Sam too.

'Ok, you're right, I surrender. You've a right to know. Sam too. I'll cook for you both tonight if you're free and we'll talk then.'

'Promise?'

'Promise' I replied with a sigh 'I'll be an open book'.

'No, I meant the cooking part. We've only really seen your ability to heat stuff up so far' she answered as deadpan as she could manage before collapsing into laughter.

Despite the dilemmas that her getting me involved in the Sarah Clark case had brought with it, Bella Maskull was a tonic that I needed much more than I had realised. Still, my own past hadn't been the only thing clouding my thoughts when I had been walking with Uther. I had some more questions for her too.

'Now it's your turn' I said, taking a seat and pouring myself a coffee.

'For what?'

'To be an open book' I answered with a wry smile, 'I have some questions about Sarah...and Cillian.'

With that the joviality disappeared. I was sure Bella had been expecting an interrogation of sorts over breakfast but not the type she was about to take part in. That was something that I hoped would work to my advantage. In a sense it already had. After all, I'd managed to avoid talking about Jess until much later in the day, though I doubted that I could keep her out of my thoughts for that long.

'Sure...ok.'

Her half smile and averted gaze didn't make it look ok though, not by any stretch of the imagination, and there it was again, my psychologist's equivalent to Peter Parker's spider sense was tingling. I couldn't work out what it was but Bella was definitely holding something back. I decided to start easy on the questions with something that I'd wanted to clarify from Sarah Clark's case file. Not before availing of some coffee and one of those delicious looking pancakes though.

'I've been wondering about the early stages of the investigation' I began, 'the file said that Sarah's belongings that she kept at Cillian's house were missing. The suggestion being that she had packed them before leaving. What I wondered though was whether or not any of her belongings were taken from her family home. There was no mention of it. Do you know?'

'They weren't. I remember Sarah's mum mentioning that at the time' she replied.

'Do you think Sarah's family would be agreeable to speaking to me about her?' I asked, already knowing that ACC Hannon had forbidden it, though asking more so as to gauge her reaction to the prospect than anything else.

'She only had her mum. She was an only child and her dad left when she was still a baby. Her Mum moved away a few years ago too. Retirement in Mallorca I think. Anyhow, I lost contact with her.'

'Ok, I'll see if I can get the PSNI to follow that up' I lied, noting that it created a flicker of fear across her face. Why was that? I needed to delve deeper and if going down the bad cop route was the only way to see what she was holding back on then that's exactly what was about to happen.

'Another thing that I wondered about was Cillian's reaction to her disappearance. The file said that he'd been continually calling Sarah through the night she disappeared but because the initial investigation didn't conclude any foul play, there wasn't really any indication of how he behaved afterward. You said that you and Cillian were a support to each other in her loss when we talked with Sam. I'm a little confused about that. It suggests you were both hurting, in which case it implies he was innocent of any wrongdoing, but yet you paint a very different picture of him. I don't get it.'

My feigned confusion was achieving the desired impact if the unconscious wringing of her hands was anything to go by.

'At, at first he was upset and worried' she stammered, 'we both were. He couldn't understand where she'd gone or what had happened to her and the more I asked him about it, the more it seemed he really didn't know. Then after a few weeks he started to get angry. I guess he believed that she really had just left by then, and as I told you before, he had a thinly veiled hatred of women. I had always put it down to abandonment issues since his Mum died, so another important female in his life leaving him wouldn't have sat well with him. Still, he took it out on everyone around him, me in particular, and I stupidly thinking that he was hurting just as much as I was, gave him comfort I guess. That was until I realised that he was just using me and then the night of her birthday he....'

With that she dissolved into tears, leaving me guessing as to what she was about to say but thinking that what she'd already said certainly seemed to ring true. I wondered if I was too close to this case and what ACC Hannon would feel about my level of "review" of the case so far. Despite my feeling that there was something that she wasn't disclosing, I believed her, though was all too aware that the view I held of Cillian Moran was a one sided one, painted almost in its entirety by her. That was something that I needed to rectify somehow, though any chance of objectivity was slim. After all, my only other contact was Sam.

'He what?' I asked flatly and waited for a response, fighting my compulsion to comfort her as she had me in the time between then and when she spoke again.

'We went for a meal and a few drinks to Rococo to commemorate her birthday' she started, dryly, ' it was fine at first, a celebration of her life, you know. Anyhow, we both had too much to drink and his mood started to deteriorate pretty quickly as the night went on.'

I had already reasoned where the conversation was going. After all, if Sarah had left him then that would have fed in negatively to the abandonment issues I'd already surmised he had from the death of his mother, issues Bella had also correctly identified.

'Let me guess, aggression, anger?' I offered.

'Yes' she continued as she tried to blink away the threat of further tears, 'his attitude was starting to garner negative attention and I knew that if any well-meaning staff member or other customer tried to intervene he would likely explode, so I encouraged him to leave, avoiding the worried look of the fatherly figure on security that night as I led him across the road to Castle Gardens.'

I winced, sensing further still where the conversation was headed, the friend in me wanting to close it down to save her reliving of it, though the detective and investigator within me willing her on.

'Bella, are you sure you want to do this, I mean, do you want to take a break?' I couldn't help but notice that from beside her Uther had managed to block out any tantalisation held for the remaining pancakes and he too wore a serious look.

'I'm fine' she nodded weakly before picking up the story, 'I figured I could calm him down by taking him there, the Castle Gardens, if not for a moonlit walk, then for the other reason couples have been known to wander across from the bar into the forested gardens to partake. It worked, the walk I mean. It took his aggression away, but he changed then. I've never seen him like that before or until he died.'

She'd certainly piqued my interest now.

'Changed how?'

'He lost it. As soon as we went into the gardens he quietened, but as we got closer to the centre point, where the statue of the Hound of Antrim is now, he started to tremble and cry. He stopped there and fell to his knees. I didn't know what to do, I'd never seen him so vulnerable and was starting to feel bad for my poor judgement of him. He grabbed my hand. He was shaking terribly and he looked more like a frightened boy than the man's man he always tried to embody. He started to squeeze my hand, pleading forgiveness. When I asked what for, he said that it wasn't his fault. He'd been forced to do it. That she was already dead.'

As she continued to recount his words and actions her face reflected every second of the trauma of the night itself and no doubt the magnification of the emotions felt in every time she had relived those moments since.

'It was then I knew' she said flatly, 'he'd virtually said as much. I didn't believe the dead already part. Then it was my turn to lose it. I lashed out at him, kicking him until he was curled up on the ground in the foetal position with me screaming for him to tell me where she was. He didn't. He clammed up and when I finally lost the strength to continue I left him lying on the ground indulging himself in sobs of self-pity and I walked home alone. He turned up at my house early the next morning, blaming the alcohol and denying everything he had revealed the previous night and from then until…'

She broke again. I'd heard enough. Now I could finally console her.

'I need to find her Carolyn. I need to find her' she half whispered.

'I know Bella, I know, and we will' I promised into her ear as I embraced her.

I couldn't be sure yet, but there was something in what she'd said that made me wonder if we were even just a tiny bit closer to doing so than she thought. Now wasn't the time to tell her that, but if my suspicions were true Antrim Castle Gardens could soon be revealing a very dark secret of its past.

PART II: "SUSPICION OFTEN CREATES WHAT IT SUSPECTS" (C.S. LEWIS)

CHAPTER
FORTY

She certainly knew how to make an entrance, ACC Brian Hannon mused to himself as he watched Dr Carolyn Harkin arrive into the situation room ahead of the briefing. There was a disarming friendliness exuding from her as she greeted the already assembled team and apologised for the tardiness in her punctuality.

'That's quite alright Dr Harkin' he answered on their behalf, 'after all, I didn't give you much notice that your presence was required this morning.'

'Thank You Sir.' She smiled in return before busying herself in the task of seeking out an empty seat or suitable ledge on which to perch herself before he got the briefing started, the latter being the only option remaining. She had turned heads within the room all right, though not just because of her only slightly late arrival. What's more she had seemingly managed to retain the attention she had garnered on entering judging by the looks on faces around those assembled. Some would, he imagined, be captivated by her beauty, others by the reputation that had likely preceded her. Regardless of their views on either of those things though, which he was sure ranged from awe and for some, through sexual attraction, to jealousy and contempt from others, she was being silently judged before she had even given any input into the briefing. Hannon had no doubt she would prove her mettle when the time came. In fact, in how she was seemingly nonchalant to the obvious stares coming from around her, she had already somewhat confirmed it. For his part though, it was time for him to prove his, again.

'Ryan Casey' were the first words of his address to the team as he moved towards the large, clear plexiglass board at the front of the situation room and attached two pictures side by side at its centre. The one on the left was a high gloss promo shot of the young star, microphone in hand, bathed in a myriad of colours courtesy of an expensive stage lighting rig and no doubt basking in glory at the adoration of the thousands of people watching as he performed. The image of Mr Casey captured in the other picture though could not have been starker in contrast. Although in this picture too his face was bathed in blushes of orange, yellow, green and red, this time they hadn't been result of ambient coloured spot lighting. This time they were the reflection of heavy bruising and blood, the outcome of his being heavily beaten and although not evident from this particular shot, stabbed to death. His face, in the still frame on the left was the picture of youth, vitality, success, happiness and angular good looks. On the right however, his face was a pale, swollen, puffy mess, his skin the unmistakeable pallor of death, and make up, an autumn palate courtesy of his injuries, a further symbol of mortality and decay.

Off to the left of the pictures with his back to the board Hannon stood silently for a few minutes letting the reality of Mr Casey's fate and the violence of his murder be completely absorbed by the assembled company. The significance of his actions was not lost on any of them. Finally, he continued, heaving out an ever so posture slumping sigh before doing so.

'My wife and daughter are fans...were fans' he said, seemingly resolved not to buckle under the weight of his own words, 'we've been to more than a few of his concerts in the last few years' he added, awkwardly pushing his glasses up on his nose as he did so.

'A bit of a fan yourself boss' a voice teased from within the group, either in effort to provide some comic relief to the situation, or an ill judged attempt at banter. Either way it fell on deaf ears. Surveying the people in front of him Hannon continued slowly, purposefully.

'I've no doubt that you will get to the bottom of this case, get the answers we need and the justice that Mr Casey and his family deserve, but I won't insult your intelligence by telling you that this is a murder case just like any other. Clearly it's not, as the pressure being put upon us by the powers that be within and beyond the force is testament to, not to mention the escalation of the ongoing trial by media that the PSNI have been subject to lately. We're going to be expected to close this one emphatically, and fast. This means added individual pressure on each of us. Pressure we can't afford to buckle under. We work efficiently but we do it right. No cutting corners. I'm not going to risk the use of unorthodox measures to get a result, only to have some jumped up defence solicitor expose them and have any prospect of conviction laughed out of court as a result. Clear?'

Aside from his final word, his voice had been low and even but the tone of its utterance left nobody in doubt that it was being spoken more in command than question. The wave of silent nods was testament to the respect that he commanded. He didn't have to say it, but they were all too aware of why he had said what he just had, aware of the need for history not to repeat itself. Harkin too, although not resident in Northern Ireland at the time, was aware of the case that he was alluding to.

'DI Stewart, could you bring everyone up to speed on what we've got so far?'

The man who rose from the assembled group had not been

the one Carolyn had expected from her face value analysis of the people in the room who she'd yet to properly meet. They of course had been doing likewise to her since her arrival, making them fair game in her eyes.

Silently taking a place at Hannon's side from where he had been previously perched on the edge of the rear of his desk, too close to the monitor of his computer for comfort, DI Shay Stewart stood straight and poised himself to address the team. As Detective In Charge or DIC to use the accepted shorthand, it would be he who would not only lead and co-ordinate the investigation, but also the actions and direction of all those involved in it. Given the gravity of Hannon's earlier words, the load associated with his role would require broad shoulders to bear, broad shoulders which he did not have, at least not in the physical sense.

With a height that would place him on the short side of average for a man and a frame that was at best, slender, he gave the appearance more of a trainee accountant who had mistakenly wandered into the wrong office building than a seasoned DI. His tailored grey suit and white, open necked shirt was complimented by smart tan brogues and matching leather belt. His trendy, carefully styled hair, the healthy glow to his skin, no doubt helped along by some tinted moisturiser and designer stubble completed the metrosexual newbie accountant look. Looks however, as Carolyn knew more than most, could be deceiving, which was why as he began to address the room, he commanded the same levels of respect and attention afforded to ACC Hannon. Every gaze, hers included, fixed upon him, every member of the team poised to give and receive information, ready to play their part.

'Ok, so we're still awaiting the full forensics report but initial feedback would suggest we're looking at a secondary crime scene. He was killed elsewhere. Where, we're still trying to establish. As you know, CCTV presence in the city centre is generally very good, particularly in Donegall Street. So far, analysis shows no sign of Casey or anything else suspicious for that matter. St Anne's Cathedral directly overlooks the scene where his body was recovered, but of course with our luck, there's a blind spot and you can guess where that is. It's most likely he was taken through the alleyway that connects North Street to Donegall Street via Writer's Square, literally yards away from where the body was discovered and in the blind spot of CCTV.'

'Chances of finding CCTV in North Street would be slim' interjected the ruddy faced older man nursing a coffee at the bottom of the table.

'Exactly Mack. Keep on it though.'

'Will do Boss.'

'Ings, what have we got from pathology?'

Running a hand through her spiky blond hair whilst stealing a glance at the folder open on the desk in front of her, Ings drew in a long breath before beginning.

'The coroner's report indicates that the primary cause of death was a traumatic air embolism as the result of a stab wound to the lung. There were several other stab wounds across the chest and abdomen at various levels of penetration. There were some superficial knife wounds too, though interestingly no defence wounds. The injuries suggest significant blood loss so there would have been a lot of bloodshed, far more than was apparent at the scene which would support it's being the secondary scene. It would also suggest that he was already dead when he was left there.'

'Same place he took the beating I guess' Mack interjected.

'I would imagine. He certainly received a hell of a beating both pre and post-mortem.'

'What about the toxicology, have they included that in the report?' Stewart asked.

'They sent an update this morning. There were high levels of alcohol in the blood but nothing else out of the ordinary.'

'What about the cocaine?'

'That's an interesting one boss. No trace found in the blood and although present around the nostrils, nasal swabs from further up the nasal cavity would suggest that none had been ingested.'

'Possibly placed there post-mortem' Stewart said to no-one in particular, 'Healy, Watson, what do we know about the victim?'

Attention turning to the two young sergeants Carolyn had first ran across when they were appraising her Mustang and subsequently its owner, one shifted uncomfortably whilst the other, the alpha male of the two Carolyn guessed, leaned back in his seat, relaxing his shoulders, causing his pectoral muscles to become more noticeably taught underneath his tailored shirt. Posturing, Carolyn decided.

'Nothing too exceptional Boss. He seems about as wholesome as his image suggests. From those we've spoken to so far he was a real gent. Treated his family well, looked after the people who worked for him, was well liked and respected on the live circuit and within the industry. A regular all round good guy. He was due to be married in four months' time. His fiancée and his family are devastated. No sign of any enemies or anyone with a motive so far. No change in his behaviour or movements either. He cooked a meal from a subscription food box with his fiancée, they ate and then he left for a meeting with his manager. That apparently was their usual weekly routine of a Friday.'

'We've still some people to interview and we're still working our way through his finances and computer. His phone was missing from the scene' added the human peacock's colleague, sheepishly.

Stewart nodded pensively before speaking again.

'I still don't get the cocaine. Why try to make it look like he had been a coke head?'

CHAPTER
FORTY-ONE

'Sounds like a question for you Dr Harkin' I heard ACC Hannon say, the unspoken call to action clearly evident.

'The floor is yours, please' DI Stewart said with a half-smile as he slowly swept his right arm out to the side of him, rolling his hand to a space beside him, the equivalent of an invisible stage spotlight, front and centre reserved for me. The fact that aside from the senior officers in the room I was the only one being called to the front of it was not lost on me. I wasn't sure if it was a show of respect or they were expecting a show. Either way I was on mettle as I took the spot.

'From what I have already observed and reported on from the scene and from what I've heard here this morning there are several conclusions which could be drawn and possible avenues of investigation to think about.'

My tone purposefully clinical, delivered on a voice that I'd deliberately softened. I paused briefly, intentionally, assured that I had their full attention and if I was being honest, toying with them as a cat might with a caught mouse before continuing.

'Firstly, the appearance of the body would lead us to believe a frenzied attack, a kill of passion if you will. Of course that suggests that the perpetrator was angry, lost control perhaps. On the face of it maybe this was the case, but I suspect differently. For one thing, if that was the case, despite the level of alcohol in Mr Casey's system, there would have been defence wounds or at least signs of a fight back. Grazed knuckles or swelling and bruising around the hands.'

I shot a glance at Ings, who busied herself rescanning the report before meeting my gaze again with a silent shake of the head. I continued.

'From what I can ascertain, the killing was pre-meditated and carried out by someone who not only knew exactly what they were doing in terms of inflicting the fatal wound, but also someone who wanted to humiliate the victim in death. He was a handsome young man and I would hazard a guess that the majority of evidence of beating would be around the face and head.'

Again I turned my attention to Ings who this time nodded agreement.

'The perpetrator wanted to damage his looks...and most likely his reputation.'

'Reputation, how?' The human peacock glared; his brow furrowed as he awaited an answer to his question.

'Well Sergeant...'

'...Healy.'

'Well Sergeant Healy, I too did a little bit of digging into the victim, hence my tardiness this morning and it's surprising what you can find on the web if you know where to look, or if you look at all. With some targeted analysis, it can be seen that despite the illusions of pre-marital bliss, rumours were rife that Mr Casey was, how would you put it, playing the field? There was a string of young women alleging such online. Interestingly, a slew of young men too. Where Mr Casey was found was not a million miles away from The Kremlin, a well-known gay club, and of course the areas around North Street appear to have a reputation for solicitation and not that of the legal variety.'

I paused to let him process what he was hearing, enjoying watching him physically wither as he did so.

'And then of course there was the cocaine. A further humiliation and undermining of the clean cut image that he had cultivated. That's before we take in the other possible significance of where he was found. Writer's Square. Again, a little digging turned up that he'd, up until relatively recently, had a writing partner. Their parting was less than acrimonious if we were to believe what can be read online. Regardless of who was responsible, I believe that not only was this a pre-meditated murder, but also that it stems from a deep seated hatred of the victim. We could be looking at several motivations for that hatred. Jealousy, revenge, greed, or even self-preservation could be amongst them. Of course I'll be able to make further judgements when I get more information from the forensic report and I have a list of questions I would like to ask of the Coroner's Office and Miss Ings here also. For now though, Sergeants Healy and Watson, I'm guessing that your interview list has just widened somewhat.'

Healy nodded almost imperceptibly, though the flushing of his face, twisted in a scowl was much more apparent. Watson, on the other hand smiled, raising his hands slightly in submission. Clearly he had decided to take my ever so slightly barbed remark on the chin.

'Thank you Dr Harkin' DI Stewart smiled.

'Please, call me Carolyn... all of you' I smiled in return, though in my head I saw it much more as a metaphorical mic drop, and of course there's only one way to follow a mic drop. A purposeful exit. I was still smiling as I stepped out into a swirling wind outside the station, a powerful gust whipping one side of my unbelted navy Mac closed tightly over my chest whilst sending the opposite side flapping like an unfurled flag. As quickly as I could manage, my sight hampered by my hair being whipped across my face by the force of the wind, I closed and belted the coat before rushing toward the car. As I reached half blindly for the door handle with one hand whilst trying to brush the tousled strands of hair from across my face with the other, a change in wind direction blasted my hair backwards from it, abruptly restoring my twenty-twenty vision. It was then I saw her, at least I thought I saw her, a fleeting glimpse before she likely realised I had become aware of her presence from her vantage point across the street before vanishing into thin air. A trick she had perfected in the time I had known her. It couldn't have been her though, my rational mind knew that. It didn't stop me diving for the interior of the car as if under fire, flinging the door wide before open before launching myself unceremoniously into the driver's seat and flailing to pull the door shut again behind me, tears already streaking my face.

Had I been applying behaviour analysis to myself as an outsider now, I would have reasoned that responsibility for my current state lay within the chemical response to a bloodstream awash with a panic induced cortisol release and trying to rationalise a response. I wasn't though, which was why I was reduced to a shuddering wreck, trying and failing to remember how to activate the central locking of the vehicle internally before abandoning the thought in favour of gunning the engine and peeling away in a flight over fight response. Of course the logical thing to have done would've been to return to the safety and security of the station, but logic abandoned even the methodical brain of this psychologist when confronted by the woman who pushed me to the brink of my sanity, the woman who had befriended me with the sole intention of destroying me. The woman who I had left for dead in a desperate fight for my own survival. Now she was back, and much as I didn't want to accept it, she was very much alive.

CHAPTER
FORTY-TWO

ACC Brian Hannon wasn't sure what had spooked Carolyn so much that she had fled the station car park in such terror, but one thing was for sure, he was resolved in making it his business to find out.

Having tried and failed to catch up with her as she left, his intention had been merely to thank her for her input and congratulate her on what had been an excellent demonstration of her skill. One which had clearly cemented her place as part of the team she had just addressed and had clearly earned her unwavering, if not in some cases grudging respect from its members. When he saw her panicked movement toward her vehicle though, then the look of abject fear on her face as the Mustang growled its way toward the exit, he knew something wasn't right, which was why he was now testing the old turbo in his faithful but protestant Volvo to the limit in his effort to keep the taillights of the Ford in his sights whilst trying and failing to reach her on her mobile at the same time.

His instincts were telling him that she was homeward bound judging by her direction of travel. He was vaguely familiar with the location of Langford Villa and decided to drop his speed down a little in order to appease the protests of the engine and in the hope that it would make at least some of the myriad of warning lights that made the dashboard resemble a set of 1980s vintage fairy lights, go out.

He'd been correct, and after around 15 minutes keeping her in sight, he was now watching as the Mustang waited for the electronic gates of the entrance to her home to open and hoping that their slow movement would allow him time to catch up before she drove in. He was in luck.

Waving at her through his windscreen as she caught sight of his car in her rear view mirror, he saw the look of shock flashing across her eyes change to one of relief as she realised who he was. Moments later they were exiting their vehicles in front of the majestic building.

'Sir!'

'Carolyn, is everything ok? I tried to catch you but...'

Hannon didn't get to finish the sentence. He couldn't. The shock of seeing the firebrand of a woman he had come to admire so in the short time he had known her, dissolve into a whimpering wreck before his very eyes had taken the words from him.

'Oh Carolyn' he said, surprised at the crack in his own voice, 'let's get you inside.'

Their conversation over the following two hours, as she unburdened herself to him, would not only bring her the support that she needed, but it would also create friendships of great strength for him. That which he had already somewhat cultivated with Dr Carolyn Harkin was one thing; the other, with his new canine ally, that was quite another. What's more, their time spent in Carolyn's kitchen snug area had allowed them to formulate a plan. Jess Farnham may or may not have returned, and that was something he would look into. Her would-be accomplice though,

Glenn McGinley, he would be Carolyn's responsibility for now, and it would be one she would be more than capable of living up to. After all, she had all the skills she needed, and in spades.

CHAPTER
FORTY-THREE

'So, IN THE SPIRIT OF LOOKING AT KILLER OPENING CHAPTERS, YOU KNOW that I always encourage you all not to be afraid to share your work with the group, nor to be afraid to read it aloud. So I guess it's time for me to practice what I preach' I pronounced from my teaching space at the front of the room; 'please be kind', I smiled before standing up and beginning to read.

To be branded a murderer, albeit briefly is one thing. For it to become a self-fulfilling prophecy, quite another. Had I any way of knowing the danger that I was exposing myself to in the snap decision I'd made to attend Daniel's funeral, I would never have gone. It had been a decision grounded in grief on some level, or more accurately, an unhealthy dose of Catholic guilt on another. Either way, the events I'd set in motion on that day would fracture my life beyond repair and end the life of another. Events that I was oblivious to, at the time. Events, it would seem that are refusing to stay buried if today is anything to go by. I should have guessed by the "welcome" I received at the Church that day, that things weren't going to go well. Despite being presented with the perfect opportunity to turn on my heel and leave, that was never going to happen. If there was one thing

I'm a slave to more than my misplaced Catholic guilt, it was my own obstinacy.

'Fuck, my little brother really did have a type didn't he' one of the mourners spat disdainfully in a voice deliberately lowered in feigned reverence to the sanctity of the Church she stood outside, but purposefully loud enough that she knew I would hear as I shakily made my way toward its nave.

I ignored the comment of course, not wishing to lower myself to her level of crassness, and as a mark of respect to Daniel didn't even offer her a look, let alone my condolences as I passed. That's definitely Margot I thought to myself, recalling Daniel's assessment of his older sister and the hatred that he held for her as he had recounted tales from his growing up to me. It appeared to have been justified.

In my peripheral vision I was aware that the others too had turned their attention to me, my senses heightened in particular to the coldness of her glare penetrating me as she took a long final drag of her cigarette before dropping it to the ground and stubbing it out with the sole of a black patent stiletto. Very classy.

'She has no right to...'

'...Please Margot, let it be. Not today.' I heard the voice of the elderly male, Daniel's father likely, in reply to the haughtiness of his daughter's remark and the spike in tension that it brought with it. His voice was weak, thick with exasperation, and at odds with his broad frame, and a visage that looked like that of a much younger man. Grief I thought, or age, or perhaps too many years spent having to keep his daughter muzzled.

'Fine! But...'

I didn't hang around to hear exactly what her response was, though I just about made out something to the effect of, 'at least the others weren't the death of him'. I'm pretty sure the word Bitch was hurled in my direction too.

Sliding in to an empty pew near the back of the church, I focused my attention on blocking Margot out of my thoughts by choosing instead to marvel at the ornate gold leaf frame surrounding the painted first station of the cross, "Jesus Is Condemned To Death", if my education courtesy of the Daughters of Charity School served me well. I would only realise the irony of this later on, long after she snapped my attention away from it.

'Do you mind if I sit here?' came the whispered voice. I looked to see a woman of similar age and look to myself smiling sheepishly at me.

'Yes, of course' I replied, returning her smile, my own voice hushed. I suddenly got what Margot meant. The woman could have been my double, both in looks and sense of dress, albeit she was considerably more pretty than I was. I felt myself blush a little at the thought. Well, at that and the realisation that I had been patting the bench beside me like a child beckoning her friend to come sit with her. Of course it was likely destined we would become friends. I hadn't counted on being her killer though.

'I'm Jess, Jessica Farnham' she whispered, offering me her hand. I took it, sealing both our fates.

I paused for breath, and if truth be told, for effect. It worked. The pause was soon broken by the sound of applause coming from the class, including that of a reluctant Glenn McGinley.

'I love it. You've linked your story to Glenn's. That's so clever' Gladys gushed realising that Jess was a common character in our writing.

'Yeah, it looks like we have a collaboration on our hands. I'm going to be quids in.' Glenn tried to hide his disdain in humour. He achieved it, with those who weren't wise enough to be looking for anything beneath face value.

'Why, Thank You' I drawled, in self-deprecation, before taking an exaggerated bow.

'Now. If you would like to indulge me further, I'll continue.'

And that was it. Two significant women in the life of Daniel Knox, former lovers mourning his passing from a shared pew in a draughty church following an icy reception. Never to meet again. At least, that was until a chance meeting on a University Campus in Ormskirk reunited them. It would be later that I would discover that there had been nothing chance about it. It had rather been orchestrated as the beginning of a campaign of stalking and terror that would make me fear for my life so much, that in a desperate act of self-preservation, I would end hers.

The fanfare and reverie that my continuation had brought with it was short-lived. Glenn McGinley's razor sharp questioning and steely glare cutting it with ease.

'How did she die? Jess Farnham. How did your character…I'm sorry, I didn't catch her name, kill her?'

'Actually, I hadn't given the narrator's name, but since I borrowed one of your characters names in Jess, and you'd originally used my name in your work, let's call her Carolyn Harkin for now. I can change it out in the final draft.'

He nodded, the faintest change in his expression betraying either amusement or controlled anger, it was hard to tell which. Either way, the game was afoot between Glenn McGinley and I, oblivious to the others in the class bar Bella.

'Touché Dr Harkin. And how did Carolyn rid herself of her would be stalker?'

'Don't you mean, how will I?' I smirked. 'I haven't written it yet remember. That'll be the denouement. I think something involving a blow to the head to end a frenzied knife attack stemming from an argument and a startling revelation. As far as the would be aspect of the stalking is concerned, there'll be no, would be about it. The exposition of the story will remove all doubt of that.'

Tilting his head slightly and pursing his lips, his face took on a pensive look momentarily, until he nodded a slow, silent approval. The fire in his eyes continuing to dance gloatingly. Did he think he was still in control here?

'I'm beyond intrigued. What was the revelation?'

'Ah Glenn, you've made the same mistake again. Not, what was the revelation, rather, what will the revelation be.' I smiled. Despite the undercurrent of danger that only he, Bella and I were aware of, I couldn't help myself. I was enjoying the verbal locking of horns and battle of wits. I continued.

'You're getting ahead of yourself. Writing spoilers for your manuscript comes much later on in the workshop series. No matter, I'm happy to share my plotting with you. I think the revelation will be that Jess had spent a large amount of the time in a secure psychiatric unit, having been found guilty of the murder of Daniel Knox, a murder that I, or rather Carolyn herself had been questioned in connection with, and almost charged for.'

'And her motive for this murder?'

'One of the oldest in crime fiction writing, and life. Jealousy. She was present when Daniel had publicly proposed to Carolyn and she accepted. She'd been livid, and with an already unhinged personality according to some, it would be a natural progression for her. Hell hath no fury and all that.'

'Ah, applying your particular set of skills, I like it' he smirked, the condescension and sarcasm almost dripping from his words.'

'Well, it'd be a shame to waste them. People would come to doubt my worthiness to be called Doctor.'

'Indeed, I'm fascinated though. You said that part of your story would be the denouement. Isn't that the part of the story that begins to draw all the plot lines together? The bit that leads to the finale. Surely what you're describing is the finale?'

'No. I haven't got to the finale yet. I'm not quite sure what that will entail, but I'm sure it'll be explosive.'

'Oh, I'm loving this, it's amazing' Gladys bleated, 'it's like both your stories have intertwined and it all sounds fabulous. It's like it could nearly have happened in real life. I can't wait to find out what happens next.'

She was completely oblivious not just to breaking the rising tension between McGinley and I, but of just how close her statement had been to fact.

'Well, Carolyn has just moved into a big house. If the character Carolyn does likewise, the ending might go down the route of a stereotypical big house novel and the usual tropes' he offered mockingly, 'The uncovering of a crime related to the place, usually involving the discovery of a body followed by the inevitable big house fire that almost, but not quite destroys the building' McGinley sneered, seemingly now incensed enough not to remember to hide it.

'It might well do. The trope of the big house fire, I like it. Though if I go down that plot route I would have to follow through on the other trope of such a plot at the end. You know, the restoration of the protagonist...and the dead villain.'

CHAPTER
FORTY-FOUR

SAM MORAN'S BOAT WAS NEITHER DOCKED AT LANGFORD VILLA, NOR visible amongst the early morning vessels drifting across the lough. That could only mean one thing to Bella. It was happening again. Her heart sank a little at the realisation and the tightening sensation around her left wrist that usually signalled a rise in her anxiety levels made itself known to her. Sam hadn't had a dark patch in a while, but if ever there was an indication that he was about to hit one, the disappearance of the boat was the surest of signs. She knew better than to call him, it would be a waste of time. Better to just keep her head down, keep things ticking over with the business and hope that this "lost weekend" as he had dubbed them, would be a short lived one. Then they could both try to get him back onto an even keel. Still, there was Carolyn. She was bound to ask questions. How could she tell her about Sam's dark passenger? Was it even her place to alert her to presence of the demon that Sam sometimes had to wrestle with? She would be vague she decided. Maybe just allude to the fact that at times the boat was aptly named and that Sam's, "Scoundrel Days" were not altogether behind him. He was a big boy. He could fill in the blanks if he chose to himself when he returned. Whenever that might be.

CHAPTER
FORTY-FIVE

The rhythmic pounding of the rain on the deck above him was a sound that Sam Moran normally took comfort from. There was something strangely reassuring in the sound, especially when he was cocooned in the warmth of his cabin bed amidst the gentle rolling of the boat against the current. This morning though the noise reflected his unrelenting sense of urgency to get inside his Broughshane home, a sense he had felt since the moment that a Belfast Live news alert had informed him of Ryan Casey's untimely demise, and one that he had realised that he must fight until daylight. Despite being the owner of the house, he knew only too well that he would be best not drawing attention to the fact that he had returned. The boat tied to the mooring point on the River Braid at the back of the property would have attracted less attention than the internal lights being turned on if he were to enter it at night. Now though, the time was right, and the rain would likely provide increased cover from the attention of any potential witnesses to his return. Finally, it was time.

Moving quickly from the mooring and across the decking area that connected it to the back garden of the house he was soon at the back door, armed with his keys and about to penetrate the lock. He stopped, hesitating momentarily, a means of trying to control the rising trepidation inside him at the thought of what he was about to encounter inside. It wouldn't be the first time that Ryan Casey had left an almighty mess for him to clear up. He would be right. There would be an almighty mess, but no amount of clearing up would ever rid him from it.

CHAPTER
FORTY-SIX

Having driven past the property many times over the years Bella had often thought of the bungalow and the memories contained within it. She had never for one moment though, thought that she would be inside it again. Yet, here she was, nosing the mini through the narrow entrance to the driveway. The place had changed hands several times since she was last here and according to Sam's diary he was due here this morning to provide a quote for the current owner on some refurbishment. A task that had fallen to her in his absence. The place was set to be listed as a holiday let but apparently needed a bit of work to make it more Air B&B marketable. She would normally have relished such a visit but for this particular place, her feelings were mixed. She'd had such happy memories of growing up here, some sad ones too, but all memories that she cherished, nonetheless. Now, if the owner agreed with her ideas and estimate, she could effectively be tarnishing those memories by the touch of her own hand. The thought of that brought with it a pang of sadness.

Arming herself with the notebook, pen, measuring tape and of course, her smartphone, all of which were the tools of the trade for the job she was about to undertake, she exited the car, trying to place her memories of the property firmly to the back of her mind as she did so. She was a professional after all, and this job should be treated just like any other. The small porch was darker than she had remembered, not helped by the dull grey cloud typical of an Autumn midmorning in Antrim, though she was still able to make out the outline of the wall mounted key box to the left of the front door. Shivering, she tucked the notebook under her arm, silently cursing her earlier choice that a gilet would be warm enough, a decision with fashion rather than practicality in mind, and not for the first time. Arming herself with her phone, she activated the torch app which turned on the light at the back of it, sending an arc of harsh white light across the face of the key box and exposing the brushed steel combination lock. Holding the phone shakily in her right hand, she used her dominant left to line up the tumblers of the lock to the combination provided in Sam's digital diary before pulling the lever that opened the box and retrieving the keys from inside. She allowed herself a little victory pump, her success in gaining the keys reminding her of one of the must see TV shows from her teens where such a challenge success would have gained her a crystal had she been a contestant from The Crystal Maze. She followed that success with gaining entry to the house which commenced an assault on her senses brought by memories associated with the sights and smells within.

The hall decor remained unchanged from when she had last crossed the threshold. The floor, a ceramic tile chequer of terracotta and cream upon which a clashing carpet runner of blush zebra print ran its entire length. In a movement of muscle memory, she moved to switch on the light. Despite the earliness of the hour, the long hall was dark, the only natural light coming from the stained glass area of the front door and either side of the frame now behind her which with the darkness of the porch and dullness of the weather only served to further preclude any natural light. The ceiling bulb immediately illuminated, though the choice of a light fitting largely made up of plates of brown tinted glass meant that it made only a marginal difference. Bella smiled. Like herself, her Aunt Molly had been a woman of style over substance, despite her advancing years. Her smile broadened still as her eyes fell upon the white, wrought iron telephone stand, the crimson velvet upholstered seat and the mustard coloured rotary telephone, all relics from the 80s, still sitting upon it. She would have her work cut out in dragging this room into the 21st century alone, and that was before she had even thought about the heating. At the moment, a tiny storage heater was charged with the job of heating the long expanse. The number of doors leading off into adjoining rooms would also be problematic. It had always reminded her of a hotel corridor because of that. She hadn't been able to bring herself to look near the last door on the left. His room. At least not until it flew open with a start, bringing her face to face with a sight that chilled her to the core. She had fully expected to be haunted by her fears of the past when she had entered. The fear she faced now was very much one of the present and her Mini, just yards away, may as well have not been there at all as her body, rooted her frozen to the spot as he approached.

CHAPTER
FORTY-SEVEN

SAM MORAN WAS WELL USED TO THE INTERIOR OF HIS HOUSE RESEMBLING a bomb site following an occasion where Ryan Casey had availed himself of their "arrangement". A crime scene though, that was an entirely different story, especially one of this magnitude. Someone had obviously lost their lives here and judging by the scene, violently to boot. Possibly Casey himself if the local and national news was to be believed. He wouldn't mourn him. After all, there had been times in the last few months where he would have happily rid the world of Casey himself. He'd seen sides to the star that few others had, and fewer still would wish to. His tendencies toward the hedonistic, arrogance, cruelty and at times, downright evil were well guarded from the fans and the majority of the industry. Casey had seen to that, and much to Sam's disgust, he had helped ensure it, facilitating outlets for Casey's darker side and clearing up the damage he left in his wake. Judging from the mess at the sitting room end of the large open planned room comprising of sitting room, kitchen and diner, Casey had received exactly the type of end that he deserved. It was the only justice appropriate after what he had done to her, and he hoped that she would now rest a little easier and be at peace in the knowledge that he had been held to account. By whom, he neither knew nor cared. Momentarily his attention wandered to the last time he'd spoken to her. The rose that was Lauren Baxter. The vision of her standing there, leaning her back against the self-same kitchen worktop that he now stared in the direction of, smiling defiantly at him with a coffee in her hand, brought the flash of a smile to Sam at its memory. She had somehow found her way back into Casey's favour, having either fallen out of it or having been victim of his insatiable desire to bed the next pretty young thing. Whether they were male or female depended very much upon his mood. She'd been determined to make a go of it with Casey though, in spite of that, and had even grander plans to oust the current incumbent of the title fiancée to him and claim that title for herself, so she had told Sam, fully aware of the daggers her words contained. Daggers that wounded more when coupled with the fact that the words were mouthed through lips wearing the lipstick that Sam himself had bought for her on one of their many dates. What's more, she was wearing her hair just the way she knew he liked it. She was even dressed in the chocolate coloured lingerie set and matching short silk dressing gown she knew he loved to see her in, and out of. She knew he would be there then. Knew what she had intended to say to him. Knew how cruel she was being. He felt the anger rise, only to be replaced by grief...and guilt. No matter how she had belittled their affair and dismissed him, she didn't deserve what had happened to her. Didn't deserve the watery grave she found herself in. Just like those before her.

CHAPTER
FORTY-EIGHT

Glenn Mc Ginley couldn't have been expected to know that Bella was already familiar with the spot beside the fire in the sitting room where he had placed her, or could he? Several permutations of how things were now going to play out were flashing through her mind, none of which didn't threaten her safety. As he moved through into the adjacent kitchen, or scullery as Molly had referred to it back in the day, she found some strength and comfort in the familiarity of her surroundings and the reassurance that it brought with it. A home advantage of sorts. She had never before felt a paralysing fear like that she had experienced when Glenn had emerged from Connor's room like that. It had been bad enough that she hadn't been expecting anyone to be in the house, I mean why have a key box there in the first place and have issued instructions and a combination code to open it? Then to have him spring from the shadows! For a long moment she had feared for her life. A not so small part of her still did. After all, he clearly had some sort of sinister intent towards Carolyn and she didn't know if she too figured in his twisted plan for...whatever it was? What's more, she still didn't know why he was here. Had he lured her here on the pretence that someone needed a quote for renovations? If so, why? Had bringing her to this particular location also been a deliberate ploy? Did he know she had a history with the place? Surely if he'd been expecting anyone it would've been Sam? There were so many questions swirling through Bella's mind. The primary one being, just what the fuck is going on here?

Snapped away from her thoughts by a mini explosion of spits and sparks brought by a log shifting within the fire, the flames voraciously licking at it as it moved, she turned just in time to see a micro avalanche of red hot coals cascade towards the grate. Surprise quickly gave way to comfort. Was it a sign from Connor? Is his spirit still here, still looking out for her? The warm glow radiating from the fireplace and the memories it brought with it certainly reminded her of him. Not that she needed reminding. She'd spent many an evening sitting in this very spot opposite him. More so in his final days when his body, ravaged as much by the medication as by the cancer it was there to treat, could no longer feel the benefit of the central heating and had drawn him here. He had been her closest childhood friend first and foremost. The fact that they were cousins had been immaterial, and from when they were mere toddlers, they had been inseparable. Until the end. It had been her caring role for him that had led her into nursing and she fleetingly wondered what he would think about what had become of her, or more importantly, what she had become. She couldn't allow her thoughts to wander too far down that path. Not now. Not ever. Besides, now needed to be very much about self-preservation. Her thoughts needed to be solely focused on one thing. Getting out of here alive.

CHAPTER
FORTY-NINE

'Here you go! A strong pot of tea and some biscuits for the shock' Glenn McGinley said jokingly as he set the tray down on the largest of a small nest of tables before sliding all three tables in unison across the linoleum floor into place between them in front of the fire.

'Joking apart, I really am sorry. I really didn't mean to startle you. If it's of any consolation, you gave me quite the fright yourself. I mean, Sarah did tell me that someone would be coming to look at the place. She wants to give it a refresh before it's listed on Air B&B, but I'd completely forgotten that someone would be coming to give the place the once over today, and I certainly wasn't expecting that person to be you.'

Bella half raised her eyebrows in response, a single wrinkle appearing across her brow. His explanation certainly sounded plausible but his having lowered himself into the seat opposite her, Connor's seat, irked her. That and the fact that he was here in the first place.

'Sarah?' She asked.

'Yes, my friend, Sarah Millen. She owns the place' he answered with a disarming smile that she was beginning to notice was a bit of a trademark of his. It might have worked on her normally, marginally at least, if she wasn't still feeling more than a little trapped.

'When my work brought me here, I needed to find a temporary base. Thankfully Sarah volunteered this place' he offered, pre-empting what would without doubt have been her next question.

'And you still haven't told me what that is. The work I mean'. Now it was her turn to flick on the charm or the appearance of it at least. She'd relaxed a little now. His manner and the credibility of his explanation had seen to that.

'No, I haven't have I' he retorted teasingly, 'I mean, I could tell you, but then I'd have to kill you.'

Bella smiled at the comment, hoping her expression didn't betray the newest spike of unease felt behind it. She wasn't sure if his flirtatious attempt at humour enamoured him to her or terrified her. Either way she was exposing herself to a situation that she was less than comfortable with. So why was she still here?

CHAPTER
FIFTY

The one advantage that ACC Hannon's official office at PSNI headquarters had over his favoured station office was the fact that here he would be much less likely to be disturbed. Today he counted on that. Absorbed since first light in finding out whether or not Jessica Farnham was indeed alive, he had found himself wading through a mound of digital files spanning her interactions with the police. He'd established early on that yes, she was in fact dead, and that her death occurred just as Carolyn had described it. The struggle that had ensued between the two women in Carolyn's then home when she had come at Carolyn with a knife had indeed ended in her receipt of a fatal wound from the blade, just like Carolyn had recounted to him.

What had actually taken up most of his time was allowing himself to get lost down the rabbit hole of reading through Farnham's entire history of interaction with the police. A history that read like a story akin to one of Carolyn's novels, and one that had placed Carolyn as the victim despite the fact that it had been she who had survived it.

Beginning in London, Miss Farnham had been tried and found guilty of the murder of Carolyn's former fiancée, Daniel Knox, a murder that Carolyn herself had been questioned in connection with. Following a plea of diminished responsibility, her incarceration had been a blend of imprisonment and psychological rehabilitation. A failed rehabilitation as it turned out.

What had followed on her release was her actively seeking out and befriending an unsuspecting Carolyn before embarking on a campaign of stalking and intimidation unrivalled by any he had ever come across. Having read what he'd read, it was little wonder that Carolyn had been so devastated at the prospect of her survival. The thought made him realise that he had been prolonging her anxiety, albeit for a few hours. Pulling out his phone from his pocket he scanned his contacts for her number before dialling. Within a few seconds the call had connected.

'Sir' she answered stiffly.

'You're not in service now Carolyn. Please, call me Brian.'

'Yes Sir...Brian' she answered, wincing at her failed attempt to shake off some of the formality of her tone.

'I'll get straight to the point. She's dead Carolyn. I've looked at the autopsy report and there's no question. Jessica Farnham is of no threat to you.'

Saying the words to her had filled he too with a sense of relief, to a level which surprised him. The silence that followed on the other end though was palpable. Until he heard the soft sobs that she had evidently been trying to stifle. If he could have reached through the phone and held her, consoled her, he would have. Instead he just found himself croakily uttering, 'She can't harm you now.'

'Thank You', her teary reply prompted him to end the call more prematurely than he intended, the emotional charge in the conversation making him feel more awkward and uncomfortable than he cared for.

Returning the phone to where it had been sitting on the desk beside her computer, Carolyn ripped a tissue from a nearby box and began to dab at the tears in her eyes.

Brian's call had brought some relief in confirming Jess' death, but his words of reassurance that she no longer represented a threat rang hollow in her ear. Even in death Jess had found a way to return. Glenn McGinley's manuscript and the woman outside the police station had confirmed that. What was more, the threat somehow remained a very real one. The realisation of it sent her blood cold and brought a pain to her chest that caused her to imagine her heart now encased in ice. Trying to shake the feeling, she rose and walked to the large dual aspect window in her study. If there was anything that could make her feel more at ease it would be her unrivalled view of Lough Neagh from this vantage point, that was for sure. Even in its mirroring the greyness of the brooding clouds above, it was beautiful. Hugging herself against the chill she felt as she watched, now transfixed by the gentle rippling movement of the water, the calm before the storm if the cloud cover was to be believed, she noticed the merest glint of sunlight breaking through the cloud. Seemingly gaining in strength it punctured a hole through the thick grey flock of the cloud until a single golden beam now illuminated part of the vast body of water. Tracking the beam from top to bottom her gaze fell to where it ended, it's transforming the already beautiful picture framed in the window to one of seemingly celestial significance as it spotlighted a single swan, the whiteness of its down glowing magnificently as the water shone little sparks of gold around it. In that moment Carolyn felt a sense of warmth and serenity return to her, and not for the first time since she'd arrived back at Langford Villa. She was definitely getting some healing from this place. A healing that she needed now more than ever.

It was then that her phone rang again, breaking her from the calm. Probably Brian calling back she thought as she moved toward her desk again to retrieve the phone. It wasn't. The name illuminating the screen was one she counted on never seeing there again. It was there though, plain as day, accompanying the shrill ringtone, her name illuminated in the light from the screen. Caller ID: Jess Farnham.

CHAPTER
FIFTY-ONE

THE SETTING HAD BEEN DIFFERENT THIS TIME, BUT WHEN IT CAME DOWN to it she had been like all the others. Would be like all the others. Glenn McGinley amused himself with the thought as he cleared away the tea tray before returning to the room he had set up as his home office.

It had been a fireside chat this time in a tired old bungalow in Antrim rather than the sparse sterile functional space that was his consultation room back at the facility, but the outcome had been the same. Unbeknownst to the lovely Bella, she had just been subject to a psychological review courtesy of Dr Glenn Addams-McGinley. He had never practiced under his double-barrelled surname, opting for plain old Dr Addams instead. In his line of work it was imperative that the patients felt he was relatable. They would have been less likely to allow him to build a rapport with the perceived impediment of differences in social status. Since coming to Antrim to accost the equally lovely (or so some might think) Dr Harkin, it had been vital that he ditch Addams in favour of McGinley, for fear that his name might trigger a memory of their shared past, or a recollection of his name as one mentioned within the medical circles they both moved within.

Specialising in the social and emotional rehabilitation of women who had been subject to sexual, physical or emotional trauma, or more often than not, a combination of all three, he was a psychologist of great repute, owing to the positivity of the outcome for his patients. Those who he chose to help. For others, the "rehabilitation" would involve abuse and ultimately trauma of a very different kind. Using his skills and training he had without fail, easily allowed himself to walk the corridors of their psyche. For some, he would apply healing as he went. For others, he reserved the right to mess them up a little more. Sometimes, a lot more. Like all abusers it was about power and control for him. Some called it a God complex. He wasn't interested in controlling their freedoms, their bodies, or even their rights. There was only one type of control that satisfied him. Control of their minds. Not just in the form of subservience. That was too crass for a man of his wit and learning. Reprogramming their minds to behaviours that they thought were routed in their own free will, now that was a feeling to behold. The first step toward which he had just taken with the unsuspecting Bella. He would savour every moment of that. For now though, it was time to break a glass ceiling, the figurative shards of which he would use to make Dr Carolyn Harkin bleed just as the fatal puncture wound she had inflicted on Jess had done. He allowed himself a smile at the thought of it before returning to his study. Within moments his fingers began flying over the keyboard and his screen filled with words.

What happened to Dr Addams on that Saturday afternoon had it been placed into a work of fiction, would have been deemed a stretch too far in its believability and would most likely have been edited out of existence. The events of that day and their aftermath, however, were all too real, and as his

professional and personal worlds collided with devastating consequence, the infamous words of Mark Twain regarding truth being stranger than fiction could never have held more resonance. Nor could his own words that Marita Melinka was not of sound mind. I told you so's wouldn't change what had happened that day though, and they certainly wouldn't bring Solomon back, that was a crippling reality that he faced anew each waking morning. He could almost forgive Marita her actions, she was in no state mentally to be on the streets. The person responsible for her being there however, that would be a different matter. The woman, Dr Carolyn Harkin would never be offered his forgiveness or anything close to it. She would feel the full force of the retribution that he would administer to her though. Of that he was certain.

Perhaps his fellow psychologist, the one of clearly more renown than he if the hype around her were to be believed, had dreamt of one day shattering glass ceilings. If so, she had definitely achieved as much. Literally, that was. That had happened as soon as the woman, who upon a technicality in Harkin's review of his practice, had been discharged from the facility and his care, had scooped 5 year old Solomon up in her arms. His beautiful Solomon, the child he thought he would never have. His miracle boy. They had both turned their heads toward where she had called from, closing the distance between them as she did so. His curious gaze was still fixed upon her when she snatched him into her arms from where he had sat at their table at the rooftop restaurant, feigning doe eyes at him as she lifted him level to her with a smile before Addams had sufficiently processed what was happening to be able to intervene.

'Hello Beautiful Boy.'

The saccharine laced tone of her voice, her wide eyes, her smile still haunts him almost as much as the broad smile Solomon had responded with. That was before time lapsed into slow motion, Addams' movements laboured as if underwater as her warm smile at Solomon was turned to him, her lips taking on a sinister curl at their edges and the glint in her eyes replaced with the deathly dullness of those of a shark. It was within that millisecond he had realised that he was already too late. His child had been taken by an equally dangerous and equally cold blooded predator and he was too late to do anything but watch. She briefly turned her attention again to Solomon before hurling the boy off the roof and sending him smashing through the atrium of the courtyard Reception area of The Edgbaston Hotel below, ending his young life on impact with the solid marble slabs that made up its floor. No parent should ever have to deal with the death of their child, let alone a devastating loss brought about in such tragic and traumatic circumstances. Dr Harkin, despite her learning, would never understand that. She would know the pain though. Feel the devastation. Suffer the way he had. That would be his revenge. He would eventually kill her too. That he would do for Solomon.

CHAPTER
FIFTY-TWO

AT LEAST THERE HAD BEEN SOME POSITIVES TO BE TAKEN FROM HER return to the property that had once been home to Molly and Connor this morning, Bella mused as she powered up the MacBook. She'd had just enough presence of mind to at least take some pictures of the interior of the old bungalow and a note of its most relevant measurements before nervously uttering her goodbyes and scampering away from there, and from him. It was only now, some half an hour after securing herself behind her own heavy front door, locking and bolting it behind her, that she had started to find some semblance of ease. She habitually locked herself inside the apartment when she returned home. This afternoon though, it had been more through conscious thought than muscle memory.

Having secreted herself into the safety and comfort of her small, second Storey apartment in Carnbeg Square, she had flicked on the kettle out of reflex rather than necessity before taking a seat at the small dining table at the front window of the open planned expanse that served as her sitting room, dining room and kitchen. It had been here that she had been sat since, her thoughts a torrent of the traumas of memories past mixed with the more recent fears, dangers, and possibilities she had been presented with this morning in the form of Glenn McGinley. Creating a new folder on the MacBook under the address of the bungalow, she started to get down to business, importing the photographs into the folder and creating a spreadsheet of the measurements. It was usually at this point that she would get most excited about a job such as this. The moment that she started to create design templates and mock ups of what the renovated bungalow could look like if she were allowed to apply her practical and creative flair. More than several hours into it now though and she still wasn't feeling it. Perhaps a run was what she needed to shake off her preoccupations and improve her mood. It might also give her time to process her thoughts on Glenn McGinley. Was he the bogeyman that Carolyn thought or was he actually a charming, funny and intelligent person underneath the exterior he presented? Was this a closer representation of the truth? She needed to work that one out and soon. Especially since she was becoming much more aware of a growing attraction she felt for him. It didn't surprise her. She seemed to have a penchant for the bad boy type. The question was, just how bad this time? She'd get the opportunity to figure it out soon enough. After all, she'd agreed to have dinner with him before the writing class in a couple of nights time. Yep, she definitely needed to pound the tarmac for a while to get her head around that one. Besides, it would be good for mind, body and soul.

After swapping the clothes she'd been wearing, still exuding the smell of smoke from her time at the fireside earlier, for her favourite Under Armour training leggings and top, she pulled on her complimenting Sketchers runners, retied her hair into a tight ponytail and headed for the door. Within moments she'd done a quick warm-up and was already headed across Carnbeg Square and jogging toward Klibegs Road at a pace, initially intent on completing her usual 3 mile circuit, before adapting it so that her run would end at Langford Villa meaning she could call in with Carolyn and Uther. The prospect of their company would help her eat the miles up a little more quickly too. So far, it was working. At least it had been until she became aware that she wasn't alone.

It wasn't unusual to come across another runner or realise there was one behind you on this road despite its rural nature. It was relatively close to several housing developments and a large town after all, so naturally some of the other inhabitants of the area would use it as a jogging trail. It was less unusual at this time of the day too. Many runners, particularly female runners would try to get their runs in as early as they could manage on Autumn evenings like this, feeling marginally safer knowing that there would be less likelihood of their being attacked during rush hour, despite the early darkness. Still, there was just something about the figure several hundred feet behind her that made her feel on edge. Her first thought was to slow her pace, or stop to feign stretching out a cramp, to let the person behind pass. She would try that. Her second thought was to wrap her hand around her keys pointing several strategically placed, claw like between her fingers so that she could defend herself should she come under attack. The first strategy didn't work, the person behind slowing their pace as she slowed hers, stopping as she stopped, maintaining the distance between them as they did so. Time for Plan B. Make the claw then take off at a sprint and hope against hope that she was faster and fitter than the person behind. That didn't work either.

CHAPTER
FIFTY-THREE

For a dead woman Jess Farnham was persistent, I'll grant her that I thought as the phone rang for the 14th time in just a few hours. With each call after the first, my abject terror at seeing her name subsided from fear through despair, anger, frustration and now irritation. I had answered diligently each time as per Brian's advice when I had called him again, this time in full meltdown mode after Jess' first call, and he had firstly ensured I had locked the doors and windows before he ordered a monitor on my mobile line. Of course, both the house and the front gate were secured. That had always been my first priority. As far as the line monitoring was concerned I also knew the drill. Try to make the call last long enough so that the signals can be triangulated and an approximate location of the caller found. The problem was that every time I answered, the call clicked off immediately.

I had been about to go leave the phone in another room to give myself some headspace when it began to ring again. This time, thankfully, it was Bella. A very breathless and anxious Bella.

'Carolyn, I'm at the gate, please, let me in. Hurry, I'm being followed' she pleaded, sending me padding toward the control panel in the hall with urgency. Moments later I had thrown open the front door and was pulling her inside before locking it again behind her and enveloping her in a reassuring embrace.

'It's ok. You're ok. You're safe now' I murmured into the damp hair at the side of her head.

It was a few moments after I'd led her into the kitchen snug before she could finally speak, panting heavily from exhaustion, red faced and drenched with perspiration while both Uther and I patiently waited, one of us wagging their tail in delight at seeing her.

'They were...were following me. They chased me' she gasped.

'What...Who?'

'I, I don't know. I was out for a run and they came behind me and followed me. I tried to run and they chased me. I sprinted until I got here. They were still behind when you let me in.'

Her words made my stomach churn. Had whoever chased her managed to follow her into the grounds? Surely the security lights that had picked out Bella would have exposed their presence too... wouldn't they? Shit!'

I moved to the security camera feed, scanning through each area in turn, my mind filled with images of the woman who had been lying in wait outside the police station, the woman who apparently wasn't Jess Farnham. The woman who had been harassing me via telephone since. Then of course there was Glenn McGinley and God only knows what he was capable of. Thankfully though, all the cameras were clear, and my most accurate form of security, Uther, was not showing any signs of agitation.

'All clear' I said, as convincingly as I could muster when I returned to her before grabbing her a bottle of water from the fridge and flicking on the coffee machine, 'Tell me what happened. Exactly what happened.'

Her account of what she had experienced during her run had me worried for her. Her recount of what had happened to her earlier in the day on the other hand, that had me worried for both of us.

'Do you think it was him who chased you?'

'It's hard to tell. Whoever it was always kept about the same distance between us and I could only ever get the occasional glance over my shoulder. I can't even be sure if they were male or female. Whoever they were, they were quick. Glenn though? My gut feeling, No.'

'It could be coincidence I guess', I thought aloud, 'but you getting a callout to that house, him being there, then being chased this evening? Something doesn't quite add up.'

'I guess now may not be a good time to tell you that I've agreed to go out for dinner with him' she offered tentatively, furrowing her brow in brace for my reaction. She was right to.

'Ok, coffee isn't strong enough for this conversation, and I still need to tell you about my communications from beyond the grave.'

'What! Jesus Carolyn. That definitely makes it Wine O Clock?'

The flicker of a smile as she moved past the initial shock of what I had initially said and her utterance of the words that had become a mantra of sorts for me in the past months brought a sense of relief. We'd both clearly had a tough day so far, Bella more so than I, and we were in need of a regroup to make sense of it.

'Have you eaten? I'll cook us something, that makes the early wine much more acceptable' I laughed.

'Sounds like a plan' she replied, 'I'll help.'

'No, you chill, I'll sort it, besides, I think Uther is after one of your ear massages by the look of him.'

I busied myself removing a Marlborough from the wine chiller, opening it and pouring two glasses whilst Bella gently rubbed Uther's ear through the thumb and forefinger of one hand while clumsily trying to unlock her phone with the other.

'Do you want to go healthy or not so much?' My opening of the refrigerator door certainly got Uther's attention if not hers judging by his movement away from her in my peripheral vision and his padding towards me. She on the other hand was now engrossed by her phone.

'What do you think Uther? Is it Salmon fillets and salad, or Pizza?' His sniffing toward the contents of the illuminated interior made me smile. Of course, he would be having his usual Science-Plan Complete Dry Dog Food, but he was smart enough to know that a treat from the fridge was not beyond the realms of possibility, which was exactly what he was rewarded with.

'What about you Bella, what do you think? Salmon or Pizza?' I turned my attention toward her in anticipation of a response that again didn't come. She hadn't heard. Still too engrossed in whatever the screen of her phone was showing and judging by the ashen look on her face and her wide eyes, it wasn't good.

'You ok? What is it?' My sense of unease grew as I moved toward her.

'I must've missed this earlier when I called you, I was so panicked' she said, a crackle of fear in her tone as she turned the phone toward me, her hand trembling slightly as she held it. A text message, likely from a burner phone, though how whoever had sent it would have known her number I wasn't sure. The message that she had just read and was now presenting to me couldn't have been more menacing. The words, capitalised, read: HOW LONG MUST I FOLLOW YOU BEFORE YOU RUN?

CHAPTER
FIFTY-FOUR

It had taken him virtually all day and the whole place now reeked of bleach, but finally Sam Moran had managed to remove all signs of Ryan Casey's bloody demise from his home. On the surface at least. God only knows what a luminol wash and some UV light might still be able to reveal. That proposition was one he didn't dare contemplate, let alone be fit to deal with ever to having to find out. Knotting the black bin bag with his PVC gloved hands he made his way to the back door again. As soon as he had disposed of the cleaning materials he would give some headspace to the questions that he had been using the distraction of his deep clean as a means to help him actively avoid. Could Ryan Casey be linked to his house? To him?

He needed a drink. At times like this he always thought better in the company of his friend, Jack Daniels. He would dump the bag and the gloves into the industrial waste bin that resided in the darkness of the short entry adjacent to the Merchant Fish & Chip Shop, before crossing the road to pay a visit to McNeill's Off Licence where he would pick up a bottle of Jack. He hadn't countenanced that someone may have been watching the house. That they had become aware of the obvious signs of life inside it; the lighting of several internal lights to balance against the loss of natural light that an early Autumn evening had brought with it. Nor had he been aware that his movements within had prompted them to alert the police. Until now.

With the door ajar, the handle still within the grip of his right hand and the rubbish bag clasped within his left, he found himself being startled by a PSNI officer, who had clearly been just as shocked at finding him on one side of the door, as he had been at finding them on the other. Both men now having to gather their thoughts quickly.

'I'm sorry to have startled you Sir' the young officer began. 'We've been called to the property after concerns were raised regarding some suspicious activity.'

'Admittedly, witnessing me cleaning up the house could be argued to be suspicious activity' Sam forced a smile. 'You know what it's like, the life of a Batchelor, I'm sure the shock of it would have been enough to worry the neighbours but it had to be done some time, I couldn't leave it much longer without people talking.'

Sam guessed from the minimal growth of stubble on the young man's face that in the local vernacular would have been described as bum fluff, that he knew little of the Batchelor lifestyle. The young officer most likely hadn't freed himself from the apron strings that fleeing the nest would have brought, especially if the razor sharp creases on the sleeves of the shirt that he wore under the protective vest of his uniform was anything to go by.

'Speaking of which.' Sam lifted the bag a little higher in front of him, before edging past the officer and opening the wheelie bin, leaning the lid against the garden wall and dropping the bag in before peeling off the gloves and tossing them in after it, hoping that his actions came across as naturally as they should have done.

The young man, his back now to Sam, spoke into his radio.

Sam had already reasoned there would have been a colleague at the front of the house.

'Sorry to have wasted your time officer' Sam said to the man's back. The young man half turned, awkwardly, wanting to face him but not entirely sure if he could take his full attention away from the open back door.

'That's quite alright Sir. Are you the owner of the property?'

'Yes. I've been away for a while. Work, you know. I came back earlier today and when I saw this mess I thought, needs must.'

'Ah, that would explain things.'

'Let me guess, a concerned neighbour? No doubt the woman at number 42. Not much gets past that one.'

'Something like that Sir.' He smiled. 'How long have you been away?'

'About a month all in.'

'Are you the only resident?'

'Yes.'

'Anyone staying over? A house-sitter or anything?'

'No.'

'That's strange.' The young officer cocked his head to the side, the light from inside the house illuminating a raised eyebrow.

'How so?'

'Because we were called out to the property by someone with concerns of suspicious behaviour in the early hours a few days ago.'

'Nothing to do with me officer I'm afraid. I suspect more the outcome of a furtive imagination and a penchant for a G&T or 10 up at number 42. I wouldn't worry about if officer.'

'In that case you wouldn't mind if we took a look around Sir' came the voice of the female officer who had emerged from the pathway that led around the side of the house linking the front and back gardens.

He did mind though. He minded a lot.

CHAPTER
FIFTY-FIVE

'Feeling better?' Glenn McGinley asked as she walked into the dining room; the distinct scent of verbena from her favourite L'Occitane shower oil permeating the air before her.

'Nothing like a long hot shower to sooth the muscles and a fresh pair of jammies after a long run' she answered as she slid into her seat at the dining table.

'You've had a busy evening my love. Wine? I've made your favourite Creamy Smoked Salmon Linguine.'

'I don't deserve you.' She smiled, taking the chilled glass of Wairau Cove from his hand.

'You're right, you deserve better. You did good today' he returned her smile before fetching two steaming bowls of pasta from the kitchen and placing one of them in front of her, dropping into the seat facing her and setting his own bowl down on the placemat.

The meal in fact wasn't her favourite but she wasn't to know that. It had been his wife's favourite, but she wasn't to know that either. Just like she wasn't to know that she wasn't in fact called Jessica Farnham, or at least she hadn't been when she had first come under his psychological care. Her former identity was of zero consequence to him. His success in his pioneering psychological rehabilitation programme, nicknamed the How To Be Dead Programme by his colleagues, that was all that had mattered. He had developed it as a means to reprogram the minds of those who had been chosen to enter witness protection, or people, who after being associated with heinous crimes or criminals, needed to be assigned new identities for their own protection and that of the public. His work with the infamous teaching assistant, Maxine Carr had been his most notable to date. At least, the most notable that his supervising authorities were aware of. The subject of which he was most proud was the one sat in front of him. The one who now believed with every fibre of her being that she was Jessica Farnham. The one who with a few image tweaks would now pass as a believable doppelgänger of Jessica Farnham. The one who with his skilled intervention, now felt every bit of hatred for Carolyn Harkin that Jessica Farnham had. He knew that. After all, it was he who had placed some of that hatred in the original Jessica Farnham's mind too.

PART THREE- "EVIL COMES FROM THE ABUSE OF FREE WILL." (C.S. LEWIS)

58

CHAPTER
FIFTY-SIX

'Thanks for coming this morning at such short notice Bella. I didn't want to disturb you but I still haven't been able to reach Sam and when I saw the puddle on the floor underneath the fridge I wasn't sure what to do.'

Uther, who had been standing guard at the side of the fridge seemingly unsure as to why it now stood considerably further away from the space that it lived in, took on an even more perplexed look as I stood and spoke into the gap behind it, addressing Bella as she worked with her back to me.

'No problem, glad to be of help. It's sorted now. It was just a slight ventilation problem that was causing the fridge motor to overheat and short out the fuse. It'll be fine now.'

Emerging from the darkness of the little alcove she had been working within, she slid the huge fridge across the slate tiled floor and back into place with ease.

'Someone's had their Weetabix this morning' I joked.

'No time for coffee though, hint, hint' she smiled.

'Payment in coffee I can do' I replied. 'Then you can explain to me why every time I've mentioned not being able to get hold of Sam, you've been evasive.'

She blushed.

'I haven't, have I?'

'Just a bit' I replied, gesturing a lengthy gap between my thumb and forefinger.

'Of course, I had to become friends with an Investigative Psychologist didn't I? Am I ever not being analysed?' She quipped with a smile.

'You're never being analysed, nobody beyond my professional life ever is…unless they set my Spider Sense tingling. Now sit!' I gave her a friendly nudge towards the snug before setting about making some coffee and getting a snack to occupy Uther as he joined her there.

'So what gives with Sam?' I asked, across the coffee tray I had placed between us.

'Let's just say that you're not the only one with a huge dog in their lives…except his is black and figurative.'

'Depression?'

'Got it in one Doc. You'll see him down sometimes. Other times he'll disappear for days on end and comes back full of beans and as if nothing ever happened.'

'Does he…?'

'…Talk about it? No. Never. And closes down without fail if you try to. I wouldn't bother if I were you. I've learned to work around it, and there's always enough going on with the business to keep me occupied until he gets back.'

'You mean like, hapless people who don't even have the wit to work out how to fix a fuse' I smiled. 'Well, that's one of my queries for the day dealt with. I've gotten to the bottom of Sam's issue, in a manner of speaking. Now for the next, how have you been?'

It had been a few days since I'd last saw her and I'd been worried after the chasing incident and text. I'd even spoken to Brian about it, only to be told that despite the fact that he would have loved to have helped, it had been an isolated incident and the speculative worst case scenario I had outlined to him, was just that, speculative. Despite his best efforts he had done little to appease my worries for her, especially since it had transpired during the conversation that until only a matter of months ago, Northern Ireland was the only part of the UK that didn't have any specific legislation around stalking.

'I'm fine Mom' she japed.

'Really Sweetie, you don't look fine' I mocked in my most saccharine laced US accent. 'Joking apart, I've been worried about you. I've lost count of how many times I wanted to call you to check you were ok, but I thought the last thing you would want was to have me pestering you.'

She half smiled but I could now see fear in her expression, and aversion of eye contact told me all I needed to know.

'What aren't you telling me Bella?' I tried to couch my words softly as I asked, though heard the worry in their delivery through my own ears. She pulled her phone from her pocket and after swiping the screen several times, handed it to me.

'Keep swiping left' she instructed. The screenshots she had taken of the messages and their content was chilling:

HOW LONG MUST I FOLLOW YOU BEFORE YOU RUN AGAIN?

YOU LOOK SO PRETTY IN THAT BLUE TOP. I CAN'T WAIT TO TEAR IT OFF YOU.

YOU'VE GOT SUCH A BEAUTIFUL BODY. YOU'LL MAKE SUCH A BEAUTIFUL BODY.

YOU SEEM DISTRACTED SITTING THERE AT YOUR WINDOW. PENNY FOR YOUR THOUGHTS.

WHAT IS A GOOD LOOKING GIRL LIKE YOU DOING IN A PLACE LIKE THIS? ALONE...PERHAPS NOT?

My mind was a whirl of worries for her and memories of what I had been through with Jess Farnham. Whoever was doing this had been obviously using a burner phone to deliver their sinister messages. That meant that they would have to have known her telephone number somehow. I also wondered if the signal from the burner phone had been triangulated with that of her own, what the proximity between the two would be. I'm calling Brian' I said simply, as we both fought back the tears.

CHAPTER
FIFTY-SEVEN

'I THINK WE'LL NEED TO CALL IN DR HARKIN AGAIN' ACC Brian Hannon, more in command than observation as he addressed DI Stewart after the team briefing. 'I'd like to hear her thoughts on what we've learned if anything.'

Stewart nodded agreement. 'Me too. She certainly brought some fresh thinking last time. I'll let the others know that she may have some questions for them.'

'I suspect she might' Brian chuckled as Stewart moved to leave. Whilst they weren't much further on in having a solid suspect, her advice on further avenues of investigation to pursue had certainly rattled a few cages and added to the list of people with means and motive to want Ryan Casey dead. What was more, they had also managed to uncover some CCTV footage that painted the young country star in a light contradictory to that of his clean cut image.

'Shall I arrange to have the recordings of the interviews and the CCTV footage sent to her Sir?' Stewart asked.

'I think so. She might be able to read more into the body language and such than we've been able to so far. Besides, she's a woman of the world. I'm sure she knows that some people use CCTV for purposes other than security.'

'Or perhaps a different type of security' Stewart said with a wink before departing.

He was sharp, Brian thought to himself. Too sharp to be lingering in the rank of DI. He should be DCI by now, though would be difficult to convince on the prospect. Still, it would be a topic that he would broach again when all this was over. The ringing of his mobile broke him from the thought.

'Carolyn, I was just about to call you.'

CHAPTER
FIFTY-EIGHT

Brian's liaison with Antrim PSNI Station and the resulting increase in patrols around the town, and in particular near Bella's house, had left me feeling more than a little underwhelmed, but realistically I knew that there was little more that he could do, and in fact should have been more grateful that he had used his position of power to do even that. Perhaps I was projecting my own negative experiences onto her, but I couldn't help but feel that this was more than some sicko getting his kicks in intimidating her. I was sure that the messages represented a real threat and it wasn't a huge leap of the imagination to have placed Glenn McGinley behind it. Him, or perhaps whoever the clone of Jess Farnham who had been trying to put the frighteners on me was. Either way, her agreeing to dinner with him didn't sit well with me. Nor did her insistence that she didn't need to come stay with me for a while.

Still, waiting for the arrival into my inbox of the CCTV footage that Brian had asked me to look at, and in an effort to distract myself from further stressing on the matter, I turned my attention to the Sarah Clark disappearance again. I'd been feeling a little guilty that my probing the matter had gone a little stale of late.

Circumstances had somehow dictated that, particularly my not being able to drill down on Sam's take on it all with his absence, but if I was being honest, there hadn't really been anywhere else I could have taken the enquiry at the moment, the trail having gone colder with each year that had passed since her disappearance, and perhaps reaching freezing point with the untimely death of Cillian Moran. Still, until I was able to speak to Sam about it, the best I could do was to look over the digital files again, which was exactly what I'd resolved myself to do before Sam's call granted me a reprieve.

'Hi Carolyn.'

'Well, if it isn't Lord Lucan. Nice of you to check in.'

I hadn't intended the barbed comment, but regardless of why he had gone off grid, a simple call would have been common courtesy and the least I deserved. Little did I realise the extent to which my words would come to bring a chill to my bones in the days ahead. Particularly my reference to Lord Lucan.

'I deserved that I suppose, though you might do well to remember Dr Harkin, that my absence has been days, not decades like your good self.'

'And I deserved that I guess' I relented. 'I'm sorry.'

'Me too.'

'You ok. Bella told me about...'

'...I'll bet she did. Anyhow, Yeah, I'm fine. At least a lot better than I have been. It's really good to hear your voice though.'

I paused, unsure how to follow that up and feeling myself flush a little.

'You still there?'

'Yeah, sorry I was...'

'...I was wondering, I mean, I kind've left you in the lurch. I was wondering if you'd let me make it up to you.'

'I've been fine, Bella has stepped into the breach with the work on the house.'

'Glad to hear it, though that wasn't quite what I meant.'

'I know. Well, I might be open to offers. What do you have in mind?' I smiled.

'Dinner. My place.'

'Sounds like an offer I can't refuse. On one condition. Only if I can bring a plus one.'

'Deal. I've been looking forward to getting to know Uther, besides, you'll both enjoy what I have in mind for you. How does around six sound? I'll text you the address, it's not far.'

'Perfect! See you at six.'

With that he was gone again and despite my flash of anger with him when I first took the call, I had to admit that hearing his voice had taken a weight off my mind. I'd been worried about him, and it would be a welcome relief to share my concerns about Bella's safety…and mine. Texting me the address though? I'd presumed that he lived on the boat, especially since it disappeared from its mooring at Langford Villa around about the same time he did.

CHAPTER
FIFTY-NINE

'Mack, what can I do you for?' Brian Hannon turned his attention from the tower of admin on his desk that he had been trying to put a dent in, having become aware of the senior detective, in vintage at least, pausing near the threshold of the open door of his office seemingly trying to decide whether to knock on the door or not.

'Sorry to disturb you Sir, I was looking for DI Stewart.'

'Sorry, I haven't seen him in a while He was here earlier though.. Anything I can help you with?'

'No, it's ok Sir, it'll be fine. I can wait.'

'Mack, you know I'm just plain old Brian to you when the young whippersnappers aren't around. Are you sure there's nothing I can help you with? You look a bit worried.'

'Nothing plain or old about you my friend, and I still can't tell you how proud it makes me to see you seated behind that desk.'

'It should be you sitting here and you know it, anyhow, come in, grab a chair. I know you well enough to know when something's worrying you. What is it?'

It was true that Clayton Macklin, or Mack as he had been

introduced when Brian first came across his slightly older colleague in his early days on the force, would one day have been considered before him for the ACC role, had it not been for his falling victim to an act of terrorism that had left him no longer physically or mentally able to meet its demands. Brian had an unwavering respect for what he considered a true gentleman of policing, and one with a razor sharp detective instincts to boot, which was exactly why he had placed him within the team he was now part of. A combination of experience and old school professionalism made him a perfect mentor for DI Stewart and a father figure of sorts for the others.

'I suppose you'll find out soon enough, but I don't want DI Stewart to think I was going above his head and I certainly didn't want to be the one adding to your burden.'

Brian took in a deep breath and held it, steeling himself for what was undoubtedly going to be bad news. Mack took the pause to be his cue.

'Ok, here goes…I could be wrong but I'm pretty sure that either Healy or Watson have been acting inappropriately with a witness. More specifically, the victim's fiancée.'

The weight of Mack's words were evident on his face as he spoke them, and despite his stating that he could have been wrong, the very fact that he was raising the concern was enough to tell Brian that he wasn't.

'Ok Mack. Thanks for that. It's fine. I'll take it from here.'

It wasn't fine though. Not by a long way, and despite the air of calm Brian was trying to exude, both men knew that the pin had just been pulled on a grenade and that the blast wave of the explosion that was soon to follow would be far reaching and potentially devastating. An internal investigation would be initiated swiftly and would be robust. For some, Brian Hannon was already sure, its outcome would be career ending at best, and more likely ending in dismissal and criminal charges being levelled at anyone found to be guilty. He would make sure of that, personally.

CHAPTER SIXTY

'Wow, what a beautiful house' I greeted Sam as I stepped out of the Ranger and onto his driveway.

'Well, we both know that it's not quite Langford Villa, but it's home' he smiled as he pulled me into an embrace.

The house was truly beautiful and despite being lucky enough to own the property that I did, I'd lost none of the grounding of my working class roots, nor my appreciation of people having bettered themselves, that others are often jealous or dismissive of, regardless of their own situation. The property, a sprawling detached, fairly new build, like those around it, backed onto the River Braid where it flowed through the affluent Mid-Ulster town of Broughshane.

Releasing me from his embrace Sam moved to the rear passenger door of the Explorer's cab, opening it for a clearly excited Uther to exit.

'Hey Big Man, at last we meet' Sam said as he fawned over him amidst showers of stolen slobbery kisses. His choice of greeting, intended as a friendly introduction was also an accurate description. Uther had certainly grown dramatically in size in the short time since he came to live with me, and now wasn't far off the height of a fully grown Irish Wolf Hound despite his youth.

'Clearly he likes you' I laughed as Sam struggled to stop Uther from jumping up on him and ultimately failed if the giant forepaw on each shoulder levelling them both in height and starting some kind of awkward dance was anything to go by.

'What a cute couple' I japed, 'I could see you two on Strictly.'

Inside I felt relieved that they were getting along and realised that it mattered to me more than I had thought. He and I were either both good judges of character, or he had a naturally friendly disposition. If the latter, it worried me and made me proud in equal measure.

'You both hungry?' Sam's question was addressed more to Uther than I.

'Starved' I replied, motioning toward the front door.

'Not quite yet Dr Harkin. We'll retire back to the house for drinks later if you like. For now though, we're off out for dinner, with a short scenic walk en-route.'

'Sounds like a plan. Lead on Macduff' I replied.

'Surely you mean, 'Lay On', Dr Harkin, and you a wordsmith too.'

I laughed, and I won't lie, his knowledge that in using the popular turn of phrase, I had misquoted Shakespeare's, Macbeth, may have made my heart do a little flip.

'Let's go. I have a couple of surprises for you between now and when we eat.'

He wasn't joking. The first surprise along the way came in the form of a community ran bird sanctuary running parallel to the banks of the Braid, a short walk away from his house. Home to all manner of avian life of wide and varied classification, from the domestic to the rare, the place was a wonder to behold for both Uther and me. The walk through it was a magical experience both in the sight of the beautiful birds and in the company. As is often the case in life though, it was to be an experience tainted by a darker aspect of nature.

After happening across a bleeding and injured young female mallard, we realised that it had just been attacked by a number of the drakes, leading us to spend several unsuccessful minutes trying and failing to prevent further attacks. In the end I was forced to witness several of the young males use their beaks to violently restrain the female whilst forcing her to mate with them whilst Sam contacted the helpline number visible throughout the signage of the sanctuary to report the issue. Watching as the situation had unfolded I felt helpless, unable to stop the attacks, knowing the only thing I could do was hope that the young female would somehow pick up on the vibes I was sending her, that what she was going through was brutally unfair and that while I couldn't stop what was happening, I was here to support her.

When Sam returned to my side he was visibly vexed.

'They told me it was fine, just to ignore it. It's all perfectly normal. It's just what the males do during mating season' he spat.

My heart sank and although his anger at the injustice was admirable, I couldn't help but feel that the voice on the other side of his call was just stating the facts. Nature can be brutal. I also couldn't help but feel that human nature could be equally brutal, especially when it came to misogynistic behaviour engrained within it. Sam may have keenly felt the injustice. Whether or not he could truly feel empathy, that was another question entirely.

'I need a drink' was my simple reply.

'I can arrange that.'

The second surprise came in the form of the location where we would get that drink, and our meal.

The Thatch Inn, located in the main street of the town had a stone cottage exterior original to its 1700's construction, and a beautiful, thatched roof, whilst inside the white walls, stone floors and roaring open fires made for the warmest of welcomes. Seated near an open fire whilst Uther sprawled across the slate floor in front of it, we were practically the embodiment of an advert for Tourism Northern Ireland, which was likely why the proprietor asked us to pose for a picture for the Inn's social feeds before we tucked in to our steaks and I reacquainted myself with a complimentary pint of Guinness after much too long an absence. The resulting image wouldn't do my writer's social profiles any harm either. As far as, "making it up to me goes", I had to admit, Sam Moran had style, and the warmth of the hospitality and his easy conversation were enough to make me forget the plight of the poor young duck. At least that was, until the conversation turned to Bella.

CHAPTER
SIXTY-ONE

THE PHOTOGRAPH OF SAM, CAROLYN AND UTHER AT DINNER THAT POPPED up in Bella's Facebook feed as she scrolled, brought a smile to her face. They looked good together. Were good together. She wondered if her ears would be burning at any stage of the evening. Probably. Part of her wished she hadn't seen the picture though. Hadn't had the visual reminder of Carolyn that brought the pang of guilt that was now growing within her. For the second time she hadn't been completely straight with her, except this time, she wasn't entirely sure why. Yes, she'd shown her the horrible texts that had been worrying her sick. She hadn't shown her the other texts though. The many many other texts exchanged between Glenn and herself. Texts, initiated by him, that if read from first to last would trace the early development of a potentially romantic relationship with the common theme of flirtation, subtle at first until it was only just a respectable distance away from sexting. Then there was tonight when he turned up at her apartment a few nights early for their dinner date. He couldn't wait any longer to see her apparently. She hadn't resisted either, which was why she was seated in the comfort of a booth in Reds

Bar & Restaurant whilst he was ordering their drinks and asking for menus.

She'd promised Carolyn she would be careful. Was she being careful? She wasn't sure. What she was sure of though, was that she wanted to be here, be with him, every bit as much as he seemingly did her.

CHAPTER
SIXTY-TWO

She was only too well aware that her true identity wasn't that of Jess Farnham. That was of zero consequence to her now. She would be Jess Farnham for as long as he wished her to be. It was worth it to feel so desired by him. So consumed by him. So empowered by him. Besides, the identity of Jess Farnham was a damn site better than the pathetic excuse for a human being that she once was. She would never go back to that. She would be whoever he wanted her to be for as long as he wanted her to be, which was why Jess Farnham was now standing at the centre of Bella Maskull's apartment, scanning around the open planned living area in the hope of finding a set of keys for Langford Villa. As it turned out, she was in luck. She needed to move quickly now in order to make the most of the opportunity that had landed in their lap.

The intention had originally been that Jess could work her magic in Bella's bedroom, arranging the "surprise" they had in store for her while he had taken her out for the evening. He had promised to ensure easy access for Jess. He'd been as good as his word on that. His supposed act of chivalry in insisting that Bella cross the threshold to exit before him, in true "Ladies First" style while he supposedly locked the door before returning the keys to her and whisking her away had worked perfectly, ensuring that the door was in fact unlocked when Jess arrived. Nice and easy... until his text arrived. Langford Villa also lay empty now, unguarded by its canine protector. If Jess could locate a spare key then a little mayhem could ensue there too. Two birds with one stone and all that. Now it was all down to her. Act One was now complete. The bedroom scene had been staged and photographed. The picture would be sent via burner phone later. Now it was time for Act Two.

CHAPTER
SIXTY-THREE

'I can't believe that the villain in your writing is actually based on your ex.' Glenn McGinley leaned closer still across small table that separated them. 'Should I be worried that I might make it in there too?'

Bella took a sip of her wine before deliberately fixing her gaze playfully on his. The cadence of the candlelight dancing in his eyes emboldened her, or perhaps it was the wine.

'Where specifically? The story or the category of ex?' She smiled.

'Hopefully neither, though I would hope to at least potentially qualify for the latter in some way if you get my drift.'

'I certainly do' she smiled, 'and anyhow, you're one to talk. I'm not the one who has not only named the writing tutor as one of their main characters but seems to be getting great delight out of having a virtual duel with her through both your stories.'

'She enjoys it, so do the old dears in the group. There's no harm in that.'

'Isn't there though?'

Bella may have been more than a little tipsy, but she still noticed the irony in his words. She couldn't fail to, especially when they had been accompanied by such change in his facial expression and the uncomfortable silence that followed them.

'Tell me about him' he finally said.

'Cillian?'

'Yes. I want to hear if he's as villainous in real life as his fictional counterpart.'

'You mean was. He's dead now, and dare I say it, deservedly so.'

'That my dear Bella, sounds like a perfect way into that particular story. What happened?'

'He was poisoned.' Her words were simple, direct. As a scorned lover he would have expected that, as he would the lack of sympathy in their tone. What he hadn't expected however, was the satisfied expression on her face and the parting of her lips into the delight of a smile. He liked it. He liked it a lot.

CHAPTER
SIXTY-FOUR

I probably shouldn't have been surprised that Sam's house had such a tastefully styled interior. He was in the trade, so to speak, after all. I suppose I'd been expecting it to have lacked a woman's touch, which it didn't. I wondered if Bella had a hand in that or if it was someone else who had sprinkled the place with just the correct amount of femininity to make it homely. What I hadn't expected was the almost clinical smell of bleach and cleaning products that permeated the air when we had arrived, and which were now being countered by the best efforts of the WoodWick candle that was working hard to replicate the aroma of the fireside at The Thatch.

The excitement of exploring the new space as it assaulted his senses had faded quickly in Uther, my huge pup now snoring lightly on the sitting room rug as Sam and I curled up facing each other on opposite sides of the large sofa, each nursing a glass of fiery amber liquid that was our whiskey nightcap.

'So when did you say Bella's date with the mystery writer is?' Sam asked.

'Tomorrow, before the writing class.'

'I'm sure she'll be fine but I'll keep an eye out, at a discreet distance of course.'

'Thanks Sam. I think she'll be fine too but with these texts, and the chase, I would just feel more at ease knowing you were somewhere nearby.'

He nodded slowly, taking on a look of preoccupation.

'What is it?'

'I was just thinking about all the stuff you told me about Jessica Farnham earlier and what had happened to you while I was.., what's happening now. It strikes me that for all your bravado, Bella is not the only one I need to be looking out for, and that's before we even factor in this Glenn McGinley character.'

He looked almost as uncomfortable in saying the words as I was in hearing them. Of course, he was right. To say that I feared for my safety was an understatement, but despite my asking him to look out for Bella, my days of needing a knight in shining armour to save me were a long way behind me, if save for my dad, they had ever existed at all.

'I'm a big girl now Sam, I can take care of myself. Besides, anyone who tries to get to me has to get past him first.' I nodded towards Uther and smiled. As if in response, he let out a low growl from his dreams.

He smiled.

'I wouldn't fancy taking either of you on.'

'I'm sorry to hear that.'

Did I really just say that? And with such a flirtatious tone too. Yes, I apparently did if his smile and the heat of the embarrassment on my face and neck were to be believed.

'I didn't mean it like that' he began, wearing a look I'd never before seen from him. He was flustered. I liked it.

'I know' I smiled, 'I was only teasing. I'm sorry.'

'Don't be' he said simply, his eyes locked on mine, taking the prickly heat blooming across my face and neck to almost thermometer bursting capacity. I was sure I must have resembled a freshly prepared lobster.

'I should get going' I stuttered.

'Let's have another night cap first' he nodded toward my glass, shifting out of his seat before I had the chance to protest. 'Besides, it would be a shame to wake him' he said as he looked down at Uther, taking up most of the mat.

'He does look comfy I suppose' I relented.

As he freshened the drinks my thoughts turned again to his depression. I didn't want to make him feel uncomfortable or to psychoanalyse him, but I did want to be sure that he was ok. I'd been surprised that I hadn't noticed any of the traits associated with the condition. Maybe I just hadn't been looking for them. After all, why would I be?

'So, the "Lost Weekend" then, are you ok?' I asked as casually as I could, as he returned to his seat and reached me my drink. Of course it didn't sound remotely casual at all. Little wonder his jaw became so taught.

'So we are going there after all. I thought you might broach the subject at some point but I expected it to be earlier. I guess you were just lulling me into a false sense of security huh?'

'I'm sorry, I don't meant to pry, I just...'

'It's fine. Yeah, I'm ok, I just needed to get away for a few days. Needed to be alone, away from everything and everyone. I get like that sometimes.'

'I get that. I mean, things can't have been easy.'

'Please Carolyn, spare me the shrink routine. I don't want to go there, and especially not with you.' His voice was suddenly gruff, his stare, deathly cold. Classic defence and avoidance tactics. He had wasted no time in putting a figurative wall between us. It was one I was determined to break through for his sake. Not in any professional capacity, but as a friend, or more, though it helped that I did have a particular set of skills.

'I wasn't trying to...I mean, I just want to be here for you that's all.' I raised my hands in mock surrender.

'I'm sorry. I didn't mean to be so harsh it's just...'

'You don't like to talk about it, I get it. It'll be the best thing for you if you do though, and believe me, I'm speaking more as a friend than a psychologist.'

He nodded, absently.

'Has it been since Cillian, or before that?'

'Before, though it has gotten much worse since we lost him.'

'Can I ask what happened? I mean, you said it was an accident on a building site but how exactly did it...'

He looked physically pained by the question, but to his credit, he didn't shirk it.

'Like you say, it was an accident. I could have prevented it though. I should have known what could happen.'

He stopped; his face ashen. I wanted to console him but my experience told me that if I interjected now he wouldn't continue to tell me what happened. I remained silent, ensuring my body language didn't betray any sense of judgement.

'I was involved in the restoration of Antrim Castle Gardens at the time. Some of the project involved renovation of the original Clotsworthy House building. The former kitchen area had a severe dampness problem. I'd put a dehumidifier in there overnight, powered by a petrol generator. I knew the ventilation wouldn't be ideal but not as limited as it turned out, plus I figured there wouldn't be anyone there overnight anyway, and the site was secured. I still don't know why he was at the site that night, but when I found him, it looked like he had taken a fall. Some of the scaffolding had failed and he'd taken a blow to the head. I guess he lost consciousness and the carbon monoxide... did the rest.'

'I'm so sorry Sam. It must've been awful to have found him like that.'

'Rather me than Bella' he half shrugged.

Setting the glass down, I reached forward, taking his hands in mine. I was about to offer some consolation when my phone pinged a message. I ignored it, despite feeling the urge to reach for it.

'You should check that. It might be Bella' said Sam. He was right, though he was probably also glad of the distraction from his demons.

The message wasn't from Bella though. It was from Jess Farnham, or at least whoever was masquerading as her. Notably, the number from the burner phone had the same last three digits as the one being used to terrorise Bella, from memory. It read:

HOW SWEET. WELL AREN'T YOU JUST THE PRETTY PAIRING. I WOULDN'T GET TOO COSY WITH THE HANDYMAN THOUGH DOC. HIS PRETTY LITTLE ASSISTANT WILL SOON BE NEEDING YOU. BTW, YOU'VE GOT MAIL.

I didn't get the chance to respond to it before the phone began to ring. This time it was Bella. And she was hysterical.

CHAPTER
SIXTY-FIVE

BELLA'S REACTION TO HER LATEST TEXT HAD BEEN ENOUGH TO CONFIRM to Glenn McGinley that phase one of tonight's strategy was so far going to plan. The look of sheer terror in her eyes as she read had been a bonus. The icing on the cake would come later, though for now he was content to be her shoulder to cry on, come protector, especially given that in not having left her company for anything other than a trip to use the restaurant facilities all night, he had given himself the perfect alibi. Jess had done a splendid job on his behalf so far, and if she had managed to get inside Langford Villa as well as Bella's apartment before sending the text, then she might very well be an improvement on the original.

Of course, he'd played his part too. The feigned look of horror after he had taken Bella's phone from her to see what had upset her so was flawless, even if he said so himself. The display of shock through anger that someone could not only be stalking her in this way, but that it had escalated into their breaking into her house, going through her possessions and laying out the outfit that they had apparently intended to dress her in after murdering her, had been BAFTA worthy. He'd even cursed the accompanying message, though his inside voice was quite impressed by Jess' chosen lexicon. AN OUTFIT TO DIE FOR I WOULD SAY, AND BELIEVE ME, I'M DRESSED TO KILL. He would resume his act of gallantry as soon as Bella finished having her breakdown call with Carolyn. If he knew her in the way that he suspected he did, she would insist on seeing Bella, perhaps even insist on having her come stay with her. Whether the good Doctor would be pleased with his chivalrous intent to offer to deliver Bella to her was another matter. Either way, phase 2 was about to swing into action.

CHAPTER
SIXTY-SIX

I HAD OF COURSE ENVISAGED BEING ON BOARD SCOUNDREL DAYS AGAIN AT some point in the near future. I'd even anticipated that Uther might one day join Sam and I on the vessel. I could never have imagined that it would be happening tonight though, and especially not in the circumstances we currently found ourselves in. Yet here we were. Sam had already convinced me to spend the night in his guest room before we'd even returned from The Thatch, given that we were enjoying the evening so, and we were both over the legal drink driving limit. I had initially planned to get a taxi home though, must confess, I hadn't thought of the impracticalities of asking the taxi driver to also accommodate a huge Irish Wolfhound in the back of their vehicle until Sam had joked about it. That was before the text from the Jess Farnham impostor that had chilled me back to sobriety. Then immediately after, our being been faced with Bella's call and the desperation to get to her that it brought. In the call, I'd agreed to McGinley's offer to drive Bella to Langford Villa, much as I hated the thought of his being near the place. Still, I was desperate to get her to the safety of my home. Now, we were en route to meet her, taking advantage of the fact that UK marine laws on drink driving were much more slack and less enforced than those of the roads, especially since the particular roads we would have been travelling on were widely known as some of the most often staffed by traffic police in Northern Ireland.

As Sam propelled the boat through the calm dark waters of Lough Neagh I huddled close to Uther, who was taking his first boat trip in his stride and enjoying the adventure by the look of him. Turning my attention to my phone I brought up the text message again. I still hadn't told Sam about it. There hadn't been the time until now. I was about to, then thought better of it. We had enough to be dealing with for now with Bella. I read it again. YOU'VE GOT MAIL, it had ended. I delved into the email app on my phone. Yes, I did indeed have mail, but only insignificant and unwanted marketing mail. Nothing untoward at all. I breathed a sigh of relief though I was still perplexed as to what it had meant.

'So, those psychologist powers of yours, do they work over the phone?'

Despite the situation Sam's choice of words still managed to rile me.

'Training Sam, not powers, and yes I can sometimes get a vibe from someone's voice from over the phone' I answered, doing my best not to sound petty.

'Good, you spoke to McGinley briefly at the end of the call. How did he seem?'

'Concerned...a little upset, worried I suppose.'

'Genuinely so?'

'It's hard to tell without seeing his facial expressions and body language, but yes, he sounded genuine' I answered.

'Not long now' he said as I saw the dark majesty of Langford Villa off in the distance behind the lights of the mooring point.

'I'd better call Brian.'

I suddenly remembered that I hadn't brought him up to speed. He had been privy to my concerns so far, as well as the stalking that Bella had been subjected to. Tonight had shown a marked progression in dangerous behaviour. It was only after Brian had answered that it occurred to me that I would also have to tell him about the text that I myself had received. I should have had the decency to tell Sam first. He would have to hear it second hand in a sense, but it was too late to worry about that now. He would just have to get over it.

CHAPTER
SIXTY-SEVEN

Much as it had made my skin crawl to have Glenn McGinley in my home, I was glad he was there for Bella's sake. Despite my feelings toward him, I couldn't deny that he had been nothing short of gentlemanly in the behaviour he displayed toward her from my observations. He appeared genuinely worried for her and protective of her, particularly when it had been time for her to go into my kitchen, which had become a makeshift incident room for the PSNI officers that Brian had sent to take statements, whilst he joined another team at Bella's apartment to manage the crime scene there. Bizarrely, I found myself thanking him as he was leaving in the early hours after the police had gone, having packed Bella off to bed whilst Sam sat sentry in the armchair in my sitting room having faultlessly assumed the role of the overprotective father figure all night.

'Glenn, I'm sorry I was so sharp with you on the phone earlier. I was just...'

'It's ok Dr Harkin...'

'...Please, call me Carolyn.'

'It's ok Carolyn. We were both worried about her. I would probably have reacted in exactly the same way in your position.

Especially after our little tête-à-têtes in the classroom. I quite enjoy those you know.'

'I know. Me too' I lied, 'Still, thanks for tonight and for looking after her.'

'I'll leave you both to it' he replied, 'By the way, you have such a beautiful home, and this guy, Wow!'

He gestured toward Uther, who I was delighted to observe, had not taken to this particular guest. In fact he had been a little out of sorts from the moment we entered the house, and that had been even before Bella and McGinley had arrived, and of course before the PSNI had gotten here.

'I'll see you out' I said.

'He was great with her but I'm glad to see him gone. Coffee?' I asked from the doorframe.

Sam nodded, trying to muster a smile.

'I'm sorry about earlier. I should have told you about the text first' I said.

'You don't have to be sorry Carolyn. I get it. There was no time and we were both worried about Bella. It's fine. It doesn't stop me from worrying about you though. Both of you.'

His expression suggested that he had the weight of the world on his shoulders. I respected him for it. Perhaps even, dare I think it, the feeling was a little bit more than respect. A feeling that I had always felt for him on some level. Except now it was getting stronger, whether I cared to admit it to myself or not.

'I'll get the coffees' I said.

Busying myself with starting up the coffee machine and fetching two mugs from the cupboard upon entering the kitchen, it was only when I was about to place them onto the marble worktop that I noticed it. It must have been then that the shock caused my grip on the mugs to be released and gravity snatched them downward to where they had exploded upon impact with the slate floor, sending a mine field of porcelain shards scattering across it. Distress rooting me to the spot, my initial thought had been of how to prevent a panic attack setting in. Thankfully, my observations had prevented it. I hadn't noticed it earlier. I had now though, and it brought with it the realisation that my world was yet again imploding around me and I wasn't sure if I was strong enough to come out of the other side of the carnage of it this time. The cause stared up at me from where it had been carefully placed, by whom I didn't yet know. The envelope, now yellowed with age, still bore the smudged lipstick kiss mark that I'd used to seal it, the siren red hue long gone, transformed into a deathly brown similar to the make-up palate I associated with use by undertakers to make death appear a little less deathly in its application to the deceased.

It couldn't be, could it? I tried to doubt it, but I already knew the answer to that question. Still, I willed myself to lift it and turn it over, removing all doubt. There it was, his name, Daniel, hastily scrawled in my handwriting. It had been opened, possibly by the original Jess I mused. Had it been before or after she had killed him? Either way, ironically, it had been her opening of this envelope that had sealed my fate in her eyes. Now Jess was back to finish what had been started. As the tears came I was again taunted by the words, YOU'VE GOT MAIL.

CHAPTER
SIXTY-EIGHT

BRIAN HANNON WAS TOO LONG IN THE TOOTH NOT TO REALISE THAT there would be some within the force both superior and inferior to him who would have questioned why he had attached himself so personally to a case of stalking behaviour against two women in Antrim, albeit that one of them was a PSNI Consultant Investigative Psychologist. Her association still didn't warrant a present in person role in the investigation from the Assistant Chief Constable by any stretch of the imagination. Here he was though, and had been so all night. Of course he wouldn't need to justify himself to those he commanded. Others though, including those within his own household, that was another matter entirely. He hadn't coped well with Karen's diagnosis. Wasn't coping with it. If he was being honest with himself, he hadn't even tried, deciding that it would be something he would bury until the time came that he could do so no longer. With the painkillers she had been able to maintain some semblance of normality. The chemotherapy would begin soon though, then everything would change. Until then, he could bury himself in work. There was that word again, bury. It wasn't like he wouldn't be needed there after all, especially since he had a high profile homicide on his hands, not to mention an enquiry into the team working it. He'd appointed Mack's niece, DI Amy Macklin, herself a rising star within the PSNI to lead it, after contenting himself that in doing so, there would be no conflict of interest.

Then there was Carolyn. For some reason he had felt himself compelled to be here. Maybe it had been her desperation in reaching out to him, or his knowledge of the trauma she had been through, or maybe it was something else. He didn't want to think of that. He was devoted to Karen, had been since their teens. He wasn't looking for a relationship. She was and will be the only woman he would ever love. At the moment though, the enormity of her diagnosis, the fact that her treatment would only prolong her life, not cure her, meant that he struggled to cope being in the same room as her. Carolyn, whether he liked it or not, somehow provided a salve to the rawness of his emotions_unbeknownst to her.

'You're lost in thought, you ok?' Carolyn asked.

'Sorry, it's been a long night, yes, I was thinking about the letter. You're sure it couldn't have been placed here after you returned?'

'I can't be 100% but I'm pretty certain it couldn't have been. Apart from when your officers arrived, the only people who had been in the kitchen were Sam and I, and he was in my sight the whole time. Your officers surely would have noticed if someone had left something on their way in or out.'

'I would like to hope so but...' He gave a slight shrug of the shoulders, 'With no sign of a break in we can't rule out that the person who broke into Miss Maskull's used the key to your home that was found there, to enter the property here. We'll continue to follow up with the door to door enquiries there but obviously that's not an option here. We can check the CCTV from the main road. It's a pity that your recording system malfunctioned. I'll send a team over to recover the disk later this afternoon.'

'Thanks Brian. I'll mention it to Sam when he wakes up too. He went back to the boat to get some rest about an hour ago, so it'll be a while yet.'

'Sure, no problem. Speaking of rest. You could be doing with some yourself if you don't mind my saying so.'

'I will. Thanks for everything Brian, I know you have a million and one other things you could be doing. Should be doing.'

'It's fine, oh, and speaking of which, I don't suppose you've had time to look over the files I had sent to you?'

I shook my head.

'The third thing on the agenda after I get some sleep. The first and second, walking Uther and getting some industrial strength coffee going to help me concentrate.'

'I'll be on my way in that case.'

'I'll give you an update as soon as I've done, and Brian, I mean it…thanks.'

His smile brought a lightness to my troubled soul, and despite the night I'd had, the warmth of the smile I returned to him was genuine. Little did I realise it would be the last time either of us would smile for a while.

CHAPTER
SIXTY-NINE

It was only on seeing ACC Hannon finally leave and Carolyn head upstairs in search of some rest that Sam Moran was finally able to close his own eyes, hoping that he too could get at least some sleep, but knowing it unlikely.

The threats that both Bella and Carolyn had been subject to in the last number of hours had been almost too much for him to bear, especially on top of the pressures he already faced in light of Ryan Casey's murder, and that it had been most likely committed in his home. Yes, he had cleaned the scene and yes, he'd managed to avoid the suspicions of the police officers who asked to look around the house the night after his return, but it didn't stop him being implicated by association with Casey and ownership of the house. He toyed again with the thought of contacting others within Casey's organisation though dismissed it. It could possibly do more harm than good. Perhaps this could be his chance to surrender that part of his life. Consign it to the past where it belonged. It would be possible, though like at other times in his past, would depend on his ability to get away with murder, despite his not being responsible for it. Not this time.

At least he had safely managed to dispose of evidence of the clean up before Carolyn's arrival, and her presence, and that of Uther at the house would be enough to keep the interests of his busybody neighbour piqued with thoughts of his love live that would distract her from her previous observations, especially now that Carolyn's pick up was currently adorning his driveway and would continue to do so until at least late afternoon. The thought made him breathe a little more easily. Just a little. There was still Bella and Carolyn to consider. It was almost impossible for them to defend themselves against what seemed to be an invisible but very real threat, more impossible still for him to protect and support them from what he couldn't see or legislate for either. He figured that the only way to help in that regard would be to do what he could to put a spotlight on the unknown assailant. He would be keeping a close eye on Glenn McGinley, as well as trying to seek out the woman purporting to be Jess Farnham. That would leave both Bella and Carolyn with just threat hiding in plain sight to face. The one that whether he liked it or not, was posed by him.

CHAPTER
SEVENTY

Tasks one and two now complete with Uther having had his fill of exercise in our walk around the perimeter of the Loughshore Park, and a fresh supply of coffee brewed beside me, it was time to tackle task three as promised. Now, holed up in my kitchen snug, a perfectly acceptable alternative to my study for fear of waking Bella, I was quite looking forward to the distraction of getting back to the Ryan Casey murder. It was to be a short lived feeling I was soon to learn. Opening the electronic folder I'd been sent, I discovered it was largely made up of video files. The first three were comprised of footage from PSNI interviews with persons of interest. The first, documented Casey's fiancée, Shannon Courtney under questioning from Healey and Watson. Watching on helplessly I began to take notes as what could only be described as a car crash unfolded before my eyes. In terms of how they handled the line of questioning around discrepancies between her account of Casey's last known movements and forensic analysis of her mobile phone, the young detectives were blundering at best, covertly misogynistic at worst. What was more unacceptable still, it didn't take any police or psychology training to see that it was clear from her reactions that she had been clearly aware of Casey's less public persona and the life he led within it. Her weak attempts at trying to explain away the content of the text messages exchanged between them as being the result of her being possessive and distrusting of him because of his celebrity status could best be described as amateur dramatics. Their probing of the details too were nothing short of farcical. It was also clear that despite the crocodile tears, she wasn't anywhere close to being as devastated as she was portraying. Another thing the keystone cops had seemingly missed. I made a note for Brian that this interview would need to be revisited. My gut feeling was that she wasn't directly involved in the murder but she definitely knew more than she was sharing.

The second and third files were of interviews conducted by Mack and Ings, and featured Casey's songwriting partner and agent respectively. Aside from a stratospheric increase in the levels of professional conduct and experience demonstrated on behalf of the officers involved, there was nothing about either interview that could be considered remarkable or relevant to finding Casey's killer in my view, perhaps placing Miss Courtney more firmly into the spotlight.

The remainder of the files in the folder were made up of short video clips or stills largely recorded by mobile devices and concealed cameras by the look and quality of them, the thumbnail pictures signalling to me that a short break for a caffeine hit, some food and a bit of quality time with Uther would be wise before I waded into them. After indulging myself and my boy I returned to my seat at the table and set myself to get started, though this time, with the weight of his head on my lap in no doubt on his part was a cunning plan to have the soft fur of his ears and scalp further petted and massaged. A ploy that worked for him in the short term. Finally, returning my attention to the task in hand I clicked on the first clip in the series, the majority of which featured Casey in various stages of undress with a slew of young women, and men. Others featured footage taken from parties at which Casey was clearly the host and at times would have barely skirted being labelled as orgies, fuelled on alcohol and drugs.

It hadn't taken long before they became so repetitive in their content that I toyed with the idea of giving up. I was far from prudish, but frankly I'd seen enough. I'd come this far though, and with just a few more to go I decided that perseverance was the most professional option. It was a decision I soon wished I hadn't taken though when the venue depicted in the penultimate recording filled my screen. I recognised the place immediately. I'd been there, and recently too. It was Sam's place. There was no mistaking it, no matter how much I wished it wasn't so. I allowed doubt to creep in, or perhaps deliberately tried to place it there. I could be wrong, couldn't I? It wouldn't be the first time after all. The more I looked though, the more sure I became. The sofa upon which acts were being committed that my mother would have described as nothing short of immoral, was definitely the same one I'd been curled up on last night, warming whiskey in hand. My stomach churned at the thought. Then came the last video clip. It too featured Sam's front room and if I'd thought I couldn't be shocked any further I was about to be proven wrong. Devastatingly wrong. This time Sam was seen sitting near Casey, romantically entangled with a semi-clad young woman, both parties engrossed so deeply in the intercourse they were engaged in, they seemed oblivious to the fact that their sexual encounter had gathered an audience, one of whom was filming it, and equally oblivious to other things going on around them, particularly Casey's careful preparation of the line of cocaine on the coffee table facing him before unceremoniously snorting it through a straw up his left nostril. That had been enough to bring tears of anger and disbelief welling in my eyes, their salty heat irritating me almost as much as my allowing them to break through my professional boundaries. It was when the young woman drew back a little from where she had been kneeling astride Sam and tossed her hair back from her face with a jerk of her head to the right however, that a cold chill gripped me, pushing the air from my lungs as it did so. Despite the odd angle, I recognised the girl. It was her, wasn't it. Again, I doubted my recollection, knowing deep down I wasn't wrong. If I wasn't, I'd seen her recently too, her photograph gazing at me through bright blue eyes from my computer screen as I read the digital report of her death, an apparent suicide, the discovery of her remains bloated and grotesque in a watery grave in Antrim Castle Gardens. My recollection stuck on the fact that she had been found by a dog walker. It was another trope of crime fiction writing that I would often mock when teaching workshops. In crime fiction, the discovery of a body, usually that of a young woman was invariably accompanied by the fact being communicated in some way to the audience or reader, that the remains were discovered by a dog walker. If it was Irish Crime fiction, the invariable inclusion of the Wicklow Mountains as the location of the "dump site" was the equivalent of lining up three gold bars in a Vegas slot machine. Hitting the trope jackpot. Of course, tropes become tropes because sadly art does imitate life; that was the awful truth. Though I had often visualised a walk through the Wicklow mountains of being reminiscent of Michael Jackson's, Thriller video, with limbs at various stages of decay protruding from the earth at absurdly awkward angles at regular intervals. Now wasn't the time for jibing or japing though. It couldn't have been furthest from it. Now, as I hastily scribed notes to share with Brian, my mind made the only mental leap that the thoughts of any reasonable person would. Sam's presence in my proximity had suddenly become a much more dangerous proposition than it had been just moments ago. Especially now that I could hear him approach from outside. It was going to take every ounce of professional experience I had to navigate a safe way through my next interactions with him, but get through it I would. After all, the safety of Bella and Uther in addition to my own could be at stake otherwise, and now he was just feet away.

CHAPTER
SEVENTY-ONE

Carolyn hadn't seemed to notice Sam Moran's presence as he entered the kitchen snug, her focus intent on the MacBook screen. That had been his first clue that something wasn't right.

'Did you manage to get some rest after ACC Hannon left, or have you been immersed in that thing all this time?' He nodded a disappointing look toward the laptop as she turned her attention to him.

'I got a few hours, you?'

'Same.'

'Is Bella awake yet?'

'No, not that I know of. I'm going to let her rest as long as I can. After all she's been through it'll do her the power of good.'

'I agree. Did ACC Hannon turn anything else up?'

'No. He was asking about the CCTV. Does it record? They couldn't access anything. They think it may have malfunctioned.'

Moving to where she was sat at the MacBook, he put a hand on her shoulder as she quickly closed down the lid, her face trying not to portray panic, and failing. His second clue that all was not as it seemed.

'I was going to log in to the cloud where the recordings are saved, I can show you.'

'Sorry, I was just about to freshen up. Can you just write the login details down and I'll send them through to Brian?'

'Sure.'

Pulling the notebook she'd been using toward him and taking the pen from her hand he was unwittingly provided with the ultimate clue. Proof if proof were needed that all was not as well as the banality of their conversation suggested. It was as he was about to leaf over the page to write down the cloud details that he noticed it. There, hastily scribbled at the foot of her notes were two words followed by a question mark, all three encircled. Pretty innocuous on the face of it. To him now though, they may as well have been represented in three feet high, flashing neon. Sam Killer?

Their eyes meeting as he raised his gaze from the page brought two new questions for him. She was clearly aware what he'd seen, despite feigned indifference. The first question, would it be a flight or fight? The second, who would flinch first?

CHAPTER
SEVENTY-TWO

I became aware of both micro-actions simultaneously. The barely visible tremor of shock that flashed across Sam's face as he saw my note, coupled with the stiffening of Uther's muscles as his hackles rose sent my cortisol levels through the roof at the very moment that a calmness in my demeanour was paramount. I needed to take control, gain the upper hand, and quickly. Just like I had the last time I'd been confronted by a potentially dangerous person in my kitchen, who I cared about but hadn't known as well as I'd thought. Except this time I needed to make sure that it didn't end in a fatal knife wound for one of us, and this time I had Uther in the mix which could prove either a blessing or a curse.

'Take a seat' I said as I pushed the closed MacBook across the table away from me as nonchalantly as I could manage. I'd pushed a purposeful calm into my words and was relieved that they sounded as intended to my own ear. He complied, placing the notebook and pen down on the table as he did so. Uther too took his opportunity to move, taking up a position of sentinel beside me, a hard stare locked on Sam that set me slightly more at ease. Even within the tension and potential danger of the moment, I couldn't help but feel a note of pride in the magnificent hound. My boy.

'Looks like we need to talk.'

He nodded, meeting my stare briefly before lowering his head and puffing his lips in a sigh.

'I didn't kill him' he said softly, 'I am glad he's dead though.' He caught my stare again, perhaps trying to gauge my response. He wasn't going to find it there. I was much too experienced for that.

'Him?'

'Ryan Casey, I know you're involved with the case.'

'We'll come to that. What about her though? How did she really meet her end?'

Admittedly I held the upper hand in terms of the information I held. Sam didn't know what I'd seen or read to reach the conclusion that he was a potential killer. He'd just made assumptions and tried to fill in the blanks for himself. I think it was more than fair to say that my reference to her had blindsided him. The look he now wore did nothing to hide the fact. It was almost like he was imploding, shock moving through disbelief and entering desperation. He began shaking his head back and forth, muttering, seemingly to himself before pushing his palms against the edge of the table and using the traction to get to his feet. I'd seen this type of reaction before. He was unravelling right before my eyes. This could only go only one of two ways and I desperately hoped that the dice would fall how I wanted them to.

'I can't do this. Not now Carolyn and not with you' he offered by way of answer, his voice raspy and the despair in his eyes shining even more brilliantly with the moisture from the tears brimming in their lower lids.

'When then? And with who?' The dice *had* fallen in my favour, there was no sign of anger or violence, yet. It was time to push the envelope a little further.

'Brian perhaps?' I continued, an unprompted low growl emanating from Uther's throat as Sam leaned forward to tower over me.

'I need to leave' he snapped, turning and pushing the chair he'd been sitting in forcefully across the slate floor to its position under the table. Uther remained still, his growl growing deeper. He could have been up close and personal with Sam within three strides. It was an observation that I imagined Sam had also made. I kept my stare fixed on Sam focusing every fibre of my being in doing one thing. Remaining silent. I could get more out of him this way.

'What about me Sam? I'd really quite like to hear what you have to say.'

I swivelled my head to see Bella stood in the door frame, her stance and stare akin to that of Uther, both looking like at any second they could tear him limb from limb.

Sam's face crumpled further if that were possible when he saw her.

'Bella...how long?'

'Long enough' she spat, 'long enough to need some answers... now.'

CHAPTER
SEVENTY-THREE

Karen Hannon was already awake when she heard the familiar growl of the Volvo's engine as he eased it to a halt on the driveway. It was now late afternoon after all. Shortly after came the equally familiar clunk of the car door as he closed it, followed by the rattle of the loose flagstone on the front porch as it took his weight. The sound brought a weak smile to her lips, knowing that he would be internally cursing the noise and the fact that she would never let him repair it. It was an extra layer of security for the wife of a police officer that a loose stone could herald an alert of a possible intruder to her ear. She knew that it irked the perfectionist within him when it came to his pride in the home that they had created together, and she entertained herself with the wry thought that he might repair it after she was gone. Perhaps she would nominate otherwise in her will, one last piece of their shared humour to comfort him from beyond the grave. She liked that idea. Within a few short moments he had padded softly through the house, shoes removed at the front door, in search of her, before seeking her out in the master bedroom.

'Hey You' she said softly as he peeked his head around the door into the semi-darkness of the room.

'Hey You' he replied, almost a whisper, 'how's today been so far?'

They had both realised that his and everyone else's persistently asking her how she was since the diagnosis had done little for anyone's mood or patience, particularly hers. It was easier all round to ask how the day had been.

'Just beginning' she answered, 'thanks to the morphine. I guess just ending in your case.'

'Nothing new there' he shrugged apologetically.

'Come to bed, keep me warm' she said, weakly folding down the duvet at his side halfway, flopping it over on itself until it resembled a soft, inviting pitta pocket awaiting its filling.

'You're cold, I'll put the heat on. Are you hungry? Isn't your medication due? Do you need anything else?'

'You Brian! I need you. That's all. Now stop fussing and get in here. You must be exhausted. You're like death warmed over, and only one of us has the excuse to look like that.'

His crestfallen look made her instantly regret her words.

'I'm sorry. I'm still allowed to worry about you, you know. Come, get some rest.'

God only knows what of the horrors we humans are capable of that he'd seen or had to deal with since she had seen him last, she thought. Sleep would help him process them at least, mentally file and recover them before again embarking upon a fresh hell of a day in the life in his chosen profession. The job he lived and breathed. Ironically, it would likely be it that would save him when she was gone. Would stop him drowning in a well of grief. He would need rest in preparation for the weeks ahead too. She was glad to hear him snore softly just moments after they had embraced under the duvet. She had a difficult conversation to broach with him later. One that could potentially devastate their last days together. She wondered if either of them would have the strength to get through it after everything else that had been thrown at them in the recent months. She hoped they would. For now though, she would hold him, appreciate the quiet warmth of their relationship while she still could, for as long as she still could.

CHAPTER
SEVENTY-FOUR

Reading over the latest part of his work in progress again had sent pulses of excitement sparking through every nerve ending in Glenn McGinley's normally controlled being. It would be just hours before he submitted it to Carolyn and would watch as she read. He would savour every moment; he was sure of that. It would be tonight in reliving, through his carefully chosen narrative, how he lost his precious boy to a psychopath on a rooftop that Dr Harkin would begin to make connections, to realise who she was dealing with and why. If she was as intelligent as he had credited her to be, she would also figure out how he had come to be connected with the original Jessica Farnham, and perhaps even realise what a threat he had posed to the good doctor's continued existence before they had even met. Tonight would take him one step closer to their endgame. In the meantime, he and Jess had some more pressing matters to deal with. Flesh pressing to be more accurate, and not in the traditional meaning of the term. She had needed little training in that regard he was pleased to report.

CHAPTER
SEVENTY-FIVE

BELLA AND UTHER HAD MOVED FOR SAM IN UNISON AS HE BOLTED, THE ensuing maelstrom, a tornado of fur and teeth, flesh and screams, sadness, violence and anxiety. All centred around me. Me struck frozen at its core, desperate for it all to end until thankfully it did, eventually, with Sam's successful break for freedom, a freedom that would be short-lived I suspected, especially after I had alerted Brian and he had dispatched officers to arrest Sam, as well as having a CSI team sent to his house. I would certainly need to deal with the fallout from that in the not so distant future. The immediate future wasn't looking rosy either with Bella stood facing me, her red rimmed eyes boring through me. Of course I couldn't and wouldn't have shown Bella the video of Sam with the girl, but I could confirm the worst for her.

'Carolyn, what the hell just happened there? He *has* killed someone hasn't he? That *is* what I walked in on him admitting to *isn't it?*'

'I think he has been involved in something sinister, yes.'

She steadied herself against the table before clumsily pulling out the seat he had occupied earlier and dropping into it, Uther now lying across the threshold of the patio doors that Sam had escaped through, ready should he return.

'I...I don't understand. I mean?'

'I can't give you any of the detail Bella, but I had reason to believe that Sam might have been involved in some way in the death of Ryan Casey, and when I confronted him, I was about to try to ask some open questions to see what he would admit to, if anything. He claimed innocence to Ryan Casey's murder before I even got to ask him anything. Then I asked him about a girl he... had been with. A girl who died. He correctly presumed I was asking if he'd had a part in that.'

'What? Who?'

'A girl I saw him with in a video sent from the PSNI. It had been recorded in his house and Casey was present. Bella...it was the girl who you thought had been murdered. The suicide at the Castle Gardens. I think you were right, and yes, I can't believe I'm saying this, but I think Sam might be involved in it in some way. I'm sorry.'

In my line of work I have often witnessed the aftermath of how a trauma can shatter a person emotionally. Never before had I been present at the moment of its occurrence. Until now.

CHAPTER
SEVENTY-SIX

EVEN ONLY A FEW HOURS IN THE COMPANY OF HIS WIFE HAD BEEN ENOUGH to replenish the reserves of strength that Brian Hannon would rely on to get him through what would no doubt be another difficult shift. The few hours rest, the shower and hot meal that his gut was now processing for fuel would also help. Now, as he purposefully strode from his reserved parking spot at PSNIHQ he couldn't help but note how the brightly lit corporate glass fronted entrance and the equally corporate, modern brick facade was at odds with the brooding, grey evening cloud that dominated the sky above it, signalling the imminent threat of a storm. He mused that if Carolyn was describing the scene in one of her books or to one of her classes, the term pathetic fallacy would certainly have been used. Maybe juxtaposition too. After all, his feelings of worry at what lay ahead for he and Karen, coupled with his professional conviction to deal appropriately with what he would now have to face were also at odds with one another, and were equally capable of causing a storm of sorts. In truth, he felt more capable of dealing with the latter than the former. What the hell had Karen been thinking about, asking him that? Well, he guessed he knew the answer to that already. He'd almost asked what had possessed her. He already knew the answer to that too. The memory of the conversation not yet an hour old made his face flush as he walked. Embarrassment and anger both bringing a red heat to his cheeks and neck. He visualised what his expression must have betrayed to her. Shock, devastation…deceit. He was sure that deep down she had realised that he could never go through with what he had promised. With what she had made him promise. Still, he had lied to appease her, to take at least some of the fear out of her eyes. Now, much like he had done with her diagnosis in general, he chose to push all thoughts of tonight's conversation to the back of his mind. He would eventually have to grasp that particular nettle again. Not tonight though, and definitely not now.

This evening he had chosen to wear the full uniform befitting his rank as ACC rather than his usual, slightly less formal attire. He wanted everyone within and beyond the building to be sure that in no uncertain terms, he would use all the powers available to him to eradicate any lack of professionalism within the force, as as well as ensuring that justice was served to those responsible for the death of Ryan Casey. The fact that few dared meet his gaze, let alone speak to him beyond the occasional, "Good Evening Sir", had been enough to indicate that the subliminal message had been received and understood. Now as DI Amy Macklin took the empty seat across the broad desk from him in his office, it was time to show the courage of his convictions.

'Ok Amy, give me the worst.'

CHAPTER
SEVENTY-SEVEN

'Bella, really, if you're not up to this evening I can go solo with the writing class, besides, your new beau will be there to have my back.'

'Have your back or stab you there?' She smiled wryly before rolling her eyes. I admired her attempt to appear ok when in reality there was nothing ok about what she was currently going through.

'I think stabbing in the front would be more his style from what I've observed so far to be fair. He enjoys watching the menace he creates after all, not to mention the reaction of others to it' I retorted, eyebrows raised.

'Still not a fan then?' She feigned a pout before smiling again, though I suspected that there was more than a grain of annoyance at my comments hiding behind it.

'I have to admit that I was impressed at how concerned he was about you last night. Very chivalrous too. Still, you can't deny that he has a knife out for me, and the way things have been going around here, it could well be literally.'

'Fair play' she nodded, her face now a mask of sobriety.

'You know I still have my guard up right?' She continued. 'I mean, it's been fun, the flirting, the messaging and the date was going great until...you know. And of course, he's not exactly hideous on the eye, but I'm not that naive, and I've seen what's been happening between you both first hand. He definitely has an axe to grind. I hope it doesn't become any more of a problem than it currently is, but I want you to be sure where my allegiances lie, and they're right here with you, and this guy.'

She leaned across the sofa to where Uther lay, running her fingers through the deep fur of his flank.

'I thought you weren't allowed on the sofa' she said softly to him, a smile creeping across her lips as she purposefully avoided eye contact with me.

'Just this once Uther' I chided mockingly.

'Just this once' Bella echoed before breaking into laughter and encouraging Uther into a playful yelp.

'Thanks' I said softly, conscious not to cloak the sliver of light that had crept into the atmosphere, 'it means a lot.'

'Family is about more than blood, and you guys are beginning to feel like family. Believe me, at the moment, I need all the family I can have around me' she sighed.

'You've never mentioned family much before. I mean, your actual family. It seems like you and Sam are family of sorts, but your real family.' She winced at the mention of Sam's name and I instantly regretted it. In fact the haunted look she now wore made me regret broaching the subject at all.

She swallowed hard.

'I'm sorry' I interrupted before she got the chance to speak, 'I shouldn't have, I mean, I shouldn't pry.'

'No, it's ok. Like I said, family is about more than blood and if you can't share your past with your family then who can you.'

I smiled as she paused, steadying herself with a sharp intake of breath before continuing.

'Not much to say really. My mum got pregnant with me when

she was still at school. She was fifteen. Not the done thing back in the day, as you would imagine. Her parents disowned her, and my dad, if you can call him that, he and his family were no better. They encouraged him to deny responsibility for the pregnancy and wasted no time in shipping him off to relatives in Sheffield to live there. Last I heard, he was settled in Rotherham, happily married and a doting father of two. They'd be in their twenties now.'

'Have you ever tried to contact him, the family?'

'I thought about it, but no' she answered, a casualness to her tone that I hadn't been expecting. 'I mean, I don't blame him, not really, at least not as much as his family. He was only sixteen at the time himself. Just a kid. It wasn't his fault. Well it was, but you know what I mean. His parents on the other hand, now they were obviously a special kind of heartless. I mean, it's one thing to protect your son, give him the best chance at life. It's quite another to treat the mother of your first grandchild like something you'd stepped in.'

I shook my head, knowing only too well the types she was describing. The archetypal parents of their day ruled by the iron rods of Catholicism or some variation of Presbyterianism and the disapproving looks of their neighbours, content to tear their families apart from the inside in order to spare their blushes and maintain what they perceived as the moral high ground, in hope of avoiding the attentions of the hypocrites who deemed themselves Christian. A dying breed thankfully, best consigned to the pre-historic where their views belonged.

'And your Mum?'

'My Aunt Molly took her under her wing. Helped her raise me in the early days, even encouraged her to go to night school. We were happy with Molly and her family.' She paused, fat tears brimming in her eyes before rolling down her cheeks. 'Until one tragedy followed the other and I was left alone.'

'I'm sorry' I replied, hoping she knew how much I meant it. 'What happened?'

'It started with Mum. She was knocked down and killed by a drunk driver on her way home from college. Then within a few months, Dan, Molly's husband suffered a fatal heart attack at his desk at work. It was just me, Molly and her son Connor, my cousin then, and we learned to be happy again. The fact that Connor and I had always been inseparable helped. Then came his diagnosis and our nursing him to the end. Soon after, Molly descended rapidly into dementia. She wound up in a home and the house willed to me ended up being sold to pay for her care until I lost her in the end as well. I went to Belfast to study nursing with Sarah...and you know the rest.'

Her demeanour, as matter of fact as her tone despite the experience she recounted thus far, changed with the mention of Sarah Clark, her shoulders slumped, bearing the burden of her loss.

'The Baxter girl, are you thinking that it wasn't suicide? Was she murdered? By Sam?'

'I don't know. I promise you one thing though, I'm going to make it my business to find out.'

'I can't believe Sam...'

'Let's just wait and see, I mean, innocent until proven guilty right?'

She nodded an unconvincing agreement.

'I'd better go get ready for the class.' I rose to go shower and change.

'I think I'll come with to the class. I mean, what's the alternative, stay here and wait for my stalker to come visit?'

'Exactly, and the alternative is to come protect me from mine, and your psycho boyfriend.' I laughed, one which she thankfully joined in on before playfully lobbing a cushion at me.

'I best get my homework done though before we go. I don't want to get on the wrong side of the tutor. Can I?'

She nodded toward my laptop.
'Be my guest' I replied, 'we leave in an hour though.'

CHAPTER
SEVENTY-EIGHT

BELLA WATCHED AS CAROLYN CROSSED THE ROOM BEFORE TURNING HER attention to the laptop. She was glad they'd had the conversation that they just had. Being able to talk about her family and her past had made her feel the load lighten a little of a burden that she hadn't been consciously aware that she'd been carrying. One from her past. Not the only one though. The others, she now bore the weight of, she was keenly aware, had become heavier than ever. Perhaps it was time to unburden herself there too, the harsh white light provided by the empty word document illuminating the screen gave her just the place to do so after all. The question that remained now, was she brave enough. Placing her fingers lightly atop the keyboard, she decided to find out.

"First do no harm." It's the core belief of the Hippocratic oath, one of the first things drummed in to trainee medical professionals, right? Wrong! Yes, whilst the famous quote can be attributed to the teachings of Hippocrates, surprisingly it can be found nowhere within his equally famous oath. That was one of the first lessons Sarah and I had learned in our first year of medical training at Queens University, Faculty of Medicine, our particular course of study being based within the Royal Victoria

Hospital in West Belfast. Our course leader, Dr. Trainor, or Dr. Crippen as we had affectionately renamed him, had taken great delight in pointing it out to us as his very first utterance, a lesson in things not always being what they seem, or what we have been conditioned to believe. I hadn't given it much thought at the time, seeing it as more a declaration, on his behalf, of his academic prowess being without depth in comparison to that of his lowly charges. In the last few hours though, his words have returned to me with a resonance so strong, they almost feel like they have been branded onto my very soul. I deserve no less.

You see Dear Reader, those very words, "First Do No Harm" were the ones that my inner voice was screaming at me as I took his life in vengeance for hers. The words that I had wilfully ignored. In fact my intention was the very opposite. I fully intended to do harm that night. I did do harm that night. I became a killer that night. Now, I suspect that I have fallen victim to what Crippen had tried to warn us against. I had acted on what I had believed to be the truth. Now, my Dear Reader, as I speak to you tonight, I fear that I may have killed the wrong man. For which I will pay a heavy price, of that I'm sure. I won't be the only one though, you can rest assured of that. For you see, Dear Reader, it seems now that there is still a wrong to be righted, justice to be served. For that reason I can tell you something without fear or hesitation, right here and right now. I will kill again.

CHAPTER
SEVENTY-NINE

From his vantage point at the Broughshane Wild Bird Sanctuary, Sam Moran could see that the PSNI had cordoned off his house, allowing an ant like army of police officers and CSI investigators free rein in crawling all over the property. He suspected that his boat, moored at Langford Villa was currently being subjected to a similar level of scrutiny, and surmised that his van was being pored over with a forensic fine tooth comb by a team of Socos too. He'd always associated the hooded white overalls they wore to make them look ghoulish and thought that they would need to have something of the ghoul about them to have chosen the career path they now tread. He'd only had a matter of hours to weigh up the way forward from here, but despite his constant frantic efforts at rationalising possibilities that didn't involve the total unravelling of his life, he could only ever reach one conclusion. He hadn't been able to find a reasonable way forward, because simply put, there wasn't one. The voice of his conscience, adopting the overused Anglicised, American phrase, "Man Up", had been making itself heard with no trouble since almost immediately after he fled Carolyn's. Now, he reasoned, it was time to start listening to it. Time to give in to the inevitable. Time to hand himself in. Which was exactly why he now found himself trudging towards his home, resolute, before complying with the instructions being barked at him by the armed officers who had become aware of his approach.

CHAPTER
EIGHTY

'We're going to blow your mind tonight Doc, and no mistake' Glenn McGinley joked as the teacups were placed down, everyone settled, and the class came to order. The others laughed, Bella joining them, though a little uneasily. I had no doubt they would, him in particular, his threat only thinly veiled in a pathetic attempt at humour in an even more pathetic display of male ego that had wowed his audience.

'Bring it on' I replied, my smile worthy of a Hollywood blockbuster. It was still my class though, and my class meant my terms, which was why, despite the best efforts of his OAP fan club and probably the relief of everyone else, he was to be last to offer a reading of his work for critique tonight. Which as it would turn out, was probably just as well.

At my invitation Gladys and her friends had in turn taken us through the latest updates on their works in progress before others in the group were offered the opportunity, some of which I was delighted to see, were beginning to take shape and demonstrated a definite progression in the confidence and competence of their writing. I doubted that any of them were writing for anyone other than themselves as a hobby, which was likely just as well given that the stories thus far could be best described as tributes to the latest efforts of Richard Osman's Thursday Murder Club, an episode of Grantchester, or indeed took their cues from some of my own work. Still, I was delighted at the distance that they'd travelled on their writing journeys under my guidance. Gladys had also put a considerable amount of time and effort into plotting out some ideas as to where she thought the shared narrative of Glenn's and my stories could go. The discussions they raised at our mid-session tea break amused me, though the thought that they were leading to me being no doubt blind-sided again by Mr McGinley with his latest "fictional" gouge into the flesh of my past was never far away. What I hadn't been prepared for though, was the fact that before he would have his chance to sharpen his claws, Bella would have lobbed a literary hand grenade in my direction. Clearly her having chosen to pull the pin was something she felt prepared to do, despite the truth, not only could the words she read aloud never be unsaid, they could equally have the potential to unmask her as a real life killer.

'I love the way you've changed the narrative viewpoint. It's so creepy, and your tone when reading it, I'm hooked. I would definitely want to read on' I heard the others, though notably minus McGinley, gush after she had finished. For our part, he and I now seemed to have something in common. The WTF thought that I was sure was rampaging through our minds like a hurricane.

'Bella...'

'I'm fine Carolyn, it's just a story. I'm fine.'

She didn't look fine though. Her eyes now shone with the tears that had formed there and her face had taken on a stony pallor.

'Are you sure?'

'Yes. We'll talk later. Besides, I want to hear what Glenn has for us this week.' She smiled weakly at me, then at him, before lowering her head. I watched as he glared at her before turning his attention to the typed page on the desk in front of him, taking it up in his hand and beginning to read aloud. The crater that had been left from Bella's bombshell paled into insignificance in comparison to that which his writing left. Still, as soon as his narrative reached the point where a child had been thrown to their death from the balcony of a restaurant, I was sure of exactly who I was dealing with, and why. It would seem that Mr McGinley had intended to pen a tale of vengeance, rooting it's ending in a real life act, no doubt involving my demise. His reading had made everything click into place for me. He may have thought he had my measure. I was determined he would be mistaken in that regard, just as much as I suspected that he was mistaken in his reasoning for targeting me in the first place. A little research and a few phone calls at a later stage would no doubt substantiate my suspicions. For now though, I was pretty sure that I had the measure of him, and the order of the moment for me was to be non-plussed by his "revelations". Ignoring the obvious would send him seething. Make him unpredictable. Provoke him, and despite everything I had come through and how badly I'd been damaged by it, that was exactly what I wanted to do.

'Well done Glenn. I can't wait to see where it goes next' I said simply before turning my attention to the others, 'I'm afraid that's it for tonight gang, we'll be getting our marching orders soon.' I didn't afford him another look despite being desperate to, to confront him about what I now suspected, and his relationship with Jess Farnham, his connection to my current stalker, possibly Bella's too, and the letter left at my home, the letter most of all. I felt his gaze locked on me for every second he remained there, willing my destruction, plotting it. He could try. He wouldn't be the first after all.

CHAPTER
EIGHTY-ONE

Despite her initial upset at having shared her secrets aloud, albeit shrouded in fiction, Bella now felt beyond exhilarated. The way Glenn had reacted afterward when they were alone possibly had a lot to do with that. That deep, hard kiss as he pressed his body unapologetically close against hers was electrifying. No comfort for her tears, just a raw passion and an unspoken understanding of her anger, her desire for vengeance, and her desire for...him. It had empowered her more than she had ever felt before in her life. He'd had everything to do with that. That was why, despite Carolyn's polite protestations and the deep set expression of worry on her face, she was now in Glenn McGinley's car, en route to a house from her past, to do things she never would have imagined doing there, and with someone she had already fantasised about doing them with. The thought of it, the anticipation of it, the danger of it sent her dopamine levels to the stratosphere, where she hoped he would keep them. At least that was until her phone pipped a text alert.

DON'T DO ANYTHING YOU WILL COME TO REGRET MY PRETTY. BELIEVE ME IF YOU DO, YOU WILL REGRET IT. I CAN PROMISE YOU THAT.

CHAPTER
EIGHTY-TWO

'You would need to do better than that' I called over my shoulder as I stood beside the Mustang searching frantically in my bag for my keys and silently cursing myself for not having the presence of mind to have them in my hand before exiting the building. Still, I had good cause. I was mad as hell with Bella's opting to go off for post-class, "drinks" with McGinley. Worried sick too. Mostly pissed at her colossal lack of judgement when it came to him. Now, given that my vain attempts at trying to persuade her to return back to the Villa with me meant that I was now alone in the dark isolation of the car park at the heart of the forested gardens, my anger had deepened beyond the capacity of fear, and frankly I didn't have time for this shit. I called again into the shadows behind me.

'Call yourself a stalker? Please! Jess Farnham would be turning in her grave. You may as well show yourself' I taunted, surprising myself in that it had worked. Stepping out into the hazy orange glow of the streetlight she faced me. Dressed in biking leathers and with the visor of her motorcycle helmet mirroring my own shadowy likeness back at me, she now stood. Whoever she was.

'You have her height and frame ok I guess. Why don't you do me the honour of letting me see you face to face.'

It was about to be Game On with Jess 2.0, and I was going to use every bit of experience in my psychology armoury to make sure I was to gain the upper hand.

I watched as she silently undid the chin strap of the helmet before pushing it purposefully upward off her head and striding forward to place it carefully onto the roof of the Mustang with a reverence and care akin to a crown being placed upon a velvet cushion. I wasn't sure if the care was being taken for the sake of the helmet or the car, either way it was nothing more than a failed attempt to gain control of the situation on her part. That I'm afraid, was never going to happen, as I was confident she would soon learn. As if oblivious to my presence, she shook out her tousled hair before making eye contact with me, indicating that either she was naturally vain, or well up on her knowledge of the person she was masquerading as. She had every movement and gesture down to a tee. I'd seen Jess do that very same thing dozens of times and whoever this woman was, she was inch perfect.

'It's hard to tell in this light, but you do look a lot like her. Not quite as pretty, but passable I guess. So what do I call you? Should we go for Tesco Value Jess perhaps?'

'Just Jess' she snapped.

'Ok, Just Jess' I mocked, 'We'll play it your way. I guess you sound like her too, though again, your voice is slightly less appealing to the ear. Not quite so elegant. From your tone though, I'm guessing that you're as easily wound up. Question is, are you a psycho like the original?'

'I'd say you're about to find that out.'

The calmness in her voice, unnerved me. The lack of emotion in it since her last utterance was, in my experience, a red flag trait of a psychopath, though equally could have been her trying to keep her emotions in check, not rising to my mocking of her. My money was on the former. Still, I knew I had to keep pushing her.

'I'm shaking in my boots, or to be more specific, my Sketchers trainers' I mocked, looking down at my feet, then slowly, deliberately shifting the line of my sight to her biker boots, then upward the full length of her body to her face, exaggeratedly taking in everything about her as I went, then angling my head to one side, as if studying her, as a flourish. Despite the low level light, the anger in her eyes was unmistakable.

'What's the matter? Don't you like being watched? Pretty ironic for a stalker don't you think?'

I smiled and levelled my head again as her jaw tightened.

'I'm not making you cross am I, Just Jess? Should I be scared, Just Jess? Would you like me to run the way Bella did, Just Jess? What's the matter, cat got your tongue?'

Her silence remained. Her glare intensified. Her slight wince became more pronounced each time I deliberately emphasised the alliterative J sound in Just Jess. I had retained the upper-hand as hoped. Time to kick things up a gear.

'Never mind, I hadn't quite finished anyhow. Have you ever heard the saying, "if looks could have killed, I'd be dead", Just Jess? You see it pretty much sums up the look on your face at the moment. The only problem is that your look is the only thing capable of killing. You see, from where I stand, you've already shown yourself to be a second rate Jessica Farnham, a bad cover version if you like. If the real Jess wasn't able to kill me, I doubt her discount doppelgänger would get any closer to success.'

'I wouldn't be so sure' she spat, 'but don't worry, you won't die tonight. That's not part of the plan.'

'Really, and what pray tell is the plan?'

'To let you know it isn't over. To let you know without mistake that I'm back and that this time I will kill you. Not before making you suffer first though.'

I stared hard at her as she spat her words with venom. There was an unmistakable conviction to what she said. Something else too though. Fear perhaps? Did she actually believe that she was Jess Farnham? Had she been so head-fucked by McGinley that her own identity had been supplanted by that of my dead stalker? Was he that good a psychologist? I doubted from what I now remember of the rumours about him, but still? The most likely explanation is that she, whoever she really was, had become submissive for some reason. Maybe becoming Jess Farnham, fucked up individual that she was, had been better than being a possibly even more fucked up individual, and McGinley had offered her a way out, a fresh start. Along with whatever else was anybody's guess. I wondered if she knew it would come at a high cost.

'You really think you're Jess Farnham don't you? Or at least you really want to be her. I can't decide which. I'm not sure which would be more pathetic either if I'm being honest.'

I moved forward a few paces, narrowing the distance between us and entering the periphery of her personal space just enough to rile her a little more.

'You, my dear are not Jess Farnham. You're either deluded, or a pathetic tribute act. Either way, your strings are being pulled and we both know who by.'

'I'm nobody's puppet I can assure you.'

I'd hit a nerve though. The low, even voice now had a definite hint of controlled anger. Time to turn up the heat even further. Perhaps to a level where I might get burnt, but it was a chance I was willing to take, despite myself.

'So you came here, right here, right now of your own volition? You're not fucking him right? And of course you're your own woman. A smart one too, I'd hazard a guess. The question I'm asking myself is, was our little tete a tete, part of the plan as you called it, or was that just a way to keep you offside while he fucks my friend in your little love nest? Was fucking her part of the plan? Did he get you to buy into that too, Just Jess?'

I became aware only too late from my peripheral vision of her snatching the helmet. Far too late to react before I felt it smash hard into the side of my head, knocking me to the ground, dazing me into a stupor that would render me powerless to defend myself against the onslaught of kicks and punches until the darkness took me. A darkness that in the moment I embraced.

CHAPTER
EIGHTY-THREE

'YOU'RE LOOKING AT SERIOUS TO GROSS MISCONDUCT IN A PUBLIC OFFICE without exception, not to mention a litany of breaches of the PSNI code of ethics in each case.' DI Amy Macklin's words were still reverberating around Assistant Chief Constable, Brian Hannon's head long after she had finished taking him through the damning report that now sat thick and imposing on his desk. Between its many pages there had been a comprehensive analysis of each and every piece of evidence found. It made for grim reading. From blatant sexual harassment and misogynistic behaviours toward colleagues, to sharing of crime scene pictures with inappropriate comment, group chats containing derogatory and often sexualised dialogue about colleagues, witnesses and victims, not to mention evidence of inappropriate relations, or the garnering thereof, between officers and those in often vulnerable positions. Those things in and of themselves were career ending and would likely result in criminal charges being brought against those responsible, and that was even before the discrepancies between personal body camera footage and written statements was taken into consideration, that was of course, when the cameras had been used, which more often than not they had not been, despite being mandatory.

'You look like you could use a coffee' Mack announced from the threshold of the open office door, attracting Brian's attention away from his present worries.

'That, and the benefit of a wise head' Brian answered, relieved for the distraction and glad of the support of an old friend. An old friend, who in his wisdom, came armed with two steaming cups of coffee.

'Amy caught up with you then?' Brian asked as Mack carefully placed the white porcelain mugs onto coasters adjacent to each other at each side of the heavy oak desk, before lowering himself into the seat opposite with a soft groan.

'She did' he acknowledged with the nod of an already furrowed brow.

For a few moments the two men sat still, an easy silence between them despite the gravity of the situation, punctuated only by the occasional knock of a cup being returned to the laminate cork coasters between sips of coffee.

'It's not easy being in the big seat is it?' Mack finally mused; his words mere observation as opposed to malice.

'It certainly isn't my friend, especially when as far as disciplinary issues are concerned, the buck stops at this particular big seat.'

'No better man to make such big decisions' Mack smiled.

'No decision to make Mack, the evidence leaves me no other course of action than to instigate disciplinary actions, and in some cases, arrange for arrests to be made. I'll need to inform the Chief Constable and prepare a report for the Policing Board. Then there'll be the press to handle.'

'Anything I can do, you know that Brian' Mack assured, reaching across and gripping his forearm, the faces of both men grey at the prospect of what lay ahead.

'I appreciate that Mack. When the shit well and truly hits the fan as it's about to, I'm going to need it. Friends are going to be thin on the ground' Hannon frowned, the wrinkles on his forehead much more deep set than Macklin had ever noticed before.

'That'll be first in a long while, I'll have been associated with the word thin' Mack joked as he patted the ample girth of his stomach. An attempt at light relief that brought a weak smile from Hannon. Both men exchanging a knowing look that they were about to open the policing equivalent of Pandora's box.

'I best leave you to it' said Mack, rising to leave.

'Thanks Mack. I best let the powers that be know what's about to happen and see if I can make a start at drafting a press release before the media office crew arrive in the morning.'

'You know where I am if you need me' Mack gestured back toward his desk.

'Yes, at home' Brian replied, gesturing in the opposite direction, 'and that my friend is an order.'

'But I can…'

'Be back, rested and refreshed for when I need you tomorrow morning' Hannon interrupted.

Mack nodded wearily, more acutely aware of his advancing years of late, despite his reluctance to acknowledge them, even to himself. He moved for the door just as the phone on Hannon's desk began to ring. He waved a silent farewell, as Hannon moved to answer. He'd barely crossed the threshold of the doorway when Hannon called him back.

'Mack!'

'Sir?'

'Sorry old timer, there's been a change of plans. I'm going to need you a bit longer. Apparently Sam Moran has just been taken into custody in Ballymena. He's en route here for questioning.'

'Interrogation Room 4?'

'You know me so well my friend.'
'I'll get it set up and ready for our guest.'

CHAPTER
EIGHTY-FOUR

UTHER'S EXUBERANT LICKING OF MY FACE ON MY RETURN TO LANGFORD Villa was of more comfort to me than he would ever know. Having been met by him in the hall I was now safe under his protection and that afforded by the security of my home. It was only now, having barely made it to the sofa, and with two heavy paws across my aching limbs, that I could let the tears come. Until now it had all been about self-preservation, about fleeing the scene. Scurrying away from the place where I had again allowed myself to become a victim. The place where my life once more came under threat in the name of Jessica Farnham. The place where I had regained consciousness in the greyness of night's transcendence into morning, my mind numb and body broken, to seek the sanctity of home. Of him.

I'd pushed Jess too far. I had naively convinced myself that I was in control. She may be an imposter in the identity she was assuming, but I hadn't factored that it didn't make her any less dangerous. In fact, if anything, it may have made her more of a threat if Jess had been subject to a psychological upgrade courtesy of McGinley, or, if my vague recollection from his revelation at the class earlier had refreshed my memory correctly, Dr Glenn

Addams PsyD. I would return to that thought, that amongst many others vying for the attention of my now overwhelmed mind. Now though, I just needed to fall apart. To cry until I could cry no more under the dutiful care of Uther. Only after I had allowed that to happen could I allow myself to heal, both physically and emotionally. As soon as I'd done that, as the motto of Dad's beloved Elvis decreed, I would solely be about "Taking Care of Business". The thought of my Dad too was a comfort. He would have loved it that I had made this place my home, despite my current circumstances, been delighted that I had returned here to Langford Villa, and ecstatic that despite his loss, I had been able to divorce myself from the outdated and emotionally debilitating brand of parenting practised by my mother. It also occurred to me that in that moment that I had become a parody of one of the characters that I had been talking about at the writing workshop over the last few lessons. The archetypal hero character that the writer deliberately destroys in order to completely restore them, or in Conservative political parlance, to "Build Back Better", in order that they may emphatically save the day. At the moment though, I could barely save myself from a complete emotional breakdown at the thought that I had put myself in life threatening danger, and yet again, more through luck than judgement, survived to tell the tale. Not that I'd planned to tell this particular tale to anyone...until my phone began to ring and when I retrieved it, now sporting a heavily cracked screen, from my pocket, I could just about make out Brian's name within the spiderweb of fractures weaving out from its centre.

'Hi Carolyn, apologies for the early call. I have some news. I thought you would want to hear straightaway.'

It was at that point that the floodgates truly opened.

CHAPTER
EIGHTY-FIVE

Glenn McGinley watched intently as Bella lay still in the bed beside him. Still deep in slumber, only her head was visible above the duvet cover clutched at her neck, insulating her against the damp cold of the Autumn morning whilst simultaneously protecting her modesty. Carefully he brushed away the loose strands of her blond hair partially covering her face. She certainly was something else. He was becoming more acutely aware of that with each moment he spent in her company. Now though, things had become complicated. His initial intent had been to use her as a pawn in his plan for the unravelling and eventual death of Carolyn Harkin. He had planned to destroy her too in the process. Now though, he was finding himself increasingly enamoured by her. His plans would have to change. That was fine though. He could work with that. She'd revealed a darkness in her last night that enthralled him. It would be relatively easy to help her embrace it further, encourage and perhaps facilitate the revenge she sought. She would still play a part in Carolyn Harkin's destruction too, and if his revised plan worked, she would relish it just as much as he planned to.

He was already mentally adjusting his intended strategy when the phone on his nightstand alerted him to a text message.

'Jess?' He questioned softly. Why on earth would she be texting? Surely she was only in the next room, though he hadn't heard her come in. Still, he'd been a little preoccupied at the time. Holding the iPhone a little closer to his face to allow the facial recognition to unlock the screen, he was able to read her words.

I didn't mean to do it. Please forgive me. I'm so sorry. I lost control. I'm sorry.

'Fuck' he growled, causing Bella to partially stir, 'What the fuck has she done?'

Quickly his thumbs hovered over the screen as he keyed his reply. It was brief. Menacing in tone, but brief, nonetheless.

Get back here. RIGHT NOW!

CHAPTER
EIGHTY-SIX

SAM MORAN HAD ONLY A LITTLE TIME TO STRATEGISE AHEAD OF HIS questioning by the police but it had been sufficient. In fact, if he was being honest with himself, he'd been planning for the eventually that he might one day face a very similar set of events, though admittedly he hadn't been prepared for the transfer to PSNI headquarters, and he certainly hadn't anticipated that he would be interviewed by the big guns. Still, he would try to play it out as planned. The long term goal would be a diminished responsibility plea. For now though, he would need to feign a lack of mental fitness for questioning. It would mean subjecting himself to the scrutiny of a psychological evaluation, but he was sure he could manufacture his desired outcome there. Just so long as the psychologist in question wasn't Carolyn, which he surmised would be highly unlikely, given that it would represent a conflict of interests on the part of the PSNI.

If anything, he would love to have Carolyn fighting in his corner, from both a personal and professional perspective. He had well and truly burnt his bridges there though; of that he was positive. He doubted now that he would even have Bella in his corner either. The bond they shared had definitely been severed in their last interaction. A reconnection very much depended on how things progressed with the PSNI. He didn't hold out much hope. Now he had potentially lost another two important women in his life and yet again it was of his own doing. Perhaps he should just accept the inevitable. It was no more than he deserved.

CHAPTER
EIGHTY-SEVEN

The phrase "coming down to earth with a bump" had been a massive understatement for Bella this morning. Since waking, for her it had been more like the cataclysmic impact of an asteroid striking her world, losing her in the plume of smoke that bellowed from the crater it had left. The Glenn, in whose strong arms she drifted off to sleep last night after hours of talking, amongst other things, had been replaced by a very different Glenn entirely. This one, brooding, pacing and preoccupied with something else, someone else, and doing little to hide the fact that for him she had outstayed her welcome. Had she done something to upset him, or had something happened? She wasn't sure, and he certainly wasn't giving her the opportunity to find out.

Stealing away from what had at one time been her family home, or as near as she would perhaps ever get to one, like a student fleeing a one night stand, which she reflected now quite literally in the cold light of day, that perhaps this in fact was. Then of course there was the revelation dressed in fiction that she had been responsible for Cillian Moran's death. It had seemed like the right thing to do last night. Just like locking lips with Glenn McGinley on the very place on the glass mezzanine that had once been the kitchen area where it had happened, had been. Not to mention her rejecting the sage advice of Carolyn to remain with her in favour of what now seemed a reckless abandonment of her senses, most likely rooted in the hatred and anger she now felt towards Sam. The man she thought better than most others, held to a higher standard than others, and had been wrong. The thought of facing Carolyn now rightly filled her with guilt and dread, which was why she was now passing Langford Villa en route to a destination she had been dreading returning to, her apartment. From there she would reset. From there she would process her thoughts. From there she would begin the fight to regain control of her life. Before any of that could happen though, there was one thing she needed to do. Slotting the car into its allotted space in the square that faced the apartment's entrance she took her phone and began to text.

"I'm sorry. My behaviour was deplorable. Please forgive me. Can I call with you later? I need to explain, and to apologise in person."

Her reply was instantaneous.

CHAPTER
EIGHTY-EIGHT

'I THINK YOU'VE MISSED YOUR TRUE CALLING BRIAN. YOU WOULD HAVE made an excellent medic' I winced as he expertly applied pressure to various points in my side in an attempt to ascertain whether or not I'd sustained any fractures to my ribs. My protests had been sufficient to ward him off calling an ambulance or taking me to hospital, but not enough to appease him from his insistence in patching me up himself, which thus far, he'd made a pretty good job of.

'The medical world's loss is policing's gain I guess' he smiled, 'I'm guessing in your own policing days, you've had your fair share of instances of being patched up by a colleague.'

'You could say that' I replied, trying my best not to laugh, knowing the physical pain it would bring, 'still, never by someone with such a gentle bedside manner as you.'

He flushed.

'You were lucky I think. No signs of any fractures to the ribs or any worrying trauma to the head. I still think you should go get checked out properly but if you're still insisting otherwise then you're going to need lots of rest, and a shedload of painkillers.'

I nodded my agreement, keen to be seen to be accepting his

advice in order to further appease his instinct to seek medical help on my behalf. I knew the physical bruising would heal in its own time. The emotional bruising would be a different matter entirely.

'Actually, speaking of your policing days, I think I'm going to need you in a bit more of a hands on capacity when you've had a few days to heal' he continued.

'With Moran in custody and the medic on duty referring him for psychological evaluation, we'll have at least a few days for you to recuperate, but beyond that, it could well be Mack, you and I bearing the brunt of the workload, and we'll need to manage things carefully to ensure that your role is not considered a conflict of interest.'

'What about the others? I mean, there were some levels of incompetence that I noticed from my review of the interview recordings you sent me but...'

'Incompetence only scratches the surface I'm afraid' he began, pushing his glasses higher up the bridge of his nose before beginning a tale of corruption, misogyny, negligence and unacceptable behaviour relating to the majority of the unit investigating the Ryan Casey murder. A litany of what I could only describe as a former police officer myself, as filth. When he informed me of his decisions regarding discipline of those involved I found myself not only agreeing wholeheartedly, but out of a sense of anger toward them and the injustice they had perpetrated toward their victims, I agreed to a more hands on role with as much vigour as I could muster given my injuries.

'I'm in.'

'Thank you Carolyn, I appreciate that more than you know.'

His face was a picture of angst that until now I'd only seen with reference to his terminally ill wife. I smiled, hoping it would set him at ease if only just a little. It seemed to work. At least until his phone rang. His brow furrowed at the identity of the caller.

'I'd better take this.'

I nodded then watched as he answered, expecting him to leave the room, given that my lack of mobility hampered my ability to.

'Sir'. He said plainly, before being addressed by the person at the other end, as it happened, loudly enough for me to be able to hear. I wondered if that had been Brian's intention.

'Brian, I won't keep you. I've read your report and have taken some counsel on it. I won't beat about the bush Brian; you're a seasoned officer of current good standing. You will of course wish to keep it that way. With that in mind, I have instructed on your behalf that any criminal charges you proposed to level against those within your report to be overturned along with any records of them. Major elements of your report have also been redacted. I've also taken the decision to have the evidence sealed. I will speak to those whose behaviour has been called into question in the coming days and issue appropriate sanction before returning them to duty.'

I had felt my stomach rise to meet my heart as the words were delivered, the threat and menace within them delivered with a tone that I could only describe as snide. I could only begin to fathom what Brian was thinking as I watched the colour at first drain from his face, then return in a wave of crimson.

'But Sir...'

'I appreciate that this isn't how you expected this to go Brian but I've made my mind up and my decision is clear.'

I had to credit Brian for his professional integrity. Whilst he bore the look of a volcano on the verge of eruption, his tone remained measured, only belying a fraction of the anger he was clearly feeling.

'With the greatest of respect Sir, you would know that the decision you have made was not yours to make. Matters such as those I reported to you out of professional courtesy, are solely my responsibility to deal with.'

'That's as may be ACC Hannon, but the fallout from actions such as those you had proposed fall squarely under my remit. You would do well to remember that.'

'But...'

'But nothing ACC Hannon! Frankly, I do not need to justify my actions to you. All you need to know is that I must act to protect the integrity of the PSNI and the safety of the public which we serve.'

'And that's all it is Sir, an act' Brian stated calmly in response to the hissed narrative of his superior, 'I think we both know your decision is nothing short of political, the P being of both the lower and higher case varieties in this case. You do what you think you need to do and I'll do likewise, but please don't insult my intelligence by expecting me to swallow your line about protecting the integrity of the force and the safety of the public. The course of action you have chosen does neither.'

'We will speak no further of this business. Like I have already said, you are a seasoned officer, currently in good standing, and might I add, not far away from early retirement...'

'I'm just going to cut you off there Sir. You see, unlike you, I've served all my time in the police force in Northern Ireland. People like us, people like me, we don't respond well to threats.'

With that Brian ended the call and I couldn't have felt more proud of him.

He smiled.

'I best be off. I'll stay in touch. See you in a few days.'

There was a bounce in both his voice and his step as he moved to leave. ACC Brian Hannon was one of the good ones and I was now more determined than ever to work closely by his side.

CHAPTER
EIGHTY-NINE

CLICHED AS IT WAS, THIS PARTICULAR KILLER HAD AGAIN RETURNED TO the scene of the crime. Of course she had done so dozens of times in the intervening years since that awful night, in fact she passed it every single time she came to Carolyn's class and had brought Glenn McGinley here just last night. Now, unable to settle at her apartment, Bella found herself sitting in the art gallery area of Clotsworthy House on a wooden bench adjacent to the glass mezzanine under the construction of which she had killed Cillian Moran. She had never intended to do what she'd done that night, at least that was what she had deluded herself into thinking for long enough. She had intended it though. It had been pre-meditated and that's exactly how it would be viewed in a court of law if she ever found herself in that position. That had been another of the notions that haunted her dreams. That, and the twisted mask of anguish that his face contorted to form as he fell, still worn in the throes of death as she stood over him.

She had been the one to notice the fault in the scaffolding earlier in the day as she inspected the newly fitted steel support beams for the mezzanine structure. She had been the one to almost topple over the ledge as a result. She had also been the one to further loosen the ill-fitting inter-clamp tube connector, knowing exactly what her intentions were. The rest had been easy. Summoning him there under false pretences had been a piece of cake. He was predictable like that. He hadn't reckoned on the confrontation though and that too was as she wanted it. He wasn't that quick witted after all and wouldn't be able to outsmart her in his defence. His continued denial and refusal to talk about what he had earlier revealed had frustrated her. In truth, if he had've just admitted his guilt she would like to have thought she would have spared him. Though possibly not. It hadn't mattered in the end. He continued with his denials even after she had recounted to him what he had told her on their evening out to celebrate what would have been Sarah's birthday. That she was not missing, but dead, and that he had disposed of the body. She may as well have been talking to the bare-brick wall. It was then that she had lost it, lurching forward at him with a primal scream, then watching as he lost his footing, panicking as he realised what was about to happen. He was beyond saving now, even if she had wanted to. She didn't. She could only watch now, witness his demise. Watch as she made things right. For Sarah.

Except she hadn't made things right, had she? The recent death of Lauren Baxter had put that into doubt. Now, Sam Moran's potential involvement in that death had clouded the truth further. Had Sam and not Cillian been responsible for the murder of Sarah Clark? It now seemed a plausible possibility. It also raised a further question in her mind. Reminded her of something about Cillian's death that had bothered her ever since. Yes, she had left him for dead, and yes, she was not thinking clearly. The thing was though, she had never recalled the generator being running at the time. After all, there had been sufficient natural light despite it being late evening, and there had been no other work going on onsite for several hours before. At the discovery that Cillian had died of carbon monoxide poisoning, the only thing it meant to her was that it had not been injuries caused by her that had killed him, and that the evil bastard still got what was coming to him. Now she wondered, did Sam have some involvement there too?

CHAPTER
NINETY

Having prepared myself a "care-tray" of sandwiches, drinks and snacks that I would not normally have described as healthy but were exactly what I needed to aid my recovery at the moment, I made up a bowl of food and treats for Uther before we both retreated to my bedroom where we gorged ourselves, me in the bed, pillows propping me up in preparation for some laptop work, Uther spread across the entire width of the bottom of the bed. Of course, he wasn't allowed up there either and I'm sure Bella would have laughed, but we both deserved the treat, and the company. I hoped she would be true to her word and come around later. We definitely needed to clear the air between us, and she wasn't aware of what had happened to me since we last spoke. I hoped she was safe and had the fleeting notion that her stalker and Jess were likely one and the same, being almost certain that texts to both of us from the burner phone had been from the same number. That made me all the more anxious to see her for myself, and of course, the fact that she could walk Uther as part of her making things up to me would be perfect.

Uther's turning toward me, mid-mouthful of gravy bone

biscuit treats and giving me a knowing look made me smile. Was he thinking about his walk or was he giving me a wary look that I should be resting instead of contemplating work? I wasn't sure which, but what I was increasingly sure of was that there was a definite mental connection between myself and my magnificent hound, and that he possibly was more cognitively aware of me than I was of myself.

'Ok Boy, time to unleash our inner Lt. Columbo and Dog. It's time to go after Mr Glenn McGinley.' Finally breaking with the temptation of the continued fulfilment of Uther's pampering desires I finally got to booting up the laptop, secure in the knowledge that he would be in pre-walk snooze mode before I had managed to type in my password.

I'd already been given my jumping off point courtesy of Glenn McGinley, or as the rumblings of my memory had stirred me toward at the class last night, Dr Glenn Addams. The true life version of the "fictional" incident he had described of a child being thrown from a balcony to their death had happened in Birmingham. Although I hadn't been physically present, I had been involved in it to a degree. As it turned out from my landing on the relevant webpages from BBC Birmingham, the gaps in my recollection were about to be refilled, and then some.

According to the coverage, the child's death had been the result of the actions of what had been described as a "deranged young female"; not words I would have chosen. The child was survived by his parents (divorced), Dr Glenn Addams-McGinley and Dr Louise Wood. The report thread, consisting of both text and videos followed the sequence of events as they unfolded. They didn't, however, include how I came to be involved, though that part I had remembered. Based in Ormskirk at the time, I had been asked by a colleague in the Midlands to review Psychological Evaluation Reports of some patients under the care of a Doctor under her supervision. A Doctor Addams as I now recalled. The evaluation outcomes as suggested by him hadn't rang true with my colleague at the time, though her field of expertise was not as closely aligned to his as mine would have been. She had been a little concerned. Perusal of the reports in question proved that she had been right to be. My review had subsequently led to several patients being released from care that he had proposed the continued treatment of, one of whom, it transpired, had been the person responsible for the death of his son. That much I could have guessed and given that I had received no further contact from either my colleague or the authorities, it had been clear that in obviously upholding my view on the patients in question, something had likely happened to further cast a shadow over his. I was keen to find out what. Some further probing around relative news threads revealed that in the investigation that followed parallel to the inquest into the child's death, an allegation had been uncovered that he had been administering an experimental combination of anti-psychotic drugs to the patients in question in addition to the use of pioneering techniques in psychosomatics and hypnotic suggestion as part of a research project codenamed the "How To Be Dead" protocol.

Unsurprisingly, as I read on, it was further alleged that his superiors were aware of the existence of the project and his work within it. Speculation also linked the funding of the project directly to Westminster. All of which, both West Midlands University and Government representatives actively distanced themselves from.

As I processed the gravity of everything that I had just read, I realised that my actions in reviewing those reports had been the direct cause of the implosion of both the personal and professional lives of the man I now knew as Glenn McGinley, albeit a situation of his own making. He truly hated me with every fibre of his being. Now at least I knew why. I also suspected now that I knew what his likely connection to Jess Farnham was, though what happened next meant I would have to wait a while to prove it.

CHAPTER
NINETY-ONE

His explosive response to her return, both physically and psychologically was only the beginning of the reparative process, that much she knew. Her further, "treatment" would be comprised of much worse. Still, it was better than the alternative for her she knew that, and she still had him. She was his chosen one. The one he had deemed worthy, and just knowing that was enough to make everything she would endure, had endured, worthwhile. Though it didn't stop Carolyn Harkin's crass words about his fucking Bella Maskull from reverberating through her head.

'You know what you need to do' he said softly, 'get yourself into position, send the text, then do whatever needs to be done to engage her. Remember though. Do not go off script. It needs to go exactly as I've told you. Right?'

She nodded, defeatedly.

'It won't happen again.'

'You're fucking right it won't. If it does...well, you know that outcome. Isn't that right, Jess?'

The malevolence of his words brought a shiver to her.

'I won't be here when you get back' he continued, 'but I shouldn't be too much longer afterward.'

She wondered where he was going and her mouth began to form the question before she thought better of it. Whether he had noticed or not she wasn't sure, but he answered as if he had.

'I'm going to work. I've been asked to do some consultative evaluation. From what I can gather, it might prove to be a very worthwhile appointment, in more ways than one.'

His words brought with them that wicked grin of his. The one that she so hated and loved.

CHAPTER
NINETY-TWO

THE ANXIETY ATTACK THAT HAD WRENCHED ME FROM MY FINDINGS ON Glenn McGinley had taken a greater toll upon me than normal. My other injuries hadn't helped. Whether it had been visited upon me as the result of those findings or as a delayed reaction to Jess' attack on me I wasn't sure. What I did know was that it had never caused a complete blackout before. Now I was coming to terms with my second shattered screen in a number of hours, this time my laptop, and an agitated Uther, clearly concerned for my wellbeing. He wasn't the only one.

'It's ok boy, I'll be ok' I reassured.

I would be ok too, I knew that. Still, I would be better if Bella was around, as would he. Reaching for my phone I text her.

I need your help. Can you come over as soon as you can?

The response was almost immediate, and chilling.

Sorry, Bella can't come to the phone right now. She's a little tied up. Don't worry though, she'll be there soon. We both will. Love. Just Jess.

CHAPTER
NINETY-THREE

Bound by cable ties to an office chair and gagged by her own scarf, Bella watched helplessly as the woman responded to the text that her phone had just alerted them both to, a leering smile tight across her lips as she amused herself with the response she had composed. The woman, Bella assumed to be the person purporting to be Jess Farnham. Carolyn's stalker, and confirmed as of just a few moments ago, hers too.

Shock was starting to give way now to anger as she took in the features of her attacker, a distinct echo of Carolyn's looks within them. Anger, directed mostly toward herself at this stage. It was her own actions that had led to her current predicament. Her own stupidly brazen actions having been emboldened by the thought of avenging the deadly deeds of Sam Moran, and to hell with the consequences. The text she'd received just now, within minutes of returning to her apartment, spurring her into action.

IT WAS NICE TO SEE YOU APPRECIATE THE ART AT CLOTSWORTHY HOUSE EARLIER. I LIKE ART TOO. MY FAVOURITE IS THE SCREAM, WHICH IS EXACTLY WHAT I'M GOING TO MAKE YOU DO AS SOON AS YOU OPEN YOUR FRONT DOOR.

As it happened, when she angrily flung open the front door, she hadn't expected to find anyone there. She hadn't accounted for coming face to face with the woman, and she definitely hadn't accounted for the attack that followed. An attack that she was pretty sure was a long way from being over.

Placing the phone back down onto the table, the woman moved across the open planned space to the kitchen where she took a large knife from the knife block before returning to face Bella.

'You scream, I will kill you, clear?'

Bella nodded agreement before the woman used the knife to cut the scarf that gagged her, an action designed to create a little drama Bella realised, orchestrated to illustrate that the woman was not afraid to use the knife.

'Jess?' Bella's voice came as a croak.

'Yes, as far as you're concerned anyway' came the menacing reply before the woman crossed to the kitchen again, this time returning with a glass of water which she held to Bella's lips as she gulped a welcome drink. Setting the water down on the table the woman lifted a chair from Bella's dining table, placed it in front of Bella, turning its back facing her, before seating herself upon it the wrong way round and folding her arms across its back.

'So, what was it like?' Her glare on Bella intent.

'What?' Bella asked, bemused.

'You know! Being stalked. Being hunted. Being intimidated. Being emotionally abused. Being physically abused. What were all those things like?'

'What, you get off on victim impact statements, are you actually that perverse?'

Her response to Bella's words came in the form of a sharp crack across her face, leaving a distinct, hand shaped red mark that smarted and stung Bella more than her stony reaction betrayed.

'Let me answer for you. It's terrifying', Jess spat, 'terrifying, degrading, sickening, need I go on?'

Bella shook her head in compliance to the expected answer.

'Here's another question for you, given your current predicament. Here you are, having been tied, bound and beaten by someone wielding a knife, but I'll bet part of you is still relieved that I'm not a man. The thought did occur, yes?'

Bella nodded again.

'Say it!' She bellowed.

'Yes.'

Admittedly the thought had flashed across Bella's mind. Was she now much less likely to be sexually assaulted and murdered? Perhaps. Statistically at least.

'And I'm guessing you know why, yes?'

'Yes.'

'You, more than most know what men are capable of. You've challenged the behaviour of men all your life. Admirably too from what I hear. Oh, and I know what you did by the way. Kudos!'

'Some men' Bella corrected defiantly, 'not all, just some.'

Her words went unacknowledged as Jess stood, calmly and returned the chair to its place at the table.

'You deserve everything I've done to you. Everything I'm going to do to you. How can you, you of all people run around after Carolyn Harkin like a little lap dog?'

The anger had returned now, as had the menacing tone and exaggerated wielding of the knife. Things were about to get worse for Bella she realised. Much worse.

'Her, the woman responsible for enabling so many men to create so many female victims, to ruin and in more cases than not, end the lives of so many women. The woman responsible for the physical and mental suffering of so many women and young girls.

She's not fit to be a Doctor any more than she was fit to be a police officer. Her incompetence is every bit as sickening as her arrogance, and ignorance. I wish I had managed to end her back in Ormskirk. I'll manage it this time though. No mistakes this time. For now though, there's you. You, the woman who radiates the persona of a confident little ball breaker. Except you were the one broken. Pathetic! Did you enjoy the sex with Glenn? He is good isn't he. It was all part of his plan though. All part of how you would be introduced to the program while I was adding to the trauma of your precious friend. Maybe I'll pass on visiting Harkin for now. It'll be a pleasure best savoured at another time. Perhaps you could pass that message on for me.'

'You feel better now you've gotten that little rant off your chest? Just one thing though. You weren't in Ormskirk. You're just a facsimile of Jess Farnham, and a poor one at that. How does that make *you* feel?' Bella asked, unable to help herself, 'You can get off your brainwashed, inaccurate little soap box sweetie. I don't fall for that kind of shit.'

They were words Bella knew she would regret the consequences of, but not her having said them. They were also words that drove Jess to silent action, her now lifeless eyes focused on the job in hand with a laser sharpness. In a swift series of fluid movements, she used the tip of the knife to roughly remove the buttons of Bella's blouse before using the blade to slowly unfold each side of it, leaving her torso exposed, save her bra, and relishing in the sheer panic apparent in the young woman's eyes as she did so. Next came the part that would never leave either of them. The moment when she would create a lifelong scar both physically and emotionally. Mark Bella Maskull for the rest of her life. The best part, there was nothing she could do about it. A master stroke you might say, just as he had instructed. She had gone off script just a little, but he wasn't to know that. At least not yet.

CHAPTER
NINETY-FOUR

THE MAN NOW SEATED FACING GLENN MCGINLEY WITHIN THE SPARSE confines of an interview room in the secure unit bore little resemblance to that which Bella had described. Not so much the pop star looks of Scandinavian heart-throb, Morten Harket, more a zombified effigy of the 80s idol. A greyness to his pallor and the cadence almost extinguished from eyes deep set into shadowy dark sockets, it was clear that he had reached the lowest ebb of his existence. In many ways that was exactly the way Glenn liked it. They were much easier to work with when they were this docile. This defeated.

'Hi Sam. My name is Dr Glenn Addams-McGinley. You can call me Glenn.'

Sam nodded slightly, if barely perceptibly. With that the process commenced and McGinley adopted his most caring persona. The one who dealt in soft calming tones, caring eyes and open gestures. The one he liked to think of as the wolf in sheep's clothing.

'Sam, I've been made aware of your predicament. My colleague has assessed that you are medically fit to face questioning. Your legal representative, however, has managed to persuade both them and the police that in your current state you are mentally vulnerable and that you need some psychological intervention to help you get strong enough to face the rigours of the interview process. That's why I'm here. We'll be spending some time together and I don't want you to worry. I promise that I can help you. To be able to do that though I'm going to need you to take me through it all. You can tell me *everything*.

Part Four- "You Can Make Anything by Writing." (C.S. Lewis)

CHAPTER
NINETY-FIVE

THE LAST FEW DAYS HAD BEEN SOLELY ABOUT BRIAN'S ADVICE TO BOTH Bella and me. Since he and one of his officers had finally returned Bella to me from the hospital his orders had been clear. Rest and recuperation had been top of the priorities list, in forms largely comprising of short walks around the grounds with Uther, bathing in the lough as he found his swimming legs, binging on Netflix and takeaways, cooking together, more than a little wine, and most importantly lots of chat. I could empathise with some of Bella's recent trauma, having been through similar myself. The physical scar though, that I couldn't even begin to comprehend. I had alerted the police as soon as I had received the text message that night. Though by the time they got there it had still been too late. They had found her there, alone and bleeding out in the apartment. That hadn't been the worst of what they had found though. Her top had been cut open and I had never known the name for it before but I did now. The aptly named centre gore of her bra had been cut through, exposing her breasts, before a long, deep cut had been made from her breastbone to her navel, reminiscent of the beginnings of the Y incision that commenced a post-mortem examination. The thought of it still sickened me and I could only imagine would torment her for the rest of her days. The physical wound would heal, leaving the faintest traces of a scar. She'd been lucky, if you could call it that. Very lucky in terms of the scarring. The emotional wound, that would be a different matter altogether. Which was exactly why we only talked about it when she broached the subject.

We'd been good for each other and the time to heal was exactly what we both needed, though neither of us were naive enough to see this as anything other than the calm before the storm. She had blocked McGinley's phone number and we had ensured the main gates to the grounds and the doors and windows of the house had remained locked to anyone other than Brian. We still had a few days before the next writing class too. Still, the time to return to reality and its cruelties was almost upon us. As it turned out, it was Bella who broke cover first, over a lazy morning coffee.

'It was all my fault you know. I realised that last night.'

'You can't blame yourself Bella, it was her who...'

'No, I mean it was my fault she was able to contact us. The WhatsApp group, the group emails from the writing class, it was me who shared our mobile details. That's how she got them. Through him. He had obviously kept Jess Farnham's phone, the SIM card at least. From there on it was only a matter of buying a few burner phones and he and his new protege were good to go.'

She was right. It made perfect sense. I followed her logic onward.

'I never got to check the security system here for the night the envelope was left and you were threatened. I couldn't find the details and was about to ask Sam when...'

'I know them' she replied, pulling the laptop toward her. Within less than a minute we were watching as Jess made her way from the front door, through the hallway and into the kitchen before returning a short while later.

'Is that her? The woman who...'

'Yes. No mistaking it. That's her alright.'

The look on her face was one of abject hatred.

'The next time I meet that bitch it'll be on my terms. She'll soon know all about being a female victim.'

Her words reminded me of what Bella had described as the explanation for the attack on her. My supposed lack of sisterhood for the female cause. The thought of it had left me livid when I first learned of the twisted reasoning and the irony of it. Now it brought a fresh wave of anger. If anything it was Jess and no doubt her predecessor who had been guilty of what I was being accused of. It was likely that had been part of the twisted narrative that McGinley had used as part of the psychological conditioning that he'd subjected them to. He had made victims of them before perpetrating the additional cruelty of transforming them into casualties of dissociative personality disorder to further his evil. Clearly his twisted mind had targeted me for revenge for the death of his son, but it was ultimately he who had been responsible as the result of his dabbling in the development of his dangerous, "How To Be Dead Programme" and the vile acts it had allowed him to indulge in beneath the radar. He'd also clearly used a warped view of my professional past to court hatred for me in his victims. The worst thing was, he'd been toying with me the entire time since the start of the writing course. He was controlling the narrative there too, cherry picking some of the biggest cases of my career. Ones where the victims were ultimately female and framing it to sound like I was somehow complicit.

'Don't worry, we'll happily cut the strings of that particular puppet as soon as the opportunity presents itself. Then we'll deal with the puppet-master.' I finally replied, the expression on my face mirroring hers.

'Something else has been bothering me' I said, pulling the laptop away from her and placing it in front of me. Navigating my way through the police file on the original Jessica Farnham it didn't take long to see that she had been placed under psychiatric care whilst in prison. Two clicks of a mouse later and boom, there it was. Her Dr, one Glenn Addams. A little further delving and it was clear to see that he had been attached HM Prison, Askham Grange, in Yorkshire whilst the original Jess Farnham was there. No doubt perfecting his particular twisted skill set in manipulation.

Another google search had him as an associate psychologist with Merseyside Police when I was working with the Faculty of Psychology at Edge Hill University in Ormskirk. The place where Jess had apparently turned up just by chance, and the place where my stalking ordeal first began. Through this role he would have had access to my case history as a police officer, as well as that of my associate psych work. His means, motive and opportunity, were all there, if only his involvement could be proven.

CHAPTER
NINETY-SIX

THE DETAILS OF GLENN MCGINLEY'S PAST AS CAROLYN OUTLINED THEM to her had made perfect sense to Bella. The things she couldn't get her head around was that despite all of it, Carolyn's experience was telling her that all evidence against McGinley was merely circumstantial at this stage, and that the only thing that the police had to go on with Jess was the video of her entering the house. This too was problematic as she appeared to have done so with a key and alarm fob, which again they couldn't prove was likely taken from and returned to Bella's apartment. They bigger problem was that they were yet to discover her true identity or where she lived, though it was likely she was at Molly's, with him.

'Penny for your thoughts' Carolyn said as she began to clear away the coffee cups.

'I just can't get my head around how someone could do the things that he has done and to have gotten away with it so far.'

'It was the same with Jess first time round. It says a lot about our justice system I'm afraid. Stalking laws offer little, if any, protection to the victim.'

'And even then, they've only just come into legislation here in

Northern Ireland. No test cases, no experience, nothing' Bella replied, defeated.

Her shoulders fell and her head lowered, crestfallen.

'It's more than that isn't it?'

I let the question hang there in the ether, watching as she struggled to frame her response.

'She was acting under his instruction that night. Him. I was falling for him Carolyn, and like every single other time I've fallen for someone I've been left damaged as the result. She could have killed me. Probably would have if he'd told her to.'

'Bella, like I've said, you can't blame yourself for what happened.'

'I can though Carolyn. I can because it's my fault. Just like before, there were warning signs and just like before, I chose to ignore them. What if he had been lining me up to be one of his victims like she said? Lining me up to be the next Jess Farnham or whoever she is? What if he'd managed to turn me on you? I mean he tried that night we spent together, and she was much less subtle in her attempts'

She nodded down toward her wound before beginning to shake, a mixture of fear and anger I suspected. I took her forearms, lightly gripping them and echoed how she nodded toward where her wound was.

'Bella, my love. You've already become his victim. There's nothing can be done to change that now. It's ok to have been a victim. It's not ok to stay one. He didn't get to do his worst on either you nor I, nor did his fucked up little minion.'

I felt my own anger rise again as I spoke, then felt the movement through her body as she began to sob uncontrollably, bringing me to hold her tightly in an embrace.

'We'll right this Bella. We'll make sure they pay for what they've done, both of them, I promise you. Sam too.'

She smiled as I released her from my embrace, her eyes bright with tears, and anger.

'I know' she said flatly, wiping away a fat tear.

'I know you do. After all, you're not a stranger to vengeance.'

I smiled ruefully as I turned my back to her. We hadn't yet broached the conversation of her "story" about being responsible for a homicide. The moment I'd heard it the penny had dropped for me. She had killed Cillian Moran in revenge for Sarah Clark. I wasn't sure if it had been an act of impulse or pre-meditation but I was sure she had been responsible. The death of Lauren Baxter had thrown his guilt of Sarah's murder into doubt which was why she had been so keen for me to investigate it. I placed the coffee cups into the sink before turning my attention back to her.

'Cillian's death wasn't an accident' I said, flatly, 'You killed him, didn't you?'

She averted my gaze for what seemed like an eternity, the silence growing between us before finally looked at me directly in the eye.

'Yes. I mean, I thought I did. Now I'm not so sure.'

CHAPTER
NINETY-SEVEN

IF BRIAN HANNON WAS IN POSSESSION OF THE POWER TO REWIND THE DAY back to the beginning he would have. He would also have taken to his car and driven to the serenity of the North Coast post haste. Of course he knew he could never outrun his problems, but watching the waves crash onto the shore at Castlerock Strand may have at least given him some perspective on it all.

As the day so far had actually played out, his morning had been spent addressing DI Stewart and the team he had originally assigned to the Ryan Casey murder investigation, this morning being the first day back on duty for those he had put under investigation for improper conduct. They had of course been given some, "sick leave" after the Chief Constable had overturned his decision to discipline them. Talk about adding insult to injury. It had been a short meeting. To the point. He may have to put up with having them among the rank and file of his officers at the moment, but their behaviour would not go unpunished, despite the views of his boss. The news that he had reassigned each of them to other teams and administrative duties for the foreseeable future had hit like a pile driver. The parting shot, that they had been reassigned to rural stations on the furthest outposts of the

Province had sent them seething, much to his satisfaction. The prize for him had been that not a single one, DI Stewart included, tried to stand up to him or his decision, knowing that doing so would raise the temperature in their particular pond even further. They hadn't seen anything yet. He wasn't about to be bullied by the Chief Constable, which was exactly why the reports from Amy Macklin's investigation had been updated to include the Chief's decision to overturn the outcomes before he had sent it to the Northern Ireland Policing Board. He would deal with the fallout from that when he absolutely had to, not a minute before, and hopefully not before finding justice for Ryan Casey.

It had been a stressful morning alright. It now paled into insignificance as he sat in his armchair in the front room of his house, a plate of sandwiches on his lap and a steaming mug of builders tea in his hand as his wife and daughter, newly returned from a stint on the West End in London planned the "party".

When Karen had first said she had a difficult conversation to have with him he assumed it would have been around assisted dying. He'd hoped she would never broach the topic, as apart from the illegality of it and his professional position, he honestly didn't think he would have it in him. Now, he'd half wished that it had been what she had asked of him rather than what she had railroaded both he and their daughter into agreeing to. In fairness, Imelda was much like her mother. They "got" each other, which is, he supposed, why she had followed in Karen's footsteps into acting; Karen having at one stage being a much sought after stage and screen actor, renowned for her penchant and skill for method acting before giving it all up, much to his chagrin, to allow him to pursue his career.

Karen's idea, that she didn't wish for us to see her suffer the final stages of her illness, was to have a farewell party for us and a few of her closest friends in order that we may celebrate her life together with her. After that, at some point, she would simply disappear from ours, check herself into a hospice or similar facility at a location undisclosed to us, then, when the time came we were to be informed of her passing...after the cremation. It was mad, every aspect of it. Yet that's what they'd agreed to. He'd supposed at first that it had been the morphine talking and he'd been preoccupied with work. With Ryan Casey. With Carolyn. It had been easier to say yes. Now he was devastated and just wanted to get the hell out of there, as far away as possible.

'Brian, oh for goodness sake, please try to keep your head in the room. Now what's it to be for the fish course, salmon or cod?'

'You choose, it's your funeral.' It was an attempt to inject a little comic relief into the situation, and though his attempt at humour was appreciated by his wife, Imelda was less enamoured by both his lack of tact and emotional distance it would appear, as she wore a scowl he'd seen a thousand times before on her mother.

CHAPTER NINETY-EIGHT

'What do you mean you aren't sure?'

In different circumstances I would have been more shocked at the revelation that Bella had indeed thought she'd killed Cillian Moran. In light of recent events I was more aghast that she now doubted it.

'Carolyn, not a day has passed since the night I left Cillian there that I haven't replayed everything that happened thousands of times in my head. I just wanted the truth. He'd all but admitted to burying someone. I wanted to know if it was Sarah. If he'd killed her and where he had buried her? I wanted to scare him, and yes, based on what I thought, I wanted to punish him *and* I was prepared to kill him. I still see his face in my mind as I pushed him, clear as day, dozens of times per day. I watch him fall over and over again; each time powerless to change the outcome. I know I was probably in shock at the time, and I know that I probably wasn't fully aware of everything that was happening around me, but not in any single replay was I ever aware of a generator running.'

'It was started up after?' I asked, eyebrows arched.

'I don't know. Like I say, I can't remember. I always just

presumed after it had been cited as a contributing factor in the cause of death, that it must have been on all along, but since I heard you confronting Sam, I can't think anything but that it was started after.'

'Had you suspected Sam's involvement before?'

'Only in perhaps trying to cover for what Cillian had done. Now though, I can't help but wonder if Cillian was innocent all along. That it was perhaps Sam who killed Sarah. That Cillian knew and when I attacked Cillian, Sam saw an opportunity to free himself from any suspicion of guilt.'

'By murdering his own son though?' I got where she was going on her train of thought, and her thinking was plausible. I just didn't want it to be true I guessed.

'Carolyn, he was like a father to me, but you showed me the video of him with Lauren Baxter. She was dead within days of that video. Dead and alone in the water. She looked just like Sarah. What else do you want me to think?'

She was right. Of course she was right. I just didn't think either of us wanted to believe that Sam Moran wasn't the man that we thought he was.

CHAPTER
NINETY-NINE

Dr Glenn Addams-McGinley, to give himself his full title, was fully aware that if they truly knew him, that society would deem him a monster. It was an identity he had craved from an early age, and one that he had carefully, purposefully cultivated and crafted, and if his name came to be associated with the words, notorious, sociopathic, evil, and dare he even think it, genius, he would wear those badges with pride.

His patient though, he was a whole different kind of monster. A much scarier one in his professional opinion. This one actually thought he was one of the good guys. It was a state of mind that had been verbalised several times throughout this afternoon's therapy session, each time by the patient himself, and each time forcing his doctor to have to resist a powerful urge to scream into the man's face that dead bodies tend not to pile up around good guys. That good guys don't seduce then murder young women. That good guys don't have a hero complex, and what good guys most certainly don't do is murder their wife, and later, their son, making those murders look like a suicide, then the handiwork of someone else respectively. Not to mention making someone close to them believe they were responsible for the killing. Those my friend were not the actions of a good guy. They were the actions of a psychopath. Still, his notes from today's session and those preceding it would make a great character profile to present to the lovely Dr Carolyn at the next writing class. Of course he would see her before that, but it would be in a very different context, and one in which he was very much looking forward to seeing the shock on her face.

CHAPTER
ONE HUNDRED

'We've a strict, "No Dogs Allowed" policy in the building Dr Harkin, but I think we can make an exception for your friend', Mack smiled, watching us as we crossed into the briefing room, Uther carrying himself with an air of importance that made me smile too.

'Soon to be your friend also Mack, I would hazard a guess' Brian answered.

'I don't doubt it Sir. He looks like he's reporting for duty.'

I beamed again.

'Constable Uther reporting for duty Sir' I answered on his behalf.

'Actually Dr Harkin' began Mack, 'he would be of much higher ranking than that. Traditionally he would hold a rank higher than that held by his handler and given you were DI, he would be...'

'One of the highest ranking in the room' Brian joked.

'And the most intelligent' Mack echoed.

'You speak for yourself Uncle Mack' DI Amy Macklin laughed, 'Dr Harkin, Constable Uther and...'

'Oh, sorry, this is Bella, Bella Maskull. I hope you don't mind; I've asked her to join us. She would have a fair amount of inside knowledge of Sam Moran, so I thought perhaps she could be interviewed, then she's very kindly going to take Uther for a walk while we chat. I mean, I know it's not exactly orthodox to turn up with a civilian and a dog in tow but...'

Saying it out loud made it sound ludicrous to my ear, but Bella's presence would indeed prove useful in my view.

'Perfect, we need all the input we can get believe me' Brian interjected, 'you're very welcome Miss Maskull. Mack here will make you a coffee and take you for a chat about Mr Moran if that's ok?'

'Not a problem' Bella beamed, putting a brave face on what would no doubt be a difficult conversation for her.

As Bella and Mack left, Amy Macklin stood, extending her hand.

'Dr Harkin. Nice to finally meet you. I've heard a lot about you.'

'All good I hope' I laughed, a little more nervously than intended.

'Most certainly. ACC Hannon here speaks very highly of you, as does our mutual friend.'

'Our mutual friend?'

'Yes, sorry, I thought you knew. Beth Shaw is a good friend of mine, and I gather of yours too.'

'Oh, yes of course, I should have realised. Yes, I remember Beth telling me about you. You consult with Farset Investigations right?'

'For my sins' Amy laughed, 'It's lovely to finally make your acquaintance.'

'Sit ladies, please' Brian gestured toward the large conference style desk dominating the open planned expanse, 'I'll grab us some coffee and we can make a start.'

Within moments he had returned with a coffee pot, some milk and some cups.

'No sugar needed if I remember correctly. You ladies are sweet enough, and as per usual, I'm watching my figure, or at least Mrs H is on my behalf.'

He patted his tummy with a laugh that we returned. He had a remarkable knack of putting people at ease and I wondered how many senior officers, particularly male senior officers would have fetched hot drinks in such circumstances rather than depositing the task upon one of their junior officers or asking one of their female colleagues to do the honours. When we were seated however, the joviality of his manner changed to that of the consummate professional he had proven himself to be time and again since I've known him.

'Carolyn, I really appreciate you coming in, especially at such short notice. I'm afraid that's the only type of notice I've ever afforded you thus far. It won't always be like that, I promise.'

'That's quite alright Sir.'

'Brian please, both of you.'

Amy and I nodded simultaneously.

'Carolyn I won't beat about the bush. You're obviously aware that I've had to disband the team investigating the Ryan Casey murder with the exception of Mack. I've been able to draft Amy into the investigation and I'm taking an active role myself, but that's literally it, just us three. I was hoping that we could persuade you to join us. We could be doing with your experience both as a former DI, and in your current capacity to help us out on this.'

I was already aware of his predicament via the telephone call he had made to ask me to come in. He had also fully appraised me of the reasons why then too, I'm guessing, taking advantage of the privacy of his office and of the one to one conversation, so I'd had a feeling that I already knew why I was here. I had been correct. Thankfully our phone call had also given me an opportunity to update him on what I'd found out regarding Glenn McGinley.

'I'd be happy to help, though I must remind you that there is a potential conflict of interest in that I have a personal friendship with the man you currently have in custody, as does Bella.'

'We're aware of that' he gestured towards Amy, 'that's one of the reasons for DI Macklin's involvement. Part of her role will be to ensure that what is currently only a potential conflict of interest does not become an actual one.'

'I don't anticipate any issues Dr Harkin. After all, you're extremely experienced and have a highly respected professional reputation.'

'In that case, count me in, and please, call me Carolyn.' The young woman exuded professionalism and I found myself liking her, though I vaguely recalled Beth telling me that despite their friendship, that she and Amy sometimes rubbed each other up the wrong way. I suspected the reason was because they were a little too alike.

'Excellent' said Brian, 'in that case, let's get down to business. Amy, can you brief Carolyn and bring me up to date?'

'Certainly. If you can just allow me to...'

She rose to retrieve a small stack of manilla folders from a nearby desk before passing one each to Brian and me.

'As you're aware Carolyn, we have Sam Moran in custody. Under the direction of the GP on duty, when his arrest was processed and at Mr Moran's request, he was referred for psychological evaluation. The GP at the time had believed that Mr Moran was mentally fit for questioning, however, both Mr Moran and his legal representative felt otherwise. In order to ensure that any interview we held with him was not subject to legal scrutiny we allowed it. He's been working with a psychologist sourced by his legal representatives for the last number of days.'

Conscious that I'd been nodding my understanding as she

spoke, I realised that she may have misinterpreted my actions as agreement, which in a way it was, though not of Sam's request.

'I completely agree with the actions taken. We certainly don't want to jeopardise any potential conviction, though we're obviously a fair way away from that. What I don't get is Sam's wish to be referred. Yes, from what I've heard, he suffers from depression, but to suggest mental instability, that makes me wonder. Is he trying to go down the diminished responsibility route? In which case it certainly suggests he has something to hide.'

'Which is why we would like you to sit in on the interview when we bring him in later today.'

'Fine' I nodded, 'what do we have on him so far?'

Amy continued.

'Despite his efforts to clear up his house, a luminol treatment and a UV light turned the place into a veritable treasure trove of Ryan Casey's blood. We also recovered a bag containing the items he used to perform the clean-up from a site nearby. Traces of both Mr Casey's DNA and Mr Moran's were found there too, as well as several partial fingerprints which matched Mr Moran.'

'He would have an alibi for around the timeframe of the murder though, in Bella and I.'

'Yes. I don't think we can put him in the frame for the murder. The clean-up on the other hand, seems like a foregone conclusion.'

'When I confronted him he mentioned a girl?' I asked.

'Yes' Brian interjected, 'the young woman, Lauren Baxter, she was the one who Mr Moran was up close and personal with in the video clip you already identified them both in. I looked into her post-mortem report. The post-mortem was conducted by the chief coroner, Dr Orr, a good friend as it goes. I had a chat to him this morning also. In his view the manner of death was drowning though the actual cause of death was inconclusive. It was the press who took it upon themselves to report it as suicide. Her blood alcohol level was verging on 40% though, so she was severely intoxicated. There were also high levels of Prozac and benzodiazepine present in her bloodstream. A fatal combination, the two can be linked to suicidal thoughts amongst other things as I'm sure you know, and that's before the alcohol is factored in. The question is, was that Lauren's intention? Did she self-administer a deadly cocktail then make for the water's edge, or was she even aware she'd taken what she had? Either way, we can't prove anything. What we can prove however, was that she has been on Mr Moran's boat and most likely within the time frame near her death, and that he has ready access to a supply of benzodiazepine.'

'What about the anti-depressants?' I asked.

'Although Moran was diagnosed with recurring bouts of depression, his GP felt that it could be controlled with lifestyle changes as opposed to medication, so no legal way of his accessing Prozac. He does, however, have a significant history with anxiety and was being treated with medication for that.'

'That would ring true of my observations. I mean on the depression. I didn't see any major signs. The anxiety surprises me though. I didn't notice any tells whatsoever. Clearly his meds were good, and of course the Prozac may have been in Miss Baxter's own prescribed medication' I mused aloud, 'still, without evidence beyond the circumstantial we can't link him to her death.'

'Ah, not so fast Dr Harkin' Brian raised a hand and smiled, 'You haven't heard everything yet. According to the post-mortem Lauren was pregnant. Dr Orr was able to extract some foetal DNA for analysis. We're not yet sure who the father was. We do know who it wasn't though. It's not a match to Ryan Casey.'

I'm sure my chin wasn't far from the surface of the table in response to that revelation, though it hadn't taken my mind long to reach the next logical conclusion. The one that brought the question pre-empted by Brian before I could ask it.

'Moran won't consent to giving a DNA sample' he sighed, 'obviously it's all over his house, his boat and his van, but without consent to getting a sample extracted directly from him we can't confirm that it's his let alone use it for paternity testing, which again he would need to consent to. Our hands are tied.'

His words made me feel sick. Not just because it seemed that justice for another young woman seemed just beyond my reach, but also at the realisation that Sam Moran was far from being the man I thought I knew. I thought of the young man from my teens and the man who was so good with Bella and with Uther. The man I was beginning to, dare I even think it, fall for all over again. My mind took me to the memory of the drinks we shared recently on the boat, where he told me of his life and his loss in our lost years. It was then it hit me. His wife died by drowning also. Framed by him as a terrible tragedy, yet by his own admission, he wasn't happy in the relationship. Looking at the loss in light of current allegations I couldn't help but wonder. If just days ago someone had asked me if Sam Moran was capable of murder, my answer would have been an emphatic, No. Now, though, not only was the answer very different, but I was also left wondering how to tell Brian that I suspected that he had possibly been responsible for the deaths of three other people without compromising Bella and her role in the demise of Sam's son.

'Earth to Carolyn' I vaguely heard Brian's voice calling me back into the moment.

'His wife. I think he's done it before. I think he killed his wife.'

Now it was Brian and Amy's turn to pick their collective jaws from the surface of the table.

CHAPTER
ONE HUNDRED ONE

For almost the entire duration of her walk through Redburn Forest Park with Uther, Bella Maskull had been completely preoccupied with her conversation with Mack. Clearly expert at his job, the old man had made her feel completely at ease in their time together. Making it feel more like a conversation than an interview, which she realised was exactly what he had been trying to do. After all, the more relaxed she felt, the more information she would be likely to convey, both wittingly and sometimes without realisation. That was the part that had her so worried now. Carolyn's advice had been succinct. She was to be truthful and accurate, but not give any scope or opportunity for Mack to even begin to suspect any involvement in anything untoward on her part. Replaying elements of the conversation in her head she was pretty sure she'd stuck to the brief ok. It didn't stop her allowing that tiny element of doubt to creep in. Now, nearing the car park where she'd left Carolyn's Ranger a little over an hour and a half earlier, after leaving Mack, she was more than ready to pick Carolyn up and go home. As well as making her feel good that her recovery from her injuries was such that she could now again manage such a walk, the exercise had stimulated her appetite and no doubt that of Uther, such that she was now more than ready for dinner, as likely was he. Sensing he was nearing the truck and the promise of a drink of cool, fresh water held within it for him, Uther's pace quickened. She was surprised therefore, that just around the bend that led to the car park, the great hound stopped dead in his tracks.

'What's wrong boy?'

He looked at her with a look she'd seen only once before. The look he gave just before his large muscular frame tensed in preparation for attacking the threat that Sam had represented that day in Carolyn's kitchen. Then came the low growl that spelt danger. From what though, or who? Perhaps Uther already knew the answer to that question. For her part, she was about to find out, despite the loud protestations of her inner voice and the scream transmitted to her brain via the nerve endings at the damage site of her still healing wound doing their best to convince her otherwise. Urging Uther onward she rounded the bend and entered the car park before being sent reeling by the sight that greeted her.

Perched nonchalantly on the bonnet of the Ranger, her feet on the bumper aiding her balance, the woman at first glance could have been Carolyn. It wasn't though, the biking leathers betrayed that immediately. It could only be Jess and it looked like they were set for another confrontation. It was one that Bella was neither mentally nor physically prepared for as yet, but it was one she wouldn't shy away from either. After all, this time she had a not so secret weapon to more than even up the odds, and by the look on Uther's face, it would only take one word to send him into action.

As it turned out there was to be no confrontation today. After smiling and waving as if greeting an old friend, Jess launched herself off the bonnet to a standing position, from which she partially unzipped the leather jacket and reached inside for a white envelope which she then placed underneath the windscreen wiper at the driver's side of the vehicle before turning to Bella, giving a mock salute, then making her way to the motorcycle she'd parked up beside the Ranger, before driving off into the late afternoon traffic.

It was only after the motorcycle had screamed past them that Bella realised that she had a huge clump of Uther's fur clutched tightly in her hand. The action and the huge animal's lack of protest to it reminded her of a scene from C. S. Lewis', The Lion, The Witch and The Wardrobe involving Aslan the lion having his mane held similarly by "Daughters of Eve", Susan and Lucy. An apt thought she later realised, given that she was not a million miles away from where the author had been born and raised. Now though, her more immediate focus was on the envelope sandwiched between the wiper blade and windscreen.

Reaching the vehicle she unlocked it and firstly poured water from a bottle into a bowl for Uther, then as he noisily gulped his fill at the rear of the Ranger, she moved to the front and carefully removed the envelope. On the front of it in bold type her name had been printed. Hands beginning to shake a little at the prospect of what was inside, she fumbled it open. The contents were surprising. In a bizarre way.

The card she now held in her hand had been personalised like those available for curation by the sender on sites such as Moonpig. On the front was a collage of photographs that looked to be of various aspects of the grounds on Langford Villa, the photograph at the centre of which was a shot of the scaled statue of the Ulster Hound. The typeface above it simply saying, Get Well Soon.

Opening the card she saw that there was writing on both sides of the divide. The words typed on the right hand side:

To Bella
Get Well Soon
With Love and Best Wishes
Glenn

X

On the left side of the dividing line was a more elaborate piece of typed text.

My Dearest Bella. I am truly sorry for what you have recently been subjected to. Despite what you have been told, what happened to you had nothing whatsoever to do with me, I can assure you of that. Your ordeal was the result of the actions of Jess and Jess alone, and yes, as I'm sure you already knew, Jess and I have a connection (she's my patient). Not like the one between you and I though. It is purely professional. It could never be like....us. I know you won't believe me and I understand why you won't take my calls, but I promise you it's true. Please let me explain everything. I haven't been upfront with you. Please let me make things right between us. Help me make you understand, what Jess did was of her own mind, unhinged as it is, and for that I suppose I must take some responsibility. For what she did though, no. I had no idea. Please, Let's talk. I miss you.

Love always
Glenn
P.S. X marks the spot.

CHAPTER
ONE HUNDRED TWO

THE RABBIT HOLE THAT I HAD TAKEN US DOWN HAD FILLED THE HOURS FOR Brian, Amy and I so much that between then and our scheduled questioning of Sam Moran, we had yet to eat, and I'd had to text Bella to tell her to go ahead home without me. The task in hand, trying to find out if Sam had indeed been responsible for the death of his wife had been a worthwhile one, fruitful in some ways, though again proved nothing more than circumstantial.

The inquest in this case had ruled her death as being accidental, though suicide had been thought possible. Sam's account had been that she was suffering badly from what he presumed to be post-partem depression. She had found it difficult to bond with Cillian and was also suffering intense bouts of insomnia. He had apparently pleaded with her over a prolonged period to seek medical help, to which she had refused. They'd been on his boat the night she died. He'd had the idea for them all to spend the night on there, out at one of her favourite spots on the lough, near Ballyronan. He'd wanted to rekindle the spark between them and they had enjoyed so much time there in the early stages of their romance. He'd also thought it might help them to bond as a family and that the rocking motion of the boat and the contentment of being somewhere she held dear, may have helped her get a good night's sleep. His account then went on to outline how they'd had a really nice night and that it had gone exactly how he'd hoped. They had put the baby down in his cot late evening. He slept soundly. They had a few glasses of wine then went to bed themselves. She had fallen asleep first. He eventually dozed off and woke several hours later to find her gone.

Her body was recovered late the following evening. The post-mortem indicated that she had drowned and that her blood-alcohol level was elevated. There were also high levels of benzodiazepine present in her toxicology. Sam's suggestion that she had likely taken some of his medication without his realisation was what had swung the decision away from suicide at the time.

I couldn't get his words out of my head though. The night had, "gone exactly as he'd hoped". Now I was about to come face to face with him. He wouldn't be able to say the same thing about tonight, I was about to make damned sure of that.

CHAPTER
ONE HUNDRED THREE

'DR ADDAMS, THANKS SO MUCH FOR AGREEING TO BE HERE. I'M SO GLAD you could make it. I know my client would feel much more assured at your presence.'

'Not a problem Mr Keys. It's the very least I could do' Glenn McGinley smiled down at the diminutive figure that was David Keys LLB as he gestured a bony finger toward the visibly distraught Sam Moran seated near the counter of the custody suite. Since their first meeting McGinley had been mildly amused by the idea that the tiny weed of a man in the oversized suit which bore the hallmarks of having been slept in several times, had the name Keys, given that he was charged with a legal responsibility to assert his skills in a manner that would lock or unlock the potential freedom of his clients. The man could barely be trusted to look after himself if the unkempt crop of thinning mousy hair and coffee stained loosely fastened tie, sitting right of centre underneath the buttoned up collar of what had once been a white shirt were anything to go by.

'Shall we?' McGinley flashed him a reassuring smile as he nodded toward Sergeant Mack Macklin who was waiting to bring them through. The least he could do indeed, he chuckled to himself. He wouldn't have missed this for the world, and for reasons that had little, if anything, to do with Sam Moran.

CHAPTER
ONE HUNDRED FOUR

'Dr Harkin, you seem a little surprised to see me' remarked Glenn McGinley as he entered the interrogation suite, his presence casting further shadow over the already dimly lit room.

'I am a little' I replied, though the voice inside my head was answering with something akin to, "well that was the fucking understatement of the century".

'I would have thought by now that someone with the considerable intellect you possess would have figured that we share a similar background' he smirked.

'Don't worry Mr McGinley, forgive me, Dr Addams-McGinley, I think I have you pretty well figured out. Is it *just* Dr Addams you still go by? Still trying to make the patients feel more at ease without the double-barrelled name? How's that working out for you I wonder?'

McGinley just pouted slightly and gave a small shrug of the shoulders, though remained silent for a long moment before the smirk returned.

'*Just* Dr Addams' he retorted, 'you know, like "Just Jess"'.

First blood to him I conceded, though he'd been a little slow off the mark. It was beginning to look like this interview was going to be every bit as much a locking of horns between he and I as it was between Brian and Sam Moran.

'Just before we begin' I continued, 'we may have both had training in psychology, but that's where any similarity between us ends.'

I ensured my voice was low and even. Just short of contempt and just barely on the right side of professional.

He nodded.

'Agreed. One of us is about protecting the vulnerable. The other...teaches crime fiction workshops amongst other things.'

Despite everything that has happened to me in life, I had never really thought of myself as someone who needed protecting, at least with the exception of, at times, from myself. Now was one of those times and I was grateful to Brian for taking command of the situation before I completely damaged the credibility of the investigation any further by wiping the floor with McGinley and not just in the metaphorical sense.

'Mr Keys, it would seem that your...associate is casting aspersions against the suitability of Dr Harkin's presence here today. Let me first assure you that as Consultant Investigative Psychologist with the PSNI, Dr Harkin is present at my request and with my full authority. I've also asked DI Amy Macklin to sit in on the interview as I am aware that Dr Harkin has a personal relationship with Mr Moran, and now it would seem, an acquaintance with...is it Dr Addams, or Mr McGinley, I'm not sure which?'

Despite the question not being addressed to him, it was McGinley who answered.

'I use the title, Dr Addams professionally and Mr McGinley in my civilian life, so to speak' he smiled briefly, though it looked more like a smirk to be fair.

'Seems like an unnecessary complication, but each to their own I suppose' Brian replied before turning his attention to Sam's counsel, 'So Mr Keys, as I was saying, I've asked DI Macklin to be here to ensure that any potential conflict of interest is not realised. If you have any problem with Dr Harkin's presence then please feel free to voice it now, though before you do, I would remind you that we extended you the courtesy of advance notice that this would be the case, which is more than you afforded us regarding Dr Addams's presence.'

Keys cleared his throat before answering.

'No, I have no problem with that.'

'And what about you Mr Moran, any objection?'

Sam, who thus far had been staring blankly ahead of him at the space between Brain and I, shook his head vacantly.

'Good, let's begin' Brian said, 'DI Macklin would you do us the honours of starting the digital recording device and introducing everyone.'

With the formalities out of the way, Brian began.

'So, Mr Moran, do you understand why you're here?'

Sam again nodded absently.

'For the benefit of the recording Mr Moran, could you answer the question?' Amy interjected.

'Yes, I understand' Sam replied softly. From his appearance and demeanour I almost felt sorry for him until I remembered that despite the likely conjecture of his legal representative, he was most probably a killer.

'Good', Brian continued, 'Though for the avoidance of doubt I will outline those reasons again for you. Please be assured at this stage you are not under arrest and are free to leave at any point you or your counsel see fit.'

'Thank you' Sam uttered, meekly.

'Mr Moran, you've been asked to attend today to aid our investigation into the murder of Mr Ryan Casey. Further to that, I would like you to clear up the assertion of Dr Harkin and another witness that you alluded to the murder of another person, a female, having been perpetrated also in relation to this case.'

I watched Sam intently as Brian spoke. There was nothing. No flicker of reaction. No tick, no narrowing of the eyes. He really was presenting as the classic, lights are on but nobody's home, patient. I wondered how much that had to do with McGinley. I'd already decided that I wouldn't afford him the professional courtesy of referring to him as Dr Addams.

Brian settled himself in the seat as an overt gesture that he was making himself comfortable. This was going to be a long ride for Sam. One which, I suspected, he should be strapping himself in for. In addition to being a long ride, for him it was going to be a pretty bumpy one. That much I was sure of.

'Mr Moran, in the time almost immediately after being told of Mr Casey's murder you disappeared off the radar from your employment by Dr Harkin whilst still under contract to complete building and renovation work to her home. During this time, a time referred to by your employee, Miss Bella Maskull as one of your "Lost Weekends", the police were called to your home on the report of a neighbour who suggested that there might be something untoward going on at the premises. When officers attended they found you acting strangely and in the middle of what looked to be a major clean up.'

'Having a deep clean of one's own home is not a crime is it?' Keys answered on Sam's behalf.

I couldn't help but think that judging by his own appearance, if it had been a crime, it likely wouldn't be one he would be found guilty of.

'That's as may be Mr Keys, but when you couple it with the following, it does seem a little odd.'

Brian raised his hands slightly off the desk and began to use the thumb and forefinger of his left hand, to count off the digits of the other.

'Firstly, we have the fact that evidence that has come into our possession shows what appears to have been frequent "parties", and I do use the term loosely, involving Mr Moran and Mr Casey amongst many others at the home of Mr Moran; Mr Moran and Mr Casey amongst those persistently engaged in what looks to be at best indecent and at worst illegal practises in Mr Moran's home. Secondly, we have Mr Moran's allusion to the murder of a female in relation to the Casey murder, a female who may possibly be one who he was seen cavorting with on more than one occasion. Thirdly, there was yet another disappearance after this allusion, something of an attempt to go on the run by all accounts. Fourthly, when Mr Moran did return to his home, he handed himself into police custody and later asked for psychological assessment. Finally, there's the small matter that there was more than several traces of blood belonging to Mr Casey found at the property, as well as evidence of the clean-up of what appeared to be a crime scene, let's say for argument's sake, perhaps a murder, in which the materials used for cleaning had both Mr Moran's DNA all over them, partial prints belonging to Mr Moran as well as the blood and DNA of the deceased, Mr Casey. You could see how that would merit a few questions Mr Keys. Now, if you don't mind, Mr Moran, what say you?'

I was expecting the usual, "No comment" nonsense. What we got in terms of his response was a veritable atom bomb.

CHAPTER
ONE HUNDRED FIVE

Staring at the card that she'd placed on the kitchen counter at which she sat, Bella was almost oblivious to the slurping and snorting sounds being produced by Uther, coupled with the scraping of the ceramic bowl across the slate floor as he wolfed down his food with gusto. She'd been careful not to touch it too much on the off chance that it might contain fingerprints when Brian sent it for analysis, as she was certain he would. When she told him about it that was. And Carolyn. Yet, she hadn't been able to inform either as yet. Not because she couldn't, at least not physically anyway.

She was tempted to lift it again. Read it again. Examine the typescript again. There really was no need. She'd already committed every word to memory and she was already sure that the font and script used were the ones preferred by Glenn in the written submissions he'd made to the writing group so far. As far as the meaning behind the content was concerned, she wasn't sure what to make of that. What any of it really meant. Had Jess, one of his patients gone rogue? Perhaps. It still didn't absolve him of any evil intent toward Carolyn, or indeed her, even if Jess had indeed acted of her own volition, which she heavily doubted. There were more questions than she had the mental capacity to deal with right now. Who was the real person behind the Jess persona? Why did he choose to use Jess as a messenger for the card? Was he playing with her head? Was all this meant to be some colossal, ego-driven mind-fuck? Then there was the cryptic postscript to the card. X marks the spot. The meaning had been lost on her until just a few moments ago when it had clicked and part of her wished it hadn't.

The X that was his kiss at the end of the note, when held up to the light was directly underneath the plinth of the picture of the Antrim Hound. That coupled with what she had realised was another cryptic clue in the words, "Get Well" had been all she had needed to get her started. A little internet research and some relating to Sam's company records, of which she had cloud access to, did the rest.

At the time of Sarah Clark's disappearance Sam was under contract to the then owners of Langford Villa, the family he had once been a handyman for. The contract, a landscaping of the grounds, to include the movement of the statue of the hound. The owners of the property wanted to give the statue a more prominent position on the estate, but the reason for its movement had been two-fold. They'd had a long-standing worry about a well in the grounds, and the potential for the child of a guest to fall in there. The hound was once more to stand guard as a safety measure. This time in the form of a cap for the well.

Putting the pieces together had sent shivers through Bella and now made her ache with grief and with the realisation that her missing friend's remains were barely more than 100 metres away from where she now sat.

She would of course speak to Carolyn on her return, and Brian too, since it was he that Carolyn said would drive her home when she'd text earlier to say she was running late. For now she would wait, and grieve, and ponder how in the world Glenn had been able to get that information to her. Unbeknownst to her, the subsequent conversation with Carolyn and Brian later would give her the answers she needed, and more.

CHAPTER
ONE HUNDRED SIX

THE JOURNEY HOME WITH BRIAN HAD BEEN VIRTUALLY SILENT SO FAR, most likely due to our separate contemplation of and rumination over the bombshell of allegations Sam had lobbed our way in relation to Shannon Courtney, now former fiancée of Ryan Casey. Then of course there was the small matter of having to release Sam into the protective custody of Glenn McGinley, pending further charges, having thus far only being able to charge him in relation to his attempted crime scene clean-up.

To my mind having Glenn McGinley responsible for the welfare of Sam Moran was akin to naming Charles Manson as Ted Bundy's responsible adult, a point I may have made forcefully but unsuccessfully to Mr Keys, and ultimately, to Brian.

Breaking the silence, Brian cleared his throat in preparation to speak. There seemed to be a little nervousness about it. Like he was about to broach a subject that he was reluctant to. Despite the relative darkness both inside and outside the vehicle, save for the ambient lighting and headlights, I could see his facial expression and body language betraying likewise.

'I'll have Amy and Mack do some digging on what Moran has

told us tomorrow. We'll bring her in the following afternoon. When is your next writing class?'

'Tomorrow evening' I answered, the thought of facing McGinley, and dear knows who else there, having already flashed through my mind more than once.

'I'll have some undercover units in and around the area.'

'Thanks Brian.'

'I'd be around myself but…I've a party to go to.'

'A party. You sound so glum about it you would think it was a funeral.'

'In a manner of speaking I guess it is. It's a farewell party…for Karen, my wife.'

What he then went on to explain left me aghast and heartbroken, struggling as I watched helplessly as this strong, solid, dependable man unravelled before my eyes as we drove. The poor man. The poor woman. The poor family. My heart now ached for them all and what they were having to go through. I couldn't help but be impressed with their bravery too, particularly Mrs Hannon, and the decisions she had taken selflessly for her family. I wasn't sure if I would have had that level of courage in me.

'I'm sorry. I didn't mean to burden you' he said flatly, having noticed my failed attempt at discreetly wiping away a tear.

'You're not a burden Brian. You're a friend, and one of the strongest, bravest and nicest people I've ever met. Your wife and daughter are lucky to have you in their corner. I'm sure they know that. I'm certainly thankful to have you in mine.'

'You'll be there for the interview with Miss Courtney tomorrow afternoon then?'

'Of course. Then, and any other time you need me…ever' I answered, meaning every single word.

With that the silence descended again, each of us returning to our own quiet contemplation. That was until we reached the front of the house where Bella and Uther came to greet us with a bombshell of their own.

CHAPTER
ONE HUNDRED SEVEN

With Sam Moran safely secreted back onto his boat and last seen floating out toward the centre of the lough, Glenn McGinley finally returned home. Carolyn and Hannon's interrogation of Moran had been intense but he'd weathered the storm, thanks in no small part to his interventions rather than those of his pathetic excuse for a lawyer. Now it was time for a little R&R and he knew just what he had in mind. He was going to have a great time. Jess, not so much. Before that she would give him an update as he made dinner, a dinner with some chemical accompaniment. She wouldn't suspect a thing.

CHAPTER
ONE HUNDRED EIGHT

FINALLY ALONE, AND FREE IN A MANNER OF SPEAKING, SAM MORAN TOOK a familiar seat in a familiar position with a familiar drink and watched. From his spot on the lough the softly lit Langford Villa and its grounds were as beautiful and majestic as ever, their quiet and still, a beacon of peace and refuge that beckoned to his tortured mind. He would nevermore be welcome there though. Not by Carolyn and especially not by Bella. Yet again he had ruined his own life and the lives of those he cared about by his lack of willing to confront the demon within him. Why did things like this always happen to him? Why always him? He already knew the answer, always had. Sadly, the resolution still alluded him. He would never be rid of the demon within. Not in life anyhow. Carolyn's glare had taken on an iciness on the handful of occasions when she deigned to even regard him earlier, and that was only when it had been an absolute necessity. He'd lost her having only just found her. And Bella. She would never forgive him now. Not after all this. The only consolations in the whole sorry situation was that the only charge levelled at him so far had been minimal, and that both women were alive, for the moment at least. He would do what he could to ensure that remained the case, though the irony that he was not only part of the threat to them because of his own internal demon, but also now directly linked to the other threat posed in Glenn McGinley truly sickened him. It was a sickness that was about to be magnified one hundred fold as he noticed the string of liveried vehicles with flashing lights enter the grounds of Langford Villa. Things were about to get much worse for him and soon. It was at that moment he realised how, and who he could hold responsible despite himself.

CHAPTER
ONE HUNDRED NINE

'YOU OK?' GLENN MCGINLEY ASKED JESS AS THE WOMAN'S EYES TOOK ON a vacant glassiness. He already knew the answer. She wasn't. In fact the register of fear and surprise in her face expressed that she was far from it. The way she was feeling would have been familiar to her, he mused, and that's what was probably the most frightening thing about it. Amused, he watched as she tried to comprehend how it had happened. How he'd managed to get his own special blend of psychotic drugs into her system without her knowledge, or consent. Watched as she scanned the dinner table at which they were both sat, regarding the content of the meal they had just shared. He could almost see the tumblers turn in her mind as she tried to fathom it. They'd shared all the same food. Shared the same bottle of wine. Drank from the same carafe of water, except...

'It was in the ice' he finally shared with a sickening grin, 'I poured us each some water but I only added the ice to the carafe afterward. You were the only one to pour more.'

She nodded some semblance of understanding, though in reality the drugs had already begun to take hold and would soon reach full potency. Soon he would take advantage of the fact and couple it with his sickening hypnosis routine. Within moments he would subject her real psyche to a physical and mental attack that would devastate her further if that were possible, while the second of her now dual psyches, the one that he had cultivated for her as Jess Farnham, would be forced to silently and helplessly witness.

'Let's bring Donna Louise out to play for a little while shall we? Give Jess a little rest.' Her vision was blurring now but she was only too aware of the look he wore. The mask of sheer evil and depravity. She'd seen it countless times before.

'Donna Louise has been sneaking out a little herself lately hasn't she?' He continued, 'And Donna Louise likes to play rough doesn't she? That's ok. I like to play rough too.'

He wasn't joking.

CHAPTER
ONE HUNDRED TEN

As had become our habit, Bella and I had arrived early for the class that night. As it turned out, so had Glenn McGinley. Rising from his place at his usual seat as we entered, he startled me, though thankfully not sufficiently that I wasn't able to hold it together.

'I'm not sure it's wise you're being here Dr Addams-McGinley' I chided, making no effort to disguise my annoyance at his presence.

I wasn't at all surprised that he'd had the audacity to turn up for the writing group but wanted to make him aware in no uncertain terms that his presence was not welcome, and that in being here he was creating a conflict of interest for us both in a professional capacity.

'Don't worry Dr Harkin, my presence here is entirely for leisure and I have no wish to speak of Sam Moran other than to say I'm sorry. When it was requested that I work with him I had no idea who he was, or that he had a connection to you. To either of you. Then I started to work with him and he started to talk about you both as part of his therapy and by that stage it was too late. I can assure you though, I was never anything other than professional.'

'I wouldn't doubt it. Actually, scratch that, I very much doubt it, if the number of police currently excavating a site on my property is anything to by. What happened to the Doctor-Patient confidentiality there? I still think it would be best if you weren't here, though, that having been said, I'm grateful for what you've done for Bella, if it turns out that your actions will bring her peace.'

'What, like his actions have ever once brought me peace since I had the misfortune to lay eyes on him? Tell it to the scar in my chest thanks to your sick little friend' she spat.

'Bella please, let me explain...'

'What, how you callously plotted to make Carolyn think that her dead stalker had returned from the grave to pick up where she left off, or how you put a negative slant on your fictionalised account of Carolyn's life stories to create a negative view of her, or maybe it'll be how you had Jess Farnham, or whoever she really is, stalk me too as a way to get at Carolyn, and at me because of my friendship with her. Are those things that you're going to explain? No? Maybe it's how you had her beat Carolyn almost to a pulp then leave her for dead in the middle of a forest, or how you had her slash me almost through to my breastbone and leave me to bleed to death. Is that it? There's quite a bit of explaining to be done there I would say, and that's just scratching the surface if you'll pardon the pun. What I'd really like you to explain though, is what kind of a spineless, arrogant, bastard preys on vulnerable women and uses them to attack other vulnerable women whilst dressing his motives in vengeance over the death of his child? My best guess so far is a misogynistic egomaniac with a God complex, and a small cock, but you're the expert after all, and as I'm sure you'll think appropriate, I will bow to your superior knowledge.'

His stony silence was as deafening as his stillness was telling.

It seemed that the renowned psychologist was struggling to strategise around his current situation. Still, she hadn't given him much of a chance to react before she laid into him again. Go her!

'No, wait, I know. You're going to explain how you sat alongside the man likely responsible for the deaths of my best friend and his own son at the very least, the man who you knew was like a father to me and argued his innocence and his freedom. Where is he now by the way? That model citizen that was supposed to be under your charge. Is he off drugging some other poor bitch before leaving her in a watery grave? That's ok though isn't it? Just like it's ok to attack Carolyn's reputation in the fights to protect the innocent and defend those powerless to do so for themselves.'

Her tone had gone beyond anger now, to a whole different place. I'd witnessed such behaviour many times before and knew what was coming next, what her cynical mocking tone would lead too. Rage…and violence.

'Leave. Now' I commanded him.

'Please, both of you, please hear me out. Then, if you still want me to leave, I will.'

His voice exuded a forced air of calm, no doubt using his years of training to tap into, but I was certain, he was about to break. I exchanged a furtive glance with Bella, her face a worrying combination of apoplexy and fury.

'You have two minutes. We have a class to prepare for' I answered curtly, perching myself at the edge of the desk in the confines of my teaching space whilst Bella lowered herself into the seat nearest to it expectantly, her gaze boring through him. Granting his request may not de-escalate the situation as much I hoped, but it might at least yield some answers.

'So you got my card?' He addressed Bella.

She remained silent, stony, poised.

'We're expecting an explanation not an interrogation' I

answered on her behalf, 'and now you have one minute, fifty seconds.'

He raised his hands slightly in surrender.

'Ok, I get it. Look, I just wanted to explain about all the other stuff yes, but mostly...about Jess. She's not Jess, but you knew that already.'

'You think?' I mocked.

'Her name is Donna- Louise Raybourne. She was a former patient of mine, and she knew Jess Farnham. They were both former patients of mine actually, and erstwhile best friends in fact.'

'And she just coincidentally turned up here pretending to be Jess Farnham at roughly the same time you arrive here, assuming the identity of the woman I know you know, one who had quite the connection with me. Then there's you, the man who is clearly hell bent on trying to destroy me by messing with my head' I snorted.

He clearly hadn't been banking on my having made the connections I had done, judging by the features of shock that he tried to mask. The almost imperceptible flare in his nostrils as he fought to contain his anger suggested that he hadn't been expecting a confrontation of this nature from me any more than he had done of Bella.

'Messing with your head is the least you deserve Dr Harkin. What Jess...Donna-Louise did to you though, to both of you, those things should never have happened. She's sick, and I tried to help her. I'm still trying to help her, but if it's what you wish, what you both wish, she's prepared to go to the police and admit what she's done...'

'...and what about you and what you've done?' Bella erupted again, 'you haven't denied trying to mind fuck Carolyn. Sounds to me like you have a bit of a twisted history in that regard, yet you and your little, whatever the fuck she is to you, and whoever the fuck you're saying she is now, tried to convince me that Carolyn continually failed in her duty of care to women. From what I can see there's only one Dr present who stands guilty of anything like that.'

I didn't look away from him once as she began a new verbal attack, witnessing his face turn from a flicker of shock through anger, then to what I could only describe as disgust as she continued to rain figurative punches on his ego.

'Why the hatred?' She continued. 'Do you really believe you're blaming her for the death of your son? You're pathetic! There's only one person who caused your boy to die. The person playing God with the psyches of the lost, the fragile and the truly evil. Am I wrong? And what did you learn from his death? Clearly not what a sick fuck you are. You weren't devastated by your son's death enough to stop your, what's it called... "How To Be Dead" shit. You just kept right on as you had been, transferring your anger to Carolyn so you could bear to allow your evil, sick head to rest each night on the pillow and to let you rise to look at your vile reflection in the mirror each morning. You disgust me.'

That was when he finally snapped, springing forward toward her in attack, only to slam into my expectant fist for his trouble. I was prepared for the attack this time, though albeit it was aimed at Bella rather than I. The force of the blow combined with the traction of his movement sent him tumbling off-balance and caused him to crash unceremoniously to the ground as Bella watched, reeling with the shock of what could have been.

'You don't touch her' I said flatly.

'Touch her! I will end her. I'll end both of you' he growled.

'Oh my goodness, Glenn, what happened? Are you ok?' The voice, a new voice, dripping with concern came from the doorway where Gladys now stood, the remainder of her posse of Golden Girls and the rest of the writing group crowding behind her.

'I'm fine' he groaned, pulling himself to his feet, 'I just tripped that's all.'

Watching as he dusted himself off and welcoming the ladies in, I couldn't help but marvel at his ability to slide back into the affable ladies' man with the killer smile.

He'd tripped alright. More than they would ever know. His mask had slipped in the process, albeit temporarily. Still, it was enough. I had the true measure of him now, and I knew exactly what to do next.

CHAPTER
ONE HUNDRED ELEVEN

TEARS STREAKED THE FACE OF JESS FARNHAM AS SHE SHAKILY CLEARED the remains of their meal from the table and began to load the dishwasher. He liked to have the place kept clean. "Cleanliness is next to Godliness" he had always quipped. She was no psychologist, but she recognised a God complex when she saw one. She was sure she hadn't been next to a God though, quite the opposite in fact. She would complete the ritual of cleaning she'd become accustomed to after an attack. There was something cathartic about it, and of course it helped take her attention away from the physical pain she had suffered on this occasion. She'd already stemmed the bleeding from her groin and would soon complete a more important cleaning ritual. The one that would wash away his touch. The one that would make the wounds from the scratches and bites scream and cry in protest at the hot soapy water from the shower in much the same way the woman she shared a consciousness with had done as she was so brutally attacked. The one that would bring some, just some relief.

The physical pain would abate, eventually. The wounds too would heal. The emotional trauma though, that would be another matter. Sure, the consciousness that was Jess Farnham had to bear witness to the assault. That had been traumatic enough in itself. It was the psyche of Donna-Louise Raybourne who had to deal with both the physicality of the attack, and the torture of being forced to relive the trauma of childhood abuse as he used knowledge gained from his "treatment" of her to recreate the scenario that had damaged her most. The recurring one of the times in her younger life where she had not only been subject to familial sexual abuse but had also been trafficked by her own father to his friends. Sometimes for drugs. Sometimes just for "fun". How she was feeling, Jess only had a mere inkling of. Still, whether he liked it or not, his "treatment" thus far had not been as successful as he had thought. The drugs and counselling had not rendered the psyche of Donna-Louise completely dormant. Her real consciousness had at times acquiesced with the one he had planted within her, and whether he liked it or not, punishing her would not stop it from happening again. He'd told both of them that he loved them. Donna-Louise had believed it, had been besotted for a while. The cloned psyche that was her, Jess Farnham, wasn't so sure. Artificial as her consciousness was, it, she, was fully aware of what happened to the original Jess Farnham and was suspicious of his role within it. Glenn Addams-McGinley was a very dangerous man. One who she vowed would never get to hurt anyone ever again.

CHAPTER
ONE HUNDRED TWELVE

'You look beautiful' Brian Hannon whispered as he fought back the tears. There would be time enough for those and they would form a river eventually, but not tonight. She deserved perfection tonight. In fact, she looked so stunning, she personified it.

Dressed in an off the shoulder, ankle length crushed velvet dress, in what Brian had been made aware several times after she had finally deemed it a worthy purchase for the occasion, was "Midnight Blue", and accented by the simple elegance of a pair of navy court shoes and a single strand of pearls, she beamed as she nodded approval of his tuxedo and cummerbund, also "Midnight Blue", before taking his arm.

'I'm more nervous now than I was on our wedding day' she said softly.

'You'll be fine, and it'll be every bit as special, I promise' he replied as he gently led her toward the door of the Hollywood Suite of the Culloden Hotel where their guests eagerly awaited them.

Tonight he would be strong at her side as they ate, drank and were merry with their nearest and dearest. He would afford her some privacy with each of them in turn too, to allow for goodbyes. He hoped she was up to it. He hoped *he* was up to it. They'd drawn upon the strength they had in each other before. Tonight would be another such time, and suddenly as the doors opened the stiff formality of his attire no longer bothered him. It was showtime, and as was her nature, she would thrive under the spotlight whilst he sought out the shadows.

CHAPTER
ONE HUNDRED THIRTEEN

'Carolyn, before we get into the writing and the craic tonight, I have some questions about a character I've been thinking of inserting into my story' Glenn McGinley piped up from his seat as everyone else got themselves settled and ready to start. If I hadn't known better I could have been fooled into believing the situation we found ourselves in was normal, and that the tense, violent exchange between he, Bella and I just minutes earlier had never happened.

'Sure, fire away' I replied. It was showtime, and regardless of what had just happened, it was time I took the stage.

'Well, I want to make the character believable, but he's such a conundrum that I'm not sure he would be.'

'A conundrum how?'

'He's the villain but doesn't just present as a good guy, he is a good guy.'

'Sounds like he's a complex character. People are complex, and none of us are completely black or white, good or bad. There's always room for a little bit of grey. Keep going with it.'

Sensing where he was going with his little play, I hoped that my generalised stock response was enough to close him down, though knew full well that Gladys would intervene in his favour, which of course she immediately did.

'Ooh, sounds intriguing. Tell us more.'

'No, no it's ok, I don't want to take up anyone else's valuable time, I'm sure you guys have things to ask about, and Carolyn likely has all manner of things planned for us this evening.'

And there he was again, the picture of chivalry. The wolf in sheep's clothing. Bastard!

'Oh please Glenn, just a few minutes; I'd love to hear about your character and how he fits into the story. Does he fit with the narrative that you and Carolyn seem to be creating together?'

'I'm not sure.' He looked to me, as if for permission to indulge himself and his captivated audience. I could only nod agreement.

'Well, if you picture a man in his fifties, quite a handsome man who has clearly looked after himself...'

'He has my vote already. Is he single?' Gladys gushed before aiming a bawdy wink at her entourage.

'...I haven't settled on a name as yet, but let's say something simple like Sam. I see Sam as being, oh, I don't know, like a handyman or something at the big house owned by my fictionalised version of Carolyn.'

'What a coincidence' Edith piped up, 'that sounds exactly like Sam Moran. He was a handyman at Langford Villa since he was a young man. He was doing some of the renovations there recently too I think.'

'Still is' I answered, tight lipped, 'talk about art imitating life, or is it life imitating art?'

'Coincidence indeed' Glenn continued, feigning surprise, 'anyhow, I see Sam as essentially a nice guy, but one who has been plagued with tragedy. I would like him to see himself as a nice guy too, unaware why, for some reason, the universe continually conspires to make him a killer, much against his will and nature, and more than several times, including members of his own family.'

'You should pursue the character. How do you see him develop and fit into the story?' I was surprised by Bella's question and what would sound to the untrained ear, to be warm curiosity.

'I think that whether intentionally or unintentionally dark, he should get his comeuppance. Have good conquer over evil. I'm just not sure of the type of justice he would deserve. Criminal justice and custodial sentence, or perhaps justice of a more fitting and darker variety.'

'You could have him murdered in vengeance for a life he has taken' Bella offered, continuing with what had clearly become her part of the act.

'I would want him to be exposed as the killer he was first. Perhaps unearthing evidence of his guilt.'

'I agree' Bella replied, before smiling and lightly applauding.

Knowing what was currently happening with the police at Langford Villa, I found myself in the strange position of questioning myself as to where in fact art began and life ended as we were clearly blurring the line between the two tonight. That was before I decided to blur it further.

'Now you've given me a dilemma Glenn' I began, 'You see, I had been toying with character ideas and I too have come up with a villain. Now I'm wondering if they can co-exist within the one narrative.'

Bella stepped in before he'd had the chance to reply.

'I don't see any reason why not. I mean, we've all had more than one scumbag in our lives at any given time. Is it a male? I mean it's usually a male right?'

'Amen to that Sister. You've clearly come across the now deceased Mr Lyons at some point' Gladys proclaimed, before flushing a little as her gaze settled again on Glenn.

'Can you tell us about the character you had in mind Carolyn?' Bella's tone was a model of innocence. She was good.

'Like Glenn's creation, mine too is a complex character' I began, before outlining the charmer, monster doctor, a wolf in sheep's clothing who hid in plain sight. A puppet master who violated the minds of the troubled or vulnerable women that society had trusted him to treat, nurture and protect. I wove the picture of a narcissist who set out to exact vengeance on an unsuspecting colleague who had unwittingly undermined him with devastating results. What I was careful not to do however, was bestow any positive physical description on the "character". He wasn't worthy of knowing that I'd noticed how handsome he was.

When I finally finished, the verdict was almost unanimous and unsurprisingly voiced by Gladys.

'What a bastard! That ladies and gentlemen is what makes Dr Carolyn Harkin a bestselling thriller writer' she proclaimed to the agreement of *nearly* all.

'Why thank you' I mock curtsied.

'What's going to become of him I wonder?' Bella mused.

'I'm not sure yet, though with people like him, they tend to be the instrument of their own destruction. I doubt he'll be any different.'

Chapter
One Hundred Fourteen

For a few short seconds Brian Hannon wondered where he was as he tried without the aid of his spectacles to make sense of the shaded splendour that was their hotel room at the Culloden Hotel. Realising, he shifted slightly to maximise the comfort being afforded to him by the double-king sized bed and luxurious bedding, before again closing his eyes and indulging himself in the memories of what had indeed been the perfect night. It had taken him a few minutes to realise she wasn't there. It hadn't occurred to him to worry at first, though her absence did prompt him to check the time. 10:00 am. He'd overslept. Still, it would not have been unlike her to go for an early morning swim or even an early trip to the spa whenever they had indulged themselves in a trip to the Culloden Estate, usually by way of a wedding anniversary celebration.

It was as he rose to visit the toilet, marvelling that he had somehow managed to avoid his frequent nocturnal urges to urinate during the night, that the realisation that something wasn't right hit him with the violence of a storm wave striking a coastal village. He didn't immediately process why his stomach was suddenly knotted, but knotted it was. Then he noticed the sparse empty space of the doorless wardrobe. The bare hangers upon which her clothes had been hanging. Dropping in angst to a seated position at the foot of the bed it was then he noticed it. A small, crisp white envelope leaned against the empty champagne bottle. She was gone and the thought of it devastated him, almost as much as the fact that he didn't get to say goodbye, to tell her he loved her for one last time. Fighting back the tears he stretched across the bed to his bedside table and grabbed his glasses before anxiously placing them on. Next came the envelope containing her precious final words to him. His shaking hands struggled to open it and when it finally allowed access to its priceless content, it did so with a parting wound, a deceptively deep paper cut, the blood from which quickly tainted the pristine whiteness of it. Pulling out the note with his other hand, her parting words were finally revealed to him.

My Dearest Brian,

Forgive me. I have again taken the coward's way out. I couldn't bear to watch you watch me die, and I couldn't bear to have to say goodbye to you. I hope you can understand.

Please know that I have loved you from the first moment that we met and will love you and our daughter until I take my dying breath.

Be happy Brian. Grieve if you must, but be happy.

Thank you for loving me.

Forever Yours

Karen xxx

That was it. She had gone. Not yet dead but most definitely gone. He would never see her again, and there was absolutely nothing he could do about it. The few short sentences, poignant as they were, just weren't enough for him. He yearned for more, needed more, though part of him was very much aware that even if her parting words were chapter and verse, it still wouldn't have been enough. He had to face it now. She was gone and in her parting had taken a huge part of him with her. A part that he wasn't sure he could continue life without.

The ringing of his mobile from the bedside locker sparked a spike of hope in his heart rate. Maybe it was her calling him? Maybe she couldn't go through with her hasty departure after all? It would be a spike that was to dissipate almost as rapidly as it had occurred. He hadn't even had to look at the screen of his phone. It wasn't her. It was the job. It was always the job.

'Hannon' he answered, flatly.

'Sir' came Mack's words, 'I'm so sorry to bother you, I know you're on leave until this afternoon but...'

'It's ok Mack. What is it?'

'I thought you would want to know. The team at Langford Villa have just pulled a body from the well. Dr Harkin and Miss Maskull have been informed. CSI are en route, as is someone from the Coroner's Office.'

He hadn't been entirely surprised but, like Karen's unannounced exit, the discovery of the body had shocked him. What shocked him more was the fact that it had been this particular piece of news that finally broke him.

'Shit! Ok, how did Carolyn and Bella take it?' He tried to keep the emotion from his voice, still he had been unable to disguise the quiver and hoped that Mack wouldn't notice. Of course he did.

'In shock by all accounts, but otherwise ok', he answered before pausing, 'Sir...Brian, are you ok? It's just you sound a bit...'

'No Mack, I'm not' he continued trying to keep his voice from breaking further as he fought back the tears, 'Mack it's Karen, I'm going to need a little time. Just a little.'

'I'll handle it Sir. Take all the time you need. Oh, and Sir... Brian, I'm so sorry for what you're going through.'

The words spoken by Mack, much like those written by Karen

sent a devastating wave of emotion through him. He admired the words of his dear friend and colleague, which is why he knew Mack would understand his inability to answer further . Instead, he ended the call and tried to process the shock of being alone. Although on a technicality, he had just become a widower and it was something he needed to try to process, regardless of the pain, loneliness and emptiness that it created.

CHAPTER
ONE HUNDRED FIFTEEN

BRIAN'S ABSENCE FROM THE INTERVIEW HAD SURPRISED ME A LITTLE, particularly because neither Mack nor Amy had offered any explanation of it, making me fear the worst. In fairness there hadn't been time, or perhaps there had and I just hadn't taken it in. After all, it wasn't like I didn't have a million other things on my mind, not least of which being the very recent discovery of human remains in the shaft of an old well in the grounds of Langford Villa. A body, which although wrapped in plastic, clearly betrayed the figure of a human of roughly the size and build of the young woman Bella had described as Sarah Clark. The PSNI of course would not speculate. Neither Bella nor I needed an autopsy or formal identification to know who it was though. We were pretty sure of that, though I worried that if decomposition had been halted enough by the wrapping of the body, Bella may well be asked to make a formal identification. That had been at the forefront of my mind on the journey here. That and the fact that the dual threats that were represented by Glenn Addams-McGinley and Sam Moran loomed large. Then there was the other thought. The one that lurked in the shadows of my consciousness in an attempt to hide itself there. The search for and excavation of the remains had caused a small but significant amount of damage to the statue of the Hound of Antrim that guarded the villa and its ground. Since learning of the damage, I was fully aware that I would fall into the trap of worry that the old folklore may indeed have a grain of truth within it, and perhaps Langford Villa would no longer come under its protection, and that both it and its inhabitants now lay exposed to danger. It didn't bear thinking about, which was why I chose to try not to. I had thus far been failing miserably and found myself glad of something new to worry about. Brian's absence in that case, had become a big deal. Still, I was confident that Amy would more than ably deputise for him and supposed this wasn't exactly my first rodeo either. I'm pretty sure we were more than a match for the would-be widow, Shannon Courtney, though from looking at her, I wasn't sure she would have agreed.

The coldness of the glare aimed at Amy and I as she entered had been her only acknowledgement of our existence, if it could even be deemed as such, as Mack directed her into her seat in the interrogation room where we waited.

Clearly an advocate for the mantra of "Tits, Teeth & Hair Darling", I couldn't help but wonder if she was in possession of the most important T that a musician should have in her armoury, Talent. I suspected not from what I'd heard and read prior to this morning. In my further observations she called to my mind the well-known line from Country Music's legendary, Dolly Parton, that it, "costs a lot of money to look this cheap", as she edged the chair backwards a little before turning almost sideways in it and folding one skinny fit, faux leather clad leg over the other and slowly rotating the pointed toe of rhinestone clad, black cowboy boot with distinct nonchalance. Not that I would have called myself a fan, but she reeked of Tesco Value Dolly at best in my opinion.

As her silence continued alongside her determination not to

look us in the eye, I was tempted to ask if she had been expecting Watson and Healey by way of a conversation starter. After all, the tousled blonde hair cascading off the shoulders directing attention downward to the black vest top and what lay beneath, it was hardly wardrobe decision made for our benefit. Nor, I suspected was the vixen-red lipstick that maximised the sultry pout, the heavy eye make-up and the biker style leather jacket that like everything else about her it seemed, was fake. Of course I could have been wrong. Perhaps she was every inch the C list Irish Country Star and maybe it wouldn't do to be out in public without donning some semblance of stage clothing, though I must admit that I struggled to see her in a pair of manky track bottoms and a baggy tee and without a pick of make-up.

'Miss Courtney, thanks for coming in this morning, we really appreciate it. I'm DI Macklin and this is Dr Harkin, my associate' Amy began.

'Believe me, if I'd known what was going to happen when I got here, I wouldn't have come anywhere near the place' she scowled, her eyes now locked on Amy with contempt.

'Sergeant Macklin served the warrant then. Good. Of course it's just procedure you'll understand. Nothing to worry about, it's mainly for elimination purposes' Amy continued, her voice cheery but business like.

'Unless you have something to hide' I added, unable to help myself.

The plan, having clearly been executed with precision by Mack, had been to serve her with a warrant to search her property whilst she attended interview with us. Thus far she'd had no indication that she may be a suspect so who knew what an unforeseen search of her house could bring to light.

'No I don't', she snapped, 'I want to know exactly what happened to Ryan just like everyone else.'

Her response interested me. Defensive, and the only emotion

on display was anger. She spoke of her fiancé like he was a mere acquaintance, not the man who was the love of her life. Not one visible sign of grief whatsoever.

'Of course' I answered, my tone deliberately straddling the line between agreement and disbelief.

'Let's get started then, shall we? Can you tell us a little bit about your relationship with Mr Casey?' Amy asked.

'What is there to tell? He was my partner. We were about to get married' she shrugged dismissively, her expression again reflecting contempt towards us.

'How about telling us about how you met?' I offered.

'We've known each other for years. We've both been on the Country Music circuit since he was a kid, me a few years before that. We've always been close. I mentored him in the early days and we became friends. We were always close and spent a lot of time together. The fans always speculated about our relationship. Some wanted us to be a couple and eventually they got what they wanted.'

Again, she'd betrayed more information to us than her words. It wasn't hard to join the dots, especially since we had the information Sam had provided us in his interview. Information she didn't know we had. What had been noteworthy to me was that her features had softened at the mention of fans. It was only at the thought of them that there appeared to be signs of happiness evident. Not at the friendship, mentorship or relationship with Ryan Casey. Clearly it was a relationship built on mutual convenience as Sam had insinuated. Now I was setting myself to prove as much.

'What was your relationship like?'

'Like I said, we were due to get married in a few weeks, what more do you need to know' she replied.

'More than that', I replied, 'that's why I asked. Did you love him?'

'Of course, what sort of a stupid question is that?' She snapped.

'Oh, I wouldn't say it was at all stupid Miss Courtney. In fact I would say it was a very reasonable one under the circumstances, with Mr Casey being dead and whatnot' Amy quipped.

'Really' came the droll answer, accompanied with an eye roll.

'Oh, maybe you think we're wasting your time Miss Courtney? Maybe I should just cut to the chase! You see Shannon, I can call you Shannon right?'

She nodded her response, slowly, as her gaze tightened on me.

'You see Shannon, I've formed my own view on your relationship and I hoped you would give me more insight but you haven't so far. Maybe I'll give you my take on it and you correct me if I'm wrong. That might work.'

In the short gap I gave her, she moved to mouth a response. I wasn't about to let that happen.

'Here's what I think! I think you were doing your thing on the circuit, probably doing well too, for a while. You'd probably been beginning to break into the big leagues, almost achieving a young girl's dreams of being a star. Almost!'

It was working. Her face was beginning to flush with anger. Time to push the envelope even further.

'Then there was a plateau and your career started to stagnate. Nothing to be ashamed of, of course, I mean, it happens to the best of us right?'

Despite the protestation in her face, other aspects of her body language, like the involuntary nod of her head indicated that I was exactly on the money. No reason, therefore, not to continue.

'Then of course, this young kid came along. A wet behind the ears kid who had talent to burn, and likely a huge crush on you. Probably had pictures of you all over his bedroom wall back in the day. Maybe even spent some personal time with those pictures too, if you get my drift.'

I winked, though inside I was wincing at the image I was forcing upon her.

'I mean, you had a few years on him right, and you know what teenagers are like. Anyhow, I digress. Your career was on the slide, his was rising stratospherically, and to boot, he fancied the pants off you, of course it would only be natural for you to cash in on that. Am I right?'

'You couldn't be more wrong' she answered matter of factly, a steely glare fixed firmly upon me.

'Actually, it sounds like it rings of the truth to me' Amy answered, giving me scope to continue.

'Then after being a star couple for some time, he eventually realises that he's the *true* star, not you. It must've really hurt when that conversation happened I would imagine. Then of course there were the accolades...and the lifestyle. Younger women, parties, drugs. He didn't need you anymore. You needed him though, so you needed to get him up the aisle. The question is, how would you do that? Obviously not with pregnancy, I mean, that would've ended any sliver of a career you had left.'

'You're making lots of presumptions and assertions that are lies, untruths you can't prove, you know that, and to be honest, I'm not sure where any of this is going.'

Judging by her turn, the bolt upright seating position she now adopted and her laser focus on me, it was clear that the nonchalance that she displayed when she had first entered the room was still present, except now it was being faked, and badly at that. Miss Courtney was now scared nearly out of her limited wits, which was exactly why I was going to keep piling on the pressure with an unspoken consent from Amy.

'Then let me enlighten you a little further', I smiled, 'Your beau was seriously losing interest, all the while becoming a bit of an egomaniac, drunk on his celebrity. The parties, the sex, he was humiliating you daily. You needed revenge, and an insurance policy to boot. So here's my theory, and of course you're right, we can't prove any of this, yet!'

I cleared my throat, then paused for effect, much to her displeasure, though I'm sure I caught the faintest of smiles from Amy.

'I think you still have the power to turn the head of many a young man Miss Courtney, and luckily for you, such was his ego, Mr Casey had become partial to bedding both young women *and* young men at his parties. Those who no doubt were on the fringes of the "scene", hoping for their own big break, and maybe naive enough to think that bedding the right people may get them one step closer. My guess is that *both* you and Mr Casey unbeknownst to him, seduced at least one such young man, perhaps more, then you used your influence, and in turn theirs with their peers, to ensure that all the exploits at the parties, including the sex and drugs, were recorded and delivered to you. That way you could blackmail Casey into wedlock, knowing you would be well looked after in any future divorce. I would further guess that you had half the industry by the balls because of the footage you had of them in highly compromising situations, making you the Queen of Country, though not for your singing talent. What I can't work out was when blackmail became murder, or at least, when you convinced someone else to commit murder on your behalf? Care to enlighten me?'

'No comment. Actually, forget that, I do have a comment. I want my solicitor, now!'

'We can certainly arrange that Miss Courtney' Amy started, 'though you're not currently charged with anything. You're here of your own volition and can leave at any point. Before you do though, I have a theory to add to Dr Harkin's. Again, I can't prove it, but if you'll indulge me?'

Following my example before her, Amy gave Courtney no time to answer before continuing.

'You see, despite the hedonism, what you hadn't counted on was Mr Casey falling in love with one of his admirers, and we know what young men are like when they're in love. They'll do anything for their soul mate, including ending their engagement and threatening to expose you for what you are, a manipulative has-been who has had to resort to blackmail. Of course it would've ended your career and your freedom, so your potential replacement had to go, right? You probably manipulated Sam Moran to facilitate that I would guess. I'm pretty sure we can prove it too with time. After all, Mr Moran has been *extremely* co-operative so far. Even with her out of the way though, her grieving beau, I would guess was boldened with rage and grief, in a very Romeo and Juliet way likely, and thinking that his world had already caved in anyway, he was set to happily ensure that yours did likewise. That was when his very existence became such a problem for you. One that you manipulated your own love struck beau to solve I'd bet.'

'This is nonsense. I'm leaving now. I will be contacting my solicitor as soon as I do and I'll be lodging a formal complaint against both of you about how I was treated today.' She was pissed alright, but it was not at how she'd been treated, it was because we were barking up the *right* tree, I was sure of it.

Little did I realise; Mack was about to give us everything we needed to nail her.

Chapter
One Hundred Sixteen

The look on Mack's face as he interrupted the interview had been enough to indicate to Amy Macklin that issuing the warrant had been a good call. Clearly the team there had hit pay dirt. 'Sorry to interrupt DI Macklin, Do you mind if I have a quick word?'

'Of course Sergeant.'

Pausing the recording, she eased her way out from behind the desk and left to learn the reason for the interruption.

'What've we got Uncle Mack?'

'Probably another step up the career ladder for you young madam. Good call on the warrant' he smiled.

'I learned from the best' she squeezed his arm.

'The team are bringing you back a guest.'

'What?' Her eyebrows arched.

'Turns out there was a young man at the property. A young man who as it goes, had wounds on his knuckles and on the palms of his right hand that would suggest he has perhaps been up to no good with his fists and a knife in the fairly recent past. He's a singer too, so they've said, which is probably just as well because he's already singing like a canary by all accounts.'

'Excellent!' Amy punched the air in triumph, to the delight and pride of Mack.

'You haven't heard all of it yet. They've recovered some very interesting IT equipment, including several hard drives and a few laptops. I'm guessing the tech guys will be able to retrieve some interesting information. There were also a few bank statements found that made interesting reading. You might want to get a warrant for a spot of forensic accounting for that.'

'I will' Amy answered.

'Just as soon as you've charged her and told her she's now being detained' Mack winked, 'ACC Hannon will be impressed. Not as impressed as your old Uncle here of course.'

With that he leaned forward and placed a gentle kiss on the top of her head, bringing a smile to her face that widened further when she re-entered the interview room and met the gaze of Carolyn.

Miss Courtney was about to achieve fame alright, just not in the manner that she had dreamt of.

CHAPTER
ONE HUNDRED SEVENTEEN

If Imelda Hannon had known or suspected last night that she would never again see her mother, her reaction to the news as Brian broke it to her would not have betrayed it. Holding his daughter tightly as she wept had transported him back to her early years at the Grammar School where she had initially struggled to fit in and he'd often held her in a similar manner when things had gotten too much for her. Holding her again now reminded him that beneath the confident exterior of the beautiful young woman, she was still his little girl at heart. It also reminded him that he couldn't allow himself to fall apart. He needed to be strong for her, just as he always had been. That much he would do for her, and for Karen wherever she may be.

'You up for going home chicken?' He asked as her sobs began to subside. Breaking from his embrace, she looked up at him, nodding.

'Yes. She told me where to find a letter she would leave for me there when the time came.' Her voice caught at the thought of it.

'Ok, let's get you home then.' His voice was soft, gentle, as always. Of course he had broken news similar to this to dozens of families over the years. Never before though to a member of his own family, and never whilst he himself was feeling like he had been ripped apart from the insides. He'd always been able to walk away from it before too. He would simply break the news that would more often than not, devastate a family, then return to the bosom of his own. That wasn't going to be the case this time though. Yes, he had Imelda and they would always be there for each other, but she was a young woman with her own life in London. When things settled a little she would return to that life and he would be alone...and bereft.

CHAPTER
ONE HUNDRED EIGHTEEN

Bella Maskull really had no idea where she was headed as she led Uther to the rear cab of Carolyn's Ranger. All she knew was that she couldn't bear to be at Langford Villa without Carolyn present and that both she and the great hound could probably be doing with a walk. She needed to clear her head. To process what the removal of the remains from the well had meant. She was still in shock she guessed, still not knowing if she could grieve properly for Sarah now. Would it finally bring closure? Was it even Sarah's body? Of course, it had to be. Then there was Sam, and Cillian...and what she'd done. What a bloody mess the whole thing was. How could she ever expect closure? She would never be able to make things totally right. Never be able to totally walk away from this. She could make things right for Sarah though. And she would.

The walk as it turned out, had become a series of strolls, taking in Loughshore Park, Castle Gardens, the village of Broughshane and the river walk behind it. Of course Uther didn't complain. If he'd known that Bella had been actively seeking out danger however, his outlook may have been different. She hadn't realised herself initially, but her leaving Langford Villa hadn't just been about headspace. It had also been about finding Sam Moran. A task that was proving unsuccessful as yet. That'd been ok as it went. It gave her time to think, to plot. Not for her writing work in progress though, this was a very different plot entirely. A plot that now had both she and Uther stood in the porch area of what had once been her home, waiting for Glenn McGinley to answer the door. It was a risk to her safety, especially after the pre-class confrontation she, Carolyn and he had been involved in just last night. She was past worrying about that now though. Now, the way she was feeling, it should be him that should be worried. Something he surely must have realised from the first moment he set eyes on her after opening the door.

'You're explanation last night was a shit-show' she spat, 'but if you want to make it up to me, really make it up to me you'll get a message to Sam. Tell him to be at the jetty at Langford Villa at 10pm on Friday night. I'll be alone. No police, I guarantee that. I just want to talk.'

She'd tried to keep her voice as even as possible, tried to contain her emotions. It hadn't worked.

'I'll see what I can do. I mean, I'll contact him, but just because I'm supposed to be responsible for him doesn't mean I can control him' McGinley answered, a note of concern in his voice that had surprised her.

'Really! I thought you were all about control. Just make it happen.' Forcing ice into her voice and gaze as she snapped her response, she was sure she'd made herself clear. Still, it didn't stop her trembling from within, and without Uther she probably wouldn't have been brave enough to even come here. But she had. What was more, from the look on his face, McGinley understood that, and bizarrely, respected it.

'He'll be there' came his response from behind as they strode off, 'I guarantee it.'

He knew what he was agreeing to, she was sure of that. He also knew exactly what he was enabling her to do as a result and was relishing every single second of it.

CHAPTER
ONE HUNDRED NINETEEN

Whilst it wasn't the same without Brian, I had to admit that it felt good for Amy, Mack and I to be celebrating what we were sure was the near conclusion of Ryan Casey's murder investigation. My unexpected visitor to the station however, ensured that the celebrations in my case were to be short-lived.

'I figured this would be the only way you would agree to speak to me' she uttered, gesturing around her as I found myself in an interview room for the second time that day.'

Arms folded across my chest, I answered.

'Fine, I'll speak to you, but only if you agree to the conversation being recorded.'

She nodded.

'Whatever you need.'

Something was different about her. It was immediately obvious in her voice. Gone was the cockiness in her tone that had been apparent the last time we had met. Gone too was the self-assured manner, and perhaps most notably, gone was the sharpness in her features, apparent even in the semi-darkness of our last meeting. It was almost as though she were a completely different person, and from what I'd learned of Glenn

McGinley's "practice", suspected that she could very well be just that.

Taking my seat opposite her, I first flicked on the recording equipment before introducing myself. With angst written all over her face, and after a long pause, she did likewise.

'Donna-Louise Raybourne' she almost whispered, before repeating herself, this time more resolutely, 'my name is Donna-Louise Raybourne.'

As she spoke, my mind flashed back to the confrontation with McGinley before the last writing class. He'd mentioned then that he would have Jess come confess to the attacks on Bella and me if Bella had deemed it necessary. This wasn't Jess though. She'd already said as much. She was though, likely the person who shared a consciousness and physicality with her. My training and recollection of what I'd read of McGinley's recent work was leading me to believe that the woman I now faced was the true personality, rather than that of Jess Farnham that he had fabricated and developed within her. Still, I couldn't rule out that she might still be acting under his command.

'Miss Raybourne, what made you come here today?'

'I, I needed to talk. I needed to talk to you Dr Harkin, to explain... because of the terrible things that we've done to you, and to Miss Maskull. We knew that you wouldn't see us unless it was within a secure environment.'

I nodded my comprehension slowly.

'We?' I suspected that I knew what she meant, but still, I needed to hear it.

'Jess and I' she answered, her voice aquiver, 'we've done some terrible things. He made us do some terrible, terrible things.'

I had a million and one questions but I knew that from the point of view of the recording, and it's potential to be used within a legal context in any future trial, I had to keep the conversation progressing slowly, getting the facts without forcing them.

'He?'

'Dr Addams. Dr Addams-McGinley' she answered, simply.

'Did Dr Addams send you here today?'

'No, I mean, yes, but not in the way you think.'

I arched my eyebrows in question.

'He wanted Jess to come and frighten you again. He told her to find you, wait for you and then tell you when she was going to kill you. She was to give a set date and time.'

Feeling my stomach lurch a little at what she was saying and its implications for me, I purposefully forced all thoughts of panic and hysteria to the back of my mind. I needed to stay in the moment. To remain professional.

'Do you know what that date and time was?'

'Yes' she answered, innocently, 'Friday at 10pm.'

Her words chilled me to the bone. My last altercation with the real Jess Farnham had been on a Friday evening. Her time of death had been called as 10pm. Clearly this time around, it was intended that the outcome would be reversed. I wasn't about to allow that to happen. It'd be over my dead body, so to speak.

'Donna- Louise, is Jess here with you today?'

She nodded, apprehensively.

'Can I speak to her please?' I asked, forcing a lightness to my tone.

Again, she nodded, worry in her eyes before the shine in them dulled and her features again took on a sharpness. The physical change, though on the surface subtle, was immense.

'Jess?'

Her eyes narrowed, head tilted slightly, her visage was similar to that which she wore when I had last met her in Antrim Castle Gardens. The look of a predator regarding their cornered prey. I wasn't sure if she was deliberately trying to achieve the same affect or if that had merely been the way he had conditioned her to be, though either way I wasn't going to allow it the desired effect.

'Jess, why did you come here today?'

'I had to, for her sake?'

'Donna-Louise?'

'Yes.'

'Did she make you come?'

'No, he did. He wanted me to threaten your life. She wanted us to talk to you. We want to stop him. Want you to stop him. He did terrible things to her. She loved him. She let him put me into her consciousness. Then he made her, us, do terrible things. He's done terrible things to us too, to her especially.'

Despite her best efforts to stop them, tears had formed in her eyes, threatening to make her meticulously applied mascara run. My knowledge of dual personality disorder was limited, and the fact that one of those personalities had been created by someone other than the person afflicted was unheard of. I'd never come across a case where the personalities had bonded with one another either. They normally remained very distinct and independent of one another, usually disparaging and distrusting of one another. These two however, had bonded, over a combined hatred of him, one that lead here, to rebellion against him, risking mortal danger in the process.

'It's ok' I reached across the desk despite myself, taking her hands in mine, 'I can help you. I will help you.'

She half nodded before breaking down completely, her sobs revealing her desperation and vulnerability, their vulnerability.

'You know, despite how it ended, the original Jess and I were friends, I bet he never told you that' I said, surprised to feel the threat of tears prick the back of my own eyes.

'Will you tell me about her?' Her words were soft, murmured between sobs.

'Of course I can tell you about her, about you' I offered, bringing a short laugh between heaves of grief.

'I never knew Jess when I first knew her if that makes sense. I suppose I never truly did.'

Beginning to compose herself, she smiled wryly at my remark, poised to hear the remainder of my tale, as I suspected was Donna-Louise, the other inhabitant of her consciousness.

'In another time and place, and with I too as another person of sorts, Jessica Farnham was on the fringes of the friendship group of my boyfriend and me. She was his friend really. Actually, his ex, it turned out, though they remained friends, sometimes with benefits I was later to learn.'

'Daniel?'

'Yes.'

'That's where it all started. Her hatred for you' she offered, having obviously learned as much from Mc-Ginley.

'She was obviously ill in some way, I mean mentally' I hesitated, 'anyway, he proposed and I said yes. That'd been too much for her. I've often wondered if he had led her to believe that they might one day get back together, that maybe she would one day become the future Mrs Knox. Of course that wasn't to be. Ironically, she'd seen to that herself by murdering him.'

'She didn't know you'd just jilted him. She hated you for that. Hated herself for it too' said Jess.

'I know. The irony of it all. She killed him to stop me having him, not knowing that I'd discarded him just moments before. If it hadn't been so tragic it'd be funny.'

'The stuff you told Glenn. I mean the stuff that you said in the class, he told me about it. I hadn't known about that before. He hadn't either.'

I swallowed what I was about to say, thinking it best not to remind her that if he hadn't known, then of course she wouldn't have.

'You mean our meeting at Daniel's funeral. No, I guessed he hadn't by his reaction. Anyhow, I didn't see her after that, not until she turned up on campus in Ormskirk.'

'You said you became friends?' Clearly McGinley's "programming" of her memories was not without flaws, apart from the obvious ones. She clearly craved more knowledge, to understand the real Jess more, herself more.

'Yes. We became friends. Fated we said. Fated I thought. I suppose it had been too, though just not in the way that I'd thought. She started as an admin assistant in the Faculty of Psychology where I worked. We chatted, small talk at first, though I got the feeling that I'd known her from somewhere before. She'd said likewise and our friendship had already begun to flourish before we made the connection that we had indeed met before. That knowledge brought us closer. Soon we were inseparable. She was single and I'd sworn off men having just come out of yet another failed relationship, so we spent lots of time together, got to know each other really well. We were best friends for a while, until it started to turn sour. Sometimes her mask would start to slip, particularly with alcohol on board. She would show her jealousy that Daniel and I had been engaged. Then I would catch her following me or turning up at places where she knew I would be. It creeped me out so I challenged her on it.'

'And?'

'She denied it of course. Said it was all my imagination. It wasn't. Other people started to notice it too. Other friends and colleagues started to raise red flags about their observations of her and how she obsessed about me. Then my professional life started to turn to shit. Accusations of malpractice and fraud, seemingly with supporting evidence coming from within the faculty. I didn't make the connection that she might have something to do with it at first. I did think her behaviour around it all odd enough to start asking questions of colleagues within HR and doing a little digging of my own.'

'She'd been responsible.'

'Yes, but I guess you already know that. Anyway, I found out then that she had been the one responsible for Daniel's death. Had served time for it. Logic then dictated she was also responsible for what was happening to me. Stupidly, I again confronted her, receiving a beating for my trouble.'

'There's more though, yes? What happened next?'

'I reported her to the police. They charged her with assault but she was bailed. She disappeared then, though that's when things really began to become traumatic. She made her presence felt every day, until the end.'

'How?'

'My car was vandalised. Then things started to be moved around my house when I wasn't there. Then there was Maisie, my cat. I came home one day to find a wet holdall in my house. She was inside, dead. She'd drowned her I guess. The phone calls and threats started after that. Hundreds of them at all times of the day and night. I would soon go the way of my cat. She meant it too. She proved that just days later when I awoke one night to find her stood at the end of my bed. She just stood there, watching the fear consume me. Then she told me I was safe for now. She just wanted to let me know she could kill me at any time she chose to. A few weeks later she made that choice. My time was up. My fight or flight instinct kicked in then. As she cursed me for ruining her life, plunging the knife at me as she did, I decided to fight for my life, and won.'

My final words brought tears. From both of us.

CHAPTER
ONE HUNDRED TWENTY

As the two women shared a tear across the table, Amy Macklin too found herself dabbing away tears from her eyes as she observed from behind the two-way mirror in the small room adjacent to where they sat. What she had just witnessed had been harrowing, and whilst she couldn't fully comprehend the intricacies of what it meant to have dual personality disorder, she was sure that the person facing Carolyn needed help, and that she was going to do everything in her power to get her or them or whatever that meant, that help. She'd also seen Carolyn Harkin in a very different light. She'd come to admire her in the time they'd been working together. The last hour had multiplied that admiration one hundred fold.

Leaving her observation point she moved to the doorway of the interview room before knocking and entering.

'I'm sorry to interrupt Dr Harkin, Miss Farnham, would you mind if I joined you?'

Carolyn nodded.

'Jess, this is DI Macklin. She was listening in through there' she explained as she pointed to the mirror, 'she's also going to help you.'

Jess nodded her acknowledgement; her face still tear streaked and eyes red rimmed.

'Of course you can join us DI Macklin, but I'm not here looking for help. I'm here to help you.'

With that Amy stopped the recording and started a new one, commencing a more formal interview. One which through the combined experience of both she and Carolyn, they were able to illicit statements from both Jess and Donna Louise regarding the illicit activities of the, How To Be Dead programme, and the atrocities committed against them by Glenn McGinley, the so called Dr Addams both as part of the programme and beyond it. By the time they'd reached the end of the interview Amy had everything she needed to launch several UK wide investigations into McGinley, his medical practice and criminal activity. Donna-Louise had also consented to a physical examination to gather evidence of her most recent assault, and both she and the consciousness that was Jess Farnham had agreed that they would testify to the truth of the allegations made, in a court of law if required.

'That can't have been easy for you' Amy acknowledged when the interview finally ended. She was emotionally drained, so she couldn't even begin to comprehend the toll taken on the others present.

'I think we've got everything we need for now, but it certainly wasn't easy' Carolyn agreed.

Shaking her head and gesturing toward the recording device, Jess again took on a determined look. One which Amy picked up on immediately, formally ending the interview and stopping the recording.

'You don't have everything you need Dr Harkin. That's why we're here. You need help.'

CHAPTER
ONE HUNDRED TWENTY-ONE

Two letters and two half cups of rapidly cooling tea sitting on the kitchen table between them, Brian and Imelda Hannon sat in stony silence, each trying to comprehend the sudden wife and mother shaped void that had appeared in their lives. Each wondering where they go from here and how they could face a future without her.

'We could track her down' Brian half-heartedly offered, knowing that his daughter would never go against her mother's last wishes. She shook her head in a silent no.

'I just wasn't expecting it to happen so soon' she finally spoke, 'and I thought we would have had the chance of a proper goodbye.'

She was still in shock, angry too, he knew that, and although she hadn't discussed the content of the letter with him, he'd seen enough of the length of the text to know that it had been brief. Too brief. It had surprised him. How had Karen managed to concentrate a lifetime of the love between a mother and daughter into a two line parting he couldn't believe. The thought of it made his own anger grow.

'I know love. I'm still struggling to get my own head around it too. Still, we don't know what frame of mind she was in. I mean what she's going through, it must…'

'Don't you dare try to defend her Dad' Imelda interrupted, 'please, there's no defending this.'

She was fighting back angry tears now. Grieving for a mother who had denied her the sharing of her final moments with her. She didn't deserve that grief. Not now. Not yet.

'I need to get out of here Dad. I need a drink.'

'Good idea. A change of scenery and some liquid healing will do us both good. I'm up for that.'

'I think I need a complete change of scenery Dad…maybe with some of the girls. Why don't you see if Mack can meet you for a pint.'

His face dropped a little, bringing a pang of guilt to her.

'Dad I need you; I'll always need you, more than ever now. Tonight though, I need a friend more. So do you.'

He nodded and smiled a weak smile, and as if on cue his phone rang. It was Mack.

'Sir, Sorry to intrude. I just thought you might want to be kept in the loop. The remains from the well have been identified as those of Sarah Clark. We've got some early feedback from forensics too.'

'Thanks Mack. You can hit me with the details. Not now though. Not yet. I'd prefer you to do it in person, here at the house. Oh, and Mack, bring some whiskey with you. That's an order.'

'Certainly Sir…Brian.'

CHAPTER
ONE HUNDRED TWENTY-TWO

THE ABSENCE OF BELLA AND UTHER FROM LANGFORD VILLA WHEN I returned, was palpable. The place seemed cold, soulless without it's resident great hound. The void left sent my thoughts to the damage to the statue of the Antrim hound and brought the worry of whether or not the legend was true. Was Langford Villa, my home, no longer under its protection? I balked at even entertaining the idea.

'Save the melodramatics for your books Carolyn' I scolded myself. Still, having someone just informing you that your murder was imminent, naming the time, date and location, probably could excuse one a little melodrama. Deciding on distraction via the medium of cooking I made a start on dinner, figuring that they'd probably be back by the time it was ready, even if their walk had been a lengthy one. Besides, if Uther's food radar didn't ping on the beginning of the food prep, then Bella's certainly would. The thought made me smile. Uther really was the heart of the home, and if I was being honest, I'd more than become accustomed to having Bella around the place. The time between now and their return would be spent profitably in putting my acquired knowledge into practice with the making of James Martin's, now mine, signature cottage pie. That and putting the finishing touches to the plan hatched between Jess, Amy and I. Friday, 10pm was set to be a night that Glen McGinley was never going to forget. He'd already set the wheels in motion for that himself. There would be a dramatic ending alright. Just not the one that he'd planned.

CHAPTER
ONE HUNDRED TWENTY-THREE

It had taken several measures of his preferred single malt before Brian Hannon had been able to give full disclosure on why he was now grieving the loss of his wife, despite the fact that she was not yet dead. Of course Mack had been aware of Karen's terminal diagnosis, but the rest had been a closely guarded secret, only a select few were aware of until now. Hannon's explanation smacked of the faintly ridiculous to his own ears as the words tentatively left his mouth and were left hanging in desperation between the two men, suspended above the whiskey bottle, awaiting a response. When it finally came, his older colleague, former mentor, had not only absorbed the information with a non-judgemental calm, but his choice of words and actions had placed him comfortably back into what Brian had often considered as the role of the big brother that Mack had played with grace over the years of their friendship. That was exactly what he needed now. Someone who would let him break the dam on his grief and be there to pick up the pieces afterward, which was exactly what had happened there across the table in the relatively dim light provided by the fluorescent tubes nestled underneath the kitchen cabinets. There, where they waked Karen Hannon in a manner more in keeping with tradition than her loss had been, and there where it had been inevitable that the conversation would invariably return to work.

'I think I might be ready for that update now Mack. I could use the distraction, and another drink.' Mack nodded before picking up the bottle and refilling both their glasses, took a sip from his, then began.

'As I said on the phone, the remains have been identified as those of Sarah Clark. The cause of death is not yet clear, though they've ruled out the obvious, asphyxiation and the like. Barry Orr is conducting the post-mortem himself. It's scheduled for tomorrow morning, first thing.'

'Whatever the cause it's a sinister one. She didn't wrap herself in plastic and put herself down the well' Brian replied.

'Nothing from toxicology yet, but forensics have identified the plastic sheeting as being typical of that commonly used on building sites in the form of rubble disposal bags. It possibly puts Sam Moran, or indeed his son back in the frame. Both worked the site at the time of Miss Clark's disappearance, though that's circumstantial as things stand.'

'Are they doing latent fingerprint testing?'

'First thing tomorrow morning.'

'Looks like it's a waiting game for now. I'll head up to Langford Villa first thing and let Bella and Carolyn know officially. We'll place a call to Dr Addams-McGinley too. The so-called, responsible adult will need to bring Moran in tomorrow. We currently have enough to at least speak to him, and hopefully by tomorrow, enough to lay further charges of the type he can't walk away from.'

'There've been some developments with that according to Amy', Mack replied, 'I think we'll soon have Mc-Ginley in custody too, but I don't know the in's and out's. Amy and I think Carolyn wanted to brief you on that themselves.'

'Excellent. Looking forward to it. I hope they've enough to nail the not so good doctor to the wall.'

'She certainly seemed pleased with herself.'

'Rightly so. Speaking of which, I'm guessing the Ryan Casey investigation is all but tied up?'

'Yes. The would be Widow Casey's bit on the side was also a singer as it goes. That's exactly what he did too. Sing, like a canary. All very Shakespearean as it played out. Reminiscent of a modern day Macbeth, well if Macbeth was actually called Liam McCullough and harboured a dream of finding fame as a Country Music Star whilst serving an apprenticeship in his father's chain of butchers shops. He was blackmailed and bullied by her to rid the world of Casey on her behalf. He inflicted the fatal wound, then immediately lost his bottle. She, of course was waiting in the wings ready to take over. They're both in custody and the press department is drafting a statement to the media, scheduled for early afternoon tomorrow.'

'Sounds like tomorrow is shaping up to be a busy day for me' Hannon replied.

'Not as busy as you might think boss. The Chief has put himself above the parapet to front the press conference.'

'Of course he did. A bit of positive PR for him to swoop in and take the credit for, I should've known. No doubt he's benched Amy?'

'Would you expect otherwise?'

'Bastard!'

'I'll drink to that.'

Toasting the successful wrapping of the case and the fact that the Chief Constable was indeed a bastard was exactly what both men needed, Brian thought, the alcohol, company and conversation numbing the rawness of his emotions albeit temporarily. Come tomorrow morning Karen will still be gone and he and Imelda will still be devastated by her loss. A loss he wouldn't wish on anyone. It was that thought that prompted another to push through the fog of his alcohol addled brain. The supposed suicide of Lauren Baxter. Had that been resolved as part of the closing of the Casey investigation? The answer, a disappointed no, had made him wince. He would find the truth himself, and whether he liked it or not, Sam Moran would give it to him.

CHAPTER
ONE HUNDRED TWENTY-FOUR

BELLA WAS ON BOARD WITH THE PLAN ALMOST FROM THE GET-GO, AND MY unveiling of it, post my recount of what we'd learned from Jess, had lasted beyond our evening meal, the finer points being honed by us both long into the night. Now, with Uther's early morning constitutional as we crunched a frosty circuit of the misty perimeter of the Villa's grounds, the topic was still a hot one. As could be seen from the clouds of condensation that billowed every time we exhaled in chat.

'I wish I could see his face when he gets the group message.' Bella flashed a smile at the thought.

'We'll see his face when it counts. That'll more than make up for it. I just hope we can get the plan past Brian.'

'Are you kidding, have you not seen the way he dotes on you?'

Her words made me feel uncomfortable. Of course I'd noticed, but Brian was a married man, one going through a horrendous ordeal to boot, besides, he was a friend, nothing more. A small part of me did wonder if things would have been different under different circumstances, I admit, but then there was Sam. If the current circumstances had been different, that too could have presented a scenario I had allowed myself to entertain. Did allow myself to entertain I suppose.

'I'm sure Amy will have more sway with him if we need it.'

'How you feeling? You know, the cold light of day and all that. Literally in this case. It can't be easy processing that someone has planned your murder and saw fit to herald the news to you?'

'I'm trying not to think about it, but every time I slept last night I dreamt of it. I kept waking up in a cold sweat.'

In truth it had been much more than a few instances of waking up in a cold sweat in the night. The reality translated into full blown panic attacks, so frequent that even Uther had eventually become accustomed to them.

Each time, the dream had been so vivid, playing out exactly as was described. There I was, mid-flow in delivering the writing workshop, the delegates, including McGinley enthralled. Then she arrived. Casual, bold as brass. Jess. The knife appeared before anyone could do anything about it; before I could do anything about it. Within seconds I was prone, bleeding profusely from the three accurately and callously inflicted wounds that would end my life, watching as she left as calmly as she had arrived, amid a maelstrom of screams and cries, none of which were mine. It was always at this point I woke up to a different type of attack, one induced by sheer terror.

'Don't worry, we've got you covered, even Jess. McGinley's plans are set to backfire spectacularly.'

'I know', I smiled, 'I hate to say it, but part of me actually admires his thinking. Bringing the plot of the fictional work we've duelled within, to a real life conclusion. Life imitating art in human tragedy. He's clever.'

'He's an egotistical, psychotic bastard is what he is, and he'll get no credit from me' Bella spat, 'He will get what he's due though, we'll certainly see to that.'

'Best get back then. You've a message to send.'

CHAPTER
ONE HUNDRED TWENTY-FIVE

GOOD MORNING ALL. BELLA HERE. JUST WANTED TO PASS ON A LITTLE note from Carolyn. More of an invite actually. As you know, Friday coming is our final session of the crime writing workshop. Carolyn was wondering if you would like to have the final session at her house. Her plan, if you're all agreeable, is to have a dinner party after as a celebration of your achievements-come-housewarming gathering. She hasn't had the chance to show off the place as yet, and it'll give us an excuse to get our glad rags on. Plus, rumour has it that there will be a very special guest. Let me know what you think.

Bella xx

Reading the group message brought a smile to Glenn McGinley. One of the few of late that had actually managed to reach his eyes. The machine gun response of positive replies to it, predictable as it was, also pleased him. Rising from his seat, he leaned across the breakfast table and planted a kiss on the top of the head of Jess.

'The girl did good.'

'She fell for it. Really?'

Lifting her chin so her gaze met his, he regarded her. The excitement on her face genuine. Her happiness in her actions having pleased him, pathetic. Satisfying. Tightening his hold on her jaw slightly, to the point where he knew it was borderline uncomfortable, painful, he observed as she fought hard not to show any flicker of pain, or fear. He smiled.

'She certainly did my pretty one. She certainly did.'

Carolyn Harkin's reaction to the knell of her death had been a predictable one. Just as he had counted on.

PART FIVE- "COURAGE, DEAR HEART"- C.S. LEWIS

CHAPTER
ONE HUNDRED TWENTY-SIX

'What do you mean am I happy to sanction this, Carolyn? You know I'm not happy, not even a little bit.'

'But you will sanction it Brian.' I tried to push as much authority into my words as I dared.

He paused, pushed his glasses a little further up across the bridge of his nose then trained a withering look directly at me.

'No. No, not without a reformulation of your entire plan and most certainly not with my taking a back seat as a guest. I'm happy to go under the radar but you need to be clear Carolyn, we'll be playing the entire proceedings my way and only even then because I'll be there to lead the proceedings, and because I have a very capable deputy in Uther, don't I boy!'

Sliding the coaster that held his now empty coffee cup across the table, he reached for Uther, rubbing the great hounds jaw and chin bringing a yelp of delight.

'Your Mum is playing with fire with this grand plan of hers. She's lucky she has us to give her a reality check. Any potential victims here would be real, not like in her fiction books.'

As it turned out he would be right...on all counts.

CHAPTER
ONE HUNDRED TWENTY-SEVEN

HAVING READ IT SO MANY TIMES PREVIOUSLY THAT HE HAD ALREADY committed it to memory, Sam Moran again found himself drawn to opening the last text message received on the burner phone, staring intently at it until the screen returned to darkness.

Your company has been requested, actually demanded by one Miss Bella Maskull. Info as follows:
Day- Friday
Time- 20:00hrs
Place- Langford Villa (The Jetty)
She said she would come alone. I see no reason to doubt her word.

Perhaps no reason to doubt Bella's word, Sam mused. The word of the messenger though, that was a whole other story. After all, Dr Addams-McGinley had form. "You can tell me everything. I can only help you if you tell me everything", he'd said. Foolishly Sam had agreed. Help, that as it turned out, involved breaching his trust, a breach that brought almost half of the local constabulary onto the grounds of Langford Villa. Whatever had happened to Doctor-Patient confidentiality? Perhaps that was reserved for the morally scrupulous, of which McGinley evidently didn't belong. Still, he himself wasn't in a position to judge anyone. Her body had likely been recovered by now. Dear, Sweet Sarah. It hadn't been like before with Helen. She had deserved to die. How could a mother not bond with her own child after feeling the little life grow inside her? Not love the baby she had longed for. He and Cillian were all the better for her death. Sarah on the other hand. That was different. He could see why Cillian had been smitten with her. He too had succumbed and to his eternal shame, it was he who had initiated the affair. He hadn't expected her to fall for him, and he certainly hadn't expected to fall for her. Hadn't expected to be planning a new life together with her. A life that would devastate Cillian. He hadn't intended to kill her either. Still, it was he who had encouraged the drug usage. It was he too who had witnessed the seizure amidst the throes of their passion. Finally, it was he who had underestimated its outcome, putting the heightened sexual gratification it brought to him before her need for intervention. Until she was gone. Her life ended, his and Cillian's devastated. Both forced down a much darker path than that either man would have ever dared embark upon. One that would include familicide on his part and bring him to his current position, options severely limited.

He'd thought several times in the last number of days of tossing the burner phone into the lough and sailing off, not quite into the sunset, but enough to escape justice. Equally he'd seriously entertained the idea of ending his own life several times. He had the means to do it after all. The drugs, the alcohol, the water, just like his wife before him, with one exception: He had choice. She hadn't. Neither had Lauren. The police had no doubt made that connection too, or at least weren't far from it. He was yet to reply to the message and Friday was drawing ever closer. In that moment his mind was made up. He would try to evade justice, but Bella deserved to hear the truth from him. If she was as good as her word, which he knew her to be, she would be alone. That in itself was not without risk. She would know the truth by now and he'd witnessed first-hand how she went about exacting justice the last time she'd reached a conclusion on the identity of Sarah's killer. It was a risk he felt compelled to take, if only to see her one last time...and perhaps, Carolyn.

Waking the phone once more he finally typed a reply.

I'll be there.

CHAPTER
ONE HUNDRED TWENTY-EIGHT

It had taken every ounce of emotional resilience she could muster for Bella to be able to continue to focus on ACC Hannon's words after he had confirmed the identity of the remains taken from the well as indeed being those of Sarah. Now, as he and Carolyn remained downstairs, her no doubt trying to bring him on board with the plan for Glenn McGinley's endgame, Bella had taken refuge upstairs in the guest room that both she and Carolyn now referred to as her room. Although working to Carolyn's exacting specifications, she'd had a hand in the design of all the rooms in the house during the refurbishment, and of them all, this room, the smallest of them all had been her favourite. She'd had the most control over this one, and with its Lily pad Green paint, dark oak wooden floor and range of well-chosen accessories, she always felt it had a calming effect on her. Its ability to do so at the moment was being tested to the limit as she lay across the bed, gazing past the tasteful accent curtains framing a view of the lough beyond, trying to process what Hannon had said.

He'd used the term, "The Perpetrator", he'd had to, she supposed. She knew what he meant though, and in her head had substituted his words for the name, "Sam Moran". Sam Moran had taken such great pains to tightly wrap Sarah's body in plastic, he had unwittingly preserved it against the elements, so despite it's having been partially submerged in the water contained at the bottom of the well, the relatively low water table and the tightly sealed plastic meant that the body had not been subject to water damage. The tight seal had also preserved the body for forensic excavation, as had the inside of the plastic wrapping, which had already delivered some well-preserved latent fingerprints under testing, prints, some of which matched those that Moran had given before being released under the charge of tampering with a crime scene. Early findings from the post-mortem examination suggest the cause of death to be a fatal seizure, most likely drug induced. Then there were the traces of semen present. Had it been Cillian's or Sam's? So much about this just didn't make sense, yet on some level it had made perfect sense. Drugs a likely factor in her death? Sarah abhorred drug use. Yet her will could be easily bent, particularly by Cillian. Had Cillian been responsible? Had Sam helped him cover it up or was the opposite true. Her heart of hearts said yes. Sam was, is an attractive man. Sarah could be easily swayed by the father figure he represented, and she had liked older men. If she'd been having an affair she would have told her though. They shared everything, right? Perhaps not, and she had seemed happier in the weeks leading up to her death. Then there was the undeniable association of Sam Moran with dead young women and water. A sudden need to retch exploded in her stomach, sending her racing for the bathroom. She hadn't seen what had been going on right under her nose all those years ago. She'd failed Sarah. Let her down. Even when she'd tried to avenge her murder, she'd let her down again. What's more, she'd worked and practically lived with her actual killer, believing him to be a good man. Flawed yes, blinkered by unwavering devotion to his son, yes, but one of the best, or so she'd thought. Not so though. One of the worst in fact. Heaving over the bowl she violently rid herself of the contents of her stomach before moving to the sink and running the cold water to splash over her face. A few short minutes later as she towelled the wetness from it she caught sight of herself in the mirror. Eyes bloodshot, their red rims puffy, skin ghostly pale, she was a mess. She was still here though, unlike Sarah. She could come back from this. She will come back from this, and no one would ever be a victim of Sam Moran's ever again.

133

CHAPTER
ONE HUNDRED TWENTY-NINE

THE SOUND OF BELLA DASHING TOWARD THE BATHROOM AND HER subsequent retching echoed through the stillness of the old house, breaking Brian and I from our conversation and eliciting Uther's movement toward the stairs.

'I'd better...'

'...leave her Carolyn. She'll be fine. She just needs to process what's happened. She's probably best left alone.'

I nodded agreement. He was right. He was always right, sometimes irritatingly so, though his sagacity was one of the things I admired most about him.

'What about you Brian? Are you alright? You're processing too, aren't you?'

I instantly hated myself for what I'd said and how I'd said it. My words came from genuine concern, our conversation having turned from Glenn McGinley to Brian's personal circumstances but came out as defence of his unwitting attack on my emerging maternal instincts to go to Bella, their tone biting and cruel.

'I'm sorry Brian. I didn't mean to say that the way I did. It's just...I'm concerned about you, and Imelda.'

'It's ok Carolyn. You're right. I'm processing, we both are.

We're both devastated too, but we're battling on, each in our own way. My work is what's getting me through at the moment, just like Karen had said it would, and Imelda, she's taking solace in her friends and her social life.'

Shakily lifting the coffee cup and draining its last remaining contents he paused before continuing.

'I know what you're probably thinking. We're avoiding the pain. Avoiding each other because we remind each other of the pain. That we should be dealing with it. You'd be right, but we can't, not yet. It's too raw and it hurts too much, so we'll avoid it until it becomes bearable, if it ever becomes bearable.'

He'd fought back the tears admirably thus far, but the dam had broken now and I was glad for him that it had.

'I completely understand Brian. More than you realise. I'm here for you though, you know that.'

He nodded, then choked a laugh through the tears.

'Not for much longer if you keep coming up with crazy assed schemes like, "Operation Endgame", he snorted, giving us both a much needed laugh, which as it turned out would be but a brief moment of comic relief, ended by his phone ringing.

His face was ashen as he had ended the call. His work, the support mechanism that was the only thing that had been keeping him together since Karen's vanishing act, had just been unceremoniously snatched from him by the Justice Minister of all people.

I'd listened as she'd offered her support having heard of his recent personal tragedy, suggesting compassionate leave. Leave which he had politely refused, bringing a swift change in her tone as it transpired that if he would not take leave as suggested, he was to be suspended pending investigations of a complaint into his handling of disciplinary proceedings involving several serving PSNI employees and an accusation of corruption against the Chief Constable. The final irony came when the Justice Minister, a woman I had held in high regard from what I'd known of her, dispensed the ultimate injustice of offering early retirement on medical grounds and demanding his use his "leave" to consider the option seriously.

'What a bitch' I spat as he returned the phone to his pocket, the bereft look on his face echoing what I was sure was the expression it had borne when learning of Karen's disappearance, 'she has no right.'

'No, but perhaps she is right' he answered dejectedly, 'maybe the time is right and I should stand down. I was already thinking about doing so soon anyhow.'

I tried to reflect his calm back at him, despite the fact that I was seething at what I had just witnessed.

'Perhaps so Brian, but that should be your decision to make, not one that's been forced upon you. Brian, you have to fight this. You're too good a man to leave under a cloud. It's just not right.'

'I know Carolyn, but I've been in policing long enough to know that sometimes the bad guy wins, and that sometimes the bad guy comes disguised as the good guy. Besides, I'm getting too old for this, and with Karen...Carolyn I'm not sure I've much fight left in me.'

'She was right about one thing', I answered, 'you do need a bit of time. To contemplate your future yes, to heal and recharge yes, but to turn your back on a hard won reputation and well deserved professional status, fuck no.'

'We'll see' he conceded, 'in the meantime, the billing of your special guest at the dinner party might need to be downgraded from ACC Hannon to just plain old Brian.'

'Just plain old Brian is good enough for me.' I smiled.

CHAPTER
ONE HUNDRED THIRTY

As news of what seemed to be the professional demise of ACC Brian Hannon spread like wildfire among the rank and file at PSNIHQ, the common consensus was that the writing had been on the wall from the very moment Hannon had decided to tackle the corruption known to many as being so deeply bedded within the force that his stance would invariably lead to his falling on his sword in one way or another. For two members of the Macklin family who formed part of that rank and file, the view was very different. Despite their working class background, they didn't sing along with the common people, never really had. Which was exactly why the news had brought with it a vow to change the news story. It was likely in Brian's current situation and knowing him as Mack did, that he would have no fight left in him. For them though, they were loyal to the core to their ACC and friend. If he couldn't fight then they would, and they were more than a match for the challenge. In fact they were already strategising for it.

CHAPTER
ONE HUNDRED THIRTY-ONE

It was safe to say that Glenn McGinley had awoken with that #FridayFeeling. Tonight was the night and despite the anticipation of it, he had slept like the proverbial baby and was feeling the benefits of having had his full eight hours sleep. He didn't do nerves, or sleepless nights for that matter. Such frailties were the reserve of the emotionally wanting. A breakfast of eggs over easy, some granary toast and a freshly brewed coffee would be just the ticket. Speaking of over easy, where was Jess? She was usually first to rise but there was no sign of her in the kitchen. Padding through each room in the small bungalow only served to prove her absence without doubt. Had Donna-Louise dared come to the fore again? Had she encouraged the normally obedient Jess to deceive? Surely after the punishment meted out to her last time she wouldn't dare. If she had though, she would pay more dearly than before. It would have to wait until after tonight though. She would play her part tonight regardless. It was vital to his success.

The noise of the front door opening made him start, a feeling of relief at seeing her following. She was already in full costume for the role she would play tonight and looked perfectly placed to play it.

'We were out of milk. I got some croissants too, you hungry?'

He was, though no longer for food. The sight of her in the plain black skirt, black tights and pumps, topped with a simple white shirt, the material translucent enough to show the outline of her white bra beneath, had aroused him. The sight too of her simple make-up and hair tied back in a loose ponytail had caused the arousal to intensify. She was dressed perfectly for the modern day interpretation of a silver service waitress, dressed exactly how the other women on the website were. He had gambled that Carolyn would have used the outside catering company based closest to Langford Villa for tonight's dinner party. If he was correct she would fit in perfectly. That wasn't the reason that his temperature amongst other things was rising though. In this get up she looked more like Carolyn Harkin than ever, more than the original Jess ever had. As if reading his mind she set the milk and croissants down in the hall, took his hand a led him towards her as she took a seat in the low telephone chair, her hands sliding toward the tops of his upper thighs, drawing him closer. His meticulous planning for today had not factored in such an interlude, but it was one he was happy to entertain and Jess was certainly a very capable entertainer.

CHAPTER
ONE HUNDRED THIRTY-TWO

Having barely slept a wink I was glad to see Bella already manning the coffee machine as I came down.

'No sleep for you either' Bella said by way of good morning, 'the salon are going to have their work cut out making us presentable for tonight.'

'I'm sure you'll still be the belle of the ball, pun intended. I heard you up in the night. I was tempted to call out to you.'

'I wish you had, I ended up doing some writing. I could have been doing with your professional input into my last hurrah in tonight's class.'

'You'll be ace, but if it keeps me distracted I'd be happy to read it with the coffee you are kindly about to make.'

'Ok, you sit yourself down, I'll get the notebook, make the coffee *and* walk Uther while you critique.'

'Sounds like a win-win to me.'

I hoped it would be too, especially after the last instalment had been shared with the group. I for one could be doing without any further bombshells, not today of all days.

What would Sarah do? What would she be thinking if our roles could be reversed? Oh, how I wish they could be. That it

had been me who had been placed in that well. She could have been happy. She could have had a new life with her new love, the Disney Princess existence she had always yearned for. Me, I was never that naive, though thinking on it, actually neither was she. It didn't stop her trying though. It didn't stop her chasing the dream.

Would it have been a happy ever after though? Was there even such a thing? I doubted it. Knowing what I now know, I was more dubious than ever. Even if our roles had been reversed we would both still be victims. Both would have fallen foul of him, that monster, in one way or another. Would I have ended up in that well though? I don't think so. I was stronger than her I suppose, though I hate to admit it. I always had been on reflection. Perhaps then it was fate that it would ultimately be me who would be the dispenser of justice to him. Just what form it would take I am yet to decide, but whichever form it takes it'll be no less than is deserved. I've killed once before in vain, wrongly as it turned out. Could I do it again? Would I do it again? In a heartbeat. Was that justice enough? Probably not. Would it make me feel better? Allow me to look my mirror reflection in the eye? Hell yeah!

'An interesting read, one I hope you aren't planning on acting on?'

I raised my eyebrows awaiting her response as she made her way back in through the door, a happy Uther in tow.

'Relax Doc, what's that they say? "Some scenes have been added solely for dramatic purposes". Besides, a chance would be a fine thing. He's done another Lord Lucan act, though I'm sure McGinley knows where he is. Even if I could get to him, I would have to join the back of a very long queue of police officers, right?'

'Right!'

'So relax, you'll give yourself even more worry lines for the salon to deal with.'

Shrugging off her playful attempt at deflection, I continued.

'Joking apart, you know you can't read this right? I mean, the stuff about the well, the police haven't released any of that information.'

'I know, I know, though the local social media forums are rife with rumours about police being on the property for some reason. Lots of speculation about the house...and its new owner. It's probably another reason for the quick responses to your invite to the group to come here for the last class. Anyways, don't worry, I doubt if anyone will worry about hearing more from me. They'll be much too enamoured by the thrilling conclusion to your battle of wits and words with the delectable Mr McGinley. Have you thought about that?'

'Not yet, but I will. Anyhow, I think the real conclusion to tonight's proceedings will upstage any fictional outcome.'

'They won't know what's hit them' she replied.

'He will though, and he'll know exactly who was doing the hitting.'

CHAPTER
ONE HUNDRED THIRTY-THREE

TAKING IN HIS REFLECTION AS PROJECTED BACK TO HIM FROM THE FULL length mirror in their bedroom, Brian Hannon buttoned the open collar of his shirt then pulled each of the cuffs of his sleeves down a little so that the amount of them visible beneath the sleeves of his tuxedo jacket were equal.

'It's the little things that make the difference' he parroted Karen's words as he looked behind him to where she would usually have been perched on the bed, watching as he put the final touches to his outfit when occasion called for it.

'You men don't know how to wear clothes' she would cluck before making some subtle change to the outfit. A collar tuck here, an accessory there which would lift the outfit entirely. He smiled at the thought of how she had kept him on the straight and narrow of making the most of his appearance, often to his dismay. She wasn't there now though. Never again would be. He wasn't ready for this. For life without her.

'You look very smart Dad. Mum would've been proud. Would be proud.' Imelda, who had appeared in the doorway, smiled before walking toward him and tying his bowtie before straightening it.

'Don't worry, I'll keep you right. Mum would never forgive me otherwise.'

'Thanks Love.' He smiled. She was every inch her mother's daughter. Maybe he would be ok after all, and they say time heals right? The love of his life may be gone, the job he so loved too. He still had her though, and that was a blessing he would never tire of counting.

Now it was time for battle. His first without the security of his rank and colleagues. He wouldn't let Carolyn down though. Glenn McGinley would be brought to justice tonight at all costs. He owed her that. Besides, DI Amy Macklin was fully aware of his procedural overhaul of Carolyn's grand plan and had already strategised for its outcome. At least, as much as she could do under the circumstances. It had already had to be adapted further, owing to Brian's current lack of office. Still, if the stars aligned, tonight might also provide an opportunity to bring Sam Moran into custody. Brian doubted he could keep away from Langford Villa for very long given his connection to Bella and interest in Carolyn. Not to mention the likelihood that his "responsible" adult had been told in no uncertain terms to inform him that he was now wanted in questioning for serial murder and must report to Antrim station immediately. Tonight they would find out if it was actually possible to kill two birds with one stone he thought. It would be a thought that would prove foreboding in its accuracy. That, he would come to learn before the night was over.

CHAPTER
ONE HUNDRED THIRTY-FOUR

IF PLANNING ALONE MADE IT SO, THEN GLENN MCGINLEY'S SPECTACULAR delivery into the hands of justice was a foregone conclusion. It wasn't though, and I had to be prepared for every eventuality, especially where someone like him was concerned. Still, the old adage, and one ACC Hannon advised, "Fail to prepare, prepare to fail" had been the order of the day. The order of several days in fact. Finally we were ready. The caterers were due in a few hours. After a chat with Brian they had been prepared to go with the cover of having a "friend" of mine do some work experience ahead of a potential career change by helping serve at tonight's party, so Jess's position was secure. Bella had arranged the rear drawing room into a stylish and cosy yet fit for purpose teaching space. The view from here was wonderful. The glass panelled patio doors at the rear of the room led to the large conservatory where we would serve our welcome drinks and canapés with views of the lough that could not fail to impress, albeit briefly before they were lost to early autumnal darkness. The house had been cleaned and tidied to show house standards at Bella's insistence, and Uther, he too bathed and brushed, was ready to welcome our guests. At least after another of his many naps. The only thing that was left was for me to write my final instalment in our shared fiction, before real life events transcended the art. If my writing could be described as art that was, which my imposter syndrome had always made me doubt. Still, making my way to my study, I fired up the laptop. It was time to get creative.

"Revenge loses sight of the end in the means, but the end is not wholly bad. It wants the evil of the bad man, to be to him, what it is to everyone else." (C.S. Lewis)

Never a truer word had been spoken, and the end in this particular case was nigh. Jess Farnham was primed and ready to go. The moment she had been waiting for, the one they'd planned for had finally arrived, right here, right now, under the roof of the beautiful Langford Villa. It would be a fitting end. The plan had been faultless, foolproof, though she was no fool. Straightening her skirt and pulling her sleeves up as far as the buttoned cuffs of her shirt would allow, she was ready for her grand entrance. All she needed now was the knife...

Reading my newest prose creation back to myself I smiled. I'd always been a fan of C.S. Lewis, and for once, at first attempt, I was happy with how my words sounded alongside his. The stage was set. The cliffhanger in place. One that would be followed by the real life entrance of Jess, and I just could not wait to see McGinley's face.

CHAPTER
ONE HUNDRED THIRTY-FIVE

In his early sessions with the original Jessica Farnham, Glenn McGinley had discovered that his arch-nemesis, the esteemed Dr Carolyn Harkin had once been a much freer spirit. One who by her own admission, had lived her life with a "What's the worst that could happen" attitude. It had almost been her undoing once before. She might live her life with much less abandon now, but if she thinks that would be enough for her to atone for the sins of her past, she was wrong. Very wrong. She wouldn't get to walk away this time. He'd made sure of that. The stage was set. Jess would assimilate into the staff easily, anonymously amongst the melee of the evening after he'd ensured her access to the property via the boot of his car. Access to the knife would merely take a trip to the generously supplied kitchen. Beyond that she would take on the role of a server. It wouldn't be fancy hors d'oeuvres or Michelin starred mains she would be serving though. It would be justice, and revenge, and all upon his command. Patting the folded paper that was his final written instalment to the fiction shared with Harkin, he smiled. It represented a literary attack on her before it was followed by a physical one. The one that would end her life, and he could not wait to see the look on her face.

CHAPTER
ONE HUNDRED THIRTY-SIX

THE RELEASE OF NERVOUS ENERGY HAD BEEN THE ORDER OF THE EVENING for Uther and me, which was exactly why Bella had banished us from the house and the grounds whilst the caterers set up and the final preparations were made for our guests. My choice of venue for our walk though, in hindsight had been a poor one. I usually adored the walk around Antrim Castle Gardens, even in the missy grey of an autumn evening. This evening though, I found it... haunting. Though not an overly Spiritual person, I truly felt I could sense the presence of Lauren Baxter and Cillian Moran, both reminding me that despite the police being poised to arrest McGinley tonight, and Sam Moran having been told via McGinley to report to Antrim Police Station for further questioning, as of the here and now, both men remained free, and every bit as dangerous; a thought that alarmed me even more than I cared to admit to myself. Then there was Lady Langford, whose presence not only radiated from the cold exterior of Clotsworthy House, it permeated the very air in the gardens, her energy, and no doubt that of her own great hound most evident near its statue at the centre of the gardens. It was an energy that Uther seemed to be aware of too, though I wondered if that was merely his connection to me, or if indeed to that of his legendary ancestor. Either way, it had sapped his youthful exuberance, and his gait had transformed from that of an excited puppy, to one of mindful protector. The look that passed between us as he lifted his head toward me as we passed the statue brought hot needles of threatening tears to the backs of my eyes. Tears of sadness, tears of pride, or love, I wasn't sure which, probably all three, all of which, for reasons I couldn't fathom, had made a well of dread and foreboding in the pit of my stomach at threat of the Langford Curse, should the statue be broken, which of course, on my property it had. It was to be a dread that would multiply a hundredfold as I parked up the Explorer at the front of the house, only to catch a glimpse of a cruiser sitting out on the lough. For a split second I thought it wasn't just any cruiser though. I, even from this distance, had managed to convince myself the nameplate said, "Scoundrel Days". On closer inspection I decided my eyes must be deceiving me. Not even Sam would have the audacity to turn up here. Besides, in spite of the fact that neither he nor the boat could be found, the maritime police who had been maintaining a presence on the lough, had thus far not seen sight nor sound of him. I'd no doubt he would resurface and that justice would be served, but I strongly doubted it would be tonight. At least I hoped not. I didn't have the mental capacity to deal with that. Not tonight.

CHAPTER
ONE HUNDRED THIRTY-SEVEN

'Ladies, so lovely to see you' Bella smiled as she air kissed Gladys and her sidekicks in welcome, 'Carolyn will be with you shortly. She's still making herself beautiful.'

'I'm sure that won't take long in her case, as I'm sure it didn't in yours my dear' said Gladys.

'Indeed, you look absolutely stunning Bella' echoed Edith.

'I wholeheartedly agree' came the deeper voice. The one she recognised instantly. The one she hadn't been expecting, having been so distracted by the arrival of the ladies that she hadn't noticed he'd been hot on their heels.

'Glenn, my goodness, you startled me. Thank you, and you too ladies. Let me show you all to the conservatory for some drinks.'

Leading them through the hallway, past the kitchen, through their "classroom" for the evening and finally to the conservatory, the chatter of conversation had been centred around how beautiful the house and its grounds were, what a great restoration had been done, and the exchange of stories around past visits. The remaining members of the class, the younger men and women who had barely engaged with the rest of the group in the previous weeks had joined the chatter and had seemingly come out of themselves quite a lot more. It was something that Carolyn had predicted would happen from previous experience, and she'd been right. Bella just hoped that she would be right about how everything else tonight would pan out. She had hoped to be back in time to see for herself. She had a prior engagement though. One which Carolyn had not been privy too, and one she was hoping would stay that way. Sam, she felt, was a man of his word when it came to her request to meet and his agreement to it , which was why, besides the red velvet halter neck midi dress that everyone had complimented her on this evening, she'd paired with the stylish functionality of her black Chelsea boots. Perfect for outdoor use and the clambering on and off of a cruiser that would be docking any time soon.

CHAPTER
ONE HUNDRED THIRTY-EIGHT

'Ladies and Gentlemen, I give you none other than ACC Brian Hannon.'

My introduction of Brian to the esteemed company was met with a combination of shock and awe, though in the minority of one, abject disdain.

'My word Carolyn, you really do have friends in high places' Edith gushed.

'That I do Edith, and I did promise you a special guest tonight, didn't I.'

'You didn't disappoint, and my, doesn't ACC Hannon look even more handsome in real life than he does on the news' Gladys interjected.

'Oh, don't Gladys, you'll be making him blush. Anyhow, ACC Hannon here...'

'I'd heard it was former ACC Hannon, no?' Glenn McGinley smirked.

'No, indeed' came Brian's confident reply, 'rumours of my professional demise have been greatly exaggerated. I am however, taking a break, which is why I have the time to speak to you lovely people tonight.'

'ACC Hannon, Brian, has agreed to give us a little talk later on interrogation techniques and the police procedure that we crime writers so often get wrong. He's also agreed to a little interrogation himself, in the form of some Q&A in exchange for joining us for dinner, isn't that right Brian?'

'Absolutely! Besides, Dr Harkin here is a hard woman to say no to, as I'm sure you'll agree.'

His response brought laughter from all, except the usual, non-notable exception. He'd hardly spoken and they were already enthralled, hanging in anticipation of his next utterance.

'Speaking of which, it's time for class. I'm looking forward to hearing what you have for me this week.'

'Us too' came the reply from one of the younger members of the group, who until tonight, had barely uttered a word, other than to share his work. Peter, I think his name was. I should really have remembered.

'I can't wait to hear if your shared narrative with Glenn ends tonight, and if so, how' he continued.

'We're all waiting for that I expect' Edith agreed, 'I really don't know how they manage it. It's like they're sitting plotting together when we're not around.'

'Maybe they do' Peter offered in jest.

'I can assure you we don't' I replied, jovially, 'we must just be on the same page of sorts, though I do sometimes need time to adapt my work to suit, which is why I prefer to hear him read before I do, and which I'm sure that, gentleman that he is, he'll oblige me with tonight.'

I tipped an exaggerated wink at McGinley, before leading everyone back into the classroom for the evening.

'For those of you who haven't met him, this is Uther', I gestured towards him where he sat, on ceremony, 'the teacher's pet. Say hello Uther.'

I hadn't expected him to oblige, but he gave a short bark, to delighted laughter.

'Now, if you'd all like to take a seat, and Glenn, you can begin when you're ready' I instructed. Moments later, he began.

'The cruiser wasn't that far offshore where it floated on the choppy grey lough. For those forced to watch from dry land as events unfolded however, it may as well have been a million miles away. Amongst the young woman's many endearing qualities, people had sometimes described her as being feisty. Others had used the word, "ballsy" as misguidedly misogynistic as it was. As of this moment though, she was out of her depth, almost literally.

She'd gone there to meet him with the sole intention of ending his life. After all, it had not been the first time she'd committed such an act. She was a killer. She didn't look like one, but as she herself had speculated through the medium of fiction, what does a killer look like? The answer in this case was very much like the man who stood facing her now on the boat. Identical in fact.

She'd underestimated him. Never truly knew who he was or what he was capable of. She'd also gravely misjudged the lengths a man could go to, to protect his secrets, and his freedom.

She'd sought to beat him at his own game, weakening his strength and resolve through ingestion of prescription medication. She'd even used her wiles to ensure the medication had been that which he'd used to similar effect on others. Her plan, to wait until he was almost at the point of unconsciousness, then, "guide" him over the side. She had taken charge of the boat before. She could guide it into the mooring again tonight with ease.

He would of course be discovered in due course. A poor man driven demented by his demons, forced down a dark path that ultimately had ended in suicide. She would grieve as expected too. Devastated at the loss of the closest thing to a father she had ever known. To those forced to witness it though, including the large Irish Wolfhound growling and barking in desperation to be her hero, this was not how events were playing out. It was the shouting that had first drawn their attention, the sound carrying easily to where they were holding their writing class. Now, as she had slapped, punched and pushed while he tried to fend her off, he seemed to snap, grasping her throat tightly for what seemed like minutes, before pushing her violently back into a seated position on the deck. Turning, he'd attempted to pour himself a drink, the whiskey bottle still in hand as she lurched at him again. Then came the sickening crack as the bottle met with her head, sending her sprawling, splayed across the deck. Hearing their cries from the shore as if for the first time, he looked at them for a long moment. It was after that he had slowly gone to her, lifted her as if to help. Then the splash came, and the sound of the boat's engine firing up. She was gone, and so was he.'

The tension in his words had compelled me to turn to Bella, in search of her reaction. She was gone though, and so was Uther.

CHAPTER
ONE HUNDRED THIRTY-NINE

McGinley had barely taken a breath to read when Bella had quietly slipped out. She'd had an unexpected escort as Uther had quietly led her to the jetty where the boat waited.

'Ok Boy! That's far enough. I can take it from here.'

He gave a soft howl before seating himself on the grass embankment, watching as she walked on, eventually stepping onto the boat. He'd stood at the helm, a silhouette, with his back to her in the moonlight. His figure mysterious, unnerving. Hearing her and feeling the boat shift, he turned around.

'Bella' he said softly, moving to embrace her, his face already streaked with tears in the moonlight.

'No Sam.' She refused his embrace, arms outstretched in a barrier to stop him.

'Bella, I'm so sorry. I wanted to tell you. So many times I wanted to tell you', his voice a quiver as he desperately pushed out the words.

'What for Sam?' She spat. 'What are you sorry for exactly?'

'Please, let's get out of here. Take a seat. We can talk out on the lough.'

'You really think I'm going to fall for that Sam. Sit there

sipping whiskey with a blanket around me while you tell me all your sad little life stories and give it the whole woe is me act. Did you do that with all the girls Sam? Your victims? Carolyn told me she'd been subject to your charms that way. Such a smooth operator, eh? Was she to be your next victim then, was that the intention, or are you going to give me the bad things happening to a good man, controlled by his demons shit?'

It took a full few seconds before he could respond, stood, stock still, in shock at her words.

'No, it wasn't like that. I'm not like...'

'Save your shit Sam! Yes, we do need to get out of here, and I've got just the place in mind. Bring your whiskey bottle with you. You're going to need it.'

The last thing she expected from him was silent compliance as she alighted the boat and began her purposeful march, Uther falling into step beside her as she passed him. He was there though, matching every stride, a few subservient steps behind her and her canine protector until she reached the recently excavated well and the statue that had once sealed it, now sitting just a few short feet away. Instinctively, Bella pulled herself up onto the plinth upon which the statue, Uther's stone counterpart sat, standing briefly at its flank before dropping into a seated position, legs hanging from the edge as Sam watched, waited, the whiskey bottle hanging from the grip of his right hand and Uther took his place as sentry by her side. For a few short moments she sat still, gaze locked on him, her face a picture of contempt before reaching out and gesturing for the bottle. Again he complied, closing the distance between them to a low growl from Uther and offering her the bottle and watching as she raised it to her mouth and took a generous mouthful before swallowing hard and handing it back to him.

'Take some. Like I said, you'll probably need it.'

'The condemned man's last drink eh?'

'Well you are a wanted man, and it just so happens that the Assistant Chief Constable and some of his people aren't very far away.'

'That's not what I meant' he answered, his eyes narrowing as he surveyed her reaction.

'What, you think I'm going to kill you? I won't lie, the thought had crossed my mind.'

'Well, it wouldn't be first time that you ended the life of a Moran man is it?'

The aggression in his tone was more than matched by another growl from Uther and the raising of his heckles, prompting Sam to take a few steps backwards and moderate his tone.

'You think I didn't know what you did to Cillian?'

'Actually, until recently I didn't, and to be clear, what I did to Cillian is something I have had to live with every second of every day since. It has consumed me just as much as what happened to Sarah. But I worked it out Sam. Worked you out.'

Lowering his gaze to the ground, though studiously avoiding the opening of the well, all fight seemed to desert Sam. In times gone by it would have been enough to bring Bella rushing to his side to offer consolation. This was now though, and she was far from done with him.

'You apologised earlier, back at the boat. You were sorry, wanted to explain everything. Now's your chance. Let's start with how you killed your son and left me to think I'd been responsible.'

Her words were enough to send a shot of anger through him, aggression again visible from his stance and the look he wore.

'I didn't, it wasn't' he growled before she interjected, a clinical chill clinging to her words.

'Except you did Sam. You see, I replay my last moments with Cillian over and over again, every, single, day! The confrontation, the push, the fall. The look in his eyes. There was something that hadn't occurred to me though, until recently. The generator. It wasn't on when I was there. There was no need for it to be. Even at the inquest when I stood there by your side, supporting you, comforting you, I hadn't realised it. Even when carbon monoxide poisoning was cited as a contributing factor in his death I didn't make the connection. He was alive when you obviously came across him. The lungs full of fumes testify to that. You could have saved him. You didn't though, and now we both know why. Is that what you wanted to explain, or was it about what you did to Sarah? Cillian knew you'd killed her. He helped you dump her here after all, which is exactly why you made the most of my having pushed him, I realise all that now.'

Her words met with silence; it was her turn to watch as he gulped down a mouthful of the whiskey before returning his gaze to her. A gaze as cold and stony as that of the statue she was leant against.

'So where is it, this great explanation of yours? Or maybe I've got it wrong and you haven't murdered my best friend and my boyfriend.'

'It was an accident. Sarah I mean, it was an accident. I didn't mean for her to die.'

He let out a short sigh before continuing, his voice ragged.

'You may not believe me but I loved her. I still love her. There's not a day that passes that I'm not crushed by her loss, by the loss of both of them. I miss them more than you could ever realise.'

'Yet, you discarded her like she was worthless and denied her any dignity in death. Denied us the chance to mourn her.'

'I'm sorry' his voice cracked and the tears began to streak slowly down his face.

'Only for yourself Sam. Save it, please. Just tell me what happened.'

'We'd been...seeing each other.'

'Having an affair. Presumably Cillian didn't know?'

'No, and I'm not proud. I didn't mean for it to happen. I tried to resist but she was always around and the more I got to know her, despite the age difference, the more I came to like her, then to love her.'

'Until you killed her.'

Ignoring Bella's barbed words, he continued in his justification.

'We were going to tell him. We were planning a life together. Then there was that night, and the drugs. She'd been pressurising me for a while. She knew the recreational effects my medication could have and she said she wanted it. Needed it. I was weak.'

'You were more than weak. You were pathetic. You didn't love her or you wouldn't have given in. You probably encouraged it. I mean you were hardly thinking with your brain were you. It sounds to me like you exploited her. You should have been a father figure not a...creep!'

Her words continued to deflect from him without reaction. He needed this, she realised. He needed to get the weight of the past off his chest and as much as she didn't want to alleviate his emotional burden, she needed to hear what he had to say, for her own sake. She would replace his burden later, and then some.

'She came to see me the night of the Halloween party, before she was due to meet Cillian. It was supposed to be just a quick drink but she took some of my meds too before one thing led to another and... Anyway, she was fine, but then she suddenly took some kind of seizure. It all happened so quickly. I tried to help but it all happened so quickly. She was gone before I could do anything. If I'd known it would have caused such a reaction I would never have...'

'But you did. No matter how you try to dress it up, this wasn't just some tragic accident. It was no more an accident than Cillian's mother's death and I'll bet you've somehow managed to absolve yourself from any responsibility for that too. Some twisted logic that makes you the victim. Poor Sam, he didn't ask for any of this, and he's such a nice guy right? I'm sure Cillian didn't think so when he found out. Maybe you can enlighten me?'

'He was livid. I thought he was going to kill me. Until he broke. Then he was heartbroken. He kept saying that he'd lost everyone he'd ever loved. Sarah and his mum were dead and as far as he was concerned, I may as well have been. He wanted to call the police, but I couldn't let him do that. I told him it was time for him to back me. Time for him to turn a blind eye to what I'd done, just as I'd done those countless times for him. He did, and for a while I thought everything was going to be fine but then he told you he knew Sarah was dead and I worried he might go to the police until...what you did.'

Slowly, Bella eased herself off the plinth and stood shakily facing him, her own face now streaking with tears that she could no longer hold back.

'So what happens now? Where do we go from here?'

Sam's words, though low and even, had an unmistakeable air of fear in them.

'We go find ACC Hannon and you confess...to everything.'

'Bella I can't' he pleaded, 'Believe me, I am so sorry for everything I've done to them and to you. I love you like a daughter. I'd do anything for you, but I couldn't survive prison. I'd rather die and believe me when I say that I've contemplated ending things, more than once.'

'Was that before or after you got yourself involved with Ryan Casey? You certainly embraced your demons *and* others when you met him, didn't you? Or was it after you let history repeat itself yet again leaving another drugged up young woman in a watery grave? I suppose that wasn't your fault either. Women who love you seem to end up that way don't they? I dread to think what could have happened to Carolyn, or me for that matter, the daughter you never had, if we hadn't realised.'

'I would never have hurt you. Either of you' he growled.

'You'll forgive me if I don't believe you Sam. Despite your delusions otherwise, you were always a very real threat to us. You see, your love doesn't seem to count for much, especially when you kill everyone you claim to love. I'm sure you'd have loved the baby too. Your future son or daughter. It was too early to tell which. We'll never know now since you murdered them when you ended their mother's life. Still, at least they were spared ever having to set eyes on you.'

It was all Bella could do not to smile as she delivered the news that Sam's most recent victim was his unborn child. Of course she felt for the child, felt for all of his victims, but she had relished every second of this, their last conversation and it's crushing effect on him. She'd looked forward to it. Planned for it. Just like she'd planned for exactly what would happen next.

CHAPTER
ONE HUNDRED FORTY

IN ACCORDANCE WITH MCGINLEY'S INSTRUCTIONS, JESS FINALLY EXITED the car. Stretching the stiffness out of her joints from where she'd lain so long under a fleece blanket on the back seat, she first noticed her reflection in the rear passenger window, her face ghostly white in the moonlight. It was an apt image. That's what she was after all right. A ghostly facsimile of the original Jessica Farnham. She would lay that ghost to rest tonight. They both deserved that.

The next thing she noticed was the noise, the commotion. Two people arguing by the sound of it, a dog growling too. Was she too late? She moved quickly towards the sound. It was Bella, and a man. Perhaps Sam Moran? They were near the statue of the stone hound. As she neared, the argument appeared to escalate. Became physical. Even as she got closer still, she remained oblivious to them. They were completely immersed in the argument, the dog's growls and snarls getting louder before escalating to a ferocious bark as its large muscular back arched, ready to pounce. She'd almost cried out when it happened. The swing of the bottle, the sickening crack of glass on bone, then the leap of the dog, followed by another sickening crack, this time louder as the skull met the concrete edge of the stone plinth upon which the statue likeness of the dog stood. It was only then her presence was noted.

'Help me' came the voice, surprisingly low and even in tone. Which was exactly what she did.

CHAPTER
ONE HUNDRED FORTY-ONE

As soon as I'd registered the absence of Bella and Uther, McGinley's words had sent me racing toward the jetty, Brian matching me stride for stride. The cruiser was there, but they weren't. It was on that realisation that we first heard Uther's cries, alerting us to his location. Hers too I hoped. It was at the statue we found them, she battered, bruised and bleeding a little. Uther, seemingly unscathed, tending her.

'Oh Thank God. You're ok.' I heard myself shakily utter before kneeling and embracing them, as hard as I could; never again wanting to let them go as Bella and I shared a river of tears.

'Was Moran here?' I heard Brian ask, his voice a mixture of sympathy and urgency. Bella, breaking gently from our embrace nodded her response before answering a tearful yes.

Brian nodded, his face grave.

'You should call Amy. Have the grounds searched' I urged Brian, 'We'll need an ambulance too. Get her checked out.'

'No, please, it's nothing, I'm ok.' Bella pleaded, 'Everything's ok'.

It wasn't though. I knew that now. We all did, from the moment I had noticed the ground around the well had been disturbed, saw the drag marks, the broken glass and evidence of bloodshed greater than that coming from Bella's injuries. The look that ran between us had confirmed it. Justice had been served, and despite my better judgement, on some level I was ok with that.

'Carolyn, we need to get him out of there' Brian commanded. He was right of course, as always. Which was exactly what we did, and with the help of Bella, to her credit. Our efforts were in vain though. We were too late. Sam Moran had already breathed his last, and despite myself, I couldn't help but think that the fact that it had been taken in the very place he had concealed the body of the vivacious young woman he'd made his victim, made it a fitting end for him.

'I'll have some questions when you're feeling able for it, and of course I'll need you to make a statement' Brian said to Bella as he briefly put a comforting arm around her as we stood over Moran's remains before withdrawing it and returning to the business of alerting Amy and Mack to the scene. I had been expecting him to arrest her, not comfort her until I realised. She might well have been guilty of concealing a crime, but she hadn't been responsible for Moran's death. That responsibility had fallen to her canine protector and I would be eternally grateful to him that it was so.

'What happens now Brian?' I asked.

'You two go back inside. Get Bella cleaned up then both get back to your guests. You might need to round some of them up first. Give them a refreshment break, of the liquid variety. I'll follow in when I get things under control here. Then back to the writing chat before we give Mr McGinley his own little surprise

CHAPTER
ONE HUNDRED FORTY-TWO

Jess Farnham exchanged a nod with the Catering Manager before checking herself over one final time and commencing duty. She'd already removed all evidence of her recent encounter from her uniform in the cloakroom and had cleaned herself up. Miraculously, she'd managed to avoid the blood and the vast majority of the mud. Lifting a tray, she began to prepare the drinks order that had just come through from the guests. She would gladly prepare them; in fact it was imperative that she did. One of the others would serve though, as per the agreement. She would remain back of house, for now. Quite literally in this case. It wasn't her time to shine. Not yet. It *was* game on though, and tonight had already been a success of sorts in one fiend being dispatched to an apt resting place where they could harm no longer. Admittedly, it was a lot colder and wetter than the hell she'd guessed he probably deserved, but it would suffice. Another demon would soon meet their fate too, and she couldn't wait to see the look on his face.

CHAPTER
ONE HUNDRED FORTY-THREE

It had been Amy's instructions rather Brian's that their fellow officers had followed in the end, given his newly bestowed civilian status. With a degree of impartiality in the case of Sam Moran that would ensure an ordered and responsible command, but with more than a vested interest in Glenn McGinley being brought to justice, it had been she, ably assisted by Mack who decided that the removal of the body from the grounds would be low key and under the radar of the public and the media alike, but for the moment, perhaps most importantly, those attending the class. Its commencement was to be vital.

'I must confess Glenn, that you had me captivated tonight. So much so that when I noticed Bella and Uther missing, I feared the worst.'

'A pretty female victim and possibly the death of a much loved animal. Two tropes of crime writing of which only one the audience could ever forgive.' To my surprise, having not quite finished what I presumed was his first drink of the evening, his words were slurred and his eyes glassy as he delivered a wry smile.

'I'm only a fire short of the "Big House" crime novel tropes that we talked about before. Still, there's time yet I suppose. We have yet to hear from the good doctor here' he continued, addressing the others as opposed to me, an edge to his increasingly slurred words which seemingly had his desired effect on his audience. The air was charged with tension as I rose and began to read.

I watched him carefully, glancing at him with increased frequency each time I lifted my eyes from the text. His glassy stare was fixed straight ahead, a look of puzzlement on his face. Something else too. Worry?

When I finally got to the line,

'All she needed now was the knife' I paused for dramatic effect. It had been Jess's cue to enter knife in hand. It was all set. All eyes on her as she entered, I waited, to see his look of shock, his reaction when as we planned, she relieved herself of the prop and levelled the allegations of his torture and abuse to his face. Except there wasn't one. Instead, as she purposefully entered and made toward him with the knife, there was merely a flicker of recognition as he watched, increasingly zoned out, as everyone, me included, waited with bated breath as the menacing looking server with a lethal looking knife crossed the room. To our collective surprise, Jess walked right up to him, knife at her side, leaned down, kissed him lightly on the top of the head then moved her mouth to his ear.

'Surprise' she said softly, before straightening up and introducing herself to the assembled company as a surprise guest. Her greeting of him and his reaction to it concerned me. Something wasn't right. I rose and moved toward them. It was then she raised the knife again, holding it across his throat.

'Relax Dr Harkin. You asked me here to tell everyone who this man is, what he's capable of and what he'd intended me to do with this knife. Your fictionalised version came remarkably close, I must say. Now I will fill in the blanks if you will allow.'

Moving the knife marginally away from the skin on his neck,

she set about telling us her story, the story of the real Jess, that of her actual personality, Donna-Louise, and what my fate tonight was set to be. All the while we sat listening, frozen, captive, perhaps in both senses of the word. I'd of course heard her words before, lived some of them. It didn't stop me being chilled to the core, as I suspected everyone else in the room was too. Except one. The one who through dulled senses I suspected was only half hearing them, his addled mind preoccupied by a very different situation. As she concluded, she again put her mouth to his ear. She spoke softly, her breathless tone deliberately flirtatious.

'You like a stiff drink don't you my love. Fixed just the way you like it. Lots of ice. Your own special ice. Made to your own recipe, kind of. To paraphrase a once great man, "it was in the ice." You don't have long my love. The girl did good, didn't she.' She smirked as she playfully dragged the knife over the edge of the skin of his throat, breaking it in part as she did so, creating a garish necklace of bloody pearls as a result.

Another kiss to the top of the head then she slowly made to leave. It was then to my surprise that he sprang at her with a primal scream only to stumble and crash across the table before tumbling violently to the floor. As if unaware, she continued, supposedly making good her escape.

'I can't let you leave Miss Farnham, you know that' Brian said calmly as I frantically fumbled with my phone to call for an ambulance as others went to his aid.

'Do what you need to do. Jess Farnham has no plans to leave here tonight. Not alive anyhow.'

'Leave her Brian' I heard myself say as the voice of the ambulance control room still spoke in my ear, 'there are no paramedics available for at least 45 minutes. We need to get him to the truck.' I ended the call, an involuntary response to the situation that directly contravened exactly what I'd been told not to do at the beginning of the call. Despite my increased levels of shock I still noted that she'd said that Jess would not be leaving. Donna-Louise on the other hand, that identity had been omitted. Deliberately I concluded.

Turning his attention from her as she swept past him, to McGinley, whose pallor was greying as he started to convulse, it was Brian's turn to spring forward.

'Help me lift him' he instructed those around McGinley.

Under their combined strength he was soon in the back of the Explorer, Brian applying his limited medical training to the best of his ability as I gunned the truck down the lane. It was as we neared the stone hound, she shot across us, at the wheel of McGinley's car, a deliberate and reckless attempt to stop us at all costs from saving her tormentor. Swerving, I managed to avoid collision with her. Not with the statue of the great Langford hound though. As the Explorer careered towards it, seemingly in slow motion, I had the fleeting thought that the class had gotten the big ending they'd been anticipating after all. A "Big House" crime story with all the bells and whistles they ever could have wished for. Still no fire though. That was until the fireball of the explosion ironically plunged Brian and I into the blackness that McGinley had already succumbed to, bathed their shocked faces in an amber glow and reflected in the ripples of the lough like an exploded firework over the dark water. As crime fiction stories go, this one, from the very start had certainly been set to end with a bang.

EPILOGUE

In the two months that had passed since Brian and I had almost lost our lives in a fireball of stone and metal, life had become full of colour again for me. I suspected likewise for him. Despite his continued grief for Karen, having come so close to death himself, it had given him a degree of perspective, as it had for me. As it turned out, the great hounds of Langford Villa both shattered stone and otherwise, had saved the lives that warranted saving that night. Lives that from then on, deserved to be lived to the fullest. Now, as we sat in the kitchen snug, plates almost cleared and sharing a rich, fruity Merlot while listening to the snores of a content Uther as he slept in front of the fire, there was a lot to live for. Though Jess / Donna- Louise had not yet been caught, I suspected strongly that we would never cross paths again. Just like I suspected that the discovery of the secret that had been buried underneath the newly restored statue of the Langford Hound had set Bella free to live her life again. I'd persuaded her to move in full time and had helped her start her own business, just where Sam's had left off. She was, in her own words, 'out-out' for the night tonight, "leaving us oldies to it", I quote. On a date, as it goes, and with a certain young man from the writing class, who as it turned out, had been so quiet all that time because he was painfully shy and had been completely smitten with her. Still was. For Brian, he'd not only avoided forced retirement, but had risen to the rank of Chief Constable, his predecessor having been removed from the role courtesy of a media storm exposing his failings and those of the force he had partaken in covering up. Despite his efforts to find out how the information had reached the media in the first place; Brian had so far been unsuccessful. I suspected that Mack and Amy may have known more about that than they had indicated to him. Particularly since I had learned from Beth Shaw that Amy's collaboration with Farset Investigations had fostered a strong friendship between her and the fiery female Editor of The Belfast Chronicle. I suspected Brian may have learned likewise, but neither of us would ever ask. We'd both be forever thankful but would never ask. Imelda too was starting to move on from the loss of her mother, having just accepted a leading role on the West End that I'm told Karen would have been immensely proud of.

Glenn McGinley had of course lost his life in the accident that night. Before it, if the truth be told. He deserved as much. Just like he'd deserved the investigation against him to continue after his demise. He'd been posthumously stripped of his medical licence, but most importantly, the lessons learned from his treatment of so many victims of trauma would positively shape the world of psychology and the treatment of the mentally incapacitated for decades to come. Finally, all seemed right with the world again. My world anyhow, and that of those who I'd come to regard as family.

Lost, contentedly as he watched the flames dance in the wood burning stove, I smiled at Brian. The reflection of the fire on the lenses of his glasses lent his eyes a cadence that had been absent for quite some time. It was returning though, slowly, with each passing day. For that I was hugely thankful. Pouring some more wine into each of our glasses I was startled when his phone came to life on the dining table, breaking both his trance and Uther's slumber and bringing him back into the moment.

'Mack' he said simply, eyeing the caller id.

'Mack.'

'Sorry to disturb your Saturday evening boss. I'm afraid I have some bad news.'

I watched as his relaxed expression was replaced with a look of concern.

'What is it?'

'I've just had a call from a colleague in Dublin. It's...about Karen I'm afraid. She's...dead.'

I watched on helplessly as he began to break physically before my eyes, whilst typically trying to maintain a professional composure.

'Dublin? Jesus!' He paused. 'Thank you Mack' he continued, his voice faltering a little, 'I'm glad it was you who brought the news. It means a lot. Can you send me through the details. Was it a hospice or a hospital? Jesus, I'll have to contact Imelda. She'll be devastated.'

'I'm so sorry for your loss Sir, and Imelda's.'

'Thanks Mack. I'd better head down there. Text me the address as soon as, can you?'

'Sir...Brian, please, wait.'

'What is it?'

'I don't quite know how to say this. She didn't die in a hospital or a hospice. Nothing of the sort as far as we're aware at this stage. In fact she was found in a shallow grave on the outskirts of Dalkey. Brian, she's been murdered.'

ACKNOWLEDGMENTS

Well, we've made it. If you're now reading this, then the chances are two things have happened. You've finished reading Write Me A Murder (I hope you enjoyed it), and if that's the case, that must mean that I've finally finished writing it. This book has been both a long time in the making and an absolute labor of love, and as with all books, has been the result of lots of hard work from lots of people, not least myself.

The spark of the idea that became Write Me A Murder happened on a Halloween night just over three years ago when just like Dr Carolyn Harkin, I too nervously crossed the car park at Clotsworthy House in Antrim to deliver my first crime fiction workshop. To the attendees of that course, and all those who have facilitated and attended the many workshops I've delivered since, I thank you for both your inspiration and your faith in me. Particular thanks to the Arts Council of Northern Ireland, Cathy Brown, Seamus Heaney HomePlace, Libraries NI and Antrim & Newtownabbey Borough Council for their ongoing support.

Speaking of ongoing support, I cannot thank my wife Heather and daughter Bella enough. Their patience and faith in me have been exceptional, as has their unwavering encouragement. I'm very lucky to have them and my family, particularly Patsy, John, Ellie and June in my corner. A further note of thanks to Heather. As with the start of my writing career, it was a chance conversation with her that set the writing of this story in motion, and it was she who helped me to responsibly navigate the choppy waters of toxic masculinity and societal attitudes towards women and girls as my fiction began to be reflected in real life by the tragic murders of Sarah Everard and Ashling Murphy.

The publication of this work would also not have been possible without the support of my colleagues within the crime fiction writing community, particularly Kelly Creighton and Vanessa O Loughlin. A huge thanks to them for their friendship, support and mentorship. A special note of thanks also to Deborah Small for her friendship and for being such an excellent beta reader and supporter of the project from the very beginning. Together they of course formed my "dream team" for my show on Belfast 247 radio, alongside Producers Heather & Bella, and what a team we were!

Special thanks also to the team at Spellbound Books for believing in me and making myself and my characters so at home. You've been fantastic.

Finally, the biggest thanks of all are to you, the readers. I do so hope you enjoyed spending some time at Langford Villa and if this is not the first book of mine you've read, apologies for the wait. I hope it was worth it. I promise it won't be so long next time. In the meantime, I sign off with a phrase those of you who listened to the radio show would be familiar, Keep er lit. Crime lit!!